PENGUIN BOOKS

TUNC

Lawrence Durrell, a British citizen of Irish parentage, was born in the Himalaya region of India in 1912. His first ten years were spent in India. After schooling in England he decided to become a writer. Throughout the 1930s Durrell devoted most of his talents to poetry, which has won much acclaim. His first novel, *The Black Book*, was published in Paris in 1938 and was cited by T. S. Eliot as "the first piece of work by a new English writer to give me any hope for the future of prose fiction." World War II temporarily interrupted Durrell's literary career. During the war years and for some time thereafter, he served Great Britain in various official and diplomatic capacities in Athens, Alexandria, Cairo, Rhodes, and Belgrade. His published works now encompass poetry, essays, and novels, including the famous Alexandria Quartet—*Justine, Balthazar, Mountolive,* and *Clea* (1957–1960)—devoted to an examination of the various aspects of love. Recognized as one of the greatest and most important writers of our time, Lawrence Durrell currently lives in the south of France. His most recent books are the nonfiction *The Greek Islands* and the novel *Livia, or Buried Alive*. Penguin Books also publishes his *Prospero's Cell, Reflections on a Marine Venus, Sicilian Carousel* (travel books about the island of Corfu, the island of Rhodes, and Sicily), the novel *The Dark Labyrinth,* and his translation and adaptation of Emmanuel Royidis's *Pope Joan*.

By Lawrence Durrell

NOVELS

THE ALEXANDRIA QUARTET:
JUSTINE, BALTHAZAR,
MOUNTOLIVE, CLEA

THE BLACK BOOK

THE DARK LABYRINTH

LIVIA, OR
BURIED ALIVE

MONSIEUR, OR
THE PRINCE OF DARKNESS

THE REVOLT OF APHRODITE:
TUNC, NUNQUAM

POPE JOAN
(translator)

POETRY

THE IKONS

THE RED LIMBO LINGO

SELECTED POEMS

THE TREE OF IDLENESS

VEGA

HUMOR

THE BEST OF ANTROBUS

ESPRIT DE CORPS

SAUVE QUI PEUT

STIFF UPPER LIP

TRAVEL

BITTER LEMONS

THE GREEK ISLANDS

PROSPERO'S CELL

REFLECTIONS ON A
MARINE VENUS

SICILIAN CAROUSEL

DRAMA

ACTE

AN IRISH FAUSTUS

SAPPHO

LETTERS AND ESSAYS

LAWRENCE DURRELL AND
HENRY MILLER:
A PRIVATE CORRESPONDENCE,
edited by George Wickes

SPIRIT OF PLACE,
edited by Alan G. Thomas

FOR YOUNG PEOPLE

WHITE EAGLES OVER SERBIA

LAWRENCE DURRELL

tunc

A Novel

PENGUIN BOOKS

Penguin Books Ltd, Harmondsworth,
Middlesex, England
Penguin Books, 625 Madison Avenue,
New York, New York 10022, U.S.A.
Penguin Books Australia Ltd, Ringwood,
Victoria, Australia
Penguin Books Canada Limited, 2801 John Street,
Markham, Ontario, Canada L3R 1B4
Penguin Books (N.Z.) Ltd, 182–190 Wairau Road,
Auckland 10, New Zealand

First published in the United States of America by
E. P. Dutton & Co., Inc., 1968
Published in Penguin Books 1979

LIBRARY OF CONGRESS CATALOGING IN PUBLICATION DATA
Durrell, Lawrence.
Tunc.
Reprint of the 1968 ed. published by Dutton, New York.
I. Title.
[PZ3.D9377Tu   1979]   [PR6007.U76]   823'.9'12   79-11706
ISBN 0 14 00.5184 8

Printed in the United States of America by
Offset Paperback Mfrs., Inc., Dallas, Pennsylvania
Set in Baskerville

For
CLAUDE-MARIE VINCENDON

deux fois deux quatre, c'est un mur

Dostoievsky. *Voix Souterraine*

Of the three men at the table, all dressed in black business suits, two must have been stone drunk. Not Nash, the reproachful, of course not. But Vibart the publisher (of late all too frequently) : and then Your Humble, Charlock, the thinking weed: on the run again. Felix Charlock, at your service. Your humble, Ma'am.

A pheasant stuffed with nominal chestnuts, a fatty wine disbursed among fake barrels in a London cellar—Poggio's, where people go to watch each other watch each other. I had been trying to explain the workings of Abel—no, you cannot have a computer with balls: but the illusion of a proximate intuition is startling. Like a buggerish astrology only more

◆◆ 13

real, more concrete; better than crystal ball or divining rod. "Here we have lying about us in our infancy" (they clear their throats loudly) "a whole culture tied to a stake, whipped blind, torn apart by mastiffs. Grrr! And here we are, three men in black overcoats, ravens of ill omen in an oak tree." I gave a couple of tremendous growls. Heads turned toward us in meek but startled fashion. "You are still drunk, Felix" (This is Nash). "No, but people as destinies are by now almost mathematically predictable. Ask Abel."

"Almost."

"Almost."

"You interest me strangely," said Vibart dozing off for a second. Emboldened Charlock continued: "I call it pogonometry. It is deduction based on the pogon (πόγον) a word which does not exist. It is the smallest conceivable unit of meaning in speech; a million pogons make up the millionth part of a phoneme. Give Abel a sigh or the birth cry of a baby and he can tell you everything."

Vibart dropped his fork on the floor, I my napkin. Leaning down simultaneously we banged our heads smartly together. (Reality is what is most conspicuous by its absence.) But it hurt, we were dazed. "I could explain what is wrong with you," said Nash all pious, all sententious, "but in psychology an explanation does not constitute a cure."

I was brought up by women—two old aunts in lax unmanning Eastbourne. My parents I hardly remember. They hid themselves in foreign continents behind lovely colored stamps. Most holidays I spent silently in hotels (when the aunts went to Baden). I brought introspection to a fine art. A cid I fell into milk; a ribonuclear cid. Where was she? How would she look if she came? Abel could have told me, but he wasn't born then. Eheu!

"And what," says Nash, all perk and arrogance, "could Abel tell *me*, eh?"

"A lot, Nash, quite a lot. I had you in frame not a fortnight ago. I've recorded you frequently on the telephone. Something about a woman who lay on your horsehair couch, eyes shut, exciting you so much by a recital of her sins that you found you were masturbating. A real psi experience. Like religious confessors knee-deep in sperm leaning forward in the confessional so as not to miss the smallest excuse for absolution. I didn't bother to find out her name. But Abel knows. Now where is your Hippocratic oath? You let her smash up the transference because she wanted to do it with you there and then. Daddy! I have your squeaks and gasps; afterward to do you justice you swore and shed tears and walked up and down."

Nash lets off a screech like a parrot; he is on his feet, scarlet, his mouth fallen open on its hinges. "Lies," he shouts.

"Very well, lies; but Abel cannot lie. You must try and

◆ ◆ 15

imagine it this way—as Abel sees it, with that infallible inner photoelectric eye of his. He X-rays time itself, photographing a personality upon the gelatine surface of flux. Look, I press a button, and your name and voice rise together like toast in a toast rack. The fasciae blaze blue, topaz, green, white. I spin the needles and they pass through the fixed points of a sort of curriculum vitae. The basic three points are birth-love-death."

Vibart gives a burst of hysterical laughter; tears crowd his eyes. We are going to be asked to leave at any moment now.

"Now if you take a simple geometrical progression, a scale, you can elaborate your graph until the needle passes through an infinity of points: whatever you choose to set up—say, jobs, skills, size, pigmentation, I.Q., temperament repressions, beliefs . . . You see the game? No, there's nothing wrong with cogito or with sum; it's poor bloody ergo that's been such a curse. The serial world of Tunc whose God is Mobego. But come, we mustn't be crybabies, mustn't pout."

I suddenly felt the need to vomit. Leaning my cold head against the colder glass wall of the urinal I continued: "As for me, scientifically speaking the full terror of death has not informed my loving. Ah, Nash, my boy. I was a gland short." Ah, Benedicta, I might have added under my breath. He holds my head while I am sick: but he is still trembling with rage at this astonishing exposure of his professional shortcomings.

I am forced to laugh. This carefully prepared hoax, I mean, about Abel. Actually I got the facts from the girl herself. At last my stomach comes to rest again. "The firm has given and the firm has taken away, blessed be the name of the firm," I intoned.

"Listen," says Nash urgently. "For Godsake don't develop a delusional system like so many have. I implore you."

"Pish! Abel has coordinated all the psi factors. A computer which can see round corners, think of it! On the prospectus it says distinctly, 'All delusional systems resolved'; now what is our civilization but a . . . ribonucleic hangover, eh? Why,

16 ◆◆

Abel could even give you a valency notion for literature. Jerk, jerk, jerk, you in your swivel chair, she on her couch."

"I've told you it's a lie," he shouts.

"Very well."

Myself I much needed to be loved—and look what happens. At full moon in Polis, when cats conjugate the verb "to be," I held the thousandth and second night in incompetent arms watching the silver climb the cold thermometers of the minarets. Ach! I yark all this gibberish up for little dactyl, my famulus; faithfully the little machine compiles it. To what end? I want the firm to have it, I want Julian to have to wade through it. When I am dead, of course, not before.

Iolanthe, in this very room, once removed the spectacles from my nose—like one lifts the lid from a jar of olives—in order to kiss me. Years later she starts to have a shadowy meaning for me, years later. While I had her, possession of her, I was quite unaware that she loved me. I had eyes for nobody but Benedicta. With her things were different, floating between rauwolfia-induced calms. Something had jumbled up her inner economy, she had never had a period: would the brain poisoning have started from this? I don't know. But I started things off. "Now," she says, "I am bleeding at last, profusely bleeding: thanks to you, my darling Felix, thanks to you. Now I know I shall have a child." Well, and what came of all that? Answer me that, gentlemen of the jury. Rolling back to the alcove table to join Vibart my mind oscillates between the two women once more. Iolanthe talking of her film husband: "Always accusing me of not loving him, of not *trying;* but just when you're trying your best to come off an irrational thought crosses your mind and freezes you: if I forgot to turn off the stove those pigeons will be cinders."

Nash trots along beside me holding my sleeve. "I have an awful feeling you are going to try and break away, make a run for it. Tell me, Felix? For goodness' sake don't. The firm would always find you, you know." I gave him an owlish glance. "I have been granted leave by the firm," said firmly. "Up to two years' sick leave."

"Ah well. That's better." Nash was vastly relieved.

"I am going to the South Seas on legitimate leave."

"Why there?"

"Because it's like everywhere else nowadays. Why not?"

Is that why I am in Athens? Yes, just to make things a little difficult for them. Vindictive Felix. Partly that, but also partly because I had a sudden desire to come back to the point from which all the lines sprang out—the point of convergence being little Number Seven in this fly-blown hotel. One candle. And by God, the little wooden pattens which recently turned up in a suitcase full of junk—the very pattens of Iolanthe. The survival value of objects never ceases to puzzle and enthrall me. People, yes, they turn up again and again, but for a limited time. But things can go on for centuries, quietly changing their owners when they tire of them: or quietly changing their owners *tout court*. I am terribly tired. Most of the prerecorded and digested stuff I have fed into Abel—for the computer is simply a huge lending library of the mind—most of it has passed through these little dactyls, as I call them. Do you think it would be possible to resume a whole life in terms of predestination? I have imagined my own so thoroughly that you can switch it on like an obituary. The two women, one dark and one graven fair; two brothers, one darkness one light. Then the rest of the playing cards, catalogs of events, humble contingencies. A sable history! Well I've brought it up to this point. Abel must be carrying it on. Just pull the lever on the sign manual and traverse across the fascia marked "contingent data." Every sensible man should make a will. . . . But only after a long, wasteful and harmful detour across the parching watersheds of celebrity, financial success. I, Felix Charlock, being sound in mind and body ha ha do hereby etc., etc. Not that I have anything much to leave; the firm has got its hands upon everything except for a few small private treasures like the dactyls here, my latest invention. I found a way to get the prototypes built without them finding out. Hardly larger than a lady's dressing case, she is a masterpiece of compression, as light as a feather. What is it?

Come closer, I will tell you. The dactyl was designed for those who talk endlessly to themselves, for Everyman that is. Also for a lazy man, such a one as myself who has an abhorrence for ink and paper. You speak and she records: more than that, she transcribes. The low feminine voice (the frequency dictated my choice) encodes the words and a tiny phonetic alphabet, no larger than a lama's prayer wheel, begins to purr. From the snout marked A the tip of the foolscap protrudes, and goes on slowly extending until with a sniff the whole page is evacuated, faultlessly typed. How is that done? Ah, that is what any firm would like to know. Nor is there any limit to the amount of dactyl's work, save lack of paper or a failing torch battery. But it is easy to see why the toy is so valuable—it could put all the stenographers in the world out of business in a matter of weeks. Moreover the machine will sensitize to an individual voice to such a degree that she accepts a code tone instead of a switch. This is arbitrary, of course. But in my case "*Konx*" will set her off, while "*Om*" will cut her out. She has made a joke of the laborious anachronism of typing. Yet I did not dare to try and take out a patent in my name, for the firm keeps a watchful eye on the Patents Office. They are at once informed when something new is in the wind . . . Julian anyway.

The reasons I have for wanting to get away are various and complex; the more superficial being self-evident, but the more profoundly buried inexpressibly difficult to expose, despite my relative experience with words. After all, the books are decently written, even though they deal with mechanics, electronics and that sort of thing. But if I were to apply a little archeology to my case I would come upon the buried cultures of deeper predispositions I suppose which determined what I was to become? On the one hand, purely superficially, I could date my existence from the moment when, with a ball of thin twine and two empty cigarette tins, I managed to make an imitation of the telephone. Ting-a-ling! Nothing very strange about that, you will say; the old Bell system was clear as daylight even to a schoolboy. But then let me take a plunge in another direction. I gradually came to equate invention with creation—perhaps too presumptuously? Yet the symptoms are much the same, are they not? Anxiety, fever, migraine, anorexia nervosa, cyclothymia (The Mother!) . . . yes, all the happy heralds of the epileptic fit. An intense strain, sense of dispersal. Then, quite suddenly the new idea breaking free from the tangle of dreams and fevers—Bang! That's how it is with me. The pain was in allowing the damned thing to ferment, to form in the imagination. In my youth I had not learned to recognize the signs. When my teeth began to chatter I suspected an attack of malaria. I had not learned to luxuriate in the convenience of a nervous breakdown. What rubbish!

Well, I have been off the map for some days now, alone in Athens with my famulus, doing a little occupational therapy every day in the form of these autobiographical notes! I have been delayed in my quest for Koepgen; the one man who could tell me where he is is out of Athens and nobody knows for how long. *Om.*

I went to see Nash in a purely formal way: I have always got on with him. He can rise to a joke on occasions, plonk! Like all analysts he is highly neurotic, leashing his hysteria with little grins and yawns and airs of omniscience. Take off glasses, cough, tap thumb, adjust paper flower in buttonhole. I make him, I think, feel a little uncomfortable; he wonders no doubt how much I knew about everything, for is not Benedicta his patient? We sparred gracefully in the fashion of well-educated Englishmen overcompensating. He was not surprised to hear I was going away for a rest. I did not mention the firm but I could see the thought flicker across his mind. Did the firm know where? Yes, the firm knew where—I took care to tell all my friends where: Tahiti. Already no doubt a message had flashed out to our agent there. I would find a large pink blotchy man in a Panama hat waiting shyly on the dock for me. Quietly, tactfully, unobtrusively my arrival would be recorded, reported upon. "I suppose you are just tired," he said. "Yet I see no cause for it. You've done nothing for months now, locked up down in Wiltshire. You are a lucky man, Charlock. Except for Benedicta's illness. You have everything." I watched him quizzically and he had the grace to blush. Then he burst out laughing with a false heartiness. We understood each other only too well, Nash and I. Wait till I tell him about Abel, just wait.

"Shall we talk syllogistically, Nash, or just talk? Causality is an attempt to mesmerize the world into some sort of significance. We cannot bear its indifference." Tears came into his eyes, comicopathetic tears, left over from laughter turned sour. "I know you are sick of your job, and just about as ill as I am, if I *am* ill." He blew out a windy lip and gave me a cunning sidelong glance. "You sound as if you have been playing with RNA. It's dangerous, Charlock. You will miss a step and go sprawling among the archetypal symbols. We'll have to reserve you a room in Paulhaus." That was the firm's private mental asylum. "It is true," I said, "that I wake up with tears pouring down my face, sometimes of laughter, sometimes of plain tears."

"There, you see?" he said triumphantly. He crossed and uncrossed his legs. "You had better take some action smartly, go on a rest cure, write another scientific book."

"I am off to Tahiti. Gauguin was here."

"Good."

"Inventors are a happy laughing breed." I stifled a sob and yawned instead. "Nash, is your laughter a cry for help?"

"Everyone's is. When do you go?"

"Tonight. Let me give you lunch."

"Very well."

"The glands all down one side are swollen—the sense of humor is grossly inflamed. Let us go to Poggio's."

He was pouring out Chianti when Vibart put in an appearance—my publisher, purple with good living: a kind of tentative affability about him whenever he spoke about the book he wanted me to write for him. "The age of autobiography." He solicited Nash's good offices in the matter. He knew too that over all these years I had been dribbling into recorders of one sort or another. A friend of twenty years' standing I first encountered here, yes, in Athens: dear old slow coach of a horse tramway buried in some minor proconsular role with his cabinets of birds' eggs. And here was Vibart persuading poor Felix to quit quasars and debouch into memoirs. I drank deeply deeply of the wine and smiled upon my two friends in clownish gag. What was to be done with them?

"Please, Charlock." He was fearfully drunk.

"Let those who have a good bedside manner with a work of art throw the first stone."

"Nash, can't you convince him?"

"Flippancy is a form of alienation," said Nash rather to my surprise; nevertheless I could not resist making dear Vibart sing once more "The Publisher's Boating Song." We were always asked to leave when he did this. I beat time with my fork.

> *Lord, you may cancel all my gifts,*
> *I feel they can be spared*
> *So long as one thing still remains,*
> *My* pompe à merde.
>
> *My books will stand the test of slime*
> *My fame be unimpaired*
> *So long as you will leave me, Lord,*
> *My* pompe à merde.

To my surprise, despite angry glances, we survive this outburst. Vibart has just been acclaimed Publisher of the Year by the Arts Guild; he owes his celebrity to an idea of breathtaking simplicity. Who else would have thought of getting Bradshaw translated into French? The effect on the French novel has been instantaneous. As one man they have rallied to this neglected English genius. Vibart bangs the table and says in a sort of ecstasy: "It's wonderful! They have reduced *events to incidents*. It's truthful to your bloody science, Felix. Nondeterministic. In Nash's terms it would be pure catatonia. Hurrah. We don't want to get well. No more novels of the castration complex. Do you like the idea of the God of Abraham advancing on you with his golden sickle to cut off your little—your all too little bit of mistletoe?" He points a ghastly finger at Nash, who recoils with a shudder. "Nevermore," continues my friend thickly. "No more goulash-prone Hungarian writers for me, no more *vieux jeu*, I spit on all your frightened freckled little minds. I'm rich! Hurrah. Bookstalls display me which heretofore were loaded with nothing but blood-cooling sex trash. No more about sex, it's too boring. Everyone's got one. Nastiness is a real stimulant though—but poor honest sex, like dying, should be a private matter."

His voice failed and faltered; I noticed the huge circles under his eyes. His wife committed suicide last month; it must do something to a man's pride. One says one is not to blame and one isn't. Still. Quickly change the subject.

We could see that he was rippling with anxiety, like wet washing on the line. Said Nash unkindly, "He needs a rest, does Felix, O yes."

Yes, this was true.

Yes, this was true.

I remember Koepgen talking of what he called the direct vision, the Autopsia. In a poem called "The relevance of thunder." In the Russian lingo. "Futility may well be axiomatic: but to surprise oneself in the act of dying might be one way to come thoroughly awake, no?" I let out another savage growl. The waiters jumped. Ah! They are converging on us at last.

Later, leaning out of the taxi window I say in a deep impressive voice. "I have left you a message written on the wall of the Gents at Claridges. Please go there and read it." My two friends exchange a glance. Some hours earlier, a bag fox drunk on aniseed, I had written in my careful cursive, "I think the control of human memory is essential for any kind of future advance of the species. The refining of false time is the issue." I did not leave any instructions about how to deal with the piggy bank. It was enough to go on with for people like Nash. I waved them good-bye in a fever of health.

In the southbound train I read (aloud) the Market Report in *The Times*, intoning it like a psalm, my breast filled with patriotism for Merlins.

MILAN

The bourse opened quiet yesterday but increased buying interest spread to a number of sectors including quicksilvers, proper-

24 ◆◆

ties, textiles, and insurances, giving way to a generally firmer trend. Towards the close there was brisk buying of leaders with Viscosa and Merlin prominent.

AMSTERDAM
Philips, Unilever and Royal Dutch opened lower but later met some demand on some local and Swiss demand.

BRUSSELS
The forward market was quiet and prices showed little change.

FRANKFURT
Reversed the recent weaker trend in initial dealings and showed a majority of gains later: the close was friendly with gains generally up to seven points.

PARIS
Sentiment improved slightly under the lead of metallurgical shares, notably Merlin, which were firm.

SYDNEY
Quiet but easier.

TOKYO
Prices moved higher. All major industrial groups, along with rails, participated in the upturn. Market quarters looking for a significant summer rally found much to bolster their hopes. Among companies reporting improved net income were: Bethlehem Steel, Phelps Dodge, Standard Oil, Merlin Group.

On the blackboard in the senior boardroom of Merlin House I had left them some cryptic memoranda for their maturer deliberations like

> motor cars made from compressed paper
> paper made from compressed motor cars
> flesh made from compressed ideals
> ideas made from compressed impulses.

They will take it all seriously. So it is. Really it is. Watching the trees go by and the poles leap and fall, leap and fall, I reflected on Merlin and on the F. of F. The Fund of Funds, the Holy Grail of all we stood for. Nash had said so often recently: "I hope you are not thinking about trying to escape from the firm, Charlock. It wouldn't work, you know?" Why? Because I had married into it? *Vagina Vinctrix!* At what point does a man decide that life must be lived *unhesitatingly?* Presumably after exhausting every other field —in my case the scientific modes: science, its tail comes off in your hand like a scared lizard. ("The response to shadow in the common flatworm is still a puzzle to biologists. Then again, in the laboratory, inside a sealed test tube the gravitational pull of the tides still obtains, together with the appropriate responses.")

Yes, he was right, I was going to try and free myself. "Start," Koepgen used to say wryly, sharply, lifting his glass, little drops of ouzo spilling onto the cheap exercise book which houses the loose nerve ends of poems which later, at dead of night, he would articulate. "Tap Tap, the chick raps on the outer shell in order to free itself—literature! Memory and identity. *Om.*"

* * *

But before leaving I did what I have so frequently done in the past—paid a visit to Victoria Station, to stand for a while under the clock. A sentimental indulgence this—for the only human fact that I know about my parents was that they met here for the first time. Each had been waiting for someone quite different. The clock decided my fate. It is the axis, so to speak, of my own beginning. (The first clocks and watches were made in the shape of an egg.) Seriously, I have often done this, to spend a moment or two of quiet reflection here: an attempt perhaps to reidentify them among the flux and reflux of pallid faces which seethe eternally about this mnemotopic spot. Here one can eat a dampish Wimpy and excogitate on the nature of birth. Well, nothing much comes of this thought, these moments of despairing inquiry. The crowd is still here, but I cannot identify their lugubrious Victorian faces. Yet they belonged I suppose to this amorphous pale collection, essence of the floating face and vote, epitome of the "90 percent don't know" in every poll. I had the notion once of inventing something to catch them up, a machine which solidified echoes retrospectively. After all one can still see the light from technically dead stars. . . . But this was too ambitious.

Perhaps (here comes Nash) I might even trace my obsession with the construction of memory tools to this incoherent desire to make contact? Of course now they are a commonplace; but when I began to make them the first recording tools were as much a novelty as the gramophone appears to have been for primitive African tribes in the eighties. So Hippolyta found them, my clumsy old black boxes with their primitive wires and magnets. The development of memory! It led me into strange domains like stenography, for example. It absorbed me utterly and led me to do weird things like learning the whole of *Paradise Lost* by heart. In the great summer sweats of this broken-down capital I used to sit at these tasks all night, only pausing to play my fiddle softly for a while, or make elaborate notes in those yellow exercise books. Memory in birds, in mammals, in violinists. Memory and the instincts, so-called. Well, but this leads nowhere I now think; I equipped myself somewhat before my time as a sound engineer. Savoy Hill and later the BBC paid me small sums to supply library stock—Balkan folk songs for example; a Scots university collected Balkan accents in dialect in order to push forward studies in phonetics. Then while messing about with the structure of the human ear as a sound bank I collided with the firm. Bang. *Om.*

Victoria, yes: and thence to the bank to transfer funds to Tahiti. Then to my club to pick up mail and make sure that all the false trails were well and truly laid: paper trails followed by vapor trails traced upon the leafskin of the Italian sky. Then to drift softer than thistledown through the violet-chalky night, skimming over the Saronic Gulf. Charlock on a planned leave of absence from the consumer's world. Second passport in the name of Smith.

> *"Hail, O Consumer's Age"* the voices boomed,
> But which consumer is, and which consumed?

As might have been expected I caught a glimpse of one of the firm's agents hanging about the airport, but he was not interested in the night passengers, or was waiting for someone else, and I was able without difficulty to sneak into the badly lit apron where the creaking little bus waited to carry me north to the capital.

The taste of this qualified freedom is somewhat strange still; I feel vaguely at a loss, like a man must who hears the prison doors close on his release after serving a long sentence. (If time had a watermark like paper one could perhaps hold it up to the light?) I quote.

Yet the little hotel, it is still here. So is the room—but absolutely unchanged. Look, here are the ink stains I made on the soiled marble mantelpiece. The bed with its dusty covers is still hammock-shaped. The dents suggest that Iolanthe has risen to go to the bathroom. In the chipped coffin of the enamel bath she will sit soaping her bright breasts. I am delighted to find this point of vantage from which to conduct my survey of the past, plan the future, mark time.

Iolanthe, Hippolyta, Caradoc . . . the light of remote stars still giving off light without heat. How relative it seems from Number Seven, the little matter of the living and the dead. Death is a matter of complete irrelevance so long as the memory umbilicus holds. In the case of Iolanthe not even a characteristic nostalgia would be permissible; her face, blown to wide-screen size, has crossed the continents; a symbol as potent as Helen of Troy. Why here on this bed, in the dark ages of youth . . . Now she has become the eighteen-foot smile.

Junior victims of the Mediterranean grigri were we; learning how to smelt down the crude slag of life. Yes, some memories of her come swaying in sideways as if searching deliberately for "the impacted line which will illumine the broad sway of statement."

The grooves of the backbone were drilled in a tender white skin which reminded one of the whiteness of Easter candles. On the back of the neck the hair came down to a point, a small tuft of curl. The coloring of Pontus and Thrace are often much lighter than those of metropolitan Greece—vide Hippolyta with her ravenswing darkness and olive eye. No, Io had the grayish green eye and the hair tending toward ash-blonde which were both gifts from Circassia. The sultans used to stock their harems with toys such as these; the choicest colorings were such, lime-green eyes and fine fair curls. Well, anyway, these tricklings through the great dam of the past cannot touch her now—the legendary Iolanthe; she may have forgotten them even, left them to litter the cutting rooms of gaunt studios in the new world. For example, I had trouble to get her to shave under the arms; in common with all girls of her class, the prostitutes of Athens, she believed that men were aroused by an ape swatch under each arm. Perhaps they were. Now however when she raised her slender arms on the screen like some bewigged almond tree the pits beneath them are smooth as an auk's egg.

The young man that I was then cannot escape the charge of exercising a certain duplicity toward her; he condescended, letting his narcissism have full sway. Well, I don't know, many factors were involved. This little angel had dirty toes and was something of a thief I believe. I found some notes from this period whose irrelevance proves that even then Charlock had an obstinate vein of introspection running along parallel, so to speak, with his mundane life of action. The second, the yellow exercise book—the one with the drawings of the cochlea and the outline for my model deafness aid—had other kinds of data thrown about in it.

Walking about Athens at night he might note: "The formication, the shuddering sweet melting almost to faintness . . . Why, the structure of the genitals is particularly adapted to such phenomena, Bolsover. (Bolsover was my tutor at Kings. I still converse with him mentally in prose and worse.) The slightest friction of a white hand will alert the dense nerve ganglia with their great vascularity. The affect disperses itself through the receiving centers of the autonomic nervous system, solar plexus, hypogastric plexus, and lumbosacral or pelvic . . . Hum. The kiss breaks surface here. The autobiography of a single kiss from Iolanthe. Note also, Bolsover, that in embryology the final organ is progressively differentiated from an anlage—which may be defined as the first accumulation of cells recognizable as the commencement of the final organ. This is about as far as one can go; but even this is not far enough back for me. Surely once in the testes of my old man, in the ape gland once, I *was?*"

These problems brought sadness and perplexity to my loving. I would light a candle and examine the sleeping figure with concern for its mysterious history; it seemed to me that it might be possible to trace back the undermeanings of pleasure and pain, an unreasonable wish I now recognize. Ass. Ape. Worm.

Her teeth were rather fine and small with just a trace of irregularity in their setting—enough to make her smile at once rueful and ravenous. She was too self-indulgent to husband her efforts in the professional sense—or perhaps too honest not to wish to give service? She could be blotted out sexually and retire into an exhaustion so extreme as to resemble death. Poor Iolanthe never got enough to eat so it was easy for a well-fed man to impose orgasm after orgasm on her until she reached the point of collapse. In our case the thing worked perfectly—indeed so perfectly that it puzzled her; we ignited each other like engines tuned to perfect pitch. Of course this is purely a technical question—one of perfect psychic and physical fit—queer there is not a science of it, nor a school in which one can try it out experimentally. If we could apply as much exactitude to sexual habits as, say, a machine turner to his toys, much unhappiness in love could be avoided. In an age of advanced technology it is surprising that no attention is given to such problems. Yes, even with her eyes closed, piously trying to think about something else in order to avoid exhaustion: even then, the surf carried her irresistibly to the other beach, rolled up her into the blessed anonymity of the fading second. Sometimes he shook her awake simply to stare into her eyes. But if at such moments she had asked him what he was thinking he would probably have replied: "The true cancer cell, in the final analysis, an oxygen-deficiency cell, a poorly breathing cell, according to Schmidt. When you coughed I suddenly saw in the field of my instrument a patch of tubercule bacilli stained with eosin to a pretty red—anemones in some Attic field." People deprived of a properly constituted childhood will always find something hollow in their responses to the world, something unfruitful. You could accuse both of us of that, in order to explain the central lack. The weakness of the marrow. A racing heart. Of course other factors help, like environment, language, age. But the central determinant of situations like this is that buried hunger which is only aggravated by the sense of emotional impotence. *Om.*

TWO

pronunciation with the stress on the third syllable. Actually I don't mind, as it makes her real name private property. She belongs, then, to Number Seven, and to the Nube, to the eternal Athens which miraculously still survives outside memory. In that mirror over there she wrestled with her eyebrows which had a tendency to grow too thickly. You should see them now—single soft lines of the purest jet. Though the room squints out on the marbles we dared not open a shutter until dusk; we lived all day in brown shadow like carp in a cool pool. Until sunset.

Sunset! Wake suddenly against the lighted wall and you have the momentary impression that the whole marble spook has taken fire and is curling up like burning cardboard. You put your hand to the hideous wallpaper and feel the actual heat of the mere reflection—or so you imagine. Up there outside the honey-colored marbles, after a full day's exposure to the sun, echo on the heat long after nightfall, temperature of mammals' blood. Gradually the light sweats dried . . . stomachs gummed together like wet leaves. Yawning and smoking they lay about in whispers. She has a toy vocabulary and an island accent.

The marbles still reflect back, translated into the whiteness of flour, the dying day's burnish. Bit by bit she keels, veers, founders. The sun slithers down the nether side of Hymettus and into the sea with a huge inaudible hiss, leaving the islands to glow like embers which the young moon will soon reillumine. (They lie beside each other as quietly as legs; no kiss but would break the curvature of the unperfected thought.) Gradually leaks up from Salamis the smell of baked bread, melons, tar, borne on the breath of the evening freshets which will soothe wet armpits and breasts.

They had been refugees from Pontus, and had trekked down with a dancing bear to settle in Crete. When the bear died (their only means of livelihood) they had a last tearful meal of the paws in oil. A small holding barely sustained her parents. To lighten the burden she had come to Athens in search of work—with the inevitable result, for work there was none. When she described these days she stood up and acted the bear, the padding and jingling of paw and bell, the harsh panting. The froth gathered at its snout where the iron ring ran through. It was half blind, the whip had struck out an eye.

The sheet had lipstick marks on it, also the tooth mug; our shoes lay side by side like fish. But she was gay, friendly, almost mannish in her directness and simplicity. A gaily colored little parrot from an island. In those days for a whole summer black fingernails were *de rigueur* among her friends and workmates. This beastly shellac stuff used to peel off onto the sheet. Her one brother had "gone to the bad"; her lip shut on the phrase, framing it instantly in the harsh rectangle of peasant judgment. Had she, then, "gone to the good"? It was an attempt at a pleasantry which miscarried; her long underlip shot out, she was in tears. During the microfield tests on Abel, I sifted a good deal of this stuff about her through the field, and the king of computers came back in oracular fashion with some chunks taken from another field— Koepgen I think. It was all about love, its scales. (After Io leaves I can watch her from the window. She takes the crooked path up the side of the Acropolis, swaying a little, as if she were a trifle tipsy, hand to heart.)

Thus Abel: "If we could only make all time proximate to reality we could see a little more deeply into the heart of our perplexities; the syzygy with its promise of a double silence is equally within the grasp of man or woman. If ever they combine forces in their field you might speak of loving as something more than a term for an unclassifiable animal. It is unmistakable when it does happen, for it feels as if the earth had subtly shifted its epicenter. How sad it seems that we, images of insipid spoon meat, spend our time in projecting such strange figures of ourselves—delegated images of a desire perfected. The mystical gryphus, the 'perfect body' of the Alexandrian psychology, is an attempt on a telenoetic field. (What space is to matter, soul is to mind.) Some saints were 'dry-visioned.' (Jerk, jerk, but nothing comes; taking the 'distressful path' toward afterimages of desire.) They were hunting, poor buggers, for a renovated meaning or an infantile adoption by a God. Unhappily words won't carry the charge in these matters, hence the deficit of truth in all verbal fields. This is where your artist might help. "A craft is a tongue, a tongue is a key, a key is a lock." On the other hand a system is merely the shy embrace by which the poor mathematician hopes to persuade his bride to open up." Koepgen never met her, I think, yet at his best he seems to be talking about her.

My frail old black recorders with their clumsy equipment were a source of the greatest concern; jolting about as they did with me on country buses, on caïques, even on mules. My livelihood depended on the accurate functioning, and this is where Said came in. The little watchmaker was a friend of Io. One-eyed, mission school, Christian Arab, he had his little workshop in a rotting hut in the Plaka, more fitting for rabbits than for a workman capable of craftsmanship of such extraordinary delicacy. Mud floor, fleas jumping in the straw and nibbling our ankles; we spent hours together, sometimes half the night, at his little workbench. He copied from any drawing. One-eyed Said with his watery optic pressed to a butter-colored barrel, among the litter of fusees and escapements and hairs. Eager and modest in discussion of trade topics such as the use of invar etc. He made my echo amplifiers in a couple of weeks. Small as a garden pea, and beautifully done in mother of pearl. Graphos now! But I will be coming to that.

It was the recorders that brought me to the notice of Hippolyta. Vivid in a baroque hat like a watering can she dispensed tea and éclairs in the best hotel, coiling and uncoiling her slender legs as she questioned me about the mysteries of the black box, wondering if I could record a speech which was to be made by some visiting dignitary. My impression squared with all I heard afterward of her public reputation. It was typical of backbiting Athens that she sounded so unsavory a figure; the truth was that she was a mixture of naïveté and wrongheadedness punctuated with strange generosities. The hard voice with its deeper tones and the fashionable boldness of the dark eyes were overcompensating for qualities like shyness which even her social practice had not enabled her entirely to throw off. The green scarf and the blood-red fingernails gave her a pleasantly old-fashioned vampire's air. "O please could you do that for me?" She named a figure in drachmae so high that my heart leaped; it would keep me for a month; and held my hand a trifle longer than formality permits. She was a warm, pleasantly troubling personage. Despite the impressive jewelery and the orchids she seemed more like a youth than a girl. Of course I accepted, and taking an advance made my way back to the Plaka delighted by such good fortune. She promised to let me know when the person in question—the speechmaker—arrived. "I can't help liking slightly hysterical women," I confided to the Parthenon.

At Spiro's tavern, under the vine trellis, I paused for a drink and caught sight of a familiar object at an empty table; the little yellow exercise book which Koepgen used for theology and musing alike. It lay there with his pen and a daily paper. He must have gone to the lavatory. At this time Koepgen was a theological student embarking on the grim path of monkhood. A typical product of White Russia, he spoke and wrote with equal ease in any of four languages. He taught me Greek, and was invaluable on out-of-the-way factors like the phonetics of this hirsute tongue; things like the Tsaconian dialect, still half anc. Doric. Well I sat and riffled while I waited.

"The *hubris*, the overweening, is always there; but it is a matter of scale. The Greeks traced its path with withering accuracy, watching it lead on to *ate*—the point at which evil is mistakenly believed to be good. Here we are then at the end of the long road—races dehumanized by the sorceries of false politics." Koepgen weeping for Russia again. I always want to shout "stop it!" At last he stood before me, full of a devout nonchalance. He was a small dapper man, contriving to look clean despite the threadbare soutane and grotesque smelly boots. His long hair, captured in a bun, was always clean. He seldom wore his stovepipe hat. He reproached me for my inquisitiveness and sat down smiling to hear my tale of good fortune. Of Hippolyta he said: "She is adorable, but she is connected with all sorts of other things. I came across her recently when I did some paid translation—O just business letters—for an organization, a firm I suppose, in Salonika. She organized it. But something about it gave me an uncomfortable feeling. They offered me very large sums to keep on with the work, but I let it drop. I don't know quite why. I wanted to keep myself free in a way. I need less and less money, more and more time."

how is narration?

◆❖◆❖◆❖◆❖◆❖◆❖◆❖◆

There are other data, floating about like motes in a sunbeam, waiting to find their place: the equipment in the abortioner's leather bag. The needle-necked appurtenances which mock the spunk-scattering troubadours of a courtly love. The fetus of a love song. ("One way," wrote Koepgen, "might be to take up Plutarch's idea of the Melisponda. This should be within the grasp of anyone.") Mara the hag with a pair of tongs worked off a car battery. I am not so sure whether in the brothels of Pireaus he did not achieve the *mare pigrum* of the philosophers and alchemists. Here one bares one's sex to a whole landscape—internal landscapes of empty sea, niggerhead coral, bleached tree trunks, olive pits burned by lye. Islands (each one a heart and mind) where the soft spirals of waves shoulder and sheathe floors awash with the disquiet of palaces submerged in folded ferns. Symbol of the search is the diver with the heavy stone tied to his belt. Sponges!

Then lying about among my own records I came upon some stone memoranda like altars and tombs; stuck in among them some moments of alarming happiness. If the portly Pausanias had seen the city's body through that of a young streetwalker his catalogs would have had more life. Names and stones would have become the real fictions and we the realities. After dark we often sneak through the broken fence and climb to the cave below the Propylaea. Her toes are fearfully dirty in her dusty sandals, as are mine, but her hair

◆◆ 41

is freshly washed and scentless. We are never quite alone up here. A few scattered cigarette points mark the places where other lovers wander, or lie stargazing. Up on these ledges in winter you will find that the southern gales carry up the faint crying of sea mews, sacred to Aphrodite; while in the spring the brown-taffeta nightingales send out their quiet call sign in the very voice of Itys. "*Itú, Itú, Itú*" they cry in pretty iteration. Then by moonlight come the little owls. They are tame. (No more!) Turning their necks in strange rhythms—clearest origin for ancient Greek masked dancing.

Down below in the later sequences of the play the tombs face east with their pathetic promise of resurrection. The modern town rolls over it all like surf. Prismatic gleams of oil patches on macadam; coffee grounds and the glitter of refuse (fish scales) outside the smelly taverns with their climbing trellises and shelves of brown barrels. Once a golden apple was a passport to the underworld, but today I am only able to buy her a toffee apple on a stick which she dips in sherbet, licking it like a tame deer.

A true Athenian, free from all this antiquarian twaddle, she knows and cares nothing for her city; but yes, some of the stories alert a fugitive delight as she sits, sugaring her kisses with her apple. It is pleasant to babble thus, floundering among the telescopic verb schemes of demotic; telling her how Styx water was so holy as to be poisonous, only to be safely drunk from a horse's hoof. They poisoned Alexander this way. Also how Antony once set up his boozing shop in the Parthenon, though his was a different sort of poisoning, a chronic narcissism. (She crosses herself superstitiously as a good Orthodox should, and snuggles superstitiously up to me.) Then . . . about embalming bodies in honey—human toffee apples: or curing sick children by making them swallow mice coated in honey. Ugh! But excited by this she responds by telling me of witches and spells which cause nausea and impotence and can only be fought with talismans blessed by a priest. All this with such earnestness that out of polite belief I also make the sign of the Byzantine cross, back to front, to ward off the harms of public utterance from us both. ("There is no difference between truth and reality—ask any poet." Thus Koepgen sternly, eyes blazing, a little drunk on ouzo.) The quiet wind blew dustily uphill among the moonkeepers. To make love in this warm curdled air seemed an act of unpremeditated simplicity that placed them back once more in the picture-book world sacred to the animal kingdom where the biological curve of the affect is free from the buggerish itch of mentation. Warm torpid mouth, strong arms, keen body—this seems all the spiritual instruction the human creature needs. It is only afterward that one will be thrown back sprawling among the introspections and doubts. How many people before Iolanthe? Throats parched in the dry air we drink thirstily from the sacred spring. She washes the sugar from her lips, washes her privates in the icy water, drying them on my old silk scarf. No, Athens was not like other places; and the complicated language, with its archaic thought forms, shielded its strangeness from foreign eyes. Afterward to sit at a tin table in a tavern, utterly replete and silent, staring at each other, fingers touching, before two glasses of colorless raki and a plate of olives. Everything should have ended there, among the tombs, by the light of a paraffin lamp. Perhaps it did?

The news of Caradoc's coming was conveyed to me by Hippolyta one fine Sunday afternoon; once more bidden to tea, I found her in a corner of the Bretagne where she kept a suite permanently available, playing patience among the palms. She looked a little less forbidding this time I thought, though she was fashionably turned out in the styles of the day. Bejeweled, yes, but this time without much war paint. Moreover she was shortsighted I noticed; raising a lorgnon briefly toward me as I advanced, she smiled. The optic changed her clever aquiline face, giving it a juvenile and somewhat innocent expression. The eyes were noble, despite their arrogance of slant. She was immediately likable, though less beautiful this time than last. I compared her mentally to her reputation for extravagant gesture and detected something which seemed at variance with the public portraits, so to speak. Somewhere inside she was a naïf—always a bad sign in a woman connected with politics and public life.

"You remember we spoke? He is coming—you may have heard of Caradoc, the architect? No? Well . . . " She suddenly burst out laughing, as if the very mention of his name had touched off an absurd memory. She laughed as far back as a tiny gold stopping on a molar and then became serious, conspiratorial. "The lecture will be on the Acropolis—will your machine be able . . . ?" I was doubtful. "If there is wind it won't be very clear. But I can make some tests in the open air? Sometimes very small things like dentures clicking, for example, ruin the quality of the sound and make the test difficult to recover on playback. I'll do what I can, naturally."

"If you come to Naos, my country house, in the garden . . . You could practice with your instrument. He will come there. I'll send you the car next Friday." I reached for a pencil to give her my address, but she laughed and waved away my intention. "I know where you live. You see, I have been making inquiries about you. I did not know what your work was or I would have offered my help. Folk songs I can get you two a penny." She snapped white fingers as one does to summon a waiter in the Orient. "On my country properties I have singers and musicians among the villagers. . . . Perhaps this would interest you later?"

"Of course."

"Then first make this speech for us." She laughed once more. "I would ask you to stay and dine but I have to go to the palace this evening. So good-bye."

That evening the fleet came in and Iolanthe was summoned back to the naval brothel in Piraeus leaving me alone to pursue my studies with Said. Three of my little Orient pearls had been manufactured now, and I was mad keen to find a deaf man to try them out on. Koepgen had said that he knew a deaf deacon who would be glad of a mechanical cure so that he would not flounder among the responses! But where was Koepgen? I left messages for him at the theological school and at the tavern he frequented.

Naos, the country house of Hippolyta in Attica, was large enough to suggest at first sight a small monastery skillfully sited within an oasis of green. By contrast, that is, to the razed and bony hills which frame the Attic plain. Here were luxuriant gardens rich with trees and shrubs within a quarter of a mile of the sea. Its secret was that it had been set down, woven round a double spring—a rarity in these parched plains: oleander, cypress and palm stood in picturesque contrast to the violet-gray stubbled hills, their fine soils long since eroded by weather and human negligence. The dangling rose gardens, the unplanned puffs of greenery made full amends for what was, at close sight, a series of architectural afterthoughts, the stutterings of several generations. Barns climbed into bed together, chapels had cemented themselves one to another in the manner of swallow nests to unfinished features like half-built turrets. One huge unfinished flying buttress poked out nature's eye, hanging in midair. One step through the door marked W.C. on the second floor and one could fall twenty feet into a fishpond below.

A series of gaunt and yet dignified rooms had been thrown down pell-mell about a central cruciform shape, rambling up two floors and petering out in precarious balconies which looked out on the ravishing mauve slopes of the foothills. On reflection one established the origins of the whole place. Clearly Hesiod had started it as a grange for his cattle; Turks, Venetians, French, Greeks had carried on the work without once looking over their shoulders, enlarging the whole place and confusing its atmospheres. In the reign of Otho utterly nonsensical elaborations had tried to render it stylish. While one corner was being built up, another was crumbling to ruins. Finally those members of the family lucky enough to have been educated in France had added the ugly cast-iron features and awkward fenestration which would, one presumes, always make them nostalgic for St. Remo in the twenties—Marseille tile, Second Empire furniture, plaster cherubim, mangy plump moldings. Yet since every feature was the worst of its epoch and kind the whole barrack had a homogeneity, indeed a rustic dignity which endeared it to all who came, either to visit or inhabit it. It was here that Hippolyta held court, here that her old friend, sheepish Count Banubula, worked in his spare time cataloging the huge library hurled together rather than collected by several generations of improvident noblemen more famous for their eccentricities than their learning. Wood rot, silverfish, death-watch beetles—all were active and industrious though nobody cared except the poor count, tiptoeing along creaking balconies or shining up precarious ladders to rescue a rotting Ariosto or Petrarch.

Here Hippolyta (the Countess Hippolyta, "Hippo," to us) lived when she came home—which was rarely; for the most part she preferred Paris or New York. Other members of the family (with whom she was not on speaking terms) also came from time to time, unheralded, to take up residence in various dusty wings. (There was one ancient and completely unexplained old lady, half blind, who might be seen crossing a corridor or scuttling off a balcony.) Two younger cousins were ladies-in-waiting at court, and also occasionally put in an appearance attended by beaky husbands or lovers. Hippo made a point of not letting her own visits coincide with theirs; it was we, the members of her little court, who usually ran into them—for there was always someone staying at Naos; permission was freely given for any of us to spend a summer or winter there.

Here then in Naos, of a spanking summer evening, I was carried to the lady with my devil machines. (Tapes A70 to 84 labeled G for Greece have been fed back into Abel.) Well, she was clad in Chinese trousers of fine shantung, inlaid Byzantine belt, and an impossible Russian shirt with split sleeves; she lounged in a deck chair by the lily pond while a hirsute peasant clumsily assuaged our thirst with whiskey and gin. She was smoking a slender cheroot, and was surrounded by a litter of fashion papers and memoranda gathered in colored folders—esoteric Greek pothooks which I feared might be the beginnings of a book. Two huge pet tortoises clicked across the paths and came bumping into the legs of our chairs, asking to be fed; and this Banubula undertook with an air of grave and scrupulous kindness shredding lettuce from a plate. My little toy was greeted with rapture and some amusement; Hippo clapped her hands and laughed aloud like a child when I reproduced a strip of conversation harshly but clearly for her consideration, while old Banubula cleared his throat in some surprise and asked whether it wasn't rather dangerous, such a machine? "I mean one could take copies of private conversations, could one not?" Indeed one could; Hippo's eye shone with a reflective gleam. The count said in his slow bronze-gong voice: "Won't Caradoc mind?" She snorted. "He knows these machines; besides if he is too lazy to write it all out, if he prefers to extemporize . . . why, it's his affair."

There was silence. "I saw Graphos today," she said, a sudden expression of sadness clouding her face. Presumably she was referring to the politician? I said nothing, nor did they. In the movement of embarrassment that followed we heard the noise of the car drawing up, and the figure of Caradoc emerged among the oleanders—the stubby frame hunched up with a defiant and slightly tipsy-looking mien; he carried a much-darned Scotch plaid over his arm, and in his hand a leather-covered flask from which he drew encouragement as he advanced. No greetings followed, much to my surprise; Hippolyta just lay, the count just stared. Staring keenly, menacingly under shaggy white eyebrows, the architectural mage advanced, his deep voice munching out segments of air with a kind of half-coherent zeal. At first blush he seemed far too sure of himself, and then as he came closer the impression changed to one of almost infantile shyness. He spread his arms and uttered a single phrase in the accents of a Welsh bard: "What it is to work for these beneficed Pharisees!" Giving a harsh bark of a laugh full of ruefulness he sat down by the pond, turning the bottle over thoughtfully in his fingers before pushing it into the pocket of his cape. A heavy air of constraint fell over the company and I realized that it was caused by my presence; they could not speak freely before me. I unshackled my machine and excused myself. But through the window of the ramshackle lavatory on the ground floor I heard, or seemed to hear, Hippo give a low cry and exclaim: "O Caradoc, the Parthenon! Only Graphos can fight it." Caradoc gave an incredulous roar in the accents of the Grand Cham. "They told me nothing, they never do. Simply to come at once and bring Pulley for costings. I was hoping to build Jocas a seraglio. But this . . . No, I won't believe it."

"Yes. Yes." Like the cry of a seabird. That was all. By the time I returned the whole picture had changed; the constraint had vanished. They had exchanged whatever they had needed to, and though there were still tears in the eyes of Hippolyta she was laughing heartily at something that Cham had said. Moreover his assistant Pulley had now joined the company—a lank North Country youth of yellowish cast, with huge hands and teeth. He said little. But he yawned from time to time like an eclipse of the sun.

A dinner table had been set out among the oleanders on a nearby terrace; the still air hardly trembled the candles in their silver sockets. Wine soon oiled the hinges of the talk. The Cham, after a short period of reservation, frankly gave me his hand.

"Charlton, you said?"

"Charlock."

"Well, Charlton, here's my hand."

Then he turned in businesslike fashion and began to mash up his food with vigor, talking in loud and confident tones as he did so. No reference was made to my function, and I made none, treading warily; but toward the middle of the meal Hippolyta made a gesture inviting me to record, and I obeyed unobtrusively, while Caradoc continued with a grumbling one-cylinder monologue. He was in a curious mood it seemed, uncertain whether to allow the wine to make him gay or whether to become testy and morose; presumably he was still troubled by whatever she had told him, for he suddenly said, in an aside: "Of course I shall never cease to be grateful to the firm—how could one not be? It has allowed me to build all its cathedrals, so to speak. But one can build cathedrals without being a religious man? Anyway I don't propose to be upset until I know for certain what is in Jocas' mind." Then, as if to pursue the metaphor he turned to me and said: 'I'm talking about Merlins, my boy. Easy to join but hard to leave. Nevertheless there comes a day . . .' He sighed heavily and took Hippolyta's hand. "Now," he said, "we must make a real effort to enjoy ourselves tonight. No good can come of worrying. I propose to lead an expedition to the Nube, and I invite the lot of you as my guests. By the navel string of the Risen Lord we shall have a marvelous time. Eh? Do you know the Nube, Charlton?"

"The Blue Danube? By repute."

"It is a home from home for us, eh, Pulley?"

He consulted the circle of candlelit faces as he barked out the phrase. There seemed little enough response aroused by this proposition. He was pained. As for the Blue Danube, it enjoyed a mild repute among frequenters of houses of ill fame. Its name, in frosted bulbs, had been changed for it by wind and weather; the letters had either fallen out of their frames or gone dead. All that remained for the wayfarer to read against the night sky now was the legend the Nube, ancing, aberet. "I should like to come," said I, and received a

50 ◆ ◆

friendly thump from the Cham. He was delighted to receive support from some quarter. His good humor returned. "It is run by an adorable personage, daughter of a Russian Grand Duke, and sometime wife to a British vice-consul, most aptly so entitled, and she calls herself Mrs. Henniker." Hippolyta smiled and said: "All Athens knows her." Caradoc nodded. "And with justice; she has the cleanest girls in Attica; moreover there is one Turk called Fatma." He embraced a large segment of air to suggest her dimensions. "A heroine is Fatma."

All this was becoming less and less esoteric. Caradoc dished us all a stoup of red Nemean and cajoled us with prophecy. "You will see," he said, "Graphos will get in and save our bacon." She smiled, yes, but sadly; shaking her head doubtfully. "I'll give you the big car," she said. "But I won't come. In case he phones or comes to see me. But I expect you'll find all your friends at the Nube, including Sipple. He knows you are arriving today." Caradoc registered approval, commended the cheese he was cutting up ("This Camembert has lain a long time, not in Abraham's bosom but in the hairy armpit of the Grand Turk himself") and added, with his mouth full: "Give me Sipple the clown any day." Pulley explained that Sipple was an "undesirable."

"But irresistible, my favorite *numéro*," insisted the Cham. "A man of parts."

"Secondhand parts" said Pulley. He seemed from his facial expressions to live in a state of furious though repressed disapproval. Caradoc, by now distinctly mellow, turned aside in disgust and confided some thoughts of the first magnitude, so to speak, to the mild and tentative count, who had registered an expression of pained alarm at the mention of a house of ill fame. It was clear that he would not be joining us in this bacchanal. Caradoc, feeling perhaps an unexpressed reservation, tried to cajole him with high thinking to concede some virtue to low living. This sort of stuff. "The Nube is the perfect place for self-examination, better than a church. Why not, after all? The nearest vicarious approach to death is

by the orgasm which produces its temporary simulacrum."
("Ow!" exclaimed Hippolyta with superstitious disgust.)
The Cham warmed to the pulpit, his tone now tinged distinctly with Welsh tabernacle. "That is why it has been surrounded with prayer, poetry, propitiation, tabu. The Greeks saw a clear relationship and in their wisdom compounded temple and brothel. We haven't the imagination. Fools! The priest has tried to harness its power, dynamo fashion, to make more brain dust. A foul repression is written all over our mugs. Look at him, him, her. *Look at me!* In the East we are told he has managed to crack the mold and liberate the statue of the silver man. But in the West our methods have failed—the silly reticule of the human brain can only generate a sterile flight of symbols and concepts which have given us certain insecure powers over matter but none over ourselves."

Pulley began to express his disapproval of all this bardic verbosity by beating himself about the chest and biceps and making animal noises and monkey faces. This delighted the Cham, who now stood up and in the pleading accents of a Welsh preacher admonished and cajoled him. "Now which is wiser, Pulley my dear fellow: to wear all nature like a suit of clothes, or to rape and tame it?"

Pulley gave a thin yowl and said: "Pack it up, Carry, like a good fellow. I've had nothing but this all day in the plane." He turned to us for support. "Can you bear it when the bloody Druid comes out in him?"

"Of course they can," said Caradoc majestically, still poised for flight. "Only just," said Hippolyta.

"It gives me the bloody shivers," said Pulley.

"Very well." Caradoc sat down unsteadily. "Very well, you Philistine. Very well." He took my hand and began to recite.

> *If a monumental mason*
> *Carved a monumental turd*
> *As a symbol of humanity at prayer,*
> *We could cast it as a bronze*

> *And distribute it to dons*
> *As an article of college table-ware*

He was sufficiently pleased with the response to threaten us with a ballad beginning:

> *How nugatory and how glum*
> *The endomorphs of scholarship*
> *Like hippos on a sinking ship*
> *Stay bum to silly bum.*

But he could push the matter no further, and submitted to Hippolyta's amused disapproval with mock contrition. She had kicked off her sandals and was smoking a Turkish cigarette in a black bone holder. Caradoc helped himself to a rose from the bowl on the table. "The moon is late tonight," he observed with petulance. He had been watching the little dab of whiteness on the horizon which marked its point of emergence. He had been here before, then? Supposedly.

The night had been still down in this garden with its unhovering candles, its slow-moving warm currents of scent. Now came a small gust which blew out the light and left us in half-darkness.

"A fitting end to our dinner," said Caradoc. "And a sign that we should be about our business. How shall we arrange matters?"

Hippolyta was staying; Banubula elected to be dropped off in Athens, "if we could face the detour." That left the three of us. I left my sacred boxes in a safe place against a future return and joined them. Pulley had taken the wheel of the car, sitting beside the chauffeur whose air of misgiving showed that he knew he was in for a long night's work. "Drive carefully," cried our hostess from the gate.

Caradoc sang softly to himself, beating time with a finger.

> *Drinking, dicing and drabbing*
> *Drabbing drinking and dice,*

You can say what you like they are nice
You can say what you like they are nice

Faces with nothing behind them
Or behinds with nothing before . . .

Pulley nearly ran into an unlighted cart and threw us all
about widdershins. Banubula made turkey noises. He was
obviously a timorous man and was relieved to be deposited
on the outskirts of the capital, pausing only to retrieve a
silver-knobbed walking stick and to bow a ceremonious good
night. Then down toward the sea we turned, and now the
young tardy moon was rising; it rode with us along the whole
circuit of the long walls, past the rabble of dingy villas
nestling in sterile palms, the beer factory, the refuse-encum-
bered Ilyssos. Below the Acropolis the olive groves melted
away downhill toward the little railway. No horizon was
ruled as yet, only a point at which stars began to prickle up
out of the darkness. The last curve of the coast road sprang
out like a branch in full blossom and elated by the moonlight
and the silver spangles of the mild sea Pulley increased speed
until we were whirling down toward Sunion—stars cool now
as cress and shining water-nibbled rock. Caradoc's rose was
black. The night was placid and reassuring. Caradoc had
decided for the time being to stop acting the rhetorical
mountebank; the lightly varnished night sky was a narcotic.
In an absentminded fashion he tried to catch a moonbeam in
his cupped hand.

Nor was it long before we swerved off the pitted macadam
of the main road onto hard dune: thence onto flaky sand
dunes, to bump and skitter and slide into the rotting garden
of the Nube and come to rest hull down under a single
balcony where the one and only Mrs. Henniker awaited us in
the attitude of a gaunt Juliet in retirement. The electric sign
throbbed weakly: though for reasons of economy or aesthetics
the current had never been taken inside where the lighting
was by paraffin lamp or candle. Caradoc announced our

arrival and at once Mrs. Henniker bobbed out of sight, only to reappear a minute later at the front door, arms extended in welcome. The long horseface with its patchy pink skin inspired confidence. She exhaled rectitude and forthrightness like the best sort of seaside landlady. Her tones were tart and martial, her back as straight as a ramrod. She was at once fearful and endearing. Behind her one could sense the long and thankless lifetime spent in putting up with the lopped-off capacities of her typical clients. ("The Goddess of Sex, who, like the multiplication table, repeats her demands, always trying to raise herself to a higher power, perhaps in order to precipitate a true self?" Who the devil was that? Yes, Koepgen.)

At any rate it was to the Nube that humanity shuffled, lugging its heavy baggage—the interior pains and massive depressions. Among Mrs. Henniker's girls they were exorcised. Not us, mind you, for we were heart-whole and in sportive mood—to judge by the tone set by Caradoc. He introduced me as Mr. Chilton and added agreeably, "He is a man of the world like us." Mrs. Henniker, who took everything with deadly seriousness, fluffed out her feathers like a bird and said, with intense feeling, "My poy. My poy"; taking as she did so my right hand between scaly palms. It was all very formal, very graceful, very relaxed. Pulley gave a German professor's bow.

We entered the Nube with well-bred enthusiasm to go through the statutory ritual with the big wooden statue of the Curé d'Arles—a cordelier with an unhealthy leer. This came as rather a surprise to me. Caradoc embraced the statue warmly, addressing it as Saint Foutain. Then he indicated a slot in its shoulder large enough to admit a drachma. "Initiate yourself," he cried jovially, tendering me the coin. It tinkled into the body of the curé and there was a whir followed by a click. All at once a hatch in his robe flew open and he thrust out a beautifully hand-painted penis the length of a sermon. "Don't reel, don't recoil that way," said Caradoc reproachfully. "Put your hand on it and wish." I obeyed, offering up a shadowy half-formulated wish, fragile yet iridescent as a soap bubble, in the general direction of the absent Io. Pulley followed suit. "He's an infallible fellow. You only have to ask him and it comes true. He was bequeathed to the Nube by a commercial traveler in French wine, as mark of his esteem and entire satisfaction." So, feeling suitably shriven, we advanced upon the candlelit interior through a succession of dusty curtains; here the girls waited, yawning—about half a dozen dressed in baggy Turkish trousers and no tops. They looked nice and tame, if rugged; and dying of boredom.

Time hung heavy, one gathered, when there were no clients in the Nube. A gramophone, yes, but the discs were few and scratched. Film magazines in plenty, but ancient. So it was that our majestic appearance on the scene evoked a burst of energy and merriment that was spontaneous and unfeigned.

But wait, we were not completely alone. In one corner of the room, on a table, lay a redheaded man apparently dead, and clad in nothing but his underpants. A large and heartless-looking fellow of Celtic cast, he was still sentient, for he breathed stertorously through his nose. Not dead, then. The girls giggled as they examined him like some entomological specimen, lifting an arm to let it drop plump, peering into a glazed eyeball, up his nose. "I don't know who he is," said Mrs. Henniker in dismay. "We will have to wait until he comes round." One of the girls explained how the eyeballs of the corpse had suddenly rolled upward into his skull like a doll; she mimed this horribly. Caradoc approached the figure with an air of medical knowledgeableness and said: "Aha! Cheyne-Stokes respiration. My diagnosis is Merchant Navy. Have you looked in his clothes?"

"He has none. He arrived on a bicycle with some money in his hand. Nothing but his underpants."

Caradoc tutted sympathetically. "You see," said Mrs. Henniker piteously, "what we are up against all the time? How to run a respectable house what I mean? Tomorrow I will ring the consul."

They submitted the corpse to a further series of tests, tickling its privates with a quill, smacking its cheeks, rubbing it with cologne—but all to no purpose. Finally with a sigh they drew a bead curtain over the figure and Mrs. Henniker led us away among the farther alcoves where, among the dusty divans, siphons and bottles awaited us together with plates of various comestibles. Here Caradoc was very much *en pacha;* Fatma had already discovered her lost love in him. I pitied and admired him, for she was a fearsome golliwog of Negroid cast, though amiable in a pockmarked way. A shelf of gold and tin teeth adorned a cheerful and matronly grin.

The girls closed in now with chatter and laughter, piling themselves around us on the cushions like stray cats. It was all very domesticated and soothing. In the far corner Miki played a tune on a tinny piano which evoked dim and far-off things. There was no disposition to hurry, except in the case of the playful Fatma who made many a playful grab at the Cham's cods to see, as she said, "if there was any fruit on the branches as yet." Pulley said with an unmerited acerbity, "She's got a hope she has"; and in truth Caradoc seemed to derive more satisfaction from conversation than anything else. The sound of his own voice filled him with a vivid autointoxication. "They always ask me," he said somewhat sadly, "if I am not married and why and how many children and so on. I try and explain that I was never convinced about the state. But at long last I got so fed up that I began to carry around a wallet full of children just to humor them. Look." He tipped out of a wallet a series of grotesque pictures of nude children of various ages. "This is my youngest," he explained, holding up the most hideous. "He must be a man of forty by now; but this poor damsel won't know any better." Fatma crooned over the pictures. They were passed round the eager circle of baby fanciers. They had the effect of increasing enthusiasm. Eager to entertain, someone started to scratch a mandolin and croon. Others in a burst of baby worship produced their knitting and fell to work in aid of an imaginary seventh-month fetus. Tina dabbed us all with scent from a bottle labeled Phul and exhorted us to have *kephi*—joy. Somewhat to my surprise Mrs. Henniker also relaxed and laid down with her head in Demetra's lap, allowing the girl to brush her harsh hair and massage her temples. She kicked off her shoes and extending thin arms in rapturous abandonment allowed two other girls to knead and palp them slowly. A fine fat peasant girl closed in on me, polite and nonchalant. Of course in those fine free presalvarsan days nobody could help being slightly nagged by syphilophobia. I thought of Schopenhauer's *"Obit anus Abit onus"* and sighed into my flowing bowl. As if she read my mind Mrs. Henniker opened one eye like a chameleon and said: "She is all right; we take no chances here; the safety of the client is our guarantee." I tried to look as if I needed no such reassurance, allowing myself to be fed like a pet bird with aromatic scraps of entrail on toothpicks. "I want to see Sipple," said Caradoc, "that velvet prick in an iron mitt, that specialist in all the unwashed desires." "Later," said Mrs. Henniker, "he always comes later"; and then as if the word had reminded her of something she consulted her watch and rose to excuse herself. "I am hiring some new girls," she explained. "The doctor is coming to examine them." So saying she filtered through a wall of curtains and disappeared. Dispersing slowly upon our various trajectories I heard, as if in a dream, Caradoc admonishing me with: "I hope Charlton that you are not one of those Englishmen who forever dream of some sodomy-prone principality with a fringe of palms where the Arabs wear nothing under their nightgowns."

Silence, dispossession, plenitude. The little rooms on the first floor of the villa were spotlessly clean and bare of all ornament. Scoured wooden floors and enormous old-fashioned beds squatting like sumpter camels, with mattresses too tough to be dented by our bodies. Outside the sea sighed along the strand. "Some magi among the barbarians seeing Harpalus despondent persuaded him that he could lure the spirit of Pythonice back from the Underworld. In vain, despite the voice which issued from the bronze bay tree." She

58 ◆◆

came from no island but from the mulberry-starred plateaus where the Vardar flows, and where the women have voices of steel wire. The fish markets of Salonika had been her only school. Pitiful black eyes of a mooncalf adorned this kindly personage. Her freshly washed hair, though coarse, was delicious as mint. But then ideas turn sideways in their sleep, seduced by the lush combing of waves upon sand, and one turns with them, sliding toward the self-possession of sleep and dreaming. Once more I saw Harpalus among the tombs. "Harpalus the Macedonian, who plundered large sums from Alexander's funds, fled to Athens; there he fell madly in love with Pythonice the courtesan and squandered everything on her. Nothing like her funeral had ever been seen, choirs, artists, displays, massed instruments. And her tomb! As you approach Athens along the Sacred Way from Eleusis, at the point where the citadel is first seen, on the right you will see a monument which outdoes in size every other. You halt and ask yourself whose it is—Miltiades, Cimon, Pericles? No. It is Pythonice's, triple slave and triple harlot."

On my way downstairs—I took a wrong turning and lost myself, blundering down at last into a sort of cellar which must once have served as a kitchen when the villa had been a normal habitation. Here a strange scene was taking place, illustrated, so to speak by the shadows which whirled and loomed upon the dirty ceiling. A group of starkly silhouetted figures stood grouped about a deal table on which lay the figure of a girl. It was their shadows which lobbed about up above like daddy longlegs: fascinating cartoons, travesties or ordinary gestures magnified to enormous size. Mrs. Henniker occupied the foreground of the animated Goya. Her friend the doctor was bent intently over the girl on the table whose parted legs suggested a fruit tree in espalier. To one side, seated along a bench, fading yellowly away from the center of lamp light sat half a dozen candidates with cheap handbags. They looked contrite and hopeful, like extras at an audition.

Abashed and curious I hesitated in the open door. Mrs. Henniker, who stood holding a bull's-eye lamp, turned with nonchalance and beckoned me in with: "Come in, my poy, we are just finishing." The doctor grunted as he inserted some kind of old-fashioned catheter with a bulb—or a swab. His bent head obscured for me the face of Iolanthe as she lay there like some taken sparrow hawk. I was handed the torch while Mrs. Henniker busied herself with some documents, reciting the name and state of the subject. "Samiou Iolanthe, maidservant in Megara." The doctor wound up his gear and threw a towel over the exposed parts. "This one is also clean," he said and sitting up abruptly the girl gazed into my startled face. Her features sketched a mute imploring expression—almost she put her fingers to her lips. The doctor seized her thumb and stuck a syringe into the ball. She gasped and bit her lips as she saw him draw off a teaspoonful of venous blood to fill a tiny phial. Mrs. Henniker explained her preoccupations to me in a series of thorny asides. "I have to be careful they don't come from other places, dirty places, what I mean. Specially the sailor's brothel in Piraeus. So I take every precaution, what I mean." I did see what she meant—for that is precisely where Iolanthe came from; nor did she, nor had she ever hidden the fact from me, for there was no promise of exclusiveness between us. On the contrary it was thanks to her that I had visited the place when the Fleet was away.

We clattered down one summer dusk in the ill-lit and musty little metro; it was not a long run to Piraeus—a ragged and echoing township aboom with sirens and factories and the whimpering of sea gulls. The place lay some way outside in a crepuscular and unsavory quarter picked out in old bluish streetlamps obviously left over from the Paris exhibitions of '88. It was traversed by a squeaky tramline so sinuous that the occasional tram bucketed and swayed about as if stricken by palsy. The establishment had more than repaid my curiosity. It was built like a barrack around three sides of a wide flagged courtyard with a fountain in the center, suggesting nothing so much as a khan at the desert's edge. The flamboyant fountain, choked and dribbling, trickled down into a basin full of green slime and moss. On all three sides of the long low blocks stood the cubicles of the girls, somewhat like a row of bathing cabins; now, of course, the place was empty, all doors lying open. One or two of the cells had been left still lit by cotton wicks afloat in saucers of olive oil—as if their tenants had just slipped out on an errand and would soon be back. But the only inhabitant of the place seemed to be the janitor—an old half-crazy crone who talked cheerfully to herself. "Soft in the head," said a gesture of Io's.

Outside every door stood a pair of wooden clogs, or pattens. It was extraordinarily beautiful in a storybook way— the dense shadow, the elfish yellow light, the dark velvety sky above. All the doors had the traditional Judas cut in them, but this time heart-shaped, which enabled the clients to peer in on the lighted girl before making their choice. Moreover on each of the doors was painted, in crude lettering, the name of the girl—all names of the Greek anthology, the very perfection of anonymity! The furniture of each cubicle was identical, consisting of a clumsy iron bed, small dressing table and chair. The only decoration was personal—tortoiseshell mirror, tinsel strips from biscuit tins, postcards of faraway ports, an ikon with a bottle of fresh olive oil beside it. The oil performed a double service both religious and laic—for the only instrument of contraception was a slip of Kalymnos sponge dipped in it. Thus the sacred juice celebrated its historic ancestry by a double burning, igniting up man and saint alike. On the back wall, innocent as a diploma on a seminary wall, was the medical certificate of health with the date of last inspection. On this figured the girl's real name.

Her cell now (Antigone) was occupied by someone called Euridice Bakos according to the chart. But she too was away on some mysterious errand, though the wick burned in the alcove before a misty Saint Barbara. This ikon was however Iolanthe's—for she blew out the wick and reclaimed it. In the drawer of the rotting dressing table with its gaudy oilcloth cover she rummaged purposefully to disinter a comb and brush of doubtful cleanliness and a few shabby articles of wear. Lastly in a corner, under the bed with its tin chamber pot she picked over a bundle of cheap magazines—*Bouquetto, Romanzo* and the like—to trace a serial she wanted to continue; also a French grammar and an English phrase book.

The pattens she had not wanted to take, although they were hers; but I was loath to surrender the clumsy things and slipped one into each pocket. Later the ikon stood upon the mantelpiece in Number Seven. They lighted an expensive candle before it and turned off the harsh electric light. The clogs served later as bookends. Then disappeared. Here they are again. The persistence of objects and the impermanence of people—he never ceased to reflect upon the matter, as he lay there listening to the distant music of the Plaka taverns and the nearer heartbeats of his watch. She slept so lightly, with such a shallow respiration, that at times she looked dead, as though her heart had stopped. Then to lie back under that shadowing ceiling and yonder into introspection once more, allowing his mind to fill up with all the detritus of thought— things far removed from fornication's rubber pedal; and yet with the idle side of his mind he could go over his points like a mare or a hare. Reflecting I should suppose upon the unconscious alchemist he might one day become, the lion man. But no, this is a perverse attempt to read back from memories which have faded. About sex? No. About death? Never. This young man never thought of making a will. No he thought in fields, fields which he hoped that one day Abel would arrange in valencies. Some document! It would ideally record how one day he, like everyone else, began to face the disruption of the ordinary appetites, the changing electric fields of the impulses, so hard to place, to tame, to convert into practical usage like, say, the orgasm of electric light in a bulb, or a wheel moving under a lever.

Koepgen used to say that human life is an anthology of states; chronological progression is an illusion. And that to be punished for what one does not remember except in dreams is our version of the tragedy the Greeks invented. The poetry is in the putty, as Caradoc used to say!

Patterns of fading music from the south; early cocks compose their infernal paternoster. Clytemnestra lopped off the heavy limbs and carefully wiped her fingers in the thing's hair. Delicate white fingers with their enormous vocabulary of gestures. The shadows on the cave of Plato lobbed and bounced now upon the walls of Mrs. Henniker's dungeon. The performance was at an end. My smile of friendly complicity had reassured Iolanthe. But to my surprise I suddenly felt the pricking of a puzzling jealousy. The scientist does not like to see his algebra get up, shake itself and walk away. I promised myself another banquet of Greek twilight soon, though it hardly allayed the absurd sensation. On the dirty wall I thought I descried moving ideograms of other love objects living in their Platonic form—"man" "rose" "fire" "star." All the furniture of Koepgen's poems, which he claimed were really "acts, the outer skin of thought." All this had passed over the head of the recumbent Charlock; now he had come back to take up the dropped stitch, so to speak, to recapitulate it all for Abel. All this vulgar data when "screened out" by the sign manuals of the computer, or "panned out" (as if for gold), would be sifted down through the spectrum of language itself, punctuated and valued, to yield at last the vatic tissue which owes little to ordinary looms. Now I know that everything is remediable, that finally somehow somewhere memory is fully recoverable. These thoughts then bursting on the surface of the mind in little bubbles of pure consciousness would provide red meat for the Lion—Abel's raw aliment.

Life is an image (Koepgen) of which everything is the reflection. All objects are slowly changing into each other—dead man to dead tree, to dead rock, to vine, to marl, to tan sand, to water, cloud, air, fire . . . a movement not of dissolution but of fulfillment. (To fulfill is to fill full.)

Chemical reincarnations by the terms of which we all become spare parts of one another—excuse the biblical echo.

Abel roars and roars. Our modern oracle like the ancient is this steel animal: bronze bull, steel lion. His diagnosis is as follows: "This young man should read Empedocles again. Complexity, which is sometimes necessary, is not always beautiful; simplicity is. Yes, but after the last question has been asked and answered there will always remain something enigmatic about a work of art or of nature. You cannot drain *la dive bouteille* however much you try."

The object of Abel's operation you see was never the manufacture of a factitious literature, no; but a way of remodeling sensation in order to place one in a position of "self-seizing." Such words then become merely a novel form of heartbeat as they do for the poet. In "real" life. Has not Koepgen always called his poems "my little prayer siphons"? Gradually I find my blundering way back through the stale curtains. . . .

Caradoc was there, musing over a drink, and looking somewhat gibbous after his exertions; Fatma had produced a manicure set and was touching up his square fingernails. He indicated a siphon and said: "Drink, boy, until you detonate the idea within you." He was I thought a trifle detonated himself already. Inconsequential ideas trailed through his mind. He stroked the golliwog and extolled her great "bubbles of plenty." Ugh! He enjoined her to give us a tune on her zither, and then without waiting for accompaniment sang softly, wearily:

> *Ah take me back once more to find*
> *That pure oasis of neurosis called*
> *The Common Mind*
> *To foster and to further if I can*
> *The universal udderhood of man.*

Obscure associations led him to speak of Sipple. "Sipple was a clown once, a professional clown. Aye! I have seen him at Olympia come on with boots like soap dishes and a nose like a lingam. His trousers furled like a sail and the whole man was held together by a celluloid dickey which rolled up like a blind and knocked him down. His greatest moment was when the second clown set fire to his privates with a torch. Talk about Latimer's ordeal: you should have heard the ladies screech. But his proclivities were not those of the refined. His habits were rebarbative. There was a scandal and he had to retire. Now he lives in honorable retirement in Athens—don't ask me on what. Even the firm can't tell me that."

He broke off and gave a surprised roar, for in the farthest alcove in the room a figure which had been lying completely buried in cushions suddenly sat up and gave a yellow yawn. It was a dramatic enough entry on cue to satisfy Sipple's sense of theater—for it was he. His pale lugubrious face was creased with sleep; his small bloodshot eyes, full of a kind of street-Arab meanness, traveled round the room in dazed fashion. Only when he saw Caradoc advance upon him with out-stretched arms did a vague smile wander into his counte-nance. "So you got here," he piped, without much relish, hitching his tubular trousers onto sagging braces, and laughed *chick chick*. His face was alive with little twitches, tics and grimaces—as if it did not know into what expression to settle. No, it was as if he needed to stretch out the sleep-creased skin. He submitted to some massive thumps of wel-come from his friend, and yawning hugely accepted to come and sit in our corner of the room. A tame sloth I would have said: with a queer pear-shaped furry head.

The Cham pushed and pulled him about as one might a pet. I was introduced and shook a damp octopod hand; bizarre was Sipple, and rather disturbing. "I was telling the boy here," said Caradoc, "about why you had to leave the motherland." Sipple shot me a doubtful and cunning look, unable to decide for a moment whether or not to pick up this gambit, an obvious comedian's "feed." His eyes were far too close together; "made to see through keyholes," a Greek would have said. Then he decided to comply. "It was all Mrs. Sipple's fault, sir," he whimpered with just the suspicion of a trembling underlip. "Yes," he went on slyly, moistening his lips and gazing sideways at me with a furtive and timorous air. "She didn't hold with my exhibitions. We had to part."

Caradoc, who appeared to hang on his lips, struck his knee with massive sympathy. "Wives never do. To the ducking stool withem all," he cried in Jovian fashion. Sipple nodded and brooded further on his wrongs.

"It was the lodger," Sipple explained to me in a painstaking undertone. "I can only do it in exceptional circumstances, and then it all goes off in spray." He looked woebegone, his underlip swelled with self-commiseration. Yet his ferret's eye still watched me, trying to size me up. I could see it was a relief when I decided to find him funny, and laughed —more out of obedience to Caradoc than from my own personal inclination. However he took courage and launched himself into his act—a recital obviously much-rehearsed and canonized by repetition. Caradoc added rhetorical flourishes of his own, obviously keenly appreciative of his friend's gifts. "You were right," he cried. "Right to leave her, Sippy, with dignity intact. Everything you tell me about her fills me with dismay. God's ruins! Covered in clumps of toc. Ah God to see her haunches stir across the moon at Grantchester. No, you were right, dead right. A woman who refuses to tie up a Sipple and thrash him with leg-irons is not worth the name."

Sipple gave the stonehenge of a smile exposing huge discolored teeth with some extensive gaps. "It wouldn't fadge, Carry," he admitted. "But here in Athens you can do as you would be done by, as the Scripture has it." I suppose you could call it extra-suspensory perception.

"Tell me again," said the Cham, eager for further felicities of this kind, and the little pear droned on. "It came over me very gradual," said Sipple, raising his arms to pat the air. "Very gradual indeed it did. At first I was normal as any curate, ask my mates. Give me an inch and I took a mile. And I was never one for the boys, Carry, not then I wasn't. But suddenly the theatrical side in me came to the fore. I was like a late-blooming flahr, Carry, a retarded flowering. Perhaps it was being a clown that did it, the magic of the footlights, I dunno."

It was funny all right, but also vaguely disquieting. He put his head on one side and winked with his right eye. He stood up and joined his fingers to say, with a seraphic sadness: "One day I had to face reality. It was quite unexpected. I pulled out me squiffer when all of a sudden it abrogated by a simple reticulation of the tickler. I was aghast! I went to see the doctor and he says to me: 'Look here, Sipple, I must be frank with you. As man to man your sperm count is low and the motility of your product *nil*.' I reeled. There I had been, so young, so gay, so misinformed. 'Sipple,' went on the doc, 'it's all in your childhood. I bet you never noozled the nipple properly. You never had seconds I'll avow.' And he was right; but then what little nipper knows how to tease the tit properly and avoid abrogation in later life when he needs all the reticulation he can get, just tell me that!" He wiped away an invisible tear and stood all comicopathetico before an invisible medico. "You have all my sympathy," said Caradoc, drunk and indeed a little moved. He swallowed heavily. Sipple went on, his voice rising to higher more plaintive register: "But that was not all, Carry. The doctor had drained away my self-confidence with his blasted medical diagmatic. Yet there was a crueler blow to come. 'Sipple,' he said to me, 'there is no way out of your dilemma. You are utterly lacking in PELVIC THRUST.' "

"How unfair," cried Caradoc with burning sympathy.

"And thank God untrue," squawked Sipple. "Under the proper stage management it is a wanton lie."

"Good."

"I have shown you, haven't I?"

"Yes."

"And I'll show you again tonight. Where is Henniker?"

"I'll take your word for it, Sippy."

Sipple poured himself out a massive drink and warmed to his tale, secure now in his hold over his audience. He must have been a very great clown once, for he combined the farcical and the sinister within one range of expression. "Someday I shall write the story of my love life from my own point of view. Starting with the dawn of realization. One day the scales dropped from my eyes. I saw love as only a clown could: what struck me was this: the *position*, first of all, is *ridiculous*. No one with a sense of the absurd could look at it frankly without wanting to laugh. Who invented it? If you had seen Mrs. Arthur Sipple lying there, all reliability, and fingering her ringlets impatiently, you'd have felt your risibility rise I bet. It was too much for me, I couldn't master myself, I laughed in her face. Well, not exactly her face. She was too heavy to turn over, you'd need a spade. It was only when her nightdress took fire that she realized that all was over. I couldn't help laughing, and that made her cry. 'Farewell forever, Beatrice,' I said turning on my heel. I sailed away and for many a month I wallowed in the dark night of the soul. I reflected. Gradually my ideas clarified, became more theatrical. I had found a way through.

"So I went back to the doctor, all fulfillment, to tell him about my new methods. He jumped and said I was a caution. A caution! 'It's very very un-British, you know,' he said. I hadn't thought of that. I thought he'd be so pleased with me. He said I was a traitor to the unborn race. He said he wanted to write a paper on me, me Sipple. I grew a trifle peremptory with him, I'll allow. But I hadn't come all the way back to Cockfosters to be insulted. He called me an anomaly and it was the last straw. I struck him and broke his spectacles." Sipple gave a brief sketch of this blow and sank back onto the sofa. "And so," he went on slowly, "I came here to Athens to try and find peace of mind; and I won't say I didn't. I'm assuaged now, thanks to Mrs. Henniker's girls and their broomsticks. No more abrogation of the tickler."

Caradoc was having one of his brief attacks of buoyancy; drink seemed to have a curious intermittent effect upon him, making him tipsy in little patches. But these were passing clouds of fancy merely from which he appeared to be able to recover by an act of will. "Once," he was saying dreamily, "once the firm sent me to build a king a palace in Burma and there I found the menfolk had little bells sewn into their season tickets—believe me bells. Every movement accompanied by a soft and silver tinkle. Suggestive, melodious and poetical it was to hear them chiming along the dark jungle roads. I almost went out and ordered a carillon for myself. . . .

> *Come join the wanton music where it swells,*
> *Order yourself a whopping set of bells.*

But nothing came of it. I was withdrawn too soon."

A large-scale diversionary activity was now taking place somewhere among the curtains; Pulley appeared looking sheepish and incoherent, followed by Mrs. Henniker who was greeted with a cry from Sipple. "What about it, Mrs. H.?" he cried. "I told you I wanted to be tortured tonight in front of my friends here." Mrs. Henniker clucked and responded imperturbably that there had been a little delay, but that the "torture room" was being prepared and the girls dressed up. The clown then excused himself with aplomb, saying that he had to get ready for his act but that he would not be long. "Don't let him fall asleep," he added pointing to the yawning Pulley. "I need an audience or it falls flat."

Nor did it take very long to set the theatrical scene. Mrs. Henniker reappeared with clasped hands and bade us follow her once more down into the same gaunt kitchen where the shadows still bobbed and slithered—but a different set of them; moreoever the dungeon now was full of the melancholy clanking of chains. More lights had been introduced—and there in the middle of things was Sipple naked. They had just finished chaining him to a truckle bed of medieval ugliness. He paid no attention to anyone. He appeared deeply preoccupied. He was wearing the awkward old-fashioned leg-irons of the cripple. But most bizarre of all were the party whips, so to speak. The three girls who had been delegated to "torture" him wore mortarboards and university gowns with dingy fur tippets. The contrast with their baggy Turkish trousers was delightful. They each held a long broom switch—the sort one could buy for a few drachmae and which tavern keepers use for sweeping out the mud-floored taverns. As we entered they all advanced purposefully upon Sipple with their weapons at the ready while he, appearing to catch sight of them for the first time, gave a start and sank kneeling to the floor.

He began to tremble and sweat, his eyeballs hung out as he gazed around him for some method of escape. He shrank back with dismal clankings. I had to remind myself that he was acting—but indeed *was* he acting? It was impossible to say how true or false this traumatic behavior was. Mrs. Henniker folded her arms and looked on with a proud smile. The three doctors of divinity now proclaimed in very broken English, "Arthur, you have been naughty again. You must be punish!" Sipple cringed. "Nao!" he cried in anguish. "Don't 'urt me. I swear I never."

The girls, too, acted their parts very well, frowning, knitting black brows, gritting white teeth. Their English was full of charm—such broken crockery, and so various as to accent—craggy Cretan, singsong Ionian. "Confess," they cried, and Sipple began to sob. "Forward!" said Mrs. Henniker now, under her breath in Greek, adding the further adornment of a thick Russian intonation. "Forward, my children, my partridges."

They bowed implacably over Sipple now and shouted in ragged unison, "You have again wetted your bed." And before he could protest any further they fell upon him roundly with their broom switches and began to fustigate the fool unmercifully, crying, "Dirty. Dirty."

"Ah," cried Sipple at the stinging pleasure of the first assault. "Ah." He writhed, twisted and pleaded to be sure; he even made a few desultory movements which suggested that he was going to fight back. But this was only to provoke a harsher attack. Anyway he would have stood little chance against this band of peasant Amazons. He clanked, scraped and squeaked. The noise grew somewhat loud, and Mrs. Henniker slipped into the corner to put on a disc of "The Blue Danube" in order to mitigate it. Bits of broom flew off in every direction. Caradoc watched this scene with the reflective gravity of one watching a bullfight. I felt astonishment mixed with misgiving. But meanwhile Sipple, oblivious to us all, was taking his medicine like a clown—nay, lapping it up.

He had sunk under the sharpened onslaught, begun to disintegrate, deliquesce. His pale arms and legs looked like those of a small octopus writhing in the throes of death. In between his cries and sobs for mercy his breath came faster and faster, he gasped and gulped with a perverted pleasure. At last he gave a final squeak and lay spread-eagled on the stone flags. They went on beating him until they saw no further sign of life and then, panting, desisted and burst into peals of hysterical laughter. The corpse of Sipple was unchained, disentangled and hoisted lovingly onto the truckle bed. 'Well done," said Mrs. Henniker. "Now he will sleep." Indeed Sipple had already fallen into a deep infantile slumber. He had his thumb in his mouth and sucked softly and rhythmically on it.

They surrounded his bed filled with a kind of commiserating admiration and wonder. On slept Sipple, oblivious. I noticed the markings on his arms and legs—no larger than blackheads in a greasy sink: but unmistakably the punctures of a syringe. The shadows swayed about us. One of the lamps had begun to smoke. And now, in the middle of everything, there came a sharp hammering on a door somewhere and Mrs. Henniker jumped as if stung by a wasp and dashed away down the corridor. Everyone waited in tableau grouped about the truckle bed until she should reappear—which she did a moment later at full gallop crying: "Quick, the police."

An indescribable confusion now reigned. In pure panic the girls scattered like rabbits to a gunshot. Windows were thrown open, doors unbolted, sleepers were warned to hurry up. The house disgorged its inhabitants in ragged fashion. I found myself running along the dunes with Pulley and Caradoc in the frail starshine. Our car had disappeared, though there seemed to be another on the road with only its dim sidelights on. Having put a good distance bewteen ourselves and the house we lay in a ditch panting to await developments. Later the whole thing turned out to have been a misunderstanding; it was simply two sailors who had come to claim their recumbent friend. But now we felt like frightened schoolboys. Concern for the sleeping clown played some part in Caradoc's meditations as we lay among the squills, listening to the sighing sea. Then the tension ebbed, and turning on his back the Cham's thoughts changed direction. Presumably Hippolyta's chauffeur had beaten a retreat in order not to compromise her reputation by any brush with the law. He would be back, of that my companions were sure. I chewed grass, yawning. Caradoc's meditations turned upon other subjects, though only he and Pulley were *au courant*. Out of this only vague sketches swam before me. Something about Hippolyta having ruined her life by a long-standing attachment, a lifelong infatuation with Graphos. "And what the devil can she think we will achieve by my giving a Sermon on the Mount on the blasted Acropolis?" Nobody cared what savants thought. Graphos might save the day, but his career was at its lowest ebb. He had had several nervous breakdowns and was virtually unable to lead his party even if the government fell, as they thought it would this winter. And all because he was going *deaf*.

I perked up. "Can you imagine a worse fate for a politician raised in a tradition of public rhetoric? No wonder he's finished."

"Did you say *deaf?*" I said.

"Deaf!" I had become very fond of the word and repeated it softly to myself. It had become a very beautiful word to me.

"And I have to sermonize on the Mount," repeated Caradoc with disgust. "Something to give ears to the deaf, something full of arse-felt greetings and blubberly love. I ask you. As if it could avert the worst."

"What worst?" I asked; it seemed to me that for days now I had done nothing but ask questions to which nobody could or would provide an answer. Caradoc shook himself and said: "How should I know? I am only an architect."

Lights were coming down the road. It was Hippolyta's car. We signaled and galloped toward it.

Somewhere here the continuity becomes impacted again, or dispersed. "I was the fruit of a mixed mirage," said Caradoc, dining Chez Vivi with a group of money-loving boors with polish. Laughing until his buttonhole tumbled into his wineglass. "We must work for the greatest happiness of the highest few." I had by then confided my Orient pearls to the care of Hippolyta for Graphos. A queer sort of prosopography reigns over this section of time. Arriving too early, for example, I waited in the rose garden while she saw Graphos to his car. I had only seen his picture in the paper, or seen him sitting in the back of a silver car, waving to crowds. I had missed the club foot; now as they came down the path arm in arm I heard the shuffling syncopated walk, and I realized that he had greater burdens to carry than merely his increasing deafness. His silver hair and narrow wood-beetle's head with those melancholy incurious eyes—they were set off by the silver ties he wore, imported from Germany. Somewhere in spite of the cunning he gave off all the lethargy of riches. I came upon exactly the quality of the infatuation he had engendered in an ancient Greek poem about a male lover.

> *He reeks with many charms,*
> *His walk is a whole hip dance,*
> *His excrement is sesame seedcake*
> *His very spittle is apples.*

Insight is definitely a handicap when it comes to loving. (His rival shot him stone dead with a longbow.) On the lavatory wall someone had marked the three stages of man after the classical formula:

> satiety
> hubris
> *ate*

"The danger for Graphos is that he has begun to think of himself in the third person singular," she said sadly, but much later. All this data vibrates on now across the screens of the ordering condensers in Abel, to emerge at the requisite angle of inclination.

Nor was my experiment with Caradoc's voice less successful; amongst the confusion and general blur of conversation there was a brief passage extolling the charms of Fatma to which she listened with considerable amusement, and which I found centuries later among my baggage and fed to A. "She may not be a goddess to everyone," he begins a trifle defensively, "though her lineaments reveal an ancient heritage. An early victim of ritual infibulation was she. Later Albanian doctors sewed up the hymen with number twelve pack thread so that she might contract an honorable union. No wonder her husband jumped off a cliff after so long and arduous a honeymoon. In their professional excitement the doctors had by mistake used the strings of a guitar. She gave out whole arpeggios like a musical box when she opened her legs. Her husband, once recovered, sent her back to her parents with a

74 ◆◆

hole bored in her frock to show that she was no virgin. Litigation over the affair is doubtless still going on. But meanwhile what was Fatma to do? She took the priapic road like so many others. She walked in peace and brightness holding the leather phallus, the sacred *olisbos* in the processions of Mrs. Henniker. Nor must we forget that these parts were *aidoion* to the Greeks, "inspiring holy awe." There is no special word for chastity in ancient Greek. It was the Church Fathers who, being troubled and a trifle perverted, invented *agneia*. But bless you, Fatma does not know that, to this very day. When she dies her likeness will be in all the taverns, her tomb at the Nube covered with votive laurels; she will have earned the *noblissima meretrix* of future ages. Biology will have to be nudged to make room for Fatma."

But the rest scattered with the talk as gun-shy birds will at a clapping of hands. Something vague remains which might be guessed to concern the Piraeus brothel where many of the names live on from the catalogs of Athenaeus—like Damasandra which means, "the man crusher": and the little thin ones, all skin and bone and saucer eyes, are still "anchovies." Superimposed somewhere in all this Iolanthe's just-as-ancient moral world out of Greek time. Skins plastered with white lead to hide the chancres, jowls stained with mulberry juice, blown hair powdering to gray, underside of olives in wind but not half as venerable. The Lydians spayed their women and did their flogging to the sound of a flute. Depilatories of pitch plaster battling desperately against the approach of old age. . . . The appropriate sounds of the fountain whispering and of a leather-covered bottle being decanted. Then amidst yawns C.'s declamation of a poem called "The Origen of Species":

> *One god-distorted neophyte*
> *Cut off his cods to see the light,*
> *Now though the impulse does not die*
> *He greets erections with a sigh.*

◆ ◆ 75

Somewhere, too, room must be made for the scattered utterances of Koepgen—his notebooks were always to hand, not a drop was spilt. Records from some Plaka evening under a vine tent, mewed at by mandolins. "First pick your wine: then bleed into it preciously, drop by drop, the living semen of the resin. Then pour out and drink to complete the ikonography of a mind at odds with itself here below the lid of sky. The differences can be reconciled for a while by these humble tin jars." Singing has blurred the rest of it, but here and there, like the glint of mica in stone, the ear catches a solidified echo. "Have you noticed that at the moment of death a man breathes in through both nostrils?"

These simple indices of acture anxiety, racing pulse, incontinence, motor incoordination (wine jar spilled, flowers scattered, vase broken) involve the loss of reflexes acquired within the first year of infant life. Iolanthe cannot be to blame. She sleeps like a mouse widow with her hair in her mouth, black fingernails extended on the pillow like grotesque fingerprints. Bodies smelling hot and rank.

Somewhere here also, among the shattered fragments recovered from old recordings. Abel has the germ plasm of Hippolyta's voice, vivacious and halting, running on like a brook in a dry riverbed. The black of that perfumed hair when set seems to be charcoal, carved and buffed—or a Chinese ink which holds its sheen even in darkness. She walks naked, unself-conscious, to the balcony to find the car keys, and when he has driven off without a backward glance she goes barefoot down the garden path to the small Byzantine chapel at the end to consult the hovering Draconian eyes of the ikons, the reproachful smile of Saint Barbara. Here to light the lamps and mutter the traditional prayers.

It never ceases to amaze me that throughout all this period, unknown to me, Benedicta was approaching; she was sliding down the mighty Danube whose feeble headspring crawls out of a small opening in the courtyard of some German castle. Lulled by the voices of the Nibelungs she sees great castles in ruins brooding on their own reflections in the running water.

Trees arch over Durnstein: then Vienna, Budapest, Belgrade and down through the Iron Gates to scout the Black Sea coast of Bulgaria in a Rumanian packet slim as a cigarette; and so down the Bosporus to where the crooked calligraphy of mosques and spires waited for her in Polis. And for Charlock.

The journey had been arranged for her by the firm; young widows must do their forgetting somehow.

Little eddies of thyme and rosemary lay about in parcels among the columns; one walked into them. There was no breeze. The sun had completed its impressive swight-lifting act and plunged into the darkness. Violet the Saronic Gulf, topaz Hymettus, lilac bronze the marbles. The oncoming night was freshening toward the dews of midnight and after. Here we were assembled, some two hundred people, at the northern end of the Parthenon. *Tenue de ville,* dark suits, cocktail dresses. It seemed a fairly representative lecture audience—members of the Academy and the Temple of Science, professors and other riffraff of this order. In this cool stable air everyone was relaxed and informal, indeed mildly gay. Except Hippolyta, who was in a high state of nerves, eating valerian cachets one after another to calm herself. On the top plinth, among the columns, stood a lectern with a lamp. It was from here that Caradoc was supposed to be lecturing. The general disposition of the chairs for the audience was pleasantly informal. They were dotted about in groups among the shattered rubble. Everything promised—or so I thought. Doubtless the site itself was responsible for these feelings, for who can see the blasted Parthenon at dusk without wanting to put his arms round it? Moreover in his honeyed oncoming of night with its promise of a late moonrise, an occasional firefly triggering on the slopes below, the owls calling?

Below the battlements glowed the magic display of precious stones which is Athens at night: a spilled jewel casket. The shaven hills like penitents bowed around us and domed the whole in watchful silence. Yes, but what of the lecturer?

"I haven't been able to reach him all day. He's been out

with Sipple, drinking very heavily. They were seen on bicycles at Phaleron this afternoon, very unsteady. I've hunted everywhere. If he doesn't come in another five minutes I shall have to call the whole thing off. Imagine how delighted the women will be to see me humiliated like this." I took her arm and tried to calm her. But she was trembling with anxiety and fury combined. It was true that a slight restlessness had begun to make itself felt in the audience. Conversation had begun to dwindle, become more desultory. The women had taken stock of each other's clothes and were becoming bored. "Give him time," I said for the fourth time. People had started to cough and cross their legs.

At this moment a vague shape emerged from among the distant columns and began to move toward us with a slow, curmudgeonly tread. At first it was a mere shadowy sketch of a man but gradually it began to take on shape as it approached. It held what appeared to be a bottle in its left hand. Head bent, it appeared to be sunk in the deepest meditation as it advanced with this lagging unsteady gait. "It's Caradoc," she hissed with a mixture of elation, terror and doubt. The figure stopped short and gazed at us with all amazement, as if seeing us all for the first time, and quite unexpectedly. "He's drunk," she added with disgust gripping my arm. "O God! And he has forgotten all about the lecture."

Indeed it was easy to read all this into the expressions which played about those noble if somewhat dispersed features. It was the face of a man who asks himself desperately what the devil he is supposed to be doing in such a place, at such a time. He gazed at the lectern with a slowly maturing astonishment, and then at the assembly grouped before him. "Well I'm damned," he said audibly. At this moment the despairing Hippolyta saved the day by starting to applaud. Everyone took up and echoed the clapping, and the ripple of sound seemed to stir some deep chord in the remoter recesses of the lecturer's memory. He frowned and sucked his teeth as he explored these fugitive memories, sorting them hazily into

78 ◆ ◆

groups. The quixotic clapping swelled, and its implications began slowly to dawn on him. It was for him, all this! Yes, after all there was some little matter of a lecture. A broad smile illumined those heroic features. "The lecture, of course," he said, with evident relief, and set his bottle down on the plinth beside him—slowly, but without an overelaborate display of unsteadiness. It was impossible to judge whether he looked as drunk to the rest of the audience as he did to us. They did not perhaps know him well enough to detect more than a desirable flamboyance of attitude—the nonchalance of a great foreign savant. Moreover his tangled mane of hair and his rumpled clothes seemed oddly in keeping with the place. He had appeared like some sage or prophet from among the columns—bearing perhaps an oracle? A ripple of interest went through us all. The Greeks, with their highly tuned sense of dramatic oratory, must have believed this to be a calculated entry suitable to a man about to discourse on this most enigmatic of ancient monuments. But it was all very well for him to remember the lecture at this late date—it must have been gnawing at the fringes of his subconscious all day: but if he had prepared nothing? Hippolyta trembled like a leaf. Our hands locked in sympathetic alarm we watched him take a few steps forward and grip the lectern forcibly, like a dentist about to pluck out a molar. He gazed around in leonine fashion under frowning eyebrows. Then he curtly raised his hand and the clapping ebbed away into silence.

"All day," he said on a hoarse and Delphic note, "I have been locked in meditation, wondering what I was going to tell you tonight about this." He waved an arm toward the columns behind. Hippo sighed with growing relief. "At least he is not completely out." Quite the contrary. His speech was thick but audible and unslurred. He was making a rapid recovery, hand over fist. "Wondering," he went on in the same rasping tone, "how much I would *dare* to reveal of what I know."

He had unwittingly fallen upon a splendid opening gambit. The hint of mysteries, of the occult, was most appropriate to the place as well as to the gathering. There was a stir of interest. Caradoc shook his head and sank his chin upon his breast for a long moment of meditation. We, his friends, were afraid that he might indeed doze off in this attitude—but we did him an injustice. In due course he raised his leonine head once more, and, with the faintest trace of a hiccup, went on in oracular fashion. "Time must inspirit us with all the magniloquence of the memories which hover here. Who were they, first of all, these ancestors of ours? Who? And how did they manage to actualize the potential in man's notions of beauty, sidestep history, abbreviate eternity? Perhaps by prayer—but if so to whom, to what?" He licked his lips with relish and raked his audience with flashing eye. Hippolyta nudged me. "This is good stuff," she whispered. "But most of them don't know English and they won't realize that it means nothing. But the tone is perfect, isn't it?" It was; he was clearly beginning to surmount his infirmity rather successfully. If only he could keep up the oracular note it wouldn't matter much what he actually said. Hope dawned in our hearts.

"Anyone can build, place one stone on another, but who can achieve the gigantic impersonality of such art? The cool thrift of that classical indifference which only comes when one has stopped caring? In our age the problem has not changed, only our responses are different. We have tried to purify insight with the aid of reason and its fruit in technics: and failed—our buildings show it. Yet we are still here, still full of sap, still trying, grafted onto these ancient marble roots. They have not disowned us yet. They are still lying in wait for us, the selfish and indifferent nurselings of matter, yes; and their architecture is the fruit by which ye shall know them. It is the hero of every epoch. Into it can be read the destiny, doctrines and predispositions of a time, a being, a place, a material. But in an age of fragments, an age without a true cosmological notion of affect and its powers, what can we do but flounder, improvise, hesitate? A building is a language which tells us all. It cannot cheat."

"The only trouble," whispered Hippolyta again, "is that all this is useless for my purposes. It's all gibberish, damn him."

"Never mind. At least he's here."

Caradoc's self-possession was gaining ground. He had retrieved his bottle by a stealthy sideways movement, and placed it on the lectern before him. He seemed to draw courage from an occasional affectionate glance at it. He pursued his way, adding judicious and expressive gestures.

"What can I tell you about him, this man, these men, who realized and built this trophy? Everything, in fact. Moreover everything which you also know full well, though perhaps without actually realizing it. For we have all done our spell in the womb, have we not? We were all inhabitants of prehistory once, we all squirmed out into the so-called world. If I can give you the autobiography of this monument it is only because it starts with my own birth; I will give you its pedigree in giving you my own.

"In the first twenty-four hours after birth we must recognize a total reorganization of the creature in question from a water to a land animal. No transformation from chrysalis to butterfly could be more radical, more complete, more drastic. The skin, for example, changes from an internal organ, encapsulated, to an external one, exposed to the free and abrasive airs. This little martyr's body must cope with a terrific drop in external temperature. Light and sound pierce eye and ear like gimlets. No wonder I screeched." (At this point Caradoc gave a brief but bloodcurdling screech.)

"Then, to pursue the matter further, the infant like an explorer must supply his own oxygen requirements. Is *this* freedom? Nor could the stimulants of his puny machine be less irksome to come to terms with—small whiffs of deadly carbon monoxide, with its inevitable slight hypoxia. *Aiee!* Can you wonder that my only wish was to retreat, not only into the sheltering maternal pouch, but right back into the testes of the primeval ape for whom my father merely acted as agent, as representative? I can tell you that Caradoc found this no fun at all. My respiratory center was laboring heavily.

I lay on the slab, the mortuary slab of my immortal life—twitching like a skate in a frying pan. But even this would have been too much if it had not been enough. Within a few hours an even more drastic reorganization was to be forced upon me. My whole cardiovascular system, so cozily established and equilibrated in the socialist state of the womb, had to change from the dull but munificent throbbing of the placental intake to a new order of things—a whole new system. From now on my own lungs were to be the primary, indeed the only source of my oxygen supply. Think of it, and pity the shuddering child." Here the lecturer provided a few illustrative shudders and took a brief pull at the bottle, as if to seek warmth and consolation against these memories.

"At birth the heat-regulating centers are sadly immature. It takes weeks of running in for the motors to improve. At birth, as I said, there is the calamitous temperature fall, but as yet no teeth to chatter with. It takes overcoming, and somehow I did it. I achieved the state known as poikilothermic—a shifting of temperatures to respond to the degree outside. The doctor was in raptures at the very word. Poikilothermic! He pushed a dynamometer up my behind and began to read off the impulses, beating time with his finger. But already I was dying to retire from this unequal struggle, to draw my pension and relinquish the good fight. But I must not deny that I had already had a little practice in swallowing during my period *in utero*. There had also been a few languid movements of the gastrointestinal tract—a mere dummy practice. But I knew no more about its meaning than a conscript knows about the intentions behind intensive arms drill; less, even, I should say, much less. He may guess—but how should I guess my own future?

"Of course some sucking motions had been present before there was anything to suck on, so to speak. Ah the teat, when it came—what an inexpressible relief! What a consolation prize for the surrender I had made!

"All this is essential to realize if we are to think seriously about the Parthenon, my friends. The inside of a baby is sterile at birth; but a few hours afterward . . . why, it has apparently taken in all the germs that make human life so well worth unliving among our mortal contemporaries. As you can imagine I found all this most distasteful, and made it plain with whatever vocal chords I possessed. In the meantime however the skin had started to influence fluid balance by evaporation. But the whole thing felt so damn precarious—the capillary system is so liable to dilatation and contraction. Yet I went on—not consciously, by my own volition but propelled by my biological shadow. Slowly the respiration began to stabilize. But how slowly the systolic blood pressure comes up during childhood. The pulse rate, so high at birth, slowly comes down to the average adult beat of seventy-two to the minute. But meanwhile I was also developing an enzyme system for digesting the various chemical entities I should be required to ingest in order to keep body and snail together. How slow! I mean the evolution of the body membrane in order to filter proteins adequately. At birth the lining of the intestinal tract is a hopelessly inadequate barrier which allows the more complex of the proteins to be absorbed in the bloodstream undigested. The key to later allergies may well be here; to this day I cannot face crab unless it is marinated in whiskey. Then, too, the filtering and concentrating powers of the kidney are woefully immature at birth.

"Up to twenty-six weeks after the fatal event I was struggling with the shift-over to an entirely different chemical type of hemoglobin. You see, my respiration was far more diaphragmatic than intercostal. I had to be patient, to let it settle into intercostal. I did. I have never had any thanks for this. Of course *some* muscle tone had been present *in utero*. I am not boasting. This is normal. At birth the infant presents itself with a hypertonicity of muscle which gradually levels off. Mine did. I will not dilate on all the other skills which had to be mastered if I was ever to hope to live on to build cities or temples: bowel control, feeding, self-feeding. I passed through all these phases until by the end of late infancy the homeostasis of my physiology had become more or less established. Biting and chewing had replaced sucking—but with great reluctance. Teeth, which begin to appear after six months, gradually reach the normal size of the first deciduous set at about two years. By then, of course, I had already marked my mother with my personality by biting her breasts to cause more than one attack of nipple inflammation.

"I should add here that by the time I could utter one word I had passed through the university of a human mother's care and absorbed from her—from her voice, taste, smell, silences—a complete, overwhelmingly complete, cultural attitude which has cost me half a century or more to modify, to objectify. A cultural stance derived from every scintilla of her own anxieties, disgusts, predilections, moral and mental prejudices. All this was conveyed to me as if by massage, by radio wave—in a fashion quite independent of the reasoning forebrain. Mold-made, then, and with the classical penis in a state of erection I capered upon the scene to play my part—a remarkable and distinguished one—in the charade of people who believe themselves to be free. 'Woman,' I cried in parody, 'what have I to do with thee?' She did not need to answer. In the confessional intimacy of these first few months of absolute dependence I had received an impress, a mold mark, a sigil which will perhaps never be effaced. My very body image I owe to her—my slovenliness, lubberliness, my awkward gait, propensity for strong drink—responses she bred in me by leaving me alone too long to cry: by going out of the house and leaving me alone. . . . How can I thank her? For all my cities have been built in her image. They have no more than the four gates necessary to symbolize integration. The quaternary of resolved conflicts—even though it is harder to construct creatively upon a rectangle than upon the free flow of a curve or ellipse.

"And yet, even here, after so much struggle, can I say that I have succeeded? What is the education of the adolescent, the adult even, compared in power to this primary school of the affect which leaves its pugmarks alike in human minds and the marble they quarry? The notion of education, used in its ordinary sense, is surely nonsense. O perhaps it once might have connoted some sort of psychic training toward freedom from this chain, this biological prison within which all mothers want their sons to be sexual bayonets and encourage them to be such, while all fathers want their daughters to be merely fruitful extensions of their wives. Yet bayonets end in battle and deep graves—look about you: and women in order to mask their satisfactions end up in lustful widows' weeds, tailored for beauty.

"How soaring an act of insolence, then, was a construct of this order, and my God, how fragile an act of affirmation! With all the dice loaded against him this man one day stood upright in his mother's shadow and evolved this terrifying stone dream. He dared not yet conceive of the existence of another shadow, an unfettered one, the soul. A meaningless but fruitful placebo. Aye! For this early conception of a soul of the dead presupposed at first a subterranean continuation of life on earth, and led inevitably to tomb building . . . the Stone Age binding up of corpses symbolizing their tethering to one dwelling place. The first house, the tomb, became the outer casing for the dead soul, just as the first house proper (its windows breathing like lungs) was a case for man—as indeed his mother's body had been a case to house the water-rocked embryo. But from all this to the temple— what an imaginative jump! It takes his soaring beyond the chthonian tie; for here at last is a bus shelter, and an ark for the immortal and the divine.

"Somehow he managed, for one brief flash, to get a glimpse of the genetics of the idea and to break the incestuous tie. Hurrah, you might well say; well, but to escape chthonos is one thing and to face your own disappearance (without Mummy there to help) is quite another. His tomb becomes a boat to sail him over the dark waters of the underworld. Poor little embryo, poor mock giant. This recurring flash of vision is eternally lost and found, lost and found. His cenotaphs are battered into ruins as this has been.

"But if you can't take it with you, you can't entirely leave it behind either—the inheritance. Now comes the big historic dilemma. His sense of plastic had to cling to the morphology of what he now, tactually as well as factually, knew. The scale of his vision, however much it might include past, present and future, had to remain human. The fruit of this struggle, and this dilemma, you can see partly resolved here in this stone cartoon. Vitruvius has told us the story—how when Ion started to found the thirteen colonies in Icaria he found that the memories of the immigrants had begun to fail them, to turn hazy. The workmen entrusted with the task of setting up the new temples found that they had forgotten the measurements of the old ones they wished to imitate. While they were debating how to make columns at once graceful and trustworthy it occured to them to measure a human foot and compare it to a man's height. Finding that an average foot measured one-sixth part of a man's height they applied this to their column by laying off its lowest diameter six times along the overall length, the capital included. Thus did the Doric column begin to mimic and represent the proportions and compressed beauty of the male body in temple building. And the female? You cannot have one without the other. Our author tells us that when they came to the problems raised by Diana's temple they thought of something which might symbolize the greater slenderness of the female form. The diameter would be one-eighth of the length in this case. At the bottom, then, a foot representing the slender sole. Into the capital they introduced snails which hung down to right and left like artificially curled locks; on the forehead they graved rolls and bunches of fruit for hair, and then down the shaft they made slim grooves to resemble the folds in female attire. Thus in the two styles of column one symbolized the naked male figure, the other the fully dressed female. Of course this measure did not remain, for those who came later, with finer critical taste, preferred less massiveness (or taller women?) and so fixed the height of the Doric column at seven, and the Ionian at nine times the mean diameter.

"How to forbid oneself to elucidate reality—that is the problem, the difficulty. How to restore the wonder to human geometry—that is the crux of the matter. I do not feel that this marble reproaches us for a finer science, a truer engineering, but for a poorer spirit. That is the rub. It is not our instruments which fault us, but the flaccid vision. And yet . . . to what degree were they conscious of what they were doing? Perhaps like us they felt the fatal flaw, saw ruin seeping into the foundations as they built? We shall never know the answer to this—it is too late. But we, like them, were presumably sent here to try and enlarge infinity. Otherwise why should we read all this into this bundle of battered marble? Our science is the barren midwife of matter—can we make her fruitful?

"But what, you will ask, of the diurnal man? What of his housing? We can of course see that the individual house bears the shadowy narcissistic image of himself embedded even in its most utilitarian forms. The head, the stomach, the breast. The drawing room, bedroom, the kitchen. I will not enlarge on this. All the vents are there. I would rather consider the town, the small town, whose shape can embody both trade and worship. Now Vitruvius, in common with the whole of classical opinion, describes the navel as the central point of the human body. For my part the argument that the genital organ forms the *real* center has more appeal to one who has always kept a stiff prick in an east wind. But I have only once met with it, and then in a somewhat corrupt text—Varro! But perhaps this was mere Roman politics, an attempt to oust the Delphic omphalos as the true center of the world? That would be very Roman, very subtle, to try and oust the deep-rooted matriarchal principle and set up father rule in order to promote the power of the state. This is as may be. Let us deliberate for a moment on the little town itself.

"Do you remember the rite practiced specially by the Mediterranean nations in town building? It was established around a previously marked-out center, the so-called *mundus*. This center was a circular pit into which they poured the first fruits and the gifts of consecration. After this the limits of the town were set by a circular boundary line drawn round the *mundus* as a center of ritual plowing. The simple pit or *fossa*—the lower part of which was sacred *dis manibus* to the spirits of the dead and the underworld Gods—was filled up and closed in with a round stone, the *lapis manalis*. Do you see the connection establishing itself between the two ideas—*urbs* and *mundus?*

"Then came other factors, deriving perhaps from old half-forgotten complexes—like the propitiatory building sacrifice, for example, which has hung on until today. On your way home look at the skeleton of the new gymnasium in Pancrati. Today the workmen killed a cock and smeared its blood over the pillars. But even closer at hand—do not the caryatids over there speak clearly of such a scarifice? If ever they should be opened or fall down will we not find the traces of a woman's body in one of them? A common and deeply rooted practice. In your great narrative poem on the bridge of Arta the same ceremony is mentioned—the girl bricked into the piers. It has hung on and on in the most obstinate fashion. Stupidity is infectious and society always tries to maintain the illness in its endemic state.

"Now comes the important question of orientation to be considered so that the inhabitants or worshipers might find themselves within the magnetic field (as we should say today) of the cosmic influences pouring down on them from the stars. Astrology also had a say in the founding of temples and towns. Spica was the marking star for the ancients—people far earlier than the sophisticates who built this sanctuary. In those times it was accurately done by the responsible agent, the king, with the aid of two pegs joined by a cord, and a golden mallet. The priestess having driven one peg into the ground at a previously consecrated spot, the king then directed his gaze to the constellation of the Bull's Foreleg. Having aligned the cord to the hoof thereof and to Spica, as seen through the visor of the strange headdress of the priestess, he drove home the second peg to mark the axis of the temple to be. Boom!

"Mobego, the god of today, does not require any such efforts on our part. Yet perhaps defeat and decline are also part of an unconscious intention? After all, we form our heroes in our own likeness. A Caligula or a Napoleon leaves a great raw birthmark on the fatty degenerate tissue of our history. Are we not satisfied? Have we not earned them? As for the scientific view—it is one which drags up provisional validities and pretends they are universal truths. But ideas, like women's clothes and rich men's illnesses, change according to *fashion*. Man, like the chimpanzee, cannot concentrate for very long; he yawns, he needs a sea change. Well then, a Descartes or a Leibniz is born to divert him. A film starlet might have been enough, but no, poor nature is forced to overcompensate. We are all supposed to be pilgrims, all supposed to be in search; but in fact very few among us are. The majority are mere vegetables, malingerers, fallers by the wayside. All the great cosmologies have been stripped of their validity by human sloth. They have become hospitals for the maimed, casualty clearing stations."

Hippolyta, understanding little of all this, was in a state of deep depression though tinged with relief. But Caradoc swept on, hair flying, voice booming. My only concern was for my devil box. I was anxious lest the faint wind in the mike should give me boom as well as rasp.

"There is no doubt in my mind that the geometries we use in our buildings are biological projections, and we can see the same sort of patterning in the work of other animals or insects, birds, spiders, snails and so on. Matter does not dictate the form but only modifies it in order to make sure that a spider's web really holds the fly, the bird's nest really cherishes the egg. And how much the whole matter is dependent on sexual factors is really a dark question. Among squids and octopods, for example, the males have a special arm with which to transfer the semen to the female, inserting the spermatophore into the cloak or mantle of the lady. In the chambered nautilus the female clutches and retains the arm which breaks off. Spiders are differently catered for; the end of the pedipalp is used as a syringe to suck up and transfer the sperm; but before this can be done the male must discharge this into a special web which he weaves for the purpose. In fact the female does not have to be present. In the axolotl, however, the female picks up the sperm case with her hind feet and inserts it—a labor-saving device which Mrs. Henniker's young ladies would be prepared to perform for elderly clients. In birds, sometimes, by fault an egg can produce weird gynandromorph forms, half male and half female. Aye! In the smallest thing we build is buried the lore of centuries.

"All this and much more occurred to me in my youth as a prentice architect playing about among the foundations of Canberra with Griffin, one of Sullivan's lads. It has occurred to me all over again here in Athens among the girdling shantytowns like New Ionia which your refugees from Turkey have run up, almost overnight. In these provisional and sometimes haphazard constructs you will find many a trace left of the basic predispositions we have been discussing. They have woven them up spider-wise out of old kerosene tins, driftwood, scraps of bamboo and fern, rush matting, cloth and clay. The variety and inventiveness of their constructions are beyond praise. Though they are unplanned in our sense of the word these settlements are completely homogeneous and appropriate to their sites and I shall be sorry to see them vanish. They have the perfection of organism, not of system. The streets grow up naturally like vines to meet the needs of the inhabitants, their water points and sanitation groupings intersecting economically and without fuss. All the essential distances have been preserved, needs sorted and linked, yet everything done unprofessionally, by the eye. A microclimate had been established where a city could take root. Streets of soft baked earth into which has soaked urine and wine and the blood of the Easter lambs—every casual libation. Flowers bloom everywhere from old petrol cans coaxed into loops and trellises, bringing shade to the hot gleaming walls of shanties. On a balcony of reed mats a cage of singing birds whistling the tunes of Pontus. A goat. A man in a red nightcap. There is even a little tavern

90 ◆ ◆

where the blue cans go back and forth to the butts. There is shade where bargainers can fall asleep over their arguments and card players chaffer. You must compare this heroic effort with the other one we are contemplating tonight. They have much in common. A city, you see, is an animal, and always on the move. We forget this. Any and every human settlement for example spreads to west and north in the absence of natural obstacles. Is there an obscure gravitational law responsible for this? We do not know. Some law of the ant heap? I cannot answer this question. Then reflect how quarters tend to flock together—birds of a feather. Buildings are like the people who wear them. One brothel, two, three, and soon you have a quarter. Banks, museums, income groups, tend to cling together for protection. Any new intrusion modifies the whole. A new industry displaces function, can poison a whole quarter. Or the disappearance of a tannery, say, can leave a whole suburb to decay like a tooth. Think of all this when you read of the shrine of Idean Zeus, floored with bull's blood red and polished—as in South Africa today.

"And now that we have spoken at length about womb building and tomb building it is time to consider tool building and perhaps even fool building."

Here the transcript became blurred and faulty for as he spoke an extraordinary interruption had begun to take place, a completely unexpected diversion.

A large white hand, with grotesquely painted fingernails, appeared around the column directly behind Caradoc's back. It advanced in hesitant snail-like fashion, feeling the grooves in the stone. The speaker, noticing the thrill which had rippled through his audience at this sight, and following the direction of everyone's gaze, turned his own upon this strange object. "So there you are, Mobego," he muttered under his breath. "Good."

We all watched with intense concentration as the hand became an arm clothed in a sleeve of baggy black with a preposterous celluloid cuff attached to the wrist. Hippolyta drew several sharp breaths of horror. "It's Sipple," she whispered with dismay; and indeed it was, but a Sipple that none of us had ever seen, for the creature was wearing the long since discarded equipment of his first profession. Slowly the apparition dawned among the columns of the temple, and the singularity of his appearance was dumbfounding in its wild appropriateness to the place—like some painted wooden grotesque from an ancient Greek bacchanalia which had suddenly stirred into life at the rumble of Caradoc's words. First the face, with its rhinoceroid proboscis of putty, the flaring nostrils painted onto it as if on to a child's rocking horse: the bashed-in gibus with the coarse tufts of hair sprouting from it: a tie like a cricket bat; huge penguin feet in bursting shoes: ginger hair pouring out of rent armpits. . . .

A shiver of apprehension ran through us all as this semicomatose little figure stepped shyly blinking into the soft lamplight. Hippolyta's shiver was naturally one of social apprehension; but the audience stayed mumchance, unable to decide whether to laugh or cry out. Here and there one heard a few giggles, quickly repressed, but these were purely hysterical reactions. We were riveted to our seats.

Still blinking, this grotesque advanced slyly on Caradoc, who for his part seemed also to be immobilized by surprise and indecision. Then, while we were all in this state of suspended animation, hardly daring to breathe, Sipple made a sudden rush in the direction of the bottle. Caradoc, awakened from his trance, tried to counter this somewhat ineffectually by grabbing at the clown's wrists. But with a dexterity one would hardly have expected from this strange batrachian Sipple secured the heavy bottle, and with a single wild leap jumped into the audience and began to run like a hare toward the north battlements, scattering deck chairs and the ladies in them on either side of his passage.

The spell was broken. There were some shrieks now from the tumbled womenfolk. Everyone else was on his feet gaping. Some began to laugh, but not many. Caradoc had lost his balance and fallen forward off the plinth, still holding onto his lectern. Knocked almost insensible he lay motionless among the historic stones. His oil lamp exploded and set fire to a chair; fortunately this was rapidly extinguished. But while a few concerned professors moved forward, impelled by compassion, to pick up the body of the lecturer, the greater part of the audience, still screaming, watching the dramatic trajectory of the figure with the bottle held high above his head as if it were an umbrella. The speed of his flight was astonishing; one wondered how he would manage to brake it by the time he reached the outer wall.

But Sipple had other ideas. With one wild cry, like a demented seabird, he gave a leap clear into the sky and . . . crashed down into the lighted city far below him. It was a tremendous acrobatic leap, his knees drawn up almost to his chin, his coattails spread upon the night sky like bats' wings. He seemed to hang up there for one long moment, outlined upon the shimmering opalescence of the capital below: and then plummeted down and vanished, his terrible yell fading behind him. More ragged screams went up and half the audience rushed to this high corner of the battlements to look down in the expectation of seeing the crumpled body lying far below. But just under the crowning wall there was a decent-sized ledge; relief and doubt began to mix, for surely this is where he would have fallen, out of sight of his audience? Or had he overshot it and actually fallen into Athens? They hung here pondering, hearing the deep burr of the traffic below and the soft honking of klaxons. From the ledge itself, too, there seemed to be no way down the cliff. Where the devil was he, then? The watchers craned, and turned perplexed faces to each other. The whole episode had been so strange and so sudden that some must have wondered if the whole thing was not an illusion. Had we dreamed up Sipple? His disappearance was so sudden and so complete. One could see nothing very clearly.

But by now the keepers had been summoned, and a number of chauffeurs as well, to examine the slopes of the Acropolis for the supposed body of the clown. Torches were pressed into service. A line of glowworms appeared along the fringes of the cliff. It was all to be in vain, however, for the clown had clambered down a steep goat track and made good his escape.

Attention turned to Caradoc who had cut his forehead slightly and had the wind banged out of him. He was too incoherent still to answer questions about the episode and showed signs of being still a trifle drunk as well. Hippolyta herself was almost weeping with vexation. But with great presence of mind she delegated some of the local savants to conduct him lovingly down the staircases and ramps to her car. He went out like a hero, to ragged applause. Meanwhile Hippolyta bade her guests good night, fighting back her tears. But in fact, she found to her surprise, the whole evening had been—for all its strangeness: or perhaps because of it—a great success. People still stood about in excited thunderstruck groups, discussing what they had seen and trying to evaluate it. Accounts differed also, and arguments followed. I collected my boxes which had unaccountably escaped damage and followed her down the long staircases. She walked at a furious pace and I feared she would sprain an ankle.

In the bushes below the winged victory a figure approached her and muttered something in an undertone. I took it, from its ragged clothing, to be a beggar soliciting alms. But no, it handed her a letter. She seemed filled now with a sudden new concern. She tore open the envelope and read the message in the light of the car, and it seemed to me that she turned pale, though this may have been an illusion caused by a beam of light. I loaded my gear into the boot. Caradoc was asleep in the front seat now. We climbed in and she laid trembling fingers upon my arm. "Will you do something for me tonight, please? It is very urgent. I will explain later."

The car swirled us away toward the country house. I smoked and dozed, listening to the rumble of Caradoc's

94 ◆ ◆

voice; he was apparently continuing the lecture in his sleep. Hippolyta sat stiff and upright in her corner, lost in thought.

At Naos all the lights were on, and she stalked rapidly through the rose gardens into the house where we found the sleepy-looking figure of the count half dozing by the telephone. She handed him the slip of paper, but it seemed that he was already *au courant*. "Yes, they phoned here," he said, and added, "What is to be done?"

"Is your passport visaed for Turkey?"

"Yes."

"Then take the car to the Salonika border; it will be easy to get him over if we lose no time."

The count yawned heavily and pressed his ringed hands together. "Very well," he said mildly. "Very well."

Hippolyta turned to me and said: "Will you find Sipple for him? You know where he lives."

"Sipple?"

"We must get him out of Athens as swiftly as possible. The count will drive him to Salonika if you can find him and persuade him to pack in a hurry."

"What has Sipple been doing?"

"I'll explain everything later." But she never did.

Banubula took the wheel of the big car after having stowed away a small dressing case, containing I presumed a change of clothing; he would be away a night at least. Somewhat to my surprise he proved a powerful and fastish driver, and it was not very long before we were back in the streets of the capital. We proposed to divide the labor; he would go to Kandili and draw oil and petrol, while I crossed the Plaka and alerted Sipple. We should meet at the Tower of the Winds as soon as may be. It could not be too soon for me, I reflected, for I was very tired and the hour was late. A faint gray pallor on the sea horizons of the east suggested that the dawn—which breaks very early in summer—was not far off. In the meantime . . . Sipple. I crossed the Plaka rapidly, using my pocket torch whenever necessary in the unlighted corners.

I had never been inside Sipple's quarters; but I had had

them pointed out to me during one of my walks about Athens at night. He occupied the whole of the first floor of a pretty ramshackle building of a faintly Byzantine provenance. Long narrow wooden balconies looked out toward the Observatory and the Theseum—a pleasant orientation. Two long wooden staircases mounted to the first floor from the street level—and these were a mass of flowers and ferns sprouting from petrol tins. There was hardly a passage to be pressed between them. As I made my way up, however, I noticed that the glass door at the end of the balcony was ajar, and that a faint light shone from somewhere inside the cluster of gaunt rooms. This would offer some encouragement—I should not have to knock and wake up all his neighbors.

The first room was dark and empty of everything except some rickety bamboo furniture. The walls were decorated with esoteric objects like pennons, flags of many nations, and photographs of Sipple in various poses. Two large birdcages, muffled against the light by a green shawl, hung in the window. All this my pocket torch picked up with its vivid white beam. I half whispered and half called his name, but no answer came out of the inner room, and I made my way toward it after a decent interval, pushing open the door with my hand.

The light—dimmer than I had supposed—came from a fanlight which marked, no doubt, a lavatory. In the far corner of the room stood a rumpled and disordered bed. I did not at first look at it carefully, deeming that Sipple himself was to be found beyond the lighted door attending to the calls of nature. Indeed I could hear him breathing. More to mark time than anything I swept the cheap deal table with my lamp. On it stood a half-packed suitcase and a British passport made out in the name of Alfred Mosby Sipple. So he was already packing! I advanced to look at a framed photograph on the chest of drawers, and then something impelled me to take a closer look at the bed. I was not prepared for the shock that followed. I suddenly became aware that there was

96 ◆ ◆

a figure in the bed lying with its face turned away toward the wall and the bedclothes drawn up to its chin. It was Iolanthe! Or at first sight it seemed to be her—so remarkable was the facial resemblance between her and the sleeping figure. One would have said her twin brother—for it was a youth, his style of haircut showed it. Intrigued, I advanced closer, feeling my curiosity turning to a vague alarm at the silence and pallor of the face—this face of Iolanthe. A glimpse of white teeth showed between bloodless lips. Then, as I touched the sheet, drawing it back, my blood began to curdle, for the youth had had his throat cut like a calf. The pallor and the silence had been those of death, not sleep. There was no immediate trace of blood, for it had all drained downward into the bed. The deed then had been carried out in this same position while the youth lay sleeping. I recoiled in horror and as I did so I heard the clumsy bang of the homemade water closet. A bar of sallow light entered the room through the open door frame in which stood Sipple, doing up his trousers. We stared at one another for a long moment, and I suppose he must have seen from my expression that I knew what had taken place in that soiled and rumpled bed. His face seemed to float in the yellow light like a great yolk. Traces of greasepaint still clung to it, grotesquely outlining one eye and his chin. His fingers depended from his wrists like cubist bananas. He gave something between a sob and a giggle; then taking a step toward me he held out a pleading hand and whispered: "I swear I didn't do it. He's mine, but I swear I didn't do it." We stayed fixed in this tableau for what seemed an age. Somewhere a clock ticked. The dawn was advancing. Then I heard the first sleepy chirping of Sipple's birds under their covers. My throat was parched and aching. Moreover something else had begun to play about the corners of my mind in disquieting fashion. In lifting the sheet I had noticed traces of something, just a few grains here and there, scattered on the sheet and pillow; I thought at first of powdered graphite which can give off a sheen. And then I was reminded of the black nail varnish of Iolanthe, the dark shellac mixture which set hard and glossy, but also chipped easily. It was not a thought or observation I pushed very far—my mind was like that of a startled rabbit. But it stayed, it nagged. Meanwhile here before my eyes was Sipple, apologetically shortening his braces and pouting at me, like a man who has been wronged and feels upon the point of tears. Behind him the sky was whitening from the sleeping city. Far off came the buzzing tang of a semantron from the theological seminary, calling the students to early prayers. The birds stirred, half asleep. Sipple said brokenly, but under his breath, talking purely to himself, "It's leaving the birds that really hurts." Now I heard the whimper of the big car climbing the steep slope by the temple, and reversing into position.

The tiredness which had been overwhelming me had been banished at a stroke. I walked about the city for more than an hour, drinking a raki or an ouzo in the few taverns which opened at dawn in preparation for the market carts rolling into the city with their produce. I could not get the picture of Sipple's empty bedroom, with its silent recumbent figure in the corner, out of my mind. I even returned and circled the quarter like a criminal returning to the scene of his crime, gazing up at the silent windows, wondering what I should do, if anything. Finally I fell asleep on a park bench and woke when the sun was up, stiff with rheumatism from the heavy dew which had soaked my clothes.

I limped back to the hotel, relieved to find the clumsy front door already open; the porter Nik, still in his under-clothes, was brewing coffee in a little Turkish coffee spoon. He jerked his head sleepily—a gesture which had become formalized both as a greeting and as an indication that Iolanthe was at present upstairs in Number Seven. Yawning with fatigue I shuffled my way up. The door of the room was ajar, and so was the door of the bathroom. Her handbag and clothes were on the bed, but I could hear her stirring next door. She had not heard me come in. I walked to the half-open door and once more my heart turned a complete somer-sault. She was lying in the dry tin bath covered from head to foot in fresh blood—for all the world as if she had been brutally murdered and cut to ribbons. I almost cried out but abruptly caught sight of her rapt and happy face. She was crooning to herself in a soft nasal tone, and I could just catch the words of an island song which was very much in vogue at that time: "My father is among his olive trees." As she sang she was dabbing the vivid menstrual blood on her cheeks, her forehead, her breasts—literally painting herself in it. I recoiled before she caught a glimpse of me, and retreated on tiptoe into the corridor whence I reentered Number Seven, this time making a characteristic noisy entrance. I heard her call my name. The bathroom door was abruptly closed, and with a swish the bath taps went on.

I took off my shoes and lay half drowsing on the bed until she had finished. She emerged wearing my old green dressing gown, her face radiant with a kind of defiant elation. "I have news," she said breathlessly. "Look!" She took up a key from the mantelshelf and held it up, tapping the air with it. "The key of a villa!" She sat down by my feet, bubbling over with joy. In the absurd phrasing of newspaper demotic she added: "at last! I have been solicited by a great personality. Think, Charlock! A salary, clothes, a little villa in the Plaka." For the girls of her persuasion this was the ultimate dream realized—to find oneself the mistress of a rich man. My congratulations seemed to her somewhat tepid—though in truth they were heartfelt enough; it was simply that I was dazed, half asleep, and with my mind swimming with the events of that evening. She put a sympathetic paw on my thigh, misinterpreting my lukewarmness, and went on: "Mind you, I would have stayed with you if you had really wanted. If you had spat in my mouth and said you owned me. . . . But it is better that we should be good friends like we are, is it not?"

Her sincerity was so disarming that I almost began actively to regret the intrusion of this "great personality" upon the blameless youthful life we had enjoyed in Number Seven. I saw, so to speak, rapidly thrown down upon one another—or fanned out like a pack of gaily colored cards—the thousand and one glimpses I had obtained of Athens entirely through her kind offices. I saw her buying fish, or Easter ribbons, or colored chapbooks containing the shadow-play texts, or swimming in a cove with towed hair fanned out behind. "It's really excellent news." She crinkled her laughing eyes up, relieved. "And it may lead to other things. This man has great influence." I could not then imagine what other things such an assignment might lead to.

"Who is he? Do you know?"

"Not yet." This was a lie, of course.

The trouble with memory, and its prolix self-seeding process, is that it can always bypass the points of intersection at which we recognize, or seem to recognize, the action of a temporal causality. Is it a self-indulgence to want to comb it out like a head of hair? Reminded of the severed heads of Turkish traitors prepared so scrupulously for exhibition—the hair washed and curled, the beard pomaded, the eye sockets massaged with cream by terrified Greek barbers. Or the shrunken heads in bottles of spirit which still fetch great sums as talismans in the High Taurus. Well, and among these fugitive snapshots I found a faded one of Io on her island, helping her old father with his small crop of maize. At one blow she could shed the city with all its spurious sophistications and revert to the healthy peasant. Once on holiday I had seen her barefoot walking the deep dust of the road, bronze-powdered from head to foot, with a poppy between her teeth. Given the means this would have been her idea of advancement—to help the little man with his walnut-wrinkled face on some burning hillside, among the banded vipers. The key to the stuffy villa in Pancrati was the sesame which might lead her homeward, though not before she had endured all the vicissitudes and privations which come from exclusive ownership. Months later appearing, dressed like a typical adulteress in a voluminous scarf and dark glasses, to announce that she was going away—traded presumably to some wealthy client on the Nile. But no, something better, far better. Then in a tone appropriate to the comic side of Athenian life—its Aristophanic simplicities. "Ouf, I can hardly sit down; he has a taste for the whip, this one."

I did not go back to Naos until I was summoned, a week or two later; nor, by some curious chemistry of the unconscious, did I mention anything at all about Sipple, or about my visit to his rooms. Neither did Hippolyta. Nor, most perplexing of all, could I find any reference to the matter in the newspapers which I so diligently perused in the reading rooms of the local library. Not a word, not a breath. It was to be presumed then that the whole thing had been a bad dream? Hippolyta was alone in the rambling house, lying almost waist-deep in newsprint, her cheeks pink, her voice crackling at the edges with triumph. She embraced me with a curious reverential, a devotional tenderness—the precise way that the Orthodox peasants salute an ikon. "Graphos," she cried, the tears rose to her blackbird's eye. "O do look. Have you read it?" I had not. The press was plastered with it. "It is the greatest speech he has ever made—all Athens is thrilled. He has found himself again."

These esoteric matters concerning the vicissitudes of Athenian political life were of no concern to me; or so it then seemed. "But you don't understand. His party is reformed at a single blow. He is certain now to carry the autumn election and that will save the day."

"For whom? For what?"

"For us all, silly."

She poured me a drink with shaking hand, wading through the bundles of newsprint with their vivid many-colored letterpress, all bannering the name of Graphos, all carrying cartoons of him, photographs of him. "He wants to see you, to thank you. He will receive you whenever you wish."

And receive me he did, in one of those high-ceilinged rooms in the ministry with polished parquet floors and beautiful Baluchistan carpets—receive me moreover at a magnificent rosewood desk containing nothing but an empty blotter and his own silver cigarette lighter. It was the sort of desk which is only used to initial an occasional treaty. He was paler, thinner and a good deal sadder at close quarters than I had imagined him to be—but the thin man gave off a sort of excited candence. It was gratitude partly, but also mixed with curiosity. Touching his ear with a tapering finger he asked if anyone knew of my inventions, and whether I had taken any steps to profit by them. I had only thought vaguely of the matter—the first thing was to perfect the idea. . . . "No. No," he said emphatically, standing up in his excitement. "My dear friend, do not lose your chance. There may be a great fortune in this for you; you must protect yourself somehow." His rapid and fluent French conveyed better than English could have done the temper of his excitement; I suppose I must have presented myself badly, vaguely, for my apparent indifference piqued him. "Please," he said, "I implore you to let me express my gratitude by putting you in touch with my associates who would be glad to help you put the whole thing on a proper basis. I am determined that you must not lose by this thing. Or must I plead with Hippolyta to convince you? Reflect." I confess I thought he exaggerated somewhat, but what was there to lose? "You could at least examine their proposals; if you agreed with them you would find yourself well protected. There could be a great fortune in this device."

I thanked him and agreed. "Let me take it upon myself to send you to Polis for a few days to meet them and discuss with them. No harm can come of it; but at least my conscience will be at rest. I owe you a debt, sir."

I was indeed a little puzzled by my own hesitation in the matter. Certes, I had vaguely thought of patenting the device one day and licensing it perhaps; but several reasons came into play here. First, it seemed to spoil all the fun, second I could not be sure that other devices of the same order had not been thought of—the principle was spade-simple. But these considerations seemed to carry little weight with Graphos who brushed them aside with the remark that within a week he could find out and have the matter put upon a professional basis. Well, I let it go at that, but before leaving congratulated him somewhat sychophantically upon the speech which I had not read. He winced and became shy, and I suddenly saw what an effort it must have cost this shy, reticent and orderly mind to launch itself into public affairs. He had the soul of a grammarian, not a demagogue. When I spoke, for example, of the poetry I pretended to discover in it he held up thin hands to his ears and protested. "Rhetoric, not poetry. You could not convince with mere poetry. Indeed there has always been something a little suspect about the latter for me since I read that Rimbaud insisted on wearing a top hat in London. No, our objectives are limited ones. If we get in again it will be to try and prove only that the key to the political animal is magnanimity. A frail hope I agree." And he smiled his pale sad smile, moistening his lips with his snaky tongue. His fine small teeth were turned inward, like the spokes of a lobster pot. "So you will agree to let me send you?" I nodded and he sighed with unfeigned relief and rose to shake my hands with a surprising gratitude. "You don't know how much pleasure it will give me to send you to see my associates; even if nothing should come of it I shall feel I have discharged my obligation to you. Certainly you will have nothing to complain of from the firm."

The blue sunlight of Athens seemed so firm and stable a back cloth to my restless ideas that I was not conscious of having made any kind of decision, far less a momentous one. Hippolyta slept in her cane chair under a fallen triumphant newspaper, showing a tip of tongue, smiling like a javelin-thrower who has scored a hit. Caradoc, beside her, put a finger to his lips and smiled. It was still early, the bees dew-capped from the flowers they visited. "An olive branch nailed to the inn door of the world." Far away in the harbor the sirens went bim and their echoes bim bim to slap the buttocky waters of the sound, scattering from one steel surface to the next. "I am going to Turkey." Caradoc gestured. "Shh!"

So we sat, hushed in sunlight, until I felt a drowsiness creeping over me—compact with fragments seeded from recent memories of conversations jumbled and jostled—switching points like express trains as they roared through deserted junctions. Hippo, for example, in a reported speech: "I cannot sleep alone, yet no one pleases me. It is a real dilemma." The turntable spinning away into sleep, lips parted. Then with equal suddenness some articles from Sipple's rooms which I was not conscious of having noticed at the time: cold prunes and custard in a chipped soup plate, a blue enamel teapot, and a large pair of dressmaker's scissors. Then some unidentified naked woman from the Anthology, "of delicate address and lovely insinuation." Dead notes on a classical keyboard—or might it have been already Benedicta? Here is a love letter. "Benedicta, I love you. The collection of delta spacings for several radiations permits the identification of spurious peaks resulting either from target contamination or incomplete filtration of K alpha radiation. Your Felix." Yes, on some mutinous machine like Abel will dawn one day the cabyric smile. Idly drifting, thistledown-wise came Koepgen with his "promissory notes drawn upon reality." Monks with impetigo, their heads shaved, arousing his pithy sarcasm with their great leather-bound octavo farts. "Must one, then, negotiate with God?" he exclaims oddly; hunting as if for a thorn one can't quite locate—this is not in my line. Some tiny tufts of north wind rise now and shuffle the roses. Caradoc is trying to keep awake by writing a mnemon, as he calls it. We have promised to collaborate on a macabre pantomime to be called *The Babes in the Food*. As sudden but less distinct comes the scorching rain of white roses in *Faust*—whole epochs of redemption or desire. Caradoc saying with much severity about K.: "He has been slumming among the Gnostics, selling his birthright for a pot of message. He will end by becoming an Orthodox Proust or a monarcho-Trappist. All monks are grotesque lay figures—figures of funk."

Then away beyond Cape Sunion toward those distant lighthouses of sorrow across the waters, memories of Leander, where the Moslem dead await us with an elaborate indifference. Sweet, aquiline and crucial rise the stalks of the women's tombs, the soulless women of the Islamic canon. In marble one can see the pointed conciseness of a death which promises no afterlife—without the placebo of soul or resurrection. My own faint snoring matches that of C.'s and the soft even breathing of Hippolyta in that Athenian sunlight.

THREE

wheeling now in a long arc to the left, to paddle into Kebir Kavak for pratique. Here, while they were hauling the yellow flag up and down and exchanging the windy garble of mariners' talk, I first set eyes on Mr. Sacrapant who had been detailed to meet me. He sat in the stern sheets of the quarantine cutter gazing with a kind of sweet holiness up into my face, watching my expression as I fingered the engraved visiting card. It had been sent aboard by a sailor and it read

Elias Sacrapant
B.Sc. Economics London (external)

I ducked and he ducked back; a faint smile illumined that pale clerkish countenance. The infernal noise of engines precluded more intimate exchanges. But presently he was allowed aboard. He negotiated the gangway with an erratic and somewhat elderly spriteliness. His hands were warm and tender, his eyes moist with emotion. "We have been waiting for you," he said almost reproachfully, "with such impatience. And now Mr. Pehlevi is in the islands for the weekend. He asked me to look after you until he comes. I cannot express my pleasure, Mr. Charlock." It seemed a bit overdone but he was charming in his white drill suit, elastic-sided boots and white straw hat. A very large tiepin gathered the wings of his collar over his scraggy neck. His eyes were very pale blue. Once they may have been very beautiful, almost plumbago. He spoke English as it is learned in the commercial schools of the Levant, a sort of Anglo tradesman; but very accurately and with a pretty accent. "You may relax, Mr. Charlock, for you are in my hands. I will answer any questions you put. I am the firm's senior adviser."

And so it was with Sacrapant as a companion that I came upwater at last to dangle in view of the Golden Horn where the immense inertia—the marasmus of Turkey—drifted out with sea damps to finger my soul. Cryptogram, yes, these huge walls of liquid dung baked by the sun into tumefied shapes. It all had a fine deliquescent charm—the coaxing palms, the penis-turreted domes, the lax and faded coloring of a dream turning to nightmare. Mr. Sacrapant pointed out all the sights and explained them carefully, with the exactitude of a bookkeeper, but in kindly fashion, chuckling from time to time as he did so. Moreover he was splendidly efficient, darting here and there with tickets and passports, buttonholing officials, exhorting sailors and porters. "For tonight the Pera Hotel," he explained, "will enable you to rest. There is every luxe. Tomorrow I will come and take you to the Pehlevi danglion—a water pavilion. It is prepared for you. It will be very comfortable. You will be just fine, fine." He repeated the word with his characteristic pious effervescence, joining his hands together and squeezing them. Very well.

It was the least I could do to offer him dinner when at last we arrived, and he accepted the invitation with alacrity. I confess that with the sinking sun on that gaunt but beautiful terrace I was glad of company, for I felt the death grip of the Turkish night settling upon me—a sort of nameless panic wafted up with the smell of jasmine from the gardens below, from the chain-mail ramparts of forts and ravelins which enclose Polis like the scar tissue of old wounds upon which the blood has dried black. Sacrapant was someone to talk to—but not until our meal was well on its way. He addressed himself to the menu with the same fervor—indeed he removed his wristwatch and placed it in a safe corner before picking up his knife and fork. Also he put upon his nose a pair of pince-nez the better to instruct me in the intricacies of the local cuisine. A small vermouth had brought a flush to his cheek. But at last, somewhat assuaged by the fare, he leaned back and undid his coat buttons. "I cannot tell you what pleasure it gives me," he said, "to think of you joining the firm—O I know that you have only come to discuss with Mr. Pehlevi." Here he pointed his long forefinger at his own earhole to show that he knew the subject of our discussion. "But if you agree with him, you will never never repent, Mr. Charlock. Merlin's is a marvelous firm to work for—or to let it work for you." He chuckled and rolled his eye. "Marvelous," he said. "Whether one is its slave or its master." I stared at him, eager to know more.

Mr. Sacrapant continued: "Excuse me if you think my feelings are excessive, but when I look at you I can't help the thought that if I had a son he would be about your age. With what joy I would have seen him enter Merlin's." He spoke about the organization as if it were a religious order. "That is why." And he gave my hand a shy pat, adding ruefully, "But Mrs. Sacrapant can only make girls with me, five girls. And here in Stamboul for girls . . ." He rubbed finger and thumb together expressively and hissed on a lower note the word "Dowries." Then he once more lay back in a sort of infantile rapture and went on. "But there again, the firm, thank God for the jolly old firm. They will look after all. No detail is too small, and no organization offers comparable status and benefits in the Levant. We are a hundred years ahead of our time." He poured himself a thimbleful of wine and drank it off like a hero.

It was puzzling, this string of homilies—as if he had been sent to soften me up before my negotiations with Pehlevi began. And yet . . . Sacrapant was so guileless and so likable. He dropped his napkin, and in retrieving it inadvertently revealed a strip of sock and calf. I was intrigued to see, strapped to his thin ankle, a small scout knife such as a girl cub might use to pierce the tinfoil on a jam pot. He followed the direction of my glance. "Shh," said Mr. Sacrapant. "Say nothing. In Stamboul, Mr. Charlock, one never knows. But if attacked by a Moslem I would give a good account of myself—you may be sure." He blushed and tittered and then all at once became grave, plunged in reverie. "Tell me more about the firm," I said, since it seemed his only topic. He sighed. "Ah the firm!" he said. "When will I ever cease to be grateful to it? But I will do better, I will show it to you. I have instructions to do so. At least as much of it as we manage from here—for we are only the Levant end. The firm is worldwide, you know, in London Berlin New York. Mr. Pehlevi's brother Julian runs the London end. Yes, you shall see it for yourself. It will take up the time until Mr. Jocas comes back from the islands on Monday." It sounded an interesting way of passing the time and seeing something of the city. As I walked him through the damp garden with its throbbing crickets he went on sincerely, rather touchingly. "You know—perhaps you don't— how hard it is in the Levant to have any sort of security, Mr. Charlock. It is hard to earn good money if you have children. That is why I am so happy. The firm has meant to me serenity for wife and loved ones. Yes, and insurance, too, we are all covered. Believe me, outside the firm it can be . . . very hard cheese I think you say in English? Very hard cheese."

Before taking the one dilapidated taxi he lingered for some further chatter, unwilling to end the evening; and I was glad, thinking of the ghastly bedroom that awaited me. I had forgotten to bring something to read. For his part Sacrapant behaved like a man who had been deprived of any social life, who was hungry for company. Yet he had only this one topic, the firm. "You see it is very wide. Old Mr. Merlin the founder did not believe in building up and cornering one market; he preferred to build horizontally." He drew his hand along his body with a stroking gesture. "We are very wide rather than very tall. There is great variety of holdings, but few are exclusive to ourselves. That is why the firm is so wide, why there is room for everyone in it—well, almost everyone." Here he stopped and frowned. "There are some exceptions. I forgot to tell you that Count Banubula is staying in your hotel. Now he is one. He has tried for years to join the firm but with no hope. It is nothing to do with his behavior, though when he is in Stamboul he behaves. . . . well, very strangely. You know him I think."

"Yes, of course. But what has he done?"

"I don't know," said Mr. Sacrapant compressing his lips and shooting me a furtive glance. "But I expect the firm does. Anyway, they will not let him in; he has exhausted his nerves in pleading but Mr. Jocas is adamant. There are one or two like him. The firm makes an example of them, and they are blocked. It is a huge pity for him for he is a gentleman, though his behavior in Stamboul would not let you think so."

"But he is a very mild and quiet man."

"Ah," said Mr. Sacrapant on a reproving note.

"And is Merlin still alive?"

"No," said Mr. Sacrapant, but he spoke in a whisper this time, and in a fashion that somehow carried little conviction. I had the impression that he was not at all certain. "Of course not," he added, trying to bolster the simple affirmative; but all of a sudden he looked startled and somewhat discountenanced, like a frightened rabbit. He took my hand and squeezed it saying: "I will come tomorrow and take you down to the offices for a look. Now I must go." On this somewhat ambiguous note we parted. I turned back into the hotel relieved to see that there were still a few lights on—notably in the bar. And here I was overjoyed to come upon Count Banubula, the only occupant of the place, gloomily consulting his own reflections in the tarnished mirrors.

His appearance had undergone a subtle change which had not been apparent when I entered the room. How to say it? He looked flushed, snouty, and somehow concupiscent. He swayed ever so slightly, almost imperceptibly, as very tall buildings do. "Ah," he said as he caught sight of me, in a new and rather insolent fashion. "Ah, Charlock!" I echoed his "Ah" on the same note, my curiosity aroused, for this was certainly not the Count Banubula I knew. "What about a little drink?" he went on sternly. It was virtually an order and I obeyed gladly. His waistcoat was undone and his monocle tinkled loosely against the buttons. The light was too bad to enable me to be sure, but it seemed to me that his lips and eyebrows had been discreetly touched up. This is, of course, a service which any barber will perform in the Orient on request. Banubula raised the sad plumes of his heavy eyebrows and closed his eyes, breathing slowly through his nose. Yes, he was drunk.

The barman produced two whiskies and disappeared through a hatch. Still with eyes shut the count said: "I knew you were coming. I have been here some time. Ah, my goodness, if you only knew. I can't leave till Thursday now." He started an involuntary spin like a top, and just managed to find his way to a chair. "Sit," he said, in the same authoritative way. "It is better so." I obeyed, and sat opposite him, staring at him. There was a very long silence, so long indeed that I thought he would drop off to sleep but no, he had been setting his mind to the problem of conversation. "Do you know what Caradoc said about me?" asked the count with slow sad tones. "He said I looked like a globe artichoke, and that I would die, a whiskey-stiffened mummy in some Turkish bagnio." He gave a sudden squawk of laughter and then sank back into this oozing gloom, eyeing me narrowly. "Cruel man," he said. "They are all cruel men. For years I have done their dirty work. There have never been the small rewards I asked for. Nothing. No hope. I go on and on. But I have reached the end of my tether. I am in despair, Charlock. At my age one can't go on and on and on and on. . . ." his voice sank into a mumble. "But who are these people?" I said.

"It isn't anybody special, it's just the firm."

"Merlin's?"

He nodded sadly. "O Lord," I said, "does no one talk about anything else in this city?"

The count had taken a leap into autobiography and did not heed my remark. "I love my dear wife," he said, "and I esteem her. But now she sits all day with her hair done up in a scarf and curl papers writing long letters about God to Theosophists. And I have become abnormal, you see, Charlock? Without wishing it. In these hot climates one cannot be deprived of one's rights without something happening. Since she became religious all is ended; yet I could never divorce her because of the scandal. My name is an ancient one." He blew his nose violently in a silk handkerchief and dibbled a finger in his right ear to clear it. Then he shook his head with equal violence, as if to clear his brain. "And then all these

negotiations, all this pleading. It has made me a very superstitious man, Charlock. I feel I must try and avert a horrible
fate—unless they relent. Look!" He threw open his waistcoat
to reveal a plump white chest to which was attached an
iodine locket. He waited for my comment, but it was somewhat difficult to find words; the iodine locket was the talis-
man of the day, much advertised in the vulgar press. It promised health to the wearer for a very small outlay. "But health
is no good," said Banubula sadly, "if one's fate is wrong. I
have been a student of Abraxas for several years now, and
I know my fate is wrong. Do you know how I defend myself?"
I shook my head. He detached from his key ring a small Chal-
dean bronze leaf inscribed after the fashion of amulets thus:

```
s a t o r
a r e p o
t e n e t
o p e r a
r o t a s
```

Banubula nodded like a mandarin. "It is only to prove to
you that I have tried everything. I even tried love potions on
my spouse, but they made her violently ill. I meant well.
That much you will grant me." I nodded, granting him that
much.

"O God," said Banubula, drinking deeply, thirstily, "my
sorrow seems bottomless, bottomless." The choice of phrase
seemed to me bizarre, but I did not comment. "Just how
would things change if . . . if all these negotiations were
successful?" I asked. At once his large hairless face changed its
expression, became animated with a fiery enthusiasm. "Ah
then everything would be different, don't you see? I should
be in!"

The officious barman started to bang shutter and door and
indicate brusquely that the bar was closing; he refused us
another drink. "You see?" said the count. "My whole life is
like that—one refusal follows another, everywhere, in every-

thing." His lower lip dipped steeply toward a self-commiserating burst of tears, but he restrained them manfully. "To bed I think," I said, with as much cheerfulness as I could muster. And I did what I could to steer the yawing bulk of the count upstairs to bed. "I won't bother to undress," he said cheerfully, falling upon his bed. "Good night."

I turned at the door to find that he was regarding me with one eye open with the air of a highly speculative jackdaw. "I know," he said, "you are dying to question me about him. But I know so little."

"Could Sipple be working for Merlin's?"

"Certainly. At any rate it was they who cabled and telephoned to Hippolyta asking her, us, to get him over to Polis as swiftly as was humanly possible."

"What on earth could Sipple do? Spy?"

Banubula yawned and stretched. "As for the boy you said you . . . found; that has nothing to do with the case. I mean it's a quite independent fact which has nothing to do with the firm. It's Sipple's own business."

"But how do you know about it?"

"Sipple told me. He denied having anything to do with it."

"There was no mention in the newspapers; somebody *must* have found the body. Who hushed the whole matter up?"

"In the Middle East," said Banubula sighing, "a London detective would go out of business; there are so many people with such unusual motives. . . . I mean, look, suppose Sipple's landlord thought that the discovery of a corpse would prejudice him letting the room to someone else. What would he do? He would put it in a sack and slip it into one of the sewers, or take it to the top of Hymettus and fling it into a crevasse—there are some hundreds of feet deep, sheer falls, never been explored." Banubula cleared his throat and went on in a shyer tone of voice. "Once I was forced to get rid of a rival for my wife's hand in somewhat the same fashion; though in my case it was complicated by blackmail and menaces."

"You killed a man?" I said admiringly.

"Yes . . . well . . . rather," said the count with modesty.

He lay back, closing his eyes and breathing coolly through his nose. Then he said in somewhat oracular fashion: "Haven't you noticed, Charlock, that most things in life happen just outside one's range of vision? One has to see them out of the corner of one's eye. And any one thing could be the effect of any number of others? I mean there seem to be always a dozen perfectly appropriate explanations to every phenomenon. That is what makes our reasoning minds so unsatisfactory; and yet, they are all we've got, this shabby piece of equipment." He would doubtless have had more to say, but sleep gained on him steadily and in a while his mouth fell open and he began to snore. I slipped off the light and closed the door softly.

❖❖❖❖❖❖❖❖❖❖❖❖❖

Sacrapant was as good as his word and appeared next morning on the dot—but this time with a big American car driven by a Turk dressed in a sort of bloodstained butcher's smock. He was all frail animation and charm as we bumped and careered down toward the waterside sectors of the town, through souks rendered colorless now by the dreadful European reach-me-downs worn by the inhabitants of this artificially modernized land. At the best the Turks of the capital looked opium-ridden, or as if clubbed half insensible; the clothes set off their mental disarray to perfection. Of course I did not voice my sentiments as strongly as this, but

118 ❖ ❖

my hints were enough to convey the general drift of my thoughts to Mr. Sacrapant. To my surprise he expressed stern disapproval. "They may be ugly," he said, "but thanks to them we brought off one of our biggest coups. The firm was in touch with Mustafa's party when it was still a secret society. It knew his plans, and that when it came to power it would abolish the fez and the Arabic script. It waited. By skillful bribing we made an agreement, and the very day the firman was launched, we had six ships full of cloth caps standing by in the roads! We swamped the market. We had also collared the contracts for printing of stamps and the national stationery—we had been importing presses for months. You see what I mean? Doing business in the Levant is rather a special thing." He bridled, flushed with pride. I could see that all right, O yes.

The old-fashioned countinghouse, down among the stinking tanneries of the yards, was rather impressive; the interior walls of three large factories had been taken out and replaced by a huge acreage of tile floor. Here, cheek by jowl, worked the Merlin employees, their desks brow to brow, practically touching one another. A deep susurrus of noise rose as if from a wasp's nest, deepened by the throaty echo of electric fans. Here there seemed to be no sleep—I could hardly see one face that did not signal itself as belonging to a Greek, Jew, Armenian, Copt, Italian. A sort of dramatic electrical current seemed to have generated itself. Sacrapant walked between the desks, bursting with a kind of hallowed civic pride, nodding to right and left. I could see from the way he was greeted that he was much beloved. He walked as a man might show off a garden, stopping here and there to pluck a flower. I was introduced to a few people, a swift sample, so to speak; they all spoke good English and we exchanged pleasantries. Also, in one corner—the only screened section—I was presented to three elderly men of Swiss accent and mien: they looked both authoritative and determined. They were dressed in formal old-fashioned tailcoats which must have been stifling to wear in summer. "They speak all our languages," said Mr. Sacrapant, adding: "You see here each man is very much head of his own section. We have decentralized as much as humanely possible. The great variety of our work permits it." He picked a bundle of ladings and C.I.F. telegrams off a desk and rapidly clipped out the words "Beirut, Mozambique, Aleppo, Cairo, Antananarivo, Lagos."

I accepted a traditional black coffee of the Oriental variety and expressed my approval of all this creditable activity; afterward we stepped out blinking into the sunlight. Sacrapant had taken the day off in order to show me something of the town and together we walked laterally across it, making clever detours to visit the choicer monuments. In the honeyed gloom of the covered bazaars I bought a few coins and some beaten silver wire of Yemeni origin, with the vague intention of presenting them to Hippolyta on my return. We sauntered through the courtyards of sunbaked mosques, pausing to feed the pigeons from a paper bag full of Indian *gram*. Thence to Al Quat for a really excellent lunch of pigeon and rice. It was late afternoon by the time we started to saunter back to the hotel, and by now I had come to see what an immense graveyard Stamboul is, or seems to be. The tombs are sown broadcast, not gathered together in formalized squares and rectangles. Graveyards were spread wherever humanity had scratched up a tombstone behind it, as in a cat box; here death seemed to be broadcast wholesale in quite arbitrary fashion. A heavy melancholy, a heavy depression seemed to hang over these beautiful empty monuments. Turkey takes time to know.

Truth to tell, I was rather anxious to leave it and get back to the noisy but freer air of Athens. "You have brought your box, of course?" said Mr. Sacrapant. "I know that Mr. Pehlevi is most anxious to see it." But of course he would not be available for another twenty-four hours; yes, I had brought my box. Mr. Sacrapant accepted tea and toast and reminisced awhile about the business community of Smyrna where he had learned his English. In parenthesis he added: "By the way, Mr. Pehlevi told me to tell you that there is a commercial counselor here and he will insist that any contracts we offer you should be seen by him. Just in case you have no business head. He wants everything to be aboveboard and clear. It is part of our policy. I have told Mr. Vibart and he agrees to advise you. So all is in order." I have no idea why this remark should have seemed slightly ominous to me but it did. He sighed, and with great reluctance excused himself, saying that he had a dinner engagement. For my part, after so long and exhausting a walk, I was glad to go to my room and siesta—which I did to such good effect that it was after dark when I awoke and groped my way distractedly down to dinner. There was no sign of Banubula in the dining room, and there were few other guests whose appearance offered hope of time-killing conversation. But later I ran him down in the sunken billiard room playing mournful Persian airs on a very tinny cottage piano. Several large whiskies stood before him—a precaution against the barman with his capricious habits of shutting up the bar when drinks were most needed. He was, I should say, a little less drunk than he had been the evening before, though the number of the whiskies boded little good; he allowed me to take one and sit beside him. He was in a morose, cantankerous mood, and was hitting a lot of false notes. At last he desisted, banged the piano shut. "Well," he said, sucking his teeth, "tonight I will be handing over Sipple, and then bye-bye to Polis."

"Handing over? Is he in irons?"

"He should be," said Banubula savagely. "They all should be."

He growled awhile into his waistcoat and then went on: "I suppose you have seen Pehlevi, eh? That swine!" Such an outburst from this mild, courteous and bookish man was astonishing.

"Tomorrow." Banubula sighed and shook his head with a gloomy star-crossed expression.

"Tomorrow you will be *in*, over my head."

It was my turn to get annoyed by this repetitive and meaningless reiteration—this eternal mélopée. "Listen to me," I said poking his waistcoat. "I am not in, not out, and will not be. This might be a commercial agreement over a small toy which may make me some money, that is all. Do you hear?"

"You will see," he grunted.

"Moreover any contracts will be vetted by the commercial consul," I added primly.

"Ha-ha."

"Why ha-ha?"

"Over whose dead body?" said Banubula inconsequentially. "Over mine, my boy. In you go and out I shall stay." He drained a tumbler and set it down with exaggerated care. Then all of a sudden the cloud seemed to lift a little. He smiled complacently and stroked his chin for a while, looking at me sideways. "Caradoc does not spare our infirmities," he said.

"Is *he* in?"

Banubula looked at me incredulously. "Of course," he said with disgust. "Has always *been* in; but he wants to get *out!*"

"It's like a bloody girls' school," said I.

"Yes," he said with resignation. "You are right. But let us talk about something pleasanter. If I had not been on duty here I might have shown you some of the sights of the capital. Things that most poeple don't see. In one of the kiosks of the Seraglio, for example, is Abdul Hamid's collection of dildoes, brought together from all over the world; all carefully labeled and dusted. He was impotent, they say, and this was one of his few pleasures."

"Is old Merlin still alive?" I asked suddenly. Banubula shot me a glance and sat up straight for a moment. Ignoring my remark he went on: "They were kept in a long row of pipe racks presented by the British Government in a vain attempt to curry favor with him. The names were so beautiful— *passiatempo* in Italian, *godemiche* or *bientateur* in French. No? They illustrate national attitudes better than anything else, the names. The German one was called the phallus phantom—a ghostly metaphysical machine covered with death dew. Alas, my boy, I have not the time to show you this and other treasures."

"It's a great pity."

Banubula consulted his watch with pursed lips. "In another half hour they will take over and I shall be free. But I think I should just make sure that Sipple is all right. Do you want to come with me?"

"No."

"It won't involve us in anything, you know."·

I looked and felt somewhat doubtful; depressed as I was at the thought of spending another evening here alone I did not want to become involved in any of the count's escapades. On the other hand I was a bit anxious for his own safety. It seemed unwise to leave him alone. I must have looked as confused as I felt, for he said, cajolingly: "Come on. It will take me a quarter of an hour. I will just peep through the curtain at the Seamen's Relief Club, and then we can return happy in the thought of duty well and faithfully done."

"Very well," I said. "First let me see that you can walk straight." Banubula looked wounded in his self-esteem. He rose heavily to his feet and took a very creditable turn or two up and down the room. His own steadiness rather surprised him. He looked somewhat incredulous to find himself navigating with such ease. "You see?" he said. "I'm perfectly all right. Anyway we will take a cab. I'll send these remaining whiskies up to my room for safety and we can go. Eh?"

He pressed the bell for the waiter, and gave his instructions in faultless Turkish which I envied him.

Once more we slanted down the ill-lit streets where the occasional tram squealed like a stuck pig. Banubula consulted a pocket notebook which appeared to have a rough plan penciled into it. Why not a compass? I wondered. So like an explorer did he behave. We left the taxi on a street corner and set off in an easterly direction, skirting the bazaars. The count walked in what I can only describe as a precautionary way, stopping from time to time, and looking behind, as if to see whether we were being trailed or not. Perhaps he was showing off? The town smelled heavily of tannin and garbage. We crossed a series of small squares and skirted the walled exterior of mosques. The city seemed to become more and more deserted and somewhat sinister. Finally however we reached a corner where light and noise abounded, where spits hissed and bagpipes skirled. A section of the sky had been cut out by the flares. There can be no mistake about the Greek quarter of any town. An infernal industry and gaiety reigns. Here we entered a large café the interior of which was full of mirrors and birdcages, and domino players, and crossing it reached a courtyard where, in the dimness, a notice could just be discerned which read "Seamen's Relief Club." Banubula grunted as he addressed himself to a flight of creaky stairs. "How does one relieve a seaman?" I asked, but the count did not reply.

On the first floor there was a sort of large drill hall full of smoke and the noise of feet and chairs scraping; there was also a good deal of laughter and clapping, as if at some performance or other. Banubula stopped outside a dirty door sealed by a bead curtain. "I'm not going in," he hissed, "but we'll just see. I think he's acting the fool for them now." And with sinking feelings I heard the flat nasal whine of Sipple, punctuated by the roars of laughter of the merry tars. "Yes, you may laugh, my sirs, you may laugh—but you are laughing at tragedy. Once I was like you all, I wore me busby at an angle. Then came that fatal day when I found myself abrogated. I found myself all slantingdicular to the world. Up till then my timbrel was normal, my pressure quite serene. I lived with Mrs. Sipple in a bijou suburban house with bakelite elves on the front lawn. Not far from Cockfosters it was. (Cheers!) Every day I rose, purified by sleep, to bathe and curl my hair, and put on a clean artichoke. I traveled to Olympia in a Green Line bus like the public hangman with my clothes in a bag. It wasn't exacting, to act the clown—a pore fart-buffeted blorque. But when me whiffler abrogated I lost all my confidence. (Clapping.) Ah you may laugh, but when your whiffler becomes a soft lampoon what's to be done? I found my reason foundering, gentlemen. I started drinking tiger drench. I had become alembicated. I had begun to exfluncticy. Then when I went to see the doctor all he said was: 'Sipple you are weak in marmite.' "

All this must have been accompanied by some fitting stage business of an obscene kind for it was greeted with roars of laughter. From where we stood we could not see Sipple; the balcony overhung him. He was immediately beneath us; all we could see was, so to speak, his reflection in the semicircle of barbarous faces, expressing a huge coarse gratification. Banubula consulted his watch. "Four more minutes," he said, "and then he's og. Phew, what a relief!" He stretched in the gloom and yawned. "Now let's go and have a drink, what?" We went downstairs again and crossed the courtyard; as we reached the lighted café a large black car drew up in the street outside and two men climbed out, yawning, and made their way directly past us, looking neither to right nor left. Banubula watched them pass with a smile. "That's the committee," he whispered. "Now we are free." And in a heavy jolting way he started to hurry along the street toward the corner of the square where the taxis were, coiling and uncoiling long legs.

"I can't tell you the relief," he said sinking back at last on the back seat cushions and mopping his brow. Indeed his face had become almost juvenile and unlined. "Now you can come and watch me pack, and I will share my whiskey with you." I was puzzled by my own equanimity, by the ease with which I seemed to be accepting this succession of puzzling (even a little disquieting) events. "I've stopped asking questions," I said aloud to myself. Banubula overheard me and gave a soft chuckle. "Just as well to save your breath," he said.

I sat on the bed and watched this infernally clumsy bear-like man trying to fold a pair of trousers and squeeze them into his suitcase. He was a trifle tipsy again, and his little performance would have almost done credit to the clown

Sipple. "Here," I said, "let me help you." And gratefully Banubula slumped into a chair and mopped his white brow. "I don't know what it is about clothes," he said. "They have always eluded me. They seem to have a life of their own, and it doesn't touch my life at any point. Nevertheless I wear them very gracefully, and pride myself on being quite smartly turned out. These shoes come from Firpo in Bond Street." He stared at them complacently.

I had shaken a batch of notepaper out of his coat pocket; it fell on the floor. "O dear, O dear," said the count, "how forgetful I am." He took the papers, set them alight in the ashtray and sat watching the flame like a child, poking at it with a matchstick until the paper was consumed and the ash broken up. Then he sighed and said: "Tomorrow I shall return to Athens and my dear wife. To resume my old life again."

"And Sipple?" I asked, curiosity getting the better of me. "What will become of him?" Banubula played with his lucky charm and reflected. "Nothing very special," he said. "No need for dramatic imaginings. Hippolyta says she was told that he was an expert on precious stones; that would give him a connection with Merlin all right. Then someone else said he was retained by the government to supply political intelligence. There again . . . much can be learned in the brothels of Athens. Politicians build up dossiers about each other's weaknesses and there is hardly one who hasn't some pretty little perversion up his sleeve which could lay him open to political pressure, or even blackmail. Graphos makes them dress up and whips them mildly, so they say; others have more elaborate needs. Pangarides insists on the 'chariot.' . . ."

"What is the chariot?"

"It's really a Turkish invention, I suppose. A sort of *en brochette* effect. I've never tried. It's having a small boy while the small boy himself is having a girl. With clever timing it is supposed to . . . But heavens, why am I telling you all this? I am usually so discreet."

126 ◆ ◆

He sighed heavily. I could see that he was possessed by a heavy sense of regret that he should soon be called upon to resume the trappings of respectability in Athens. "Why don't you stay here and live in a bagnio?" I asked and he sighed. Then his expression changed: "And the countess, my wife? How could I?" Affection for her flooded into him; tears came to his eyes. "She is devoted to me," he said under his breath. "And I have nobody else in the world." His tone touched me.

"Well. Good night, then," I said, and he shook my hand warmly.

Next morning I slept late, and when at last I came downstairs I found that the count had left for Galata; he had favored me with a last communication in the form of a visiting card with a crown below the name Count Horatio Banubula and a few words penciled on it. "Above all be discreet," he had written. But what the devil had I to reveal—and to whom?

Sacrapant was not due to appear before dusk so I lazed away the heat of the day in the garden under the shining limes watching the shifting hazes of the skyline condense and recondense as the sun reached its meridian. As it overpassed and began to decline the army of domes and steeples began to clarify once more, to set like jelly. Light sea airs from the Bosporus were invading the Horn now, driving the damp atmosphere upward into the town. It must have been some sort of festival day, too, for the sky was alive with long-tailed kaleidoscopic box kites—and by the time we reached the water under the Galata Bridge to pick up the steam pinnace which had been sent for me, I could look back and upward at a skyline prepared as if for some mad children's carnival. In such light, and at such a time of day, the darkness hides the squalor and ugliness of the capital, leaving exposed only the penciled shapes of its domes and walls against the approaching night; and moreover if one embarks on water at such an hour one instantly experiences a lift of the senses. The sea damp vanishes. God, how beautiful it is. Light winds pucker the gold-green waters of the Bosporus; the gorgeous melancholy of the Seraglio glows like a rotting fish among its arbors and severe groves. Edging away from the land and turning in a low half-arc toward the Bosporus I allowed Mr. Sacrapant to point out for me features like the seamark known as Leander's tower, and a skillfully sited belvedere in a palace wall whence one of the late sultans enjoyed picking off his subjects with a crossbow as they entered his field of vision. Such were the amenities of palace life in far-off times. But now our wake had thickened and spread like butter under a knife, and Sacrapant had to hold onto his Panama hat as we sped along, curving under the great placid foreheads and wide eyes of two American liners which were idling up the sound. It grew mildly choppy too as we rounded the cliff heads and turned into the Bosporus. The light was fading, and one of the typical sunsets of Stamboul was in full conflagration; the city looked as if it were burning up the night, using the approaching darkness as fuel. Sacrapant waved his arm at it and gave a small incoherent cry of pleasure—as if he had momentarily forgotten the text of the caption which should go with such a picture. But we were near in to the nether shore now and traveling fast; stone quays and villages of painted wooden houses rolled up in scroll fashion and slipped away behind us. Here, rising out of a dense greenery, one caught glimpses of walled gardens, profiles of kiosks smothered in amazed passion flowers, marble balconies, gardens starred with white lilies. Then higher up again small meadows shaded by giant plane trees, leading to softly contoured hilltops marked with umbrella pine or the slim pin of a cypress, eye-alerting as a cedilla in some forgotten tongue. Thickets of small shipping passed us, plodding industriously into the eye of the sunset, heading for Galata. Somewhere hereabouts, in one of the small sandy coves with high cliffs, would be the wooden landing stage which marked the entry to that kingdom Merlin had called "Avalon." Sacrapant explained that it was a ruin when Merlin bought it—part Byzantine fortress and part ruined Seraglio which had belonged to a rich Ottoman family that had fallen into disgrace. "The sultan expunged them all," said Sacrapant with a kind of sad relish. "It was named thus by Mr. Merlin himself." He made a motion with his slender hand.

It was still light when we came into the landing stage where the small group of servants awaited us, two of them with lanterns already lighted against the approaching night. They were supervised by a fat bald-headed capon of a man whom I had no hesitation in identifying as a eunuch. It was partly because of the unhealthy lard-colored pallor of his skin: partly because of the querulous spinster's voice which inhabited the fat body. He bowed in deeply submissive manner. Mr. Sacrapant waved him away with my suitcase as together we walked up a steep path into the garden of a small villa, with charming vine trellises on three sides, and a fine balcony overlooking the sound. This was apparently where I was to stay, and here I found my case already lying on the bed open; two servants under the supervision of the bald major-domo were hanging up my clothes. Sacrapant had a good look round and satisfied himself that all was well with me before taking his leave. "I am going back with the boat," he said. "Now in half an hour a man with a lantern will come to lead you to the villa where Mr. Jocas will be waiting for you—both of them in fact."

"Both brothers?"

"No. Miss Benedicta arrived last night. She is staying for a few days here in the other villa. You will meet her also."

"I see. How long do I stay?"

Mr. Sacrapant looked startled. "As long as . . . I don't know, sir . . . as is necessary to conclude your business with Mr. Jocas. As soon as you see him all will become clear."

"Have you ever heard the name Sipple?" I asked.

Sacrapant thought gravely and then shook his head. "Never to my knowledge," he said at last.

"I thought perhaps as you knew Count Banubula you might also know Sipple, an acquaintance of his."

Sacrapant looked desolated, and then his face cleared.

"Unless you mean Archdeacon Sipple. Of course! The Anglican clergyman."

It did not seem a fruitful line of inquiry to pursue, and I let it slide out of the picture. I strolled back with him toward the landing stage, along the winding paths which smelled of some powerful scent—was it verbena? "One more thing," I said, in spite of myself. "Who was the young woman watching us as the launch pulled in? Up there among the trees. She turned back and slipped into that little copse there."

"I saw no one," said Sacrapant. "But that is where Miss Benedicta's villa is; but you know, Mr. Charlock, it might have been anyone from the harem. There are still quite a lot of old aunts and governesses living there. Mr. Merlin was very generous to both relations and servants. Why, it could have been her English or French teacher—both live there still."

"She was youngish, handsome, dark."

"Well it was not Miss Benedicta, then."

He said good-bye with a shade of effusive reluctance; I felt that he would very much have liked to accept an invitation himself to the Pehlevi table. But it was not to be; he sighed twice, heavily, and once more took his place in the pinnace. The crew was Turkish, but the captain was Greek, for he spoke to Sacrapant in his mother tongue, saying something about the wind freshening. My friend answered impatiently, placing his hat safely beside him. He gave me a small genteel wave as the distance lengthened between us.

I stood for a moment or two watching the light dying out along the mauve hills and combs of the Asiatic shore. Then I walked back to the little villa. Someone had already lighted the petrol lamps and their white fizzing flames carved black shadows out of the rooms around them. I shaved my jumping reflection in the bathroom mirror and put on the only summer suit I had brought with me. I was sitting, at peace with the world, on the side terrace when I saw a lantern coming slowly down through the trees toward me. It was held by the fat majordomo who had been present at the landing stage. He bowed, and without further words spoken I followed him slowly upward through the gardens and copses toward where in some room (which I could not readily imagine) my host Jocas Pehlevi awaited to offer me dinner.

(If it gives me vague pleasure to recount all this, dactyl dear, it's because it seems about one hundred years ago.)

It was eerie as well as rather beautiful to pass in this fashion up the hill, guided only by the single cone of light which threw up silhouettes of buildings without substance or detail. Owls cried among the bushes, and in the heavy night air, the perfumes hung on, insisted. We crossed a ruined quadrangle of some sort, followed by a series of warrens which suggested kennels; ducked through an arch and walked along the side of a ruined turret on a broad flagged staircase. Now lights began and the bulk of the main house came into view. It suggested to me a huge Turkish khan built, as such caravanseries were, around a central courtyard with a central fountain; I heard, or seemed to hear, the champing of mules or camels and the whine of mastiffs. Up through a central massive door and along a corridor lighted with rather splendid frail gas mantles. Jocas was sitting at a long oak table, half turned sideways toward the door which admitted me, staring into my eyes.

In those disproportionately huge hands he held a piece of string with which he had constructed a cat's cradle. As we looked seriously at each other I received a sudden flock of different impressions—almost like a shower of arrows. I felt at once a feeling of being in the presence of someone of great virtue, of psychic goodness, if you like; simultaneously, like an electric current passing in me, I felt as if the contents of my mind had been examined and sifted, and as if all my pockets had been turned out. It is a disquieting effect that one sometimes runs into with a medium. Side by side with this however I had an impression of a naïve and almost foolish man, half crippled by nervousness. He was wearing, goodness only knows why, the traditional three-quarter frock coat and the Angora bonnet of wool—articles of attire which, on such a night, must have been a torture to support. Perhaps it was his desire to show some little formality toward a stranger? I don't know. I stared at that strange face with its swirling peruke of hair, and the tiny piratical rings in the earlobes, and felt unaccountably reassured. When he stood up one saw that, though thickset, he was on the short side; but he had extremely long arms and huge hands. The hand that grasped mine was moist with anxiety—or perhaps just heat generated by the absurd clothes? He wore a couple of ribbons—a Légion d'Honneur and something else I could not identify. He said nothing; we just shook hands. He motioned me to an empty chair. Then he threw back his head and gave a laugh which might have seemed sinister had I not already taken such a liking to him. His canines were tipped with gold points which gave his smile a somewhat bloodthirsty effect. But his teeth were beautiful and regular and his lips were red. He was of a swarthy cast of countenance—a "smoked" complexion: and while he seemed a hale middle-aged man there was quite a touch of gray in his hair. "Well," he said, "so at last you have come to us." I excused myself for my dilatory habits and the delay I had caused. "I know, but you have other things to do, and are not interested in making money." I assured him that he was in error. "So Graphos says," he said, dropping the string into the wastepaper basket and moodily cracking a knuckle. He seemed plunged in thought for a moment; then his face changed expression. He became benign. "You see he was right, Charlock; there was no time to be lost, there never is in matters of this kind. You were distributing these things free, were you not? Well, I had one copied, and took our drawings and articles on it for a patent. In your name, of course. That means that whatever happens—you may not want to let us handle it—the invention is yours and can't be stolen." He waited a long time, staring sorrowfully at me. "My brother Chewlian did it for you. He runs the European side of the firm in London. He is an Oxford man, Chewlian." A haunted, wistful look came into his eye. "I have never been farther than Smyrna, you see.

Though one day . . ." I thanked him most warmly for this kindly intervention on my behalf; he knew full well that I would not know how to go about patenting such an object. He got up to adjust a wavering gas jet, saying as he did so: "I am very glad you are pleased. Now at the same time Chewlian drew up a contract offer for you to study. Benedicta brought it with her; you will have it tonight. Myself I think it errs on the side of overgenerosity, but that is Chewlian all over!" He sighed in admiration at his brother. An expression almost maudlin in its affection crossed his face. "He behaves like a prince not a businessman." Then all at once he grew tense and serious and said: "That remark has made you suspicious. Why?" It was perfectly true; and he had read my mind most accurately. I said lamely: "I was thinking how incompetent I am to understand business documents, and hoping you would give me time to think them out." He laughed again and slapped his knee as if at an excellent joke. "But of course you shall. Anyway you have already taken your precautions haven't you?" I saw from this that he knew I had decided to take Vibart's advice before signing anything.

I nodded. "Come, we will have a drink on it," he said cheerfully, going to the corner of the room where decanters and plates glimmered. He poured me a glass of fiery mastika and placed a cheese pie beside me on the arm of the chair. "But there is something much bigger than this one small thing. Chewlian says we should try and enter into association with you to handle all your inventions. You have others in mind, have you not?" He got up impatiently and strode up and down the room again, this time in a fit of vexation, saying: "There! once again I have made you suspicious. I am going too fast as always." He spoke a curious English with a strong Smyrna intonation, slurring the words as if he had picked them up by ear and had never seen them written. "No," I said. "It is just that the idea is completely novel to me."

He snorted and said, "My brother would have put it to you much more . . . gentlemanly, I suppose. He says I am always like a carpet seller." He looked rueful and absurd in his black curate's tailcoat. "Anyway he has sent us a draft paper— articles of association—for you to look at." He fingered the dimple in his chin for a moment and stared at me narrowly. "No," he said at last, "it is not suspicion so much. You are slow. To understand."

"I admit it."

"Never mind. When you understand you can see if you want to join us or not. The terms are generous, and nobody yet has been dissatisfied with the firm."

I tried my hardest not to think of Caradoc and his strictures lest my thoughts be ready by this disarming yet determined little man. I nodded, attempting an air of sageness. He crossed to the door and called "Benedicta" once, on a sharp hawklike note which was at once humble and imperious. Then he came back and stood in the center of the room staring down at his own shoes. I looked about me studying the jumble of furniture and decoration which gave it the air of a storeroom. An expensive chronometer on one wall. A case of chased silver dueling pistols. Then I identified the slightly sickly smell of rotting meat. It one corner on a tall perch slept a falcon in its soft velvet snood. From time to time it stirred and very faintly tinkled the small bells it wore. While we were waiting thus the door opened and a dark girl appeared, holding a briefcase which she placed in an arm-chair. I thought she bore a resemblance to the girl who had watched the launch come in to shore from the grove of trees up the hill. She stopped just outside the radius of the lamp-light and said, in somewhat insolent fashion: "Why are you dressed up like that?" The note of icy contempt withered Jocas Pehlevi; he shriveled to almost half his size, ducking and joining his hands almost in a gesture of supplication. "For him," he said. "For Mr. Charlock." She turned a glance of indifferent appraisal upon me, echoing my bow with a curt nod. It was a cold, handsome face, framed in a sheeny mass of dark hair twisted up loosely into a chignon. A high white forehead conferred a sort of serenity upon it; but when she closed her eyes, which she did in turning her head from one person to another, one could see at once how her death mask would look. The lips were full and fine, but most of their expressions hovered between disdain and contempt. She was, then, as imperious as only a rich man's daughter dares to be: and noting this I conceived a sort of instant dislike for her which rendered her interesting.

Her entry had reduced Jocas to the dimensions of a small medieval playing-card figure; he scratched his head through the woolen bonnet. "Go and change at once," she said sternly reducing his self-esteem still further; he slipped away with an ingratiating bow in my direction, leaving us face to face. If she had moved forward a pace I would have been able to identify the peculiar blue of her eyes. But half in shadow like this they glowed with a sullen blue magnetism. She looked at me as if she had the greatest difficulty in mustering any interest in me or my doings. Then in a low voice she excused herself and turned aside to the dark corner of the room where the great falcon sat in the manner of a lectern eagle. She was wearing a long, stained garment of some sort of leather or velveteen. Now she pulled on an extra sleeve and worked her hand into a gauntlet. Somewhere in the shadows there came the dying fluttering of some small bird, a quail perhaps, and I saw with disgust that she was busy breaking up the body with her fingers into small tidbits. She suddenly began uttering a curious bubbling, crooning sound, uttering it over and over again as she drew a long plume softly over the legs of the peregrine; then the gloved hand teased the great scissor beak with the bleeding meat and the bird snapped and gorged. As it ate she reiterated the single word in the same crooning bubbling fashion. Slowly, with the greatest circumspection, she coaxed the falcon onto her wrist and turned to face me, smiling now. "He is the latest to be taken," she said. "I don't know as yet whether I shall succeed in bringing him to the lure. We shall see. Do you hunt? My father was a great falconer. But it takes an age to break them in."

At this moment the tall doors at the end of the room

opened and I saw a long dinner table laid upon a wide balcony. Jocas had already arrived upon the scene after a change of clothes. He wore now a comfortable Russian shirt of some soft silky material. His mane of hair was brushed back above his ears. "Lights," called Benedicta sharply, and at once the servants diminished the amount of light by blowing out half the candles. This left a small lighted area at one end, with two places set. "Don't move please." Still softly crooning the girl advanced to the balcony and crossed it toward the shadowy end of the table where she was to sit throughout the meal, eating nothing herself, but from time to time feeding the falcon. Jocas and I sat at the other end of the table, served by the expressionless eunuch. Out of the corner of his eye the little man kept glancing at the girl with a professional curiosity. For her part she now removed the easy fitting rufter hood for brief intervals, and then slipped it back into place. "It needs the patience of the devil," said Jocas. "But Benedicta is good. If you like we can take you for a day's sport—francolin and woodcock. Eh, Benedicta?" But the girl sat absorbed before her plateful of bleeding odds and ends and did not deign to look up or answer. Presently she rose—it was part of the routine it seemed—and announced that she must "walk" the falcon; bidding us good night she walked softly down the marble staircase into the garden and disappeared. It seemed to me that Jocas addressed himself to his dinner with a sort of relief after this—and he also became more voluble.

"Merlin was a great one for peregrines," he said. "And we have all taken after him—even down to small things. By the way, have you got the papers? In that briefcase Benedicta brought." He jumped up and fetched the article. "Here they are, you see, the two schemes set out separately. One is for the hearing device only; the other is a more detailed scheme—to manage all your work. You would become part of the firm, on a fixed retainer, with royalties, etc." He replaced the documents carefully in the briefcase and patted it. "At your leisure: the patent is safe—only your signature is needed. But first you must see your advisers. Tomorrow I will send you back to Polis for the day, yes?"

"Tell me about the firm," I said, and Jocas twinkled with pride and pleasure, in a manner which reminded me a little of Sacrapant. "Well," he said, "where to begin? Let me see."

"Begin with Merlin."

"Very well. Merlin was what you would call a merchant prince, a self-made prince. He arrived in Stamboul perhaps in the eighties of the last century on board a British yacht. He was a cabin boy. He deserted his ship, settled in the capital and began business. Much later when it had grown almost too big to handle he found myself and my brother and offered to let us become associates. How I bless the day." He joined his huge hands together and, laughing out loud, squeezed them until the knuckle joints cracked. "He was really a genius—you know all through the period of Abdul Hamid he never failed in his negotiations, he always got his firmans through. You know of course that Abdul Hamid was mad—mad with a fear of assassination. He lived up in the Yildiz palace in absolute terror. Loaded pistols lay in every corner, on every table. If startled by a sudden move he would open fire. Once his little niece ran into the room while he was dozing and he shot her. Merlin used to take special precautions when he went to see this madman—to walk slowly, talk slowly, sit quietly. He also worked out elaborate flatteries. Sent him a life-size sculpture of himself in butter, in ice cream. Sent him clocks of extraordinary workmanship specially designed in Zurich. It was he too who achieved other objectives for the firm by skillfully planted rumors. Abdul Hamid was very superstitious and had his horoscope made afresh each day. The firm suborned the court astrologer. In this way Merlin became in a sense the most important man in Turkey. But he was as wise as he was foreseeing. All the time he was giving money to the revolutionaries, to the Young Turks. And then the fleet—it was allowed to lie there and rot in harbor because Merlin told Hamid a pack of rumors about the use the Allies would make of it—playing on his fear and credulity. Why, I have seen those battleships rusting there all my life. They grow flowers on the decks. So gradually, even during the bad period, the firm grew and grew. Now of course times have changed, it is easier for us. Then when Merlin . . . left us, we two brothers took over the responsibility for Benedicta. We became her uncles." He laughed very heartily, wiping his eye in his sleeve. "And his wife?" I asked. All of a sudden Jocas looked nonplussed. His face grew serious. He thrust out his bearded chin and spread his hands in a gesture of inadequacy—as if he were powerless to answer the question satisfactorily. "There were many compromises made," he said, a trifle defensively. "There had to be. Merlin, for example, adopted the Muslim faith when he was in his fifties. Inevitably there were rumors of his wives and . . . ladies; but there was nothing very concise, very clear. This place was like a little walled city, and when you live *à la turque* the secrets of the harem are guarded from strangers. Benedicta was brought up in the harem, with foreign governesses first: then Switzerland for some years, that is why all her languages are so perfect." "But she is English?" Jocas nodded his head rapidly. "Yes. Yes. But I have never discussed with her, nor has Chewlian. Merlin never spoke with us about his private things. He was a very secretive man. I know that Chewlian also knows nothing because once he asked me."

Coffee, cigars and brandy found us removed to the farther end of the terrace where a sort of belvedere had been improvised out of carpets and cushions, and here the conversation turned to the recording machine which I had put at the service of Hippolyta in Athens. "I heard about it from Graphos," admitted Jocas, "and I could easily ask Chewlian to get me one and send it; but I understand that they are very hard to *drive*, no? And very delicate. So I waited to speak to you, to ask you about the matter."

"What would you use it for?" I asked, thinking of board-room meetings and the like. Jocas plucked his lips and looked sideways at me, with an air of exaggerated cunning. He considered. "I will tell you. We do not meddle in politics, as you know, but so often politics meddles with us that we really have to be up to date, to know what is afoot. At the moment there is a secret branch of the Young Turk officers having secret meetings. I do not want to spy on what they actually have to say; but I am on the lookout for one voice I know very well. If he has joined them, then I know all the rest. I would like a box to make a short talking of such a meeting. Would you do that for me? This has no connection with any of the other matters." I agreed, but with every professional reservation. My little mikes were not powerful enough to record through thick walls or at a hundred meters. He shook his head. "There is a fireplace in their room; beneath one of the big cisterns. I will have a brick removed for you to put your instrument."

"In that case very well."

"I will tell Sacrapant to take you, then," he said, with considerable unfeigned relief, touching my hand. "So very good."

He rose now and gazed out across the dark garden. A heavy sea fog had been rolling up as we talked and settling over the waters of the sound below; we could hear the muffled horns and bells of the sea traffic as it moved cautiously down toward the city. It had turned a trifle cold and damp. I thought it time to take my leave of my host, but he would not let me go without a visit to the old dark barn which had been turned into a "mews" for his hunting birds. I fell in with the suggestion out of politeness: indeed there was nothing to see, for the place was kept in almost total darkness. Vaguely I saw the shapes of the birds stirring on their wooden crossbars. Jocas went among them with the assurance of long familiarity. He made a low hissing noise with tongue and teeth as he went from one to the next, checking the jesses which bound them to their perches. The smell of rotting meat was almost unbearable; and I could feel the fleas jumping from the dirty flagstones onto my ankles. "This weekend we shall have some sport with them," he cried cheerfully. "If you are interested."

I agreed, for despite my personal indifference to the sport I found myself recalling to mind the image of the dark girl with the falcon on her wrist. It stirred me in some way—perhaps it was only curiosity taking fire. Nevertheless it would be interesting to go out with them, if only for the ride, and I said so. "Fine," he cried. "Fine."

We had a last whiskey on the terrace, and then the major-domo appeared with the light to conduct me back to the guesthouse. I found that I was quite unsteady on my legs, though my head was clear enough. We had agreed that I should spend next day in Polis consulting my advisers and return once more at nightfall by launch. The old eunuch led me slowly and steadily downhill, suiting his pace to mine, until at last I stood once more upon the little terrace. He entered the house to light the lamps. I stood, breathing the damp fogbound night air. There was no sky, no water, no stars. I floated in the swirling mist on my little balcony as if on a raft. His task completed the servant bowed and made his way up the hill. He was swallowed with the suddenness of a shutter falling. Then it was I heard the voice of the girl in the copse above the house. I could not see her in the dark-ness; but I could hear the low crooning of her voice as she addressed the bird on her wrist, *"Geldik gel ulalum,"* over and over again, varying the monotony of the phrase by small changes of intonation. The disembodied voice moved across the hill and faded on the ear. I was tempted to call her name once—and the thought surprised me very much indeed. In-stead I went to bed and lay in a tangle of damp sheets dream-ing fitful and discontinuous dreams in which the voice came from a great bird not a woman. A strange bubbling croon, like rose water agitated in its bowl by the drawing nargileh; a sound at once tender and obscene. On the one hand as sweet as the calling of turtledoves, on the other as incisive as the hiss of a snake. Great wings hovered over me in a dark sky; huge talons of iron entered my shoulders and I cried out. Then the long staggering fall earthward. But I fell into one of the kiosks of the Seraglio and was chased down dark corridors and into deserted ballrooms by three blind men. They operated by sound; when I made no move they halted, nonplussed, scimitars in hand. Then my breathing would alert them and they would rush toward me once more. I woke in a fever of perspiration and anxiety. The fog had lifted somewhat and there was a frail horned moon afloat in the water. Once more to bed where I wrestled awhile with insomnia before sinking once more into the grim quagmire of the dream.

I was awoken by the sun in my eyes. It was pouring across the terrace and into the windows of the little room. Moreover, to my surprise and confusion, Benedicta Merlin was there, sitting on the stone balustrade of the veranda, staring in at me as I slept. Beside her stood the briefcase which I had forgotten the evening before. Her face was serious, almost intense, almost as if she had been deeply concentrating as she watched me asleep. I uttered an incoherent good morning as I ran my hands through my hair, and she nodded. Her expression was still serious, almost a little puzzled. "You've been watching me asleep," said I with some vexation. "Why didn't you wake me?" She sighed and said: "I was counting up to a hundred. Then I was going to." She stood up and brushed some pollen or leaf mold from her hands. "I brought you this," she said, pointing to the briefcase. "The boat has arrived already and is waiting."

"Are you coming to Polis with us?"

She shook her head. "No. Not today. Why?"

"I don't know: we could talk."

"Talk?" she said in a higher register, and with a look of genuine surprise—as though the idea of someone wishing to talk to her was a novelty of the first magnitude.

"Why not?"

She turned on her heel almost shyly now and whispered, "I must go." She crossed the path and went slowly up the hill. I stood in my pajamas and watched her. At the edge of the copse she turned and looked back at me. I raised my hand in a greeting and she responded, but in a curious way—abbreviating the gesture, breaking it in half. Then she turned and vanished out of sight among the trees.

I retrieved the briefcase, and dressed in a hurry, knowing

that the patient Sacrapant would be waiting for me in the stern sheets of the *Imogen*, elegant yet stiff like some praying mantis or a tall crane in the docks.

I was suitably apologetic for having kept them all waiting and was heartily forgiven on all hands; soon we were skirling along the Bosporus coast, scoring deeply into a marble sea and throwing out a wake of white chips as we went. Everything—the great drop curtain of the city coming up before us—was hesitant, milky, tentative, mirage-edged. It was beautiful to sit within inches of the water, intently passive, so to speak: watching the glossy surface slide by under us. At such moments idle thoughts drift in star clusters, in cloud formations, across the nodding mind. I thought of Jocas' capacity for mind reading and compared it to my own: neither was very esoteric. If one concentrates on a human being, really concentrates, one can see his astral shape, so to speak, unfolding and progressing forward into his future: can divine the shape of what he might become. Well, I thought to myself wryly: aren't we being the little Faustus, now? And tell me *cher maître*, what would you divine in the smooth pious visage of Mr. Sacrapant who sits beside you holding the sacred briefcase which is to have such a strange effect on my life? "Sacrapant?" I replied to myself. "Hum. Let me see." All this was long before he fell out of the sky. The phrases came unbidden. "Case 225 Elias Sacrapant. He has listened all his life to Turkish music—music of a transcendental monotony. His wife loves with such piety that she has driven him steadily toward a nervous breakdown." But Mr. Sacrapant was talking, pointing out places of tourist interest. (How travel narrows the mind!) I nodded and took refuge in the steady hum of the engines. Then, still engaged with my Faustian self, I presented another figure for analysis, for an X ray, so to speak: Benedicta! Here my self-possession quite deserted me. I saw a succession of snapshots of that cold face—the unself-consciousness of beauty of its lines and planes and expressions. Case 226, so to speak. "She is living in absolute terror—and there is no reason for it. She has not

142 ◆◆

realized that just as art is not for everyone so other subjects like lovemaking or mathematics can only come to fruition in the hands of their adepts. Her case is so hopeless that one must, absolutely must, love her." These ideas frightened me so much that my hair almost stood on end.

Vibart occupied a modest but comfortable little villa in a palm-filled garden beyond Pera whence he conducted a good deal of his business which concerned businessmen for the most part. The front room had been converted into an office with a few files and a hospitable sideboard full of bottles. He scanned through the documents from the briefcase with care but at speed, his mouth open with astonishment. Then he pushed his horn-rimmed glasses up onto the top of his head and said: "Jesus Christ, man—have you read them?" I nodded, adding: "But I'm no lawyer and wouldn't spot any catches."

"Catches!" he laughed in exasperated amazement, and took an agitated turn up and down the room. "My dear sir! Have you seen the sliding royalty scale, the size of the retainer? You should have signed the articles of association *at once*, do you hear? They not only offer to pay you royally for what you do, but to market it; and as if that weren't enough to provide ways and means for you to experiment to your heart's content." He sat down and held his ears briefly. "I don't know what to say. I'll look at them in more detail if you like but really, on the face of it . . ."

"I felt it was almost too good to be true: as if there were something fishy behind it all."

"Merlin? Fishy? You must be mad, Charlock. The firm is as sound as a rock and highly respectable. You are damned lucky to have got into it at your age and in your line of business. I wouldn't hesitate if I were in your shoes. As a matter of fact I know quite a lot about Merlin because I was once asked to do an article for *The Times* on our Levant merchants, and I started to research on him. But somehow or other I got sidetracked, couldn't get enough material; Pehlevi raised some trivial objections—not this one, Julian,

◆ ◆ 143

who runs the London end. I was sorry because the story was a most romantic rags-to-riches one. It started very modestly with this naval cadet deserting his battleship, and going to ground in Polis. Then, bit by bit, with his headquarters in a wineshop he started dealing with true Scots judgment: hides, coal, corn, poppy from Lebanon, qat from the Yemen, tobacco, perhaps a touch of slaving on the Red Sea. . . . It grew up slowly but steadily into a giant he couldn't handle alone. Hence the two Pehlevi brothers, God knows where Merlin found them; they couldn't be more unlike each other in temperament and background. Jocas . . . well you've seen him. Julian I have never seen but only heard about. A tremendous career at Oxford, a spell in the Bank of England, and then he took over London for Merlin. With the disappearance of Merlin from the scene the firm divided by a sort of binary fission—rather like the division of the Eastern and Western churches: only of course they work hand in glove the two brothers. Julian is all banking, investment schemes, manufacturing, stocks and shares and so on: while this end you have chiefly trade based on marketable raw materials. Istanbul is still a conventionally strategic entrepôt for whatever comes down the Black Sea into the Med. Don't look so gloomy, Charlock. With one scratch of a pen you can secure more than financial independence, man, but *riches* as well as the security to go on doing your work in peace. It makes me feel hysterical to think of your luck."

"What of Benedicta Merlin, the brunette daughter?"

"Brunette? She's blonde—or one of us is color-blind. No, I remember now that she is given to wearing wigs of various colors. But she is blonde I swear, and very handsome. There, my boy, is another prize worth carrying off. I should say she's one of the richest women in the world."

"But she's a widow. Yet they never use her married name."

"Yes, so it seems. I never saw her husband."

I stood up and finished my sherry thoughtfully. "Well," I said, "I'll leave the papers with you for the time being, for a closer look into them. Then, if you still think . . . I don't know." I had an obscure but obstinate feeling against tying myself down with such finality—though I could bring no reasoning to bear on it. I could not elucidate it.

"Righto," said Vibart, disappointed. "Only, in a world where almost everyone has compromised and is doing a job he doesn't like or want in order to eat—one can't help envying a chap an offer like this."

"What would you do if you could?"

"Get out of diplomacy, where everything is so much smaller than life and . . . no, I won't say the word, Charlock, I won't say it."

I sighed for him, having heard all this bleat before. "I know," I said. "You want to write." Vibart groaned and ran his hand through his blond hair; he smiled that attractive smile of his and agreed shyly. "My dear Charlock," he said, "I have always been big with book, but it will never get written unless I WAKE UP." He shouted the last three words and banged on his desk so loudly that I was startled. "Sorry," he said. His wife called from the other room to ask if he was all right. "Of course I'm all right," he cried indignantly. "That is the whole trouble." Under the foolery I could sense a very real anger and frustration. Vibart was a charming and highly articulate victim of his education. "I must escape before I contract the diplomatic pruritus," he went on. "Better anything than to live forever in terror of committing a mere imprudence." I laughed and invited him to walk off his ill humor and he readily agreed to accompany me back to my point of rendezvous with Sacrapant. In the course of his long rambling self-decortication he threw in small scraps of hearsay, tidbits of information which sometimes struck me as false—or if not false, then on the face of it at variance with what I would have myself surmised as true. For instance, that Sacrapant was a crack pistol shot and had won a number of cups thereby; that Julian had ordered some Corinthian columns for the Merlin estate and had them broken up and scattered about in order to imitate a Greek temple. "But let me talk about myself," said Vibart, still seething with the desire of self-castigation. "It is my only real subject. I come, Charlock, from an interesting family with a record for profligacy, degeneracy, philistinism and selfishness which stretches back to Tudor times. But where are all these qualities? The strain has gone thin and sour, for I am wise and good. I can show you nothing worse than sloth, shoddiness, self-delusion and sanctimoniousness. Bad enough, you may say: but all negative things. What, shall I stay on forever, and lobby myself a dwarfdom by dancing the boa constrictor with a councillor's wife?"

"Well why not begin?" I asked.

"That's the whole point," he said sadly. "I would not be content with anything less than perfect. And you cannot, it seems to me, do it simply by being nice and well conducted and full of notions—though why the hell not? It's as if my parents had bought me an expensive wheelbarrow when they sent me to Winchester—and here I am too lazy to garden. It's despicable." He struck his calf with his cane and uttered an oath. "On the other hand how can one believe in literature? Nor is the contemporary scene very reassuring for the newcomer. Crowns of rhubarb first class, parsley, sage, rue. Tinsel for the new boys. Then the allocation of honorary titles like 'The Thrush of Finchingfield.' This is more than a little dispiriting."

"Well I don't know what to suggest."

"Of course you don't: nor do I. And here is time flying by and I'm putting on weight. Soon I shall be only fit to write the history of Adipose Rex—sorry!"

We arrived at last at the intersection of streets where Sacrapant had promised to meet me; Vibart hung on, talking, unwilling to relinquish a listener.

"I have mislaid myself," he announced with a grandiose gesture of his stick in the direction of the Grand Bazaar. "*E quindi uscimmo a riverder le stelle*—but where do I fit in, please tell me? Shall I carve myself a niche among the water babies of Socialism—the songsters of the back passage? Or contract criticism, that superior form of blood poisoning?

146 ◆◆

Shall I present as a Protestant Radical—one who will not take yes for an answer? Or is reticence the better part of valor? Shall I focus my two hundred rabbit power eyes on the future and stay mum?"

I persuaded him to allay his vexation somewhat by entering a café with me to have a mastika; here he continued with this unwearying self-examination for my benefit. "I have mapped out my whole career more than once. I have even written my own press book. 'Full of characteristic felicities and written at gale force. Who is this Vibart? We must know.' (*Sheffield Clarion*): or 'Subtle, thought-provoking and full of lovely mince' (*The Times*): or 'Ecstasy to riffle and give away' (*Vogue*). I am already at the height of my career. How did I achieve this transcendent position? I became so thin they gave me the Nobelly Prize and a whole page in the Literary Sacrament. . . ."

"It won't do, Vibart."

"I know it won't. Comely of form was he, but with the temperament of a field mouse. Damn. Damn."

All this of course masked a very real dilemma; I saw that to accuse himself of vainglory, narcissism, selfishness and so on was something more than just a defense; on the one hand it earned him kudos for honesty and insight—on the other it absolved him from *doing* anything about it. But then, on the other hand, why should he? I liked him the way he was. Besides one day he might shake the drops off and address himself honestly to life. "Well keep trying," I said, "and I'll get in touch with you in a day or two about the contracts." He took his leave with many a sad cautionary headshaking, and I watched the tall athletic figure slipping away through the warrens of the souk. And here, as if by magic, Mr. Sacrapant appeared at my elbow with his characteristic air of piety. He gazed moistly at me and clasped his hands together. "Have you joined us, Mr. Charlock? Have you signed?" For some reason this incessant harping had begun to get on my nerves. "No I have not," said stoutly with a mulish expression. "I have left them to be carefully examined. It will take a day or two."

He gave a disappointed sigh, and then shrugged his shoulders. He looked inexpressibly saddened and pained—I suppose by my suspicious hesitations over joining the firm. I saw him suddenly—a gray-haired, winged and ithyphallic little man off some shattered Phrygian marbles, standing there eternally with that look of sadness, but silent now, silent as rain or fleece. Elias Sacrapant Esq. He stood upon the axis drawn by intersecting arcades, silent and friendly. "Let us talk of other things," I said. "What about this political meeting you want monitored?"

Sacrapant came down to earth at once and took on the aspect of a conspirator; he leaned forward, after a glance around him, and said: "I was going to bring that up today. I knew you had been approached. It would be just a minute or two. They meet every evening, about six, all this week. So you could choose your time." I reflected. "You know," I said, "I have left one of my boxes in my room at the Pera. If you like we could get it and do the job this very evening. What do you say?"

Sacrapant's eyes kindled. "Good. Excellent. The sooner Mr. Pehlevi knows the truth the better for the firm. I will go down and tell the launch to wait for us, and then taxi up to join you at the hotel. You will walk I presume? Well, we have time, we have time."

I fell in with his wishes, and wool-gathered my way back to the hotel where I tested my machine and the spare microphone. Then I lay on my bed and dozed off incontinently—to dream a confused dream of childless bluestockings lecturing to Vibart on the novel.

> *Little bas bleu*
> *Come blow up my horn*
> *And sanction a tumble*
> *Amid the green corn,*
> *My pretty blue stocking*
> *My supercherie*
> *With prune and with prism*
> *Fandangle with me.*

I awoke with a start to find myself looking down the barrel of a pistol. I cried out incoherently and Mr. Sacrapant burst into a thin peal of delighted laughter. "It isn't loaded of course," he said. "But how was I to know that?" He became all contrition. "I am sorry. But I have been told to take some weapon with me. In case."

"In case what?"

"You never know."

I began to feel indignant. "Look here, I wasn't told that there was any danger about this performance."

"There isn't theoretically. None at all."

He slipped the weapon shyly into an inner breast pocket and pulled his coat down. "In a while we can start," he said.

It was my first introduction to the fantastic honeycomb of ancient cisterns upon which the city appears to have been built. Afterward I returned to explore them in some detail, but on this occasion we found our way to the Yeri Batan Serai—the underground palace built by Justinian under the portico of the basilica itself. Its entry was an obscure hole—like a shaft dug into a tumulus. A leather and wooden door, fastened with wire, marked the entry to the long flight of steps which led downward at a steep angle to the water's edge. Here Mr. Sacrapant, true to form, produced a couple of pocket torches. It was awe-inspiring to plunge down all of a sudden into this watery cathedral. The symmetrical rows of columns stretched away on all sides in extraordinary perspectives, picking up the light and shadow simultaneously. The depth, the gloom, the reverberation of our footsteps on the staircase swelled the sense of mystery; moreover from one of the darker corners—across the long lanes of dark water which threw wobbling shadows into the heavy vaulting overhead—I saw a light. Mr. Sacrapant whistled, but very softly; and he was answered after a pause by a replica of the sound, soft and mellifluous. The light approached us now, and I saw that it was on the prow of a small skiff, being rowed by a single old Turk who wore a fez. "Come," breathed Mr. Sacrapant, and held the nose of the boat steady for me to climb in with my gear. Then lithe as a lizard he leaped in after me, and we set

◆ ◆ 149

off down these long dark galleries of water. The rower propelled his boat noiselessly with a simple twisting motion of the oars, standing upright and never letting the blades rise to the water surface. It was fearfully damp; the least sound—crepitation of water in the caverns, peppering of sand falling from the roof—became blown up, magnified, hazy. None of us spoke. The rower seemed to know his destination. Mr. Sacrapant sat forward flashing his torch upon the darkness ahead. His lips moved. He was it seemed counting the columns, for presently he muttered a figure under his breath and tapped a signal on the back of the Turk, who turned the boat at a sharp angle, and set off down a side gallery. We came at last to a shallow flight of stairs—a sort of water gate—which led upward into the throat of the cistern, so to speak; it pierced the ceiling with a rotten trap of wood. This was our objective, or so it seemed. Here Sacrapant began to behave with a good deal of muffled circumspection, using gestures and mime wherever they might replace spoken words. The staircase was solid enough, but the heavy recorder was a clumsy thing to man-haul, particularly in the dancing uncertain light of the little torches. However we managed the operation without mishap; and now I followed the lanyard-like figure upward into the gloom, along a cobwebbed corridor, and then upward again. He was hunting along the wall of a particular place. The white light jumped and flicked along the gloomy stone facings—the ground floor of a deserted subterranean Venice I thought to myself as I followed him, by this time feeling more than a touch of apprehension. Blind man's fingers. I had not visualized this sort of exploit when Pehlevi spoke to me about my recorders. But it was now too late to withdraw and show a white flag. Sacrapant skidded along the corridors in lizard fashion until at last he came to a marked stone in the wall. He produced a pocket knife and, beckoning me to preserve an absolute silence, inserted it in the interstices of the stone to exercise leverage on it. It came away with relative ease and on his invitation I took a look into a sort of flue which I was soon to realize was that of a vast fireplace. The hole, admirably camouflaged, stood about six feet above ground level.

As far as the room was concerned there seemed to be a meeting already going on; chairs scraped, the hum of voices swelled and subsided. It was all barks and glottal stops to me. For my part all I had to do was to let a microphone dangle as low as possible above the hearth and start printing this medley of sound. Pertinacious Mr. Sacrapant seemed now to be in an agony of apprehension; he stood on one leg and then on the other. Why? The operation was a simple one and it was not very long before I saw my blue pilot nodding away at me in the gloom, and heard the soft whir of the machine "taking." Down below in the boardroom or officers' mess or whatever the place might be, new voices came up. Some sort of speech of welcome was made; measured and sententious sentences without subsidiary clauses, following one another in dactylic progression. I had copied for about ten minutes when Sacrapant signaled me to cut out. It was quite enough, he contorted; and so I began to pull in my line like some benighted fisherman and swash up my equipment. And here all at once there was a hitch. My line must somehow have dislodged a small stone or pebble from the interior of the flue—for something fell into the fireplace with a clatter, bouncing on the iron firedogs. At once I was aware that the inhabitants of the room below had been alerted by this sound. Their voices came up the flue now—they were trying to look up the chimney. I hauled in like mad; it was not a moment to hang about. Sacrapant hopped and cajoled me to hurry up. For my part I did not even wait to replace the stone, so infectious was the little man's anxiety. I hulked the stuff down and jumped into the boat; Sacrapant followed, but as he did so his little pistol slid out of his pocket and into the dark water with a splash. The Charon-like Turk was now urged to carry us away from the place at all speed; but he was typical of his leaden unhurried race, and so we set off at the same funeral pace, moving at right angles to one set of pillars. We had extinguished the light of the boat, and depended for direction on an occasional torch blink from Sacrapant. So we scored our slow way across the inky water of the cavern. Suddenly, far away to the right, there came a gleam of yellow light—as if from a door which had been thrown open—and one heard the nibble of voices. After a moment's delay—perhaps for deliberation—we heard the snickering of pistol shots ricocheting from the vaults and falling in the water. It was not clear whether they were aiming at us or not but the sound was ominous. Mr. Sacrapant with great prudence lay down in the bottom of the boat and complained about feeling seasick. The Turk was completely unmoved and plodded on toward our own landing stage. I tried as far as possible to sit in a position which would have shielded me from our aggressors, though their exact whereabouts as well as the direction of their fire was somewhat in doubt. It seemed to take an age before we grazed the landing stage and bumped to a halt. By now we were far away from the scene of our imprudence and it seemed possible to use the torches again; we paid off the old man and clambered out into a surprise—for darkness had already fallen upon the city. Nor did it seem possible even at this early hour to find a taxi so we were forced to content ourselves with a horse-drawn cab which jogged us, juddering and swaying, down to the Galata bridge where the launch waited, its captain smoking patiently on the bridge.

We dined late that night, but on the same balcony overlooking the darkened garden, and this time my host was in high spirits at the success of our operation of the evening; Sacrapant was invited to dinner throughout which he sat in a daze of self-congratulation. "We were shot at," he repeated wonderingly more than once. "Mr. Charlock and I were shot at." I said nothing about him lying in the sheets, or about my heroic attempt to shield myself behind the rower. We were heroes. Bravo, Felix! I was only sorry that the mysterious Benedicta was not there to share in all this grandeur; but she had crossed over to the Asiatic side, and was to meet us next morning for a day's falconry. "You know, don't you, that she was been very ill?" said Jocas Pehlevi in what seemed on the face of it an inconsequential aside. It had nothing to do with the preceding conversation. I could not quite decide whether his tone implied a warning or the registration of a simple price of information. But the phrase cracked open a new area of comprehension. Pausing for thought, I understood now the secret source of that striking and distracted gaze—the source of what I called her beauty. It was not simply the happy disposition of features, it was the sadness and withdrawnness of her illness—the fragmentation of neurasthenia— which gave her the air of someone distractedly listening to an interior monologue, a private musical score. The total solipsism of . . . but I won't say it: why offend the doctors? But if she had not had this she might have seemed as commonplace as half a hundred good-looking blonde girls; with it she achieved a kind of legendary quality—a sick muse embedded in a statue of flesh and bone. This realization so kindled my sympathy that I hardly heard Jocas saying: "Now can we hear your records, please?" I came to myself with a start. "Yes, of course."

I had been somewhat doubtful about the quality of my recording, but here again luck held. It was pronounced clear. Jocas listened with intense concentration, smoking a cigar, head down; but after the fourth repetition he said with a sigh of relief: "It was not Mahmud, was it?" Sacrapant shook his head joyfully. "Then we will not have to act for the time being," said Jocas. "Good. Good."

The conversation shifted crabwise to other and more impersonal matters which did not concern me, and I turned my attention adrift, not surprised that it wandered off in the direction of Benedicta, recalling all the minutiae of her behavior and appearance as if to find in each fragment a specimen of the sick beauty which had once become her master. I excused myself early that night, as we were due to set off before dawn, and made my way back to my waterside bungalow. I took off all my clothes and went over my body point by point, holding up the light in the mirror the better to study it. I did not know why I was doing this—nor did I ask myself any questions. But afterward I sat down in despair on the bed and said aloud: "Is this what it is like?" What was I talking about? I don't know. I found my beauty unconvincing I suppose! Moreover to add to this feeling of horrible dispersion and inadequacy there came its twin—the conviction that I had made a choice that was as bad as it was irrevocable! But, O dear, how clearly I saw that face! Nevertheless the realization must have cleared the air, so to speak, for that night I slept the dreamless sleep of early childhood. Iolanthe must have been dreaming about me.

As for Benedicta herself I must confess that I had seen her before, in a manner of speaking. The gesture with which Iolanthe sank down upon the carpet and drew forth the greasy little pack of playing cards always heralded a prolonged scrutiny of the auspices, an evaluation of her future and mine; she kept them separate even then, out of who knows what sad tact? And, youthful and self-sufficient boor that I was, I hardly noticed the crestfallen tones in which she might say: "Our story is coming to an end for many years. Soon I shall go from you, and the other will come, the widow. She will be sadder than I, much sadder. I see many doors around her, and all of them closed." I yawn, of course, in the manner of one who has known (as Caradoc would say) *"des femmes de toutes les catégorilles."* We scientific chaps cannot countenance divination by aces and spades. "My story is one of riches, riches, but much dissatisfaction, much unhappiness. Then look, we meet again in another country—but it will be too late to start again. Meanwhile the widow will hold you. She is fair. You will recognize her by her right foot—something is wrong with it."

"A cripple? Does she limp?"

"No. I see her dancing with you, beautifully."

Regarding with distaste the hot and crumpled sheets upon which Iolanthe gazed with such tenderness. Now when I think of it I go all-overish. All this for me was mere pleasure which never exploded into insight, couldn't disturb the egocentric flow of my hugged imaginings. The arts of introspection nourished on a junior loneliness and too much bloody education. Sentient beings for me were still almost convincing dummies, that was all. Am I typical then? A thousand little acts of attachment passed over me unnoticed. Well, later memory takes them and turns them into spears. One cries out in one's sleep, one curses. Like, I mean, taking the spectacles off my sunburned nose as one lifts the lid from a jar of olives—to kiss me. Made foolish by too much knowledge I did not see her then as she was, namely in her natural state; I only began to "see" her when she had created her artificial self, the actress. Then she hit me between the eyes. But then one can't start loving retroactively—or can one? Too little, Felix, and then too late. Matter of fact or fact of matter? With Benedicta I chewed off my own tail in a cloud of unknowing. For better or for hearse. But wait. It was not all so vague, for she had deep and pitiful experiences to chew upon, and was gifted with a strange aberrant insight, as when she was describing early sexual experiences once and came out with: "If you push passion to extremes you are bound to tumble into mere mysticism." What a strange use of the word "mere"! But wait a minute.

It was well before dawn when I woke with a jolt to find Jocas standing over me, jackbooted and spurred, holding a lighted candle and grinning like a dog. "Sea fog," he said oracularly, and I heard the engines of the pinnace warming up, ticking over, in the obscurity below. Over his arm he carried a miscellaneous collection of clothes and boots—gear more suitable for a day of riding than the suit I had brought with me. I foraged about amongst it all and equipped myself with a good pair of boots, ill-fitting riding breeches, an empty bandolier and such other sundries as seemed to me to be to the purpose. Then before climbing down the hill to the boat he poured us each a small cup of scalding sage tea backed by a sip of gasping mastika. So we careened out of harbor into an olive-drab mist which coiled around us, condensing upon hair and eyebrows. The dispirited dogs drowsed and yawned among the tarpaulins. "She went over early with the old falconers," said Jocas, "and we'll meet later today. Hullo! What's that?"

The channel even at this early hour was full of ships laboring cautiously down toward the Horn, their bells changing out warnings, soft wet lips of foghorns, etc. In smaller craft the lookout banged upon a saucepan and shouted from time to time to mark position. As we had to cut directly through the middle of this traffic to reach the Asiatic side the operations of the pinnace were delicate in the extreme, although we were equipped with engines of great power and a foghorn whose melancholy resonance was enough to set the dogs ululating. Jocas smoked a short pipe and waited patiently as his pilot trod cautiously among the indistinct shapes and sounds on this dark waterway. This funeral pace was imposed on us for nearly an hour and then, in the most dramatic fashion, the fog was peeled aside by a scurry of wind and we were in the full light of an early sunrise riding down along the low purple headlands of the nether shore where our drumming wake rippled down upon sleeping villages to set the colored boats bobbing at deserted landing stages. Everything was still sticky with fog damp and Jocas would not let the guns out of their cases until the sun was fully up. The dogs were rubbed down with straw. We drank black coffee in tin mugs and watched the chromatic scale of yellow Byzantine light loop up the eastern end of the sky—until it ran over and raced everywhere, spilling among the shady blue valleys, and touching in the vague outlines of the foothills. Sunrise. Carob, sweet chestnut, oak—and plaintive small owls calling.

We were running along the low toothy headlands of the coast now, in view of the country which we were to hunt. Clumps of swaying bamboos marked the points where shallow streams had nosed their way down into the bight. The land soothed itself away to the girdle of foothills, the shallow intervening valleys wearing their scrub and green screes bravely, pinpointing here and there a cypress plume or a regiment of olives; but for the most part dwarf oak, juniper, myrtle and arbutus—the classical combination so easily negotiable (so it seems) until one tries to follow a gundog into the impenetrable jungle of interlocking roots and thorns. Jocas swept the land with a powerful glass, grunting with satisfaction; then he handed it to me, pointing out here and there a shattered fragment of an abandoned temple, or a cluster of pruned stone where a seamark had been allowed to dribble into a heap of rubble under the rubbing water. But away to the north his blunt finger directed me to a small landing stage, a tiny harbor carved in shale, where the horses awaited us. Then, moving away to the right over the green land, he indicated a tall hillock, with a fine tall stand of oak trees where, in the shadow, one saw the movement and glitter of what seemed to be an encampment. "Benedicta is up there," he said. "She will have the birds. We won't use the guns today unless . . . I suppose a boar might be tempting. But they are not very numerous now."

We were met by a little group of horsemen whose repellent ugliness and strange attire suggested to the mind the inhabitants of remotest Tartary. They were clad in greasy duffle, with jackboots of soft leather crudely sewn. Their rifles were antiques, muzzle-loaders. Their little round hats with the shallow brim emphasized the almond-shaped eyes. They greeted Jocas with an awkward curtness which suggested not so much discourtesy as the shy manners of remote mountaineers. There wasn't a smile between the lot of them.

We mounted and set off across the fields feeling the sun hot upon our backs. I had not ridden for a long time—not indeed since a bit of mild hacking at university—and felt very much of a novice. Jocas rode sturdily but without elegance: indeed he sat like a sack of meal. But his huge hands and his grip on the reins suggested that a troublesome horse would receive no quarter from him.

We crossed a half-dry marsh and began to climb the hill. Here the sun had started to make the wet land steam, and the rising mist swept upward into the trees. It was through this abrupt dimming of our vision that Benedicta appeared, mounted dramatically on a bronze stallion, her yellow hair flying loose. She was a different woman from the dark girl with the heart-shaped face; this was someone imperative, assured, even perhaps cruel when one thought of the dense blue eyes under frowning brows: periwinkle-blue, large, fierce, finely formed. "You're damned late," she said to Jocas, reining in and turning into a slow-plunging, arse-banging reorientation in order to come alongside us. Then still unsmiling she reached out and pressed my wrist in a gesture of greeting which was, to say the very least of it, puzzling: I could not decide if it were descended from some Oriental form of greeting—or was an expression of personal intimacy. I was tempted to raise my wrist to my lips but refrained. The gesture itself may also have meant nothing; but it illuminated something for me in a flash. I understood what the meaning of my strange behavior on the night before could be: I mean examining myself so carefully in the mirror, measuring so to speak the degree of my own narcissism in the face of this reflected man, I had been thinking of something like this: "Yes, but then we are modified effectively by the contents of our skulls, by what we think. This science nonsense has reduced your ability to affirm yourself. You would, faced by a challenge like this—I mean a girl who sets herself down in front of the target—turn the whole thing into hollow propositions which you would lodge in the conscious mind. You couldn't just bite into her like a fresh apple. Yum, Yum. And if you did try to warm up your feelings in a more generous direction why you'd go soft, you'd go sentimental. Too much scientific thinking has poisoned feeling, has reduced your pulse rate so to speak. What will you do if she embraces you?" Fall off my horse, I suppose.

This is where the extraordinary melancholy came over me. (At this moment my heart was simmering, my blood had turned to quicksilver. I saw her then in some almost legendary form—this slender woman riding down upon us like some drunken queen of the Iceni.) It was the melancholy subject of the night before which reflected and told himself that perhaps we are forced to choose as lovemates, shipmates, playmates those that best match our inward ugliness—the sum of our own shortcomings. No, I did not know that as yet. Not then.

There was sweat upon her upper lips and temples; her cheek was red, little blonde hairs twinkled. The eyes didn't have any particular expression—perhaps a touch of disdain. But when they turned upon mine a whole new world of feeling darkened them. Incredibly enough, I could have sworn she was in love with me. Riding like that through the mist I had a sudden feeling that I was about to faint, to fall out of my saddle into a bush. It did not last long, this vertiginous feeling, but it altered the whole scale of my sentiment. All of a sudden I was sure of something, I knew where I was; I longed to escape as a fish longs to escape from the hook. If one could apply some rational system to subjects like these how nice it would be: instead one must always talk as provisionally as possible and in terms of poetry. But damn it Charlock is a scientist—and scientists, moved by pure reason, never let themselves get into such awkward positions. Was it Koepgen who said that science waas built upon defensive measurement and art upon propitiation?

"I knew you would have to come to me," she said in a low voice. A minatory note, a little too intense: I did not like it one little bit. This again did not need saying now: at the touch of her fingers on my wrist I had realized that she had been willing me to return once more in a slow curve to that point of reference in time at which our natures had ignited each other. Heavens, what a way to express it! But we *are* modified effectively by what we think. (Charlock, cool your mind with the calculus.) Benedicta waited for me to answer her—but what was I to tell her about the whole deathscapade of lovemaking? The soul of modern man is made of galvanized iron. She turned away, biting her lips. I felt sad to have to wound her by a silence and an awkwardness at a time when our feelings had defined themselves, grouped themselves, were waiting only to be honorably avowed and recognized. Thoughts incoherent and dispersed floated through my skull as the horses undulated up the slope. I heard for example (why?) the disembodied voice of Sipple say: "Blowed if I see any culture in the Parthenon. To me it's just a marble birdcage. They say it's old but how is one to tell? There are no maggots in marble." But if I could see her so clearly as she was that day I could also see, by simple extension of her look, her manner, the Benedicta who could sit for hours before a mirror with a finger to her lips, her eyes wide with fright; I could see those cupboards full of fancy-dress costumes, the masks. Puppetry! Among the cartoons of monks and demons there hung whips with knotted thongs. Yes, I saw Benedicta always elaborately gowned and cloaked, always wearing some fabulously expensive bracelet over a left-hand glove: Benedicta dressed like an Infanta to welcome me to the white walls and glassy balconies of the sanatorium in Zurich which her father had once endowed. If I had dared then to say simply: "Benedicta, I love you," it would have been like the report of a gun, the discharge of a firearm that blows the top of your skull off. The hero of the New Comedy will be the scientist in love, grappling with the androgynous shapes of his own desire. Wouldn't you say?

But we had come now to a shady clearing among the trees on the nether side of the hill which dipped down toward flat green country of simple brush, iodine colored. Here the old falconers were gathered about the awkward wooden cages which held their choicest birds. They looked like all specialists look—all members of bowling clubs, artisans, artists, tend to look. Old wrinkled specialists who spent their whole time hanging about the falcon market in Istanbul waiting to pick up a bargain—an eyas tiercel or a peregrine or a jack merlin (strange that should have been the name of Benedicta's father). Did he look rather like the bird? The little group talked in low moping tones, they had all of them grave bedside manners, walking among the unfidgeting birds. A single cigarette passed from hand to hand. The gunbearers stood about in dispirited fashion, but with our arrival all was animation; the horses were trimmed, girths checked. Jocas elected to fly the largest of the falcons, his favorite, while the girl chose a smaller short-winged bird—one that could be discharged from the wrist at the first sight of prey almost in the manner of a shotgun. We wound down the hill in single file before fanning out the beaters and the dogs, trained skillfully not to overrun. Once down the hill Jocas looked over our dispositions and released his hawk with a shrill musical cry, slipping the hood from its eyes. After a swift look about the great bird rose magnetically, its wings crushing down the air as it rustled upward in a slow arc, to take up its position in the sky. This one would "wait on" in the higher air to have the advantage over far-flying quarry. But as yet we had hardly begun the beat, moving with the sun at our backs; a couple of woodcock rose with a rattle and began their crashing trajectory across the lower sky. At once the shrill ululations of the falconers broke out, encouraging the great falcon: sometimes these sounds reminded one of the muezzin's call to prayer from a minaret in the old city. So the battle began. One of the woodcocks went to earth in the bracken and refused to be flushed, but the second put up a struggle characterized by tremendous speed and finish. It seemed to be able to judge the moment when the falcon had positioned itself for the stoop; instantly it would dive for cover, only to be flushed once more by the ever-advancing line of beaters. After the third or fourth repetition of this tactic it began to tire; its flights became shorter and more erratic, its plunges for cover more desperate. The hunt had now broken into several parties, interest being divided by other quarry, by new birds taking the air. I saw Benedicta discharge the short-winged hawk from her wrist at the sight of something rising among the holm oaks. It flew at incredible speed—fired like a slingshot.

But the battle between Jocas' falcon and the woodcock had drawn us on ahead of the rest. It was exciting, the gallop across the flat plain after the failing woodcock. It was after about a mile and a half that one saw the falcon shortening its gyres, closing the space between it and its quarry. It was winding it in almost, as a fisherman winds in a fish. The woodcock despite its fatigue was game and rose again and yet again, but falteringly now. It was becoming clear that the end was not far off. The falcon once more positioned itself, helped now by a slight change of the wind's direction. It took careful aim and suddenly came plummeting down at incredible speed, adding impetus to its own great weight. Too late the woodcock tried to evade it by a feint, sliding sideways as it fell. The falcon struck it a devastating blow with its hind talons—must have struck it stone-dead in fact. Down they both went now in a tangle of wings, leaving a trail of slow feathers in the amazed sky. At once the horsemen shrilled and ululating broke into a ragged gallop to retrieve. Jocas, red-faced and sweating, was radiant now. "It was that shift of wind," he said. "Game won't fly upwind under a hawk. What elegance, eh?"

So the day wore on; the quarry was rich and various, and the incidents of the kill quite absorbing. I quite forgot my saddle soreness. The longest and dourest battle Jocas fought was, strangely enough, with one of the slowest birds of all, a marsh heron. One would not have believed that this slow coach of a bird could outwit a trained hunting falcon, but this was very nearly the case. Indeed the heron proved so cunning that it had Jocas swearing with admiration. Though in lateral flight it is slow, the big concave wings give it the power of rising rapidly in the perpendicular, almost in balloon-fashion: meanwhile the falcon has the task of trying to gain sufficient height for her swoop by circling. The old heron used this advantage so skillfully that the battle ranged over several miles. Twice the hunter misjudged its distance, or the heron sidestepped it in the sky: for the falcon, missing it, lost the superiority of altitude and was forced laboriously to circle once again until it could take up the required position. But at last—and both birds were tiring—it found its site and with a swoop "bound to" the heron and both came tumbling out of the sky together with a crash and scream.

The sun was well past meridian when we broke off the sport, all parties converging once more on the hillside where, on the eastern side, there was an old abandoned marble fountain in the denser part of the wood. Here a spring boomed and swished among the rocks and the air was sweet and dense with moisture. Here we lounged and ate the food which had been sent up from the boat in a wicker hamper. The cool shade was luxurious and sleep-inducing—and indeed Jocas had dozed off for a few moments when a messenger rode into the camp from the boat and summoned him back on urgent business to the town. He left at once with a resigned good humor, promising to send the pinnace back to collect us that night. I was left alone with Benedicta. Watching her move among the falconers, smoking a cigarette, I felt the same tightening of the heartstrings as I had when she rode out of the mist toward me. That, and also an awkward sense of premonition: the sense of having embarked upon a course of action which would reward me perhaps by the very damage it might do to my self-reliance, or my self-esteem. Rubbish. And yet at the heart of it all there was a magical content—for there seemed to me to be absolutely no alternative to make me hesitate. Apart from the greed of the eyes and the mind which contemplated her bright abstract beauty there was a kind of inner imperative about the matter—as if this was what I had been foreordained to execute. Yes, I had been born to get myself into this extraordinary, this bewitching mess. So that it was with a complete calm assurance of happiness that I merely nodded and agreed when she said: "I am sending them all down to the boat this evening, but I shall stay here tonight with you. Yes?" The "yes" was quite unnecessarily wistful, and now I repaid the debt of my earlier negligence by taking up the slender fingers and pressing them back to life. So we sat side by side on the grass eating a pomegranate, surrounded by all the bustle of the encampment breaking up. They were to leave us sleeping bags, wine and food; torches, cigarettes, and horses. It took them hours to pack up. We stood side by side in the green evening light to watch the cavalcade straggle down the valley toward the sea. Then, thoughtfully stripping off her clothes, she turned slowly toward the broken marble cistern where the water drummed, she walked into it, seizing the foaming jets with her hands, crying out with joy at its intense cold. So we lay rolled about and were massaged by the icy spring, to climb out cold and panting at last, and lie down as wet as fish in each other's arms. But before making love or attempting any kind of intimacy, lying mesmerized like this, still trembling from the cold water, she uttered a cautionary phrase which to my bemused mind sounded as normal, as natural, as the bustle and boom of the water in the marble dish below us. "Never ask me anything about myself, will you? You must ask Jocas, if you want to know anything. There's a great deal I do not know. I mustn't be frightened, you see."

It seemed to me perfectly logical and I accepted the proposition, sealing the pact there and then with kisses that grew ever more breathless, refining themselves, exploding like oxygen bubbles in the blood. It was like that, the sun shone, the water drummed: everything had become explicit. We sank, deeper than pain, into this profound nescience. And here again (as always when we made physical love) her teeth were drawn back in a kind of agony under her lips, and she said: "O help me, please help me, you must help me." An awkward Galahad was born. I vowed to help her—how I did not know. And mentally I replied—as I have continued to reply ever since— "Of course, my darling, of course: but against what, against whom?" There was never any answer to my question, only the pain swelling up between us; she pressed ever harder upon me as if to blot it out, as if to still the ache of some great bruise. Thus our sensuality was touched by a kind of unconscious cruelty—kisses inflicting pain, I mean, rather than pleasure. It was all very well the "Help me": but afterward she lay like the ghost of *rigor mortis* itself, her lips blue, her heart beating so that she could hardly breathe. But at last her eyes unclouded by the invading terror. Sex cleared the brain, if only for an instant. She ached in my mind like a choice abstraction.

A flock of ignorant chattering birds, perhaps starlings, crossed our middle vision and settled in a cloud in a nearby tree. Benedicta foraged for the little carbine which they had left behind with the horses and began shooting at them. She shot in a brilliant unpremeditated way, like a woman making up her face, and with an unerring exactitude. The birds began to fall on the ground like overripe fruit. She emptied the magazine before throwing the hot gun down on the sleeping bag. How easily she could fill me with disgust. It was beautiful, the polarity. Then she went and lay face down by the spring, almost touching the foaming tumbling cataract with her lips. It seemed to me then, smoking and watching her, that she was something the heart must desire and I grew afraid of the depth of my feelings. I had never before actually feared to be parted from a woman; the novelty was overwhelming. Tomorrow I must leave for Pera, I decided; if only to get away from this suffocating network of ambiguities. After all, with her wealth, etc., etc. I could hardly keep her as a mistress. . . . The ideas rose in clouds like sparrows to a gunshot. But even before they had fallen back into place she was saying:

"I feel this is decisive—that you'll never leave me. I have never felt that before." She always said this: she felt men expected it. All introspection now seemed little more than a fruitless mental debauchery. I closed up my mind and searched ever more frantically for that tame and now touchingly tremulous mouth. We fitted into each other like Japanese razors.

I had collected a couple of huge leeches which had settled on the back of my thigh; by the time I felt the slight discomfort their bites caused, they were already gorged with my blood and fit to burst. Benedicta found a salt cellar in the basket and dosed them until they spewed out the blood they had sucked and fell writhing into the dust. She seemed to like this. I went to wash in the spring. It was her turn now to sit and watch me which she did with a discomforting intentness.

Then she nodded to herself and came to sit beside me to dangle her long legs over the marble parapet. With a long stealthy look about her—as if to make sure that there were no interlopers about in the wood to oversee her—she bent down toward her right foot. I had already noticed that the small toe was bound up with a piece of surgical tape, perhaps to protect a scratch. It was this tape that she now stripped with a small slick gesture, holding out the foot for my inspection. The last toe was double! They were both perfectly formed in their twinship, but joined together. She watched me watching her with her head on one side. "Does it disgust you?" she said. It did, but I said that it did not; I bent to kiss it. Moreover I understood why she kept it bound away, out of sight of the superstitious inhabitants of the place—for it was a clear mark of witchcraft in popular Oriental belief. The vestigial toe, known to the medievals as "the devil's teat." She flexed her feet, stretched, and then wandered away to sit under a tree with an air of morose intentness. "What are you thinking, Benedicta?" Her grave, unwavering abstraction melted; she put a stalk of grass between her teeth and said: "I was wondering what they will think when they know. But what can they do, after all?"

"Who?"

"Julian, Jocas, the firm; when they know what I have decided. About you, I mean."

"Has this anything to do with them?" She looked surprised at the question and turned her head away to frown at the darkening sea line. "Besides," I went on, "just what have you decided?"

But to this her only answer was to beckon me down among the blankets where we lay luxuriously cradled between snore and wake. For much of the night we talked quietly between snatches of sleep. She spoke about a youth spent in Polis—but haphazardly, at a venture. And from these imprecise snatches of dialogue a sort of picture emerged of a childhood full of loneliness like my own, but spent in the sunken gardens of the Seraglio, in the glittering emptiness of the harem with its shallow female sensualities. In the summer heats of the old capital she had learned everything there was to be known

166 ◆ ◆

about the sexual appetites before she reached puberty. Learned and forgotten. Perhaps this was why for her there clung about the act of lovemaking a hollow, disabused quality? I don't know. She behaved as if her feelings, her private mind, were enclosed in the frailest of eggshells easily smashed by an indiscreet question. I asked her, for example, if her father was still alive; the idle question made her stiff with anxiety. She sat upright like a frightened hare and admonished me savagely for breaking the rule she had made. I must ask Jocas, she said. I had quite a task in calming her.

At dawn, or just after, we heard the purring of the ship and saw the long white furrow lengthening toward the harbor. She bound up her toe in haste. It was time to gather up our gear and leave. Benedicta was sunk in deep thought as the horses negotiated the shallow slopes of the hill. At last she said: "When are you going to sign those contracts?" I had completely forgotten their existence, and the question startled me. "I hadn't really decided to in my own mind. Why, do you want me to?" She considered me gravely from under frowning brows. "It is strange that you should doubt us," she said. "But I don't," I protested, "my hesitation hasn't been due to doubts about the validity of the contracts, no. They are overgenerous if it comes to that. No, it was something else. You see, it isn't easy because I am in love with you." She raised her quirt and struck me across the wrist. "Reflect," she said, "reflect."

"I'll see," I said. She looked at me curiously but said no more. The ride back was smooth and uneventful. Jocas was waiting for me with a hospitably decorated table; but Benedicta disappeared, after saying that she would lunch in the harem. I tried to visualize it—a sort of glass and pink satin *bonbonnière* looking out over the calm straits, the light filtered by the intricately carved wooden screens; to this I added some cage birds singing away in melancholy fashion and a few old deaf women, all clad in black, and a few wearing clumsy and ill-chosen frocks from Paris and London. Lots of gold leaf and mirrors. There would be a horn gramophone with a pile of outdated waltzes and other jazz, and bundles of old picture papers. . . . I wondered how near the mark this was. There did not, for example, appear to be a book anywhere. "You are wrong," said Jocas sharply. "She has a very smartly decorated suite of rooms, satin and gold moldings; brilliant chandeliers, and electric pianola, two black cats, and a bookcase full of beautifully bound books by Loti and company."

"Thank you," I said ironically, and he made a mock bow.

"At your service," he said. "We are not all equally gifted, alas. I should have been a fortune-teller in the bazaars I suppose. That's what my brother Chewlian says. I was very backward as a boy; even now, do you know, I read and write with difficulty. I have to pretend that I have mislaid my glasses. It has hampered me very much. It kept me a trader whereas Chewlian is truly a merchant prince. I stayed here, but he went on to brilliant studies. He found a patron; one of the monks who ran the orphanage found him a rich man to stake his education. But I was always ill, always wet my bed until my twentieth year. Had no head and no taste for paper. Only in middle age did I calm down, when Merlin found us."

"But you were orphans?"

"Yes."

"And *brothers*—how would you know?"

"It's only presumption, partly a joke; we shared the same doorstep on the same evening. What more is a brother? I love Chewlian and he loves me."

"I think I shall go back to Pera this evening."

"Yes, why not?" he said equably, pressing my arm. He was a most lovable man. "You will see nothing of Benedicta for at least two days now. She has a treatment. But she will get in touch with you if she wants. I think she has to go back to Zurich this coming week."

I found the idea curiously chilling. "She didn't say anything?" I asked, in spite of myself.

"I am not Benedicta's keeper," he said, frowning in a chewing way.

This line of conversation seemed to come up against a brick wall; I felt that perhaps I had unwittingly offended him and strove to be a trifle more conciliatory as I went on. "Tomorrow I'll have a last session with Vibart and decide about the contracts. I will certainly sign for the little ear device—which I call a 'dolly.' About the more general terms of association I'll have to see."

"I know the cause of your hesitation," he said, and burst suddenly into a peal of clear laughter. "It is perfectly justified. Once when I mentioned something I saw from your expression that you were surprised: because it meant that someone had been through the papers you had left behind in Athens. The new device for electric Braille remember?"

He was dead right. I looked at his jutting nose and laughing eyes. "You thought it was us, didn't you? Well, it wasn't. It was Graphos, one of his hirelings who went through your stuff; what they expected to find I don't know. But they photographed everything—all the parts in shorthand and the mathematical materials. Now, when I asked Graphos for details about you after this first idea came along, he was able to supply quite a number of them—things you are working on. I saw at once that we needed you as much as you need us. We can shorten your labors by years if we give you the right equipment, by years. How, for example, can you work on the firefly and the glowworm without a chemist, indeed a big laboratory to help? We have such a place—Lunn Pharmaceuticals belongs to us. Do you see?"

"The firefly produces light without heat," I had written once, unwisely. "Note. If we could find just *how* chemically we would be on to a new light source perhaps." But of course he was right, one could hardly conduct this kind of experiment from Number Seven. Jocas was watching me intently, still smiling. He said, "The trembler fuse, the iodine and sodium bath experiment—how will you ever do it?" All of a sudden the lust for this vocation—of tampering with the universe and trying to short-circuit its behavior—grew up in me and seized me by the throat. I drank my wine off at a thrust and sat bemused, staring through him. O God! There was also the danger that they might sow these idle speculations broadcast behind my back, that other talents with bigger means might scoop me. I was ashamed of the idea, but there it was! Pure science! Where does the animal come in? "Also a passage where you ask why bats can navigate in the dark and not blind men in the light, eh?"

"Hush," I said, "I'm thinking." I was, I was furiously thinking of Benedicta, sitting here trapped between conflicting hesitations.

Jocas said softly: "I do not see that the matter of Benedicta alters anything." He was doing his mental lip-reading act again. Here he was wrong; she hung above all these abstractions and ambiguities, like a wraith, an *ignis fatuus*. That long cobra face seemed to symbolize everything that this vast organization of talents stood for. I was looking fame and fortune in the eyes, and the eyes were adding the promise of love to these other riches. "Yes," I said at last, surprised to find how very hoarse my voice sounded. "Yes, I am a fool. I *must* sign on."

In retrospect this epoch, these scenes, astonished me very much when I recalled them; I mean after everything went to wrack, the period of illnesses and confusion, the period of intemperate recriminations, quarrels, fugues. Once, when she was hovering on the outside edges of logic, I even heard her say: "I only really loved you when I thought you were determined to be free from the firm. It seemed to promise me my own freedom. But afterward I saw that you were just like everyone else." Then in my fury I shouted back: "But you made me sign on, Benedicta. It was you who insisted, remember?" She nodded her furious head and answered: "Yes. I had to. But you could have stuck to your guns and that would have altered everything. For us both."

"Then why, knowing this, did you insist on having the child? There was no need, was there?"

"There were several reasons. Partly because Julian said so, Nash said so, it was a question of cure as well. Then also the question of succession, inheritance. Then me. All those miscarriages were a challenge I had to face. Above all I wanted a Merlin of my own, of my very own." She paused and gazed about her as if to identify a small sound, audible only to her inner ear. "You see," she added tonelessly, "hardly anyone saw my father in the flesh—though everyone saw Julian at some time or another. Then the firm—O Felix, Benedicta is only a woman, she has always tried to be just." Nearly sobbing.

"You talk about yourself as if you were a *product*."

"I am. I am." That was the *tu quoque*!

Then later when I was speaking to her about love she could say with burning indignation: "But love is a reality not a recipe." As if in offering her mine under any other guise I had tricked her. Woman!

But all this lay far in the future on that day when Jocas walked down to the landing stage beside me with his choppy deliberate tread. "You will go back to Athens and wait," he said and his tone was one of delighted relief. He embraced me warmly and added, "Benedicta will come to you very soon. You may find her the key to everything. Sacrapant will deal with all the contractual details. I myself am going to the islands for a week. Felix!"

"Yes, Jocas?"

"You are going to be very happy."

But I felt bemused still and shaken by my own decision. Sacrapant gazed at me with lachrymose tenderness; it seemed that he too knew, without being told, that I had agreed to sign, but tact held him silent. We roared away across the opalescent water toward the dim horizon where the city lay half asleep, embedded in time as in a quagmire—the Orient Venice snoring its life away.

Vibart was at his habitual desk, only today he was blowing an egg to add to his collection. He had pierced the blue crown with a needle and was blowing with soft absorption into the tiny hole; from the opposite hole the yolk was being gradually expelled to fall with a plop into his wastepaper basket. "There," he said with relief, placing the tiny object in a velvet hollow among others like it. He closed the casket reverently and joined his fingers together as he gazed at me. The contracts lay on the corner of the desk among his papers. Without saying anything I picked up the pen from its slab of marble and signed in all the required places. "Well," he said in great good humor, "I should bloody well think so. Fame and fortune, my boy, and all for the price of a signature. The luck some people have." I sat, staring into the middle distance, still confused and somehow fearfully sad. Somehow he must have felt it (he was a discerning young man under his flippant exterior), for his tone changed to one of quickening sympathy; the drink he poured out with which to celebrate the event was a stiff one, and I needed it, or felt I did. Though why?

I seemed to hear the voice of Sacrapant saying: "The firm is wonderful, Mr. Charlock, sir. When I could not find anyone for my wife's womb the firm found me someone."

The telephone rang squeakily. "It's for you," said Vibart. I recognized the voice of Jocas, distant and crackly. "Felix, I forgot. I have a message for you to give your friend Koepgen in Athens. He is your friend, isn't he?"

"Yes. I didn't know you knew him."

"I don't personally. But when you see him will you tell him that we have located the ikon he has been hunting for?"

"The ikon?"

"Yes. We know the monastery now."

"I'll make a note of it."

"Thank you very much, Felix."

I drew a deep breath and said: "Jocas, I have just signed the articles of association."

"I knew it," he said. "I felt it. I was sure."

Vibart sat sipping his drink and staring at me. "I think," he said, "you need cheering up. I shall invite you to dine with me and hear all the details of my literary career. It's really moving forward. And by the way, I have found a good *French* tavern. You know the French will eat anything and everything? If the sky rained corpses' legs they would become cannibals without a second thought. Moreover it would be doubly enjoyable because it was all free. Will you?"

"Very well. But I must first take these down to the firm and draw some money."

This I duly did, walking through the crowded and insanitary streets among the snarling bands of dogs. Mr. Sacrapant was waiting for me: but oh, he looked so grave and tender, like an undertaker's mute on his best behavior. He took the documents and cashed me a voucher for what seemed to me an immense sum of money which I stuffed into my slender wallet with cold fingers.

"You'll be going back to Athens I have no doubt," he said. "I shall treasure the memory of our association, Mr. Charlock."

"Thank you. In a day or two I expect." The truth of the matter was that I was reluctant to leave the city before I had seen Benedicta once more—and yet, there seemed to be no chance of that. Should I perhaps send her a message? Perhaps the mere information that I was still in Polis might . . . "I think I shall be here another full week if you should need me," I told him. "At the Pera as usual."

Malignant tumor of a passive love! All of a sudden the gloomy steamy city seemed peopled with ghosts. I was still dumb from the astonishment of finding myself freed at a stroke from all the smaller preoccupations that beset ordinary men—financial dependence, occupation, etc. It was puzzling too because anyone in my place would have felt exultant, buoyant. I felt absolutely nothing. I took a cab back to the detestable hotel, confirmed my reservation, and ordered lunch in the garden. There were no familiar faces there, much to my regret. I would be grateful for Vibart's company while I was waiting. Waiting! But suppose Benedicta did not come? There was Zurich of course.

At dusk Vibart called for me and together we wandered through the city toward his newly discovered eating house. His wife would join us there later. As usual he was preoccupied with the building of this imaginary career upon which he was too hesitant to embark; the self-rebukes multiplied in all directions. He had decided to reverse the usual order of things and start by writing his own reviews. "Why not the obits?" I suggested. "They are always the warmest reviews. The one consolation about death is that everyone will be forced to be nice to you behind your back."

"I never thought of that," said Vibart settling his napkin round his neck with the air of a man putting on a cummerbund. "And I think it's too late. My novel *The Asparagus Tree* comes out this week. ('A novel of surpassing tameness.') The press will be very mixed. I console myself by saying that the jealousy of opinionated dunces is the finest of literary compliments. I have arranged a good sales picture however. What do you think of thirty thousand in the first week? On a sliding scale that should be a clear thousand, no?"

"Too good by half," said his wife with the resignation of one who has been forced to live with an obsession. She was a handsome brunette with shy green eyes. Her name was Pia.

The food was excellent. "I should give it up," I said, "and go for criticism. Grudge yourself off in the weeklies. Loll your way to fame. Tell yourself that you are not really a bad man, just unprincipled."

"Can I," said Vibart in envious tones, "tell my wife about your terrific coup—the new job?"

"Of course." He did so at once and at some length. She watched me curiously, surprised by my lack of animation. I suppose I looked guilty. I tried to explain. "You see, Vibart, in a sort of way I am in the same boat as you. I didn't want to be just an artificer, I wanted to go for abstractions: use the calculus as a springboard. Like you, I have not got the talent. I shall be forced to confine myself to tinkering with nuts and bolts instead of dealing with poetic abstractions, new universes. And I did *so* want to be the age's little Copernicus. Hence the apathy you criticize. I am the wrong kind of scientist. I shall have to be content to try and do something about the faulty five senses in this smaller way."

He reeled off, in quotation: " 'An eagle for sight, a hart for hearing, a spider for touch, an ape for taste, and a dog for smell."

"I would have liked to achieve in my line whatever would correspond to a work of art—which my friend Koepgen has defined as an act of disciplined insubordination. But if one isn't up to it?" My God, we were getting drunk.

"Oh dear," said his wife, "here I am surrounded by failures." But she was grateful for this self-identification with her husband's private myth.

Vibart was put into a very good humor now, and decided that all further self-recrimination should cease until he had reached the coffee. The food, he said, was too good to poison, and besides the only metaphysical problem for the gourmet was: is there a life beyond the gravy?

A freak thunderstorm had sprung up and rain was needling the tragic arcades; we sat long over our brandies, waiting for it to stop, and once more the consuming restlessness beset me. My wristwatch purred on in tireless itching iteration and I found myself wondering about Benedicta and the new equivocal pattern of relationships which she alone could disentangle and sort out. Time is the only thing that doesn't wear out. "I think I shall probably leave for Athens tomorrow," I said, since Vibart was planning a picnic for the weekend and I had suddenly tired of him. The rain was thinning off now, and a fresh wind was flapping at the awnings of the cafés. By luck we found a cab to take us back to Pera, where I dropped off at my hotel. Here all my doubts were resolved, for on the mantelpiece of my room I found a single joss stick burning in a vase and a visiting card of Jocas' with a few words written on it in that curiously shapeless and hesitant hand which I was to come to know so well—Benedicta's. She was coming to visit me on the morrow at noon. All at once—like the wind dispersing storm cloud at a single puff—I felt the whole weight of my preoccupations lift and disperse. I fell asleep almost at once, but it was to dream elaborate and intricate dreams, worthy of Vibart, about the long lifelines of the firm which channeled all the riches of the Orient into the huge granaries over which Jocas presided—furs and skins and poppy, caviar and salt and wax, amber, precious stones, porcelain and glass: dreams of such fervent inaccuracy that even while I dreamed them I was forced to correct the picture, to bring it up to date with less romantic commodities like pitprops from Slovenia, oil and wheat from Russia, bauxite and tin and coal. And somewhere in the middle of this meretricious romancing I saw the pale face of Benedicta staring down at me as if from a lofty window: and I woke with a start with a question on my lips, namely, "You must be sure that her riches play no part in any decision you make." But riches cannot be sidestepped; they mark one like a harelip. I studied her handwriting with misgiving. A graphologist would have hinted at glandular imbalances. But I loved her, I loved her, I loved her.

Then in the morning, following out in some obscure fashion the train of thought which had dribbled through my sleep, I went out to the fashionable Pera shopping area with the scientific intention of spending a very large sum of money: in order to see exactly how it felt. I thought I might buy a sporting gun or a wristwatch or a fountain pen of abhorrent splendor. Accustomed to live meagerly if decently, to find myself frequently short, not of necessities, but of luxuries, I wanted to taste the sensation of pouring out some of my own fairly earned gold over some merchant's counter. But my desire for these unnecessary objects ebbed away as soon as I sighted them. What the devil would I do with a gun? Hippolyta would always lend me one. A wristwatch? I should forget to take it off when I swam. A pen? No sooner bought than lost. In desultory fashion I mooned about the souk, allowing myself to be plucked and cajoled and lectured by the swarthies. I did not know enough then about precious stones. (Now of course my artificial diamonds flourish all over the globe.) Nor perfumes. But finally, with Benedicta in mind, I allowed myself to be tempted by a small and lovely carpet—an authentic Shiraz according to the label. With this

rolled up under my arm I walked back to the hotel in time to
see a flock of *hamalis*—the grotesque cowlike public porters of
the capital—carrying a string of black suitcases and hatboxes
all marked with the gold monogram I was to come to know so
well. But she was already there, dressed like a fashion plate,
sitting upon the terrace with her gloved hands in her lap.
Gloves! Her large fine straw hat cast dancing freckles of
amber light over her features.

She was staring at her gloves and her lips were moving as if
in prayer or in a secret conversation with her own mind.
Everything seemed to warn me, but I walked up to take her
hands—remove them from her field of vision, claim them and
with them her attention. She responded, when I uttered her
name, with a glance full of abstraction—as if she were seeing
me for the first time. "Everyone is agreed," she said softly—
the most desolating words that a man in love can hear. "But
everyone, without exception, even Julian. They are all on
our side." She trembled a little when we embraced; slender
and pliant, and fragrant with a scent I could not identify. "I
want you to say my name; to hear how it sounds: I haven't
paid attention before." I repeated her name twice. She sighed
and said, "Yes, it is just as I thought." It was as if something
had been put to the proof. I sat beside her and unrolled my
gift. "I brought you a small Shiraz," I said, proud of my
acquisition, only to be dashed by her smile as she said: "It's
Afghan. You've been cheated." She laughed and clapped her
hands as if at an excellent jest.

All my gear had been moved from my room into a very
large suite on the second floor; it mingled oddly with her
collection of shining suitcases. A Turkish maid was busy
hanging up her dresses. A lunch table had been laid upon the
balcony. She stood with her probationary eyes narrowed
critically as she surveyed the room with its huge fourposter
and velvet baldachin. Then she turned suddenly to me and
said: "I can only stay three days this time. Then I must go
north. But I will come to you in Athens or in London later.
Yes?"

"Very well."

Three nights, three days of calendar time; to the bemused (and it *was* reciprocal) it could have been three centuries, so marvelously did the spilled seconds transform my view both of her and her melancholy city of historic afterthoughts: it had become a sort of extension of her childhood and its memories, a coherent demesne. All the stagnant beauties, its repellent corners of dirt and disease, the marsh gas thrown off by the rotting corpse of Byzantium—they all coalesced into a significant shape. She walked about it with the unconscious assurance of long familiarity. It was a wicked place to fall in love with a woman, an unmanning place: or was this simply Benedicta, and the obstinate alarm bell sounding in the back of my mind, muffled by the sweet minaret calls, the sage boom of sirens from the Horn? Let us say that I saw her reflections in it—imprint of the imago which underlay the kisses which were not blithe and free, as they should have been, but concentrated, perverse, bewitching. The central enigma hasn't changed from that day to this; I could have seen her even then, if I had tried, as someone born to be loved yet doomed to die, in solitude like a masterless animal. Yet how lucky I was myself—for I was able to surrender—and this gave me the illusion that I could however briefly cross the distance that she put between us. The victories of applied science! I gave her everything that I had learned from Iolanthe! For one moment had the conviction that I had stopped the great moving staircase of the heart! I stubbornly averted my face from the notion that in all this first encounter what I really saw was the first sketch, so to speak, of a more massive alienation. Did I? I don't know. Anyway, making love with a sort of breathless resignation—or else desperately, like someone trying to pull an arrow from the flesh before the poison has time to spread. And she knew ways to excite, the praying mantis, like "tie up my wrists," or less judiciously, "O it is too big, I shall split." Incitements to the furies let loose in men when they love an aggressive woman. To couple so perfectly and yet be denied any sort of initiation! Kisses were warnings I did not recognize; but the feeling of finality was delicious, vertiginous—things could not have fallen out otherwise, could they? Gentlemen of the jury, we should tackle reality in a slightly joky way, otherwise we miss its point. It isn't solemn at all, it's *playing!* It's all very well telling poor Felix that now; he too is wise after the event. Suppose we could make the electric chair into a romantic symbol? If you section the olfactory gland of the rabbit you condemn it to impotence; snick off the salamander's head while it is coupling, and it feels nothing; caught in the divine rhythm it continues as if nothing had happened. Perhaps nothing has? Benedicta! Rapidly cooling worlds, we lie asleep in each other's arms. The mysteries do not matter. I come upon her sitting on the balcony in flood of tears. "Why, Benedicta?" She doesn't know, staring up at me with tear-laden lashes, tears running down her long subtle nose. "I don't know." Yet ten minutes later laughing heartily at the antics of a monkey on a barrel organ.

Well then, as I say, her city began to borrow some of her colors; our excursions and promenades became the unfamiliar delight, and she knew corners and nooks which escaped the industry or perhaps taste of other guides like Sacrapant or Vibart. It is not possible for me now to think of Polis again without seeing Benedicta's face superposed upon whatever it is—mosque, graveyard, tilting forest of shipping in the Golden Horn. She owns it as Io owns Athens. There were puzzles, of course, and singularities: I remember that wherever we went we found someone to receive us—someone waiting outside a mosque with the keys for example. The difficulty of gaining entry to the smaller mosques, the difficulty of tracing the guardian with the keys, is too famous an aspect of Polis to need elaboration; every visitor has complained of it. Yet wherever this fateful couple went—and so often on foot—the guardian was there waiting. Had she warned him, or caused him to be warned? I asked. "No, it is just that we are lucky, simply that."

Then again, with the same equivocal air—an expression of

pride and sorrow almost—she led me through the beautiful cemetery at Eyub, among the marble incantations with their telltale turbans and flower knots. We came to one grave set in a small grilled enclosure of its own. I could not read the flowing Arabic inscription, of course; but below it, in small Roman letters, I saw the name Benedicta Merlin. There was no date. "Who is it—your mother?" I asked; but she only turned away abruptly, picking a stalk of green with which to tease her lips as she walked down the hill. "Benedicta, please tell me." She stared at me intently, and then once more turned away and resumed her slow progress among the graves. It was useless to press her. At the edge of the cemetery she turned and embraced me, pressing me to her with a strange sort of fury, as if to extirpate some unhallowed memory of the past. But no words, do you see? And then with a soft kind intensity she took out her handkerchief to rub the lipstick marks from my mouth. Never, it seemed, had anyone looked at me with so much overflowing love, vulnerable tenderness; what did it matter that she should have her secrets? The stern mask of the priestess had slipped. Briefly I saw a woman.

So the time passed, dense with the special fulfillments of physical possession; I averted my mind from the prospect of her vanishing back into Europe—dragged by the slow Orient Express through the great walls of the city toward Zurich. Then in the middle of everything—or rather at the end, for it was the last evening—came the most singular event of all: the death of Sacrapant. It was so sudden and so unexpected that it deafened the mind—though afterward of course it was explained saitsfactorily. Events of this kind are always clothed in a factitious causality when we see them in retrospect. Was it, though?

Sunset is the finest hour; with the city nimbling softly away toward darkness while the sun fights its lion battle against the skyline driving the dense mists higher and higher into brief priceless colors and shapes. To sit in the darkening garden of the hotel quietly drinking an aperitif and waiting for the blind muezzin to climb into his perch among the buildings and send out his owl cry to the faithful—this was the best way to spend this hour, watching the lights beginning to twinkle over by Taxim, and the shipping rustle and moo on the darkening water.

This particular eloquent evening we were very silent; the express left just before midnight, her packing was done. We sat there between two worlds, neither cast down nor elated: existing in a curious abstraction of certainty about the future. One side of the mind turned toward that quiet call which must soon come from the mosque—the old blind face of a bird uttering the quiet nasal cawing of the Ebed. And I saw in the gathering dusk a slim figure in white limping among the distant trees; it walked with just a trace of unsteadiness but with resolution as if toward a predetermined destination. I recognized my friend, though I did not comment on the fact; so, I think, did she, following the direction of my gaze. There would have been nothing unusual about that; but then to my surprise I saw him pause, squint upward into the sky, and enter the circular staircase of the mosque. But now his pace had changed; he walked slowly, wearily, as if bowed under a great weight. I saw him appear at the little window slit halfway up and could not resist a puzzled gasp: "What the devil, it's old Sacrapant. . . ." She looked at her watch and at the sky.

It was still early for the muezzin. The frail figure appeared at last at the balustrade, raising small fernlike hands as in an invocation to darkening world about the tower. It was indeed an invocation, but a frail and incoherent one; the sense of the words hardly penetrated the heavy layers of the damp night air. I thought I heard something like "will find fulfillment in the firm. Give it your best and it will be returned an hundredfold." One could not be absolutely sure, of course, but among the wavering incantations I thought I heard so much. Then I jumped to my feet, for the frail figure had started to lean forward and topple. Mr. Sacrapant started to fall out of the night sky in a slow swoop toward the dark

◆ ◆ 181

ground. A crash of a palm tree, and then a thud of unmistakable finality, followed by the splintering jingle of
broken glass and small change. I was transfixed by the suddenness of it all. I stood there speechless. But already there
were running feet everywhere and voices: a crowd gathered
in no time, as flies will do about an open artery. "My God," I
said. Benedicta sat quite still with bowed head. I turned to
her and whispered her name; but she did not move.

I shook her gently by the shoulders as one might shake a
clock that had stopped and she looked up at me with an
intense unwavering sadness. "Come away quick," she said,
and grabbed my hand. Away among the trees the sounds had
become more purposeful—they were gathering up the loaves
and fishes. Blood on marble. I shuddered. Crossing the dark
garden hand in hand we moved toward the lighted terraces
and public rooms of the hotel. Benedicta said: "Jocas must
have given him the sack. O why must people go to extremes?"
Why, indeed! I thought of the pale humble face of Sacrapant
shining up there in the evening sky. Of course such an
explanation would meet the case, yet . . . The evening lay
in ruins about us. The silent dinner, the packing away of the
luggage into the office car which had appeared—these operations we performed automatically, numbed by the sadness of
this sudden death. My mind reverted continually to the
memory of that pale face leaning down from the tower;
Sacrapant had looked like someone who had been carefully
deprived of an individual psychology by some experiment
with knife or drug. For one brief moment his coattails had
flattened out with the wind of his fall giving him the shape of
a dart—like a falling mallard. But he had fallen, so to speak,
slap into the middle of our emotions; the widening rings of
his death spread through our minds now, alienating us from
each other.

We embraced, we parted, almost with disgust. The hideous
station with its milling tortoise-faced mob of Turks merci-
fully precluded speeches of farewell. I stood holding her
hands while the carriage was found and the luggage stored in
it by the chauffeur. "Or else," she said gravely, in the tones of

one continuing an inner monologue, "he suddenly learned that he had cancer, or that his wife had a lover, or that his favorite child . . ." I realized that any explanation would do, and that all would forever remain merely provisional. Was this perhaps true for all of us, for all our actions? Yes, yes. I studied her face again with care, with an almost panic-stricken intentness, realizing at last how useless it was to be loving her; she had climbed into the carriage and stood looking down at me from the open window with a hesitant sorrowfulness. We could not have been further apart at this instant; a cloud of anxiety had overshadowed all emotion. I felt my heavy despairs dragging at their moorings. Tomorrow I should return to Athens—I should be free from everyone, free even from Benedicta. My God, the only four letter word that matters! The train had begun to move. I walked beside it for a few paces. She too was looking almost relieved, elated. Or so it seemed to me. Perhaps because she felt sure of me—of her hold over me? She wound up the glass window and then, with a sudden impulse, breathed upon it in order to write the word "Soon" on the little patch of condensation. At once the pain of separation came back.

I turned away to let my thoughts disperse among those sullen crowds of featureless faces. The car waited to take me back to the hotel. That night I slept alone and for the first time experienced the suffocating sense of loneliness which came over me with the conviction that I should never see Benedicta again. This whole episode would remain in my memory, carefully framed and hung, quite self-subsisting: and quite without relevance or continuity to anything else I had ever done or experienced. An anecdote of Istanbul!

Nor did this feeling completely leave me even when, from the windy deckhead, I saw the white spars of Sunion come up over the waters. The season had turned, autumn was here, the marbles looked blue with cold: and I had turned a corner in my supposed life. It was baffling, the sense of indecision which beset me; I supposed that the novelty of this new life was what had numbed me—simply that. Simply that.

Hippolyta met me at the dock with her car, bursting with

excitement and jubilation. "We're saved!" she cried as I clambered down the gangway with my suitcase. "O come along do, Charlock; we must celebrate, and it's all due to you. Graphos! He has swept all the provinces. My darling, he's changed completely. He is certain to get back into power." Apparently something had been averted by the resuscitation of the great man's party and its electoral successes. Well, I sat by her side, letting her babble on to her heart's content. We headed for the country directly because they were all "waiting to congratulate" me. I was returning like a conquering hero to the hospitable country house. "Moreover," she said, taking my hand and pressing it to her cheek, "you have joined the firm. You are one of us now." In the back of my mind I had a sudden snapshot of Benedicta walking alone in some remote corner of an untended garden, among rare shrubs and flowers which discharged their pollen on her clothes at every step, like silent pistol shots. In the house great fires blazed and champagne glasses winked. Caradoc was there and Pulley; and the immaculate spatted form of Banubula. Everyone burst into a torrent of congratulatory rhetoric. I drank away the feelings of the past weeks, lapped around by all this human glow. It was only when, as an afterthought, I said: "By the way, I am going to marry Benedicta Merlin," that the great silence fell. It was the half second of silence at the end of some marvelously executed symphony, the mesmerized rapture which precedes the thunder of applause. Yes. That sort of silence, and lasting only half a second; then the applause, or rather the storm of congratulation in which, to my surprise, I strove suspiciously to detect a false note. But no. It rang out in the most genuine manner; Caradoc indeed seemed rather moved by the news, his bear hugs hurt. I surrendered myself to my self-congratulation invaded by a new sense of confidence. It was late when at last I gathered my kit and borrowed the car to return to Athens; I was curious to see Number Seven again, to riffle my notebooks. Yet I noted with some curiosity that all of a sudden the absence, not of Benedicta but of Iolanthe, weighed. Some obscure law of association must be at work; I had not given her a thought in Istanbul, she was not appropriate to the place. Nor would Benedicta ever be to Athens. I looked up from under the shaded light and imagined her entering the room as she always did, punctual as a heartbeat. These sentimental polarities of feeling were new to me; I disapproved of them thoroughly. Frowning I returned to my scribbles. I roughed out a schema as a basis for my work for the firm when at last I should be summoned. Then I noticed a letter on the mantelpiece, a letter addressed to me. It was from Julian, written in an exquisite italic hand; it congratulated me most gracefully on the excellent news and told me that I need not move from Athens for the time being; but I should map out a work scheme and submit it. Did I wish to start with the mechanical end of my research? A limited company called Merlin Devices would be set up as part of a light-engineering subsidiary of the firm. I would find the technicians and the tools ready to hand for whatever I dreamed up. It was a marvelous prospect, and I fell asleep happily that night in the stuffy little room, with my counterpane littered with notes and formulae and diagrams.

At seven, when the porter brought me my coffee, I found that dapper Koepgen had followed hard on his heels and had taken up his usual watchful position in the armchair. Koepgen of the elf lock and the lustrous eye. For the time of day he looked unnaturally spruce and self-possessed. "Go on," he said with ill-concealed excitement. "Tell me what it is." For a moment I had forgotten. "Jocas cabled me that he would give you a message for me." Then I remembered. Sleepily I repeated the message to him. He drew a long hissing breath, his face at once rueful and amused. "What a cunning old dog, what a swine," he said admiringly, and struck his knee. "I only worked a few weeks for them but it was enough for the firm to find my weak point. They are incredible." He chirped his loudest laugh.

"What's it all about?" I asked; there was a small bottle of ouzo on the mantelpiece; Koepgen made a by-your-leave, drew the cork and tilted a dose into a tooth mug. He drank it off quite slim and said: "He holding me to ransom, the old devil. He wants me to go back to Moscow and deal with some contracts for the firm; I refused, it doesn't interest me. Now I see I will have to go if I'm ever to get my hands on the bloody thing."

"What bloody thing?"

"The ikon."

"What next?" It sounded to me as if the firm were busy doing some elaborate trade in antiques; but no, said Koepgen, no such thing. What they were after were some contracts from the Communist Government for wheat and oil in exchange for machinery. Nothing could be more prosaic. And the ikon—where did that come in? Ah. He burst out laughing again and said with exasperation, "My dear Charlock, that is a piece of Russian folklore which will sound to you quite silly; but nevertheless it has cost me several years and hundreds of miles on foot." He sat down suddenly with a bump in the chair.

"But wouldn't it be dangerous, I mean Communists and all that?"

"No. One of my uncles is minister of trade. No, it isn't that. I just didn't want to work for the firm; but I made the mistake of telling them my fairy tale, and of course this is the result. You see, when I started this theological jag I chose one of the great mystics, a big bonze of Russia as a guide. As you know, absolute obedience is required, even if one is set a task that seems an idiocy. I was set a task which turned unwittingly into a pilgrimage on my poor flat feet. There was an ikon once in the private chapel of my mother; when the estate was confiscated it had vanished. I was to find it or else."

"Or else what?"

Koepgen grinned. "Or else no progress, see? I should be stuck in the lower ranks. Never get my stripes. Don't laugh."

"What fantasy."

"Of course you'd think that; but there is more than one kind of truth, Charlock."

186 ◆ ◆

"O crikey," I said, "don't do the theological on me."

"Well, anyway, hence this bloody long walk across Russia into Athos. I traced it there. After that I drew a blank for a while. It was a Saint Catherine of a rather special kind. And of course the woods are full of them—Saint Catherines. It might be somewhere in a wayside shrine on Olympus or stuck in some great monastery in Meteora. In spite of all the help I got I drew blank after blank. The Orthodox Church is an odd organization or perhaps I should say disorganization; what is the good for example of an encyclical when half the minor clergy are illiterates?"

"Offer a reward."

"We did all that. I sorted through hundreds of them big and small; but I couldn't get the one belonging to my mother. You see? Now the firm has stepped in found it and will tell me where it is on condition . . ."

"I have never heard such rubbish in my life," I said. Koepgen nearly burst into tears. "Nor have I," he said, "nor have I."

"I should damn well refuse to go."

"Perhaps I shall. I must see. On the other hand I suppose it isn't such an arduous undertaking; it might cost me a month or two in Moscow, and then at least I would have found it and satisfied my *staretz* old Demetrius. O dear." He took another swig from the bottle and fell into a heavy melancholy silence, turning over these weird contingencies in his mind. I drew a bath and lay in it awhile, leaving him to brood in the armchair. I had decided, on the strength of my newfound fortune, to move all my belongings today to the best hotel in the town—to take a comfortable suite. I did not need more space but I was most anxious to experiment with the notion of spending a lot of money. Yes, of course the grub would be much better. I was drying myself slowly when Koepgen appeared in the doorway. He was still sunk in a kind of abstraction, and gazed at me with unfocused eye. "You know," he said slowly at last, "I have a feeling that I shall have to obey Julian. After all sacrifices have to be made if one's going to get anywhere in life, eh?"

"Hum," I said, feeling very sage and judicial, yet indifferent.

"You will see," he said, "you will see, my boy. Your turn will come. Have you ever met Julian?"

"No." I dressed slowly; it was a lovely sunny day, and we walked across Athens on foot, stopping here and there in the shadow of a vine arbor to have a drink and a mézé. Koepgen made no further reference to his ikon and I was glad; the whole thing seemed to me to be a burdensome fairy tale. After all if a man of such sharp intelligence in his forties allowed the firm to play upon these infantile superstitions, well good luck to it. But such reflections filled me with shame when I glanced at his sorrowful and now rather haggard features. I had come to like him very much. As we parted, I to reserve my new quarters and organize the move, he to return to his seminary, he said under his breath: "I fear there is no help for it. I shall have to go. I'll cable Jocas today."

He started to walk down the winding street and then, on a sudden impulse, ran after me and caught my sleeve. He said in a humble, beseeching tone, "Charlock, can I leave my notebooks with you if I decide to go?" His manner touched me. "Of course." And that evening when I got back to my new hotel, rather aware that my shabby wardrobe would have to be replaced if I were ever to match the splendor of such surroundings, I saw the familiar pile of school exercise books on the mantelpiece. A rubber band held them together. But there was no word with them; I must presume that Koepgen had fallen in with the wishes of the firm; perhaps he was already on his way north. I rather envied him the journey in a queer sort of way. My dinner had been left in the alcove to await me. I could not help touching the smooth expensive napery which enveloped it. In Athens such costly and beautiful ironed covers and napkins were quite a rarity. I had decided to work that evening on my crystals, and had set out my white china trays in the bathroom. But the telephone rang and when I picked it up Benedicta stood before me, so to speak; her voice was so clear that I thought she must be calling me from the floor below. But no, she was in Switzerland. "Darling," the endearment made my heart suddenly turn over in its grave. Every doubt, every hesitation, was puffed away on the instant and I realized with a reviving pang how much I wanted her here, right here. The enormous inadequacy of words belabored me. "Never have I missed anyone so much. It confirms everything." So it seemed to me also as I sat, gripping the black telephone, grimacing into it. "We will be married in April. Julian has arranged everything. In London. Do you agree?"

"Why wait so long, Benedicta?"

"I have to. I am under orders. I won't be free to move until then. O how much I miss you, miss you." The clear magnetic voice took on a note of familiar despair. "Julian is arranging the terms of the settlement, the marriage contract."

"What settlement?" I said in perplexity.

"Well, about my share in the firm. We must have perfect equality in love, my darling." All of a sudden the line went dead and a thousand other voices came up, trying to restore the broken communication. "Benedicta," I cried, and I could still hear her voice, though what she was saying was indistinct. An operator squashed her out and promised to call me back. I went and lay on my bed in a confused frame of mind—a mixture of rage and euphoria.

Gentlemen of the jury, now I can tell you that I have loved a woman who sat on numberless committees for the emancipation of other women, never speaking, and with the bitten nails of her left hand sheathed in a glove. Actually what women need is to be beaten almost to death, enslaved, raped and forced to cook meals when they are heavy with child. Bite through the nape of the neck, Wilkinson, stick her with a bayonet, and she's yours forever. A bottomless masochism is all they seek to indulge; the penis is too kind a weapon by far. No, the emancipation of this creature is a joke. (Benedicta, look into my eyes.) They are waveborn, slaveborn; and yet somewhere among them may be one, just *one*, who is different, who fills the bill. But what bill, Felix Love! We never had before nor never since, seen it, I mean. Burp! Pardon my parahelion.

Perfect equality in love, I thought. God! Tomorrow I would go out and buy the most expensive microscope in the world and a Stradivarius and some strawberries and a car. . . . But in love there is never enough equality to go round. We will have to settle for equity among men and women—a humbler target. Benedicta ached on. After half an hour of futile suspense I tried to restore the broken communication from my own end, but this proved impossible. They could not trace the number from which she had called me. The hall porter brought me a bottle of whiskey and a siphon. I tried to resume the precious train of thought about crystals —the fragile line of reasoning which, after so many years, has given Merlin's a near monopoly in the field of lasers. Benedicta kept intruding among my scribbles. ("The ordering of their atoms is never quite perfect or they would not be able to form, to grow.")

Then the phone did ring again and I leaped at it. But it was only Caradoc, rather drunk and indistinct, calling me from the Nube, his gruff voice framed in a background of mandolin music. "Charlock," he said in his usual growling vein, "we are waiting for you down here. Why don't you come?" But Benedicta had covered me in a sheath, a caul of discontent. I could not think of the sweaty Nube, the dust-filled curtains, without distaste. "I am waiting for a phone call, and doing some work," I said, fearful lest our own conversation might be holding up a long-distance contact. Caradoc growled on reproachfully. "Ah you scientists in love! Soon you will be accusing nature of a moral order. Push!"

"Push to you," I said. "Now for Godsake hang up and leave me alone, will you?"

He did so, but with evident reluctance. "Well, hard cheese," he said as a parting shot, and I had the sudden vivid image of Mr. Sacrapant leaning over a desk looking gravely at me and saying, "You are right to be precautionate, Mr.

Charlock." And what was the other expression? Yes, "I have inaccurized the document, sir." Presumably he meant that he had been through it for inaccuracies. Ah, pale Sacrapant, falling out of the air like these autumn leaves tumbling into the parks. Again the phone rang and this time Hippolyta's clear youthful voice sprang from the mouthpiece as if from the ear of a goddess. "Charlock, I heard you'd moved. How does it feel to be really loved?"

"O leave me alone!" I cried in anguish, much to her surprise. "Hang up. I'm waiting for a call."

But Benedicta did not ring again.

Indeed I had no word from her throughout the months which lay ahead. However, filled with the *gai savoir* I buckled down to my plans for the little Merlin subsidiary which I should virtually run single-handed from London. Or so I thought. Two members of its hypothetical board flew out to meet me, Denison and Broad, and I was glad to find them both accomplished and experienced men. Needless to say I knew nothing about company law, patent claims and similar esoteric subjects, and was glad to delegate this side of things to them; when everything was ready I should transfer myself to London with a basketful of preliminary ideas. This little respite was useful; it enabled me to map out my own objectives more clearly and to get them down on paper. Moreover I had nothing to fear from the Athens winter while I was lodged in such warm and comfortable quarters.

I sorted not only my papers but also the vast collection of tapes, fragments, dialects, etc. and transcribed them onto matrices; many were the felicities I had culled from the conversations of my friends. (The voice of Sipple saying, gravely: "You might say that I belong to the Purple People. In the case of Mrs. Sipple now—although I didn't know this till later—she used to come up every Wednesday from Broadstairs where she had been playing with the mighty organ of a DSO with Bar.")

I saw a good deal of Caradoc who was marking time before being sent off on a new assignment. As I've said, he had invented what he called the mnemon which he insisted was a literary form— "an art form in which free Freud and solipsism marry and make merry. You might say it was a soft cotton pun dressed up in the form of a *Times* personal." They were indeed *Times* personals of a slightly surrealist tinge, and I had the pleasure of helping him father a few. To my surprise he actually had them printed in the newspaper where they doubtless passed completely unnoticed or were supposed to be an obscure code, a love call for some religious sect.

> Jewish gentleman in Romford, expert on vibraphone, urgently seeks father figure.
>
> Small pegamoid man, fond of soft clinics, seeks tangible rubber acme. Own plug.

No poet ever derived great pleasure from seeing his work printed, and Caradoc spent a good deal of money on these confections. Then came his sixtieth birthday and he woke up to find himself knee-deep in telegrams of congratulations and press cuttings. There were long articles on his work everywhere, photographs of the Hoarah Bridge, the University of Tobago, and other masterpieces of his implausible genius. To my surprise all this backslapping made him sad and plaintive, and once more he began to talk about leaving the firm. "About twice in your life you get a chance to change everything, to jump over the side; but a moment's hesitation and the chance slips away. It's late in the day for me but who knows? I might get another yet. I'm keeping my eyes skinned." Meanwhile the firm had found him a new assignment with which he could hardly quarrel: a new university and senate in the Cook Islands. He would be entirely his own master. Already his fingers itched when they were near a pencil and he spent much of his time, absorbed as any child, modeling in plasticine. "The game of volumes, my boy, the most intoxicating of them all. They've promised me aerial pictures of the site; I can't wait to get my hands on them. And think of new settings, palms, volcanoes, surf."

"When will you leave?"

"As soon as I can. There's nothing more to be done here."

The season was shifting, our little group was dispersing slowly; Hippo moved back into Paris with her sails spread and only occasionally sent us a postcard. Banubula went to the New Year's Eve ball dressed up in a quaint old-fashioned stock of Edwardian provenance with a twinkling pin, looking very much like a vampire on his evening off. "He is dark umber, the bloody count," said Caradoc who enjoyed parodying his friend's exquisite and lapidary English. "I'm sure he would subscribe himself as 'Your Umber Servant.'" The poor count made no allusion to his Turkish excesses, and nor did I. He had resumed his Athenian persona. The countess still sat alone for the greater part of the day in a dressing gown and slippers, her hair caught up in a purple scarf: playing patience, and writing letters to Gurdjieff. "Horatio has been so strange this winter," she might say stretching out long phthisical fingers toward her coffee cup. "So strange." Did she see him as we did who were not privy to his innermost secrets? I mean dark brown voice, cotton gloves, silver-capped stick with heavy rubber ferrule, one ring seal, iodine locket, rebus. . . . It was hard to say. Benedicta wrote disturbingly: "I have been ill, I have had a small absence": in French this time.

Then Caradoc was summoned to London to establish his team of draftsmen for the new project, and I realized that I was going to be very lonely without him. Worse, I did not realize that we should never meet again—though in retrospect I cannot see the logic of such a sentiment. We had a farewell party in the Nube where I successfully masqueraded as sufficiently unwell to spare myself the culminating pleasures of the bed. An idiocy, I suppose—but what is one among so many? Here Sipple intervened, or rather the memory of him, for Caradoc entertained a fantastically high opinion of his friend's gifts and much regretted not to see him before he left. I questioned him about the incident of the dead boy, but found that he knew little more than I did. It may have been something to do with blackmail. "I think Sipple must have

been working for someone, perhaps Graphos, who knows?"
"The Purple People no doubt," I said.

"On the other hand Banubula thinks it was purely and simply a family affair—an affair of honor. The boy's father had said he would punish him for soiling the family honor. This *is* the Balkans after all."

"What does Hippo think?"

Caradoc drained his glass and said oracularly, "It's like everything else in life—those who know can't tell."

And at this moment Mrs. Henniker came into the room whinnying like a polo pony and waving a tattered magazine which the girls had been reading; it was a magazine devoted to film. "Look," cried Mrs. Henniker with a triumphant flourish, waving it under my nose, "one of my girls." To my surprise there she was, Iolanthe, all sepia and deckle-edged, staring out at the world with a kind of forlorn lascivious grin. She was tricked out as some sort of Eastern houri and appeared to be bearing the head of the Baptist upon a trencher. The letterpress concerned a new film made by a Frenchman in Egypt. Apparently she had lobbied herself a small part in it. I was delighted and amused, unaware that we were witnessing the beginnings of so formidable a career. Mrs. Henniker was beside herself with pleasure. "One of my girls," she kept repeating in a dazed sort of way. I was obscurely touched as I looked at the gruesome inexperienced face of young Samiou. Why "inexperienced" though? Caradoc set the paper aside with a grunt of surprise. "Well, may they all prosper," he said at last. "The little dumplings."

Pulley came in with a huge watch dangling. It was time to be going home. It was freezing in the car, the Attic plain was all glittering under hoarfrost; the sewers steamed up through the manholes all the way along Stadium Street like so many geysers. Caradoc pressed my hand and declined a parting drink, showing unwonted resolution. "Just time to pack my traps," he said, "and then hey for the Virgin Isles. Think of me basking out there, eh? And remember that all perfected cultures have depended upon a high infant mortality." No, he wasn't drunk: he was full of the sadness of farewell. "As for you, Charlock, everything is moving in your direction now. You have only to spread your sails a bit. You are going to be very happy. O yes. Very happy indeed. A future full of sperm, my boy."

I could see nothing illogical in the proposition, and yet I was filled with a sudden nagging nostalgia for the days of solitary poverty, the days before the firm took me up. But then the memory of Benedicta swept over me like a landslide; she was worth everything. I did not feel as if I had a separate existence anymore.

"Caradoc, bless you."

"Good-bye."

Om

FOUR

Konx. Ah! the brave new chrysadiamantine world of Charlock's nuptial London! O world of delegated sympathies, of mysteries, of great achievements. The expensive cars that soothed away the roads moving like ointments; the clothes that fitted like second skins. And in the midst of it all the white wand, the blind man's dowsing rod, Benedicta. It is not I who speak, Lord: it is my culture speaking through me. It is hard to disentangle this first time from the others—for she was always going away, always coming back. In the Paulhaus everything has been catered for—chapels for six denominations. People are never too ill to pray. Either she appeared at airports clad in mourning; or else delivered in a white ambulance, laughing, cured, joking with the driver: to run up the steep steps into my arms. Try as you will, there is no explanation for madness, happiness or death. At first it would have been silly to speak of souls darkened by troubling presentiments, of dialogues bathed in strange lights. Later, of course, one has all the time in the world to study the fatal metastases of the idea of love.

I counted upon her for very much, I discovered, sorting through my emotions with a new, a rather disgusting humility bordering on self-abasement. She would develop me like some backyard province perhaps, promulgate a charter. I did not even know her husband's name: whom could I ask? And then, where should we meet at last but under the backward clock at Victoria. Yet at once the Turkish image, brilliant as a postage stamp, gave place to another; she had become very thin now, very tense. She vibrated in my arms like a high-tension wire; her eyes were over made up which increased her pallor, deeped the dimple in her cheek. But with such relief, such passion, after so long an absence. "And all this time you never wrote, Benedicta." "I know." (But afterward she would write every day for weeks on end in her mriror hand: things like, "It is snowing again. They have tied me to the same chair.") But here she only gave a small sweet groan as we broke apart to plunge our eyes into one another. "Felix!" She had managed to capture my very name and make it her own; it emerged newly printed. I had never liked it very much: now I hoped she might go on repeating it. "At last it is over." At last it had begun.

I had already been here alone for nearly a month, living at the beautiful house in Mount Street among the sumptuous impersonal furniture. There had been no signal of her arrival. I contemplated with superstitious awe the huge wardrobe which filled the glass cupboards in our room—my own new wardrobe. The devil! I recalled that one day long ago Jocas had asked me, as a personal favor, to allow his tailor to take my measurements: and though puzzled, I had complied. As one among so many ambiguous happenings this small trifle had hardly seemed worth troubling about. Now I understood. I stood, biting my lip, and contemplating myself in the mirror both ashamed and delighted at my own splendor. The silver-backed brushes were good to the scalp; the bathroom was crowded with expensive toilet waters and monumental soaps. It was perfectly understandable, I told myself, that I should dress appropriately, to match my new, my enormous new salary, and in general my new role in affairs. For Benedicta's sake, as well as the firm's . . . nevertheless. Nor was it too soon, for I had already taken possession of my new suite of offices at Merlin House in the City; I had already met everyone—except of course Julian who was away. Things had begun to move forward with irresistible momentum. Yes, I had even seen the fangled Shadbolt and initialed the preposterous marriage settlement. And now all these scattered elements were knitted together and resolved by her phone call from Victoria. "I'm here at last. Please come to me at once." It was a familiar creature of course, her perfume was the same. All the signals of recognition the same. Yet a difference lay perhaps in the fact that so much time had passed and circumstances had subtly altered—this foggy soot-bellowing grime tank of a station. And then her tremendous assortment of luggage which followed in a second taxi with her maids and manservant. Some lines of Koepgen drifted idly across the back of my mind like these mushrooming winter clouds. Something like "the human face upon its stalk perpetuates only the type of a determined response; there are so few elations and so few dismays to wrinkle between a laughing or a crying death, between a truthful or a lying breath." Benedicta sat gripping my manicured hand and staring unseeingly out of the window watching London lumber by, keeping its viscous slow coil. "You have seen Shadbolt, haven't you?"

"Yes."

"He explained and you agreed. Now we are really one." It was only the context that made the phrase sound extraordinary.

"I signed the document, though really I remained unconvinced inside. It's too generous, my dear. Why should I share everything so completely?"

"O God!" she cried vehemently. "I was afraid you wouldn't see."

"It was too generous; after all I'm earning my own way now. Why shouldn't you keep your fortune? We could have had a *separation des beins* arrangement."

"No. Never. Besides didn't he tell you that I have no personal fortune outside the firm? It's all I have, the firm. Darling, I want to possess you utterly, without reserves of any kind. I can't believe in myself in any other way." Well, so did I, so did I. "But I also wanted you to feel a little independent. Room to breathe."

She began to mutter under her breath, as if she were swearing *sotto voce*. Her knuckles grew white as she gripped my hand. A strange, rather ominous sense of impending misunderstanding cast its shadow over us. It might be possible to embrace it away, to exorcise it. As I kissed her I thought of Shadbolt. He was one of the five solicitors who dealt with the firm's affairs; he had presented for my perusal a thick handbook listing all the firms holdings and all its subsidiaries. A heavy-breathing slothful little man with plum-colored countenance, whose spectacles were attached to his lapel by a heavy black ribbon. When he put them on he did so reverently, as if he were in mourning. Voice of an old bugle full of spit. The marriage contract was an elaborate document couched in the sort of phraseology which made the trained mind swim. I was too intimidated by his air of being a papal emissary to prevail upon him to explain in too great detail. His grinding humorless voice grated upon me. "Everyone in Merlin's seems to be obsessed by contractual obligations," I said somewhat peevishly. Shadbolt removed his spectacles and stared at me reproachfully. "How else shall one do business?" he asked with surprise, almost tenderly.

"But this isn't business," I said.

"Frankly," said the little man rising with infinite slowness to gaze out of the window, "I would have hesitated had I been in Miss Benedicta's place. You will allow me to be frank? But she insisted. From your point of view, Mr. Charlock, you have everything to gain and nothing to lose by it. It's a most generous gesture, a gesture of faith and trust and if I may use the word without immodesty, love. It fully incorporates you in all her fortunes. But if you wish we can tear the document up."

He crossed the room cumbrously with his penguin-like gait. I hesitated for a long moment, feeling very much out of my depth. "I somehow don't like to think about relationships, our marriage, in these terms." Yes, that was really the full extent of my reservations. The lawyer gave a bleak smile. "The sentiment does you much credit. I understand your feeling as you do. On the other hand there is nothing so very strange about making a marriage contract. Many people do. I was rather more concerned about her position than yours. All this," he tapped the white papers against his knee, "would not be easily revoked if ever there were need. She is, in a sense, putting herself entirely at your mercy and the firm as well."

"That is what worries me; there isn't any need."

But, after all, since the whole thing was merely a whim on her part . . . I took up my new gold fountain pen and signed the document. Shadbolt sighed slowly as he pressed the blotter down upon the wet ink. "You are a lucky man," he said, "a very lucky young man."

Now it seemed to me, as I sat beside her with her slender arm through mine, that the phrase might qualify as the nadir of understatement. Those nervous, tender blue eyes turning to gray in this pallid cloudlight met mine with such burning candor that I felt ashamed ever to have felt doubts or reservations about these paper conventions.

"What is it, Benedicta?" But still staring at me she only shook her head as she continued to explore her own inmost feelings—preoccupied, like someone trying to locate a hollow in a tooth. It was in this euphoric trance that we drew up at last in Mount Street. Baynes opened for us and ran down the steps to greet her; but she hardly acknowledged his presence, stalking past him into the hall with what might have seemed an insolent air, had her preoccupation not been so evident.

She threw her gloves onto the table and consulted her appearance in the tall mirror with a careful disdainful air. There was a big bowl of flowers on the side table by the wall, near the silver salver which held some engraved visiting cards and tradesmen's bills. "I told you I did not like the smell of flowers in the house," she said icily to the butler. "Take them out at once." As a matter of fact it was I who had ordered the flowers; but the kindly Baynes, after a glance at me, simply swallowed and decided to take the blame. "Yes, madam."

Benedicta turned with a dazzling smile and said: "Now let's go through the house, shall we? I love coming back here." And so we went from room to room in order to greet the more choice of her possessions—the little statue of Niobe, for example, and the wonderful gallery of golden heads of Greek gods and Roman, modern work by *cire perdue*. It was only when we were climbing the staircase that she said: "There's no one else here is there?"

"Of course not. I'm quite alone."

But now she walked with an air of quaint precaution, letting me enter each room ahead of her to draw the curtains. Nodded smiling, as if satisfied; so we perambulated the densely carpeted floors to come at last to the fine bedrooms where I had been sleeping. Here, at last, she experienced a sort of relief, clapped hands softly before my face and laughed as I trapped them. Well, then, whatever it was we had outwitted it. She walked about, opening cupboards, bed-bouncing, opening cupboards full of my gloatworthy clothing. Then abruptly she paused and said: "My God, I'm tired and dirty. I must have a bath."

I locked the door and drew her one in my scarlet bathroom, tossing in bunches of salts; simple and swift she undressed and stepped into it, and all of a sudden I was carried back in a flash to the Benedicta who had once walked into the foaming cistern of "The Copious Waters" in distant Turkey; her preoccupations were gone. I sat beside her, touching the pale shoulders with my fingers. Afterward she rolled herself in the great toweling caftan and lay on the bed, flushed rosy from the heat. "Tell me now." And so I told her all about the thrilling activities of Charlock in London, unable to disguise the triumph and excitement in my voice. She listened nodding from time to time, but the nods were only part approval —she was like to doze off at any moment. Well, about the two small factories which had been set up near Slough to start production on two of my "devices"; about a study group which had been convened to test the more nebulous experimental stuff. I really could not blame her if her eyelids fluttered and drooped. "And as soon as Julian gets back I shall make contact and . . ." But she was suddenly snapped sharp awake. She looked at me curiously for a moment and then, yawning, ran her fingers through my hair with a queer little gesture—that of a mother, ever so faintly commiserating, who hears her small son boasting about matters he could not as yet understand. "Ah Julian," she said, and I thought of the empty chair in the boardroom faced by the little marble plaque and the virgin blotter. "He's amazing really," I said, "despite his absence in New York; you know, he gets the minutes of all our meetings, annotates them and bangs them back within twenty-four hours sometimes. He must be a glutton for work. One feels his presence very strongly despite the empty chair."

Yawning, she went to the telephone, unlocking the door en route; Baynes answered hoarsely from the kitchen. She ordered him to bring some champagne in a bucket and to tell the office that she would use her box at the opera. "Do you agree?" over her shoulder. "It's my first night in London for so long? And Baynes bring us *The Times*. We must see what's on; and a car, please." A patrician simplicity, both authoritative and endearing. I consulted my watch. There was lots of time. She began her lingering toilet, slipping through the secret panel into her own mirrored rooms. Soon

Baynes came, bringing all these trophies of a fashionable life, and I scanned the paper absently. "Ah!" I said. "An obvious mnemon by Caradoc! I wonder where he is now." And I read out: " 'Continental-type orgy sought by plain-living British family, Hornchurch area. No agents.' "

"Ask the office; they'll tell you," she said, and then in the same breath, "You know they want to send us round the world for our honeymoon? Think, round the world."

"Who do?"

"The firm. Julian. Everyone." I reflected on this a moment. "Isn't it a marvelous idea?" She eyed me.

"Yes," I said, but rather doubtfully, and my tone seemed to puzzle her, for she stopped in front of me as she combed out her hair. "Well, isn't it?" she insisted. I lit a cigarette and said: "Yes, enormously kind of them. But, you know, I was rather hoping we'd sneak off all alone, by ourselves, like a couple of students. I know a dozen little places in Italy and Greece where we could be quite alone, quite out of touch—even with the firm. Besides, why put them to the expense? Think of the cost!"

"Cost?" she said on a chilling note of interrogation, and with a singular expression on her face. "How do you mean—'cost'?" I would perhaps have laughed had her strange expression not struck me so forcibly. All this became clearer later on when, after the marriage, I made the intoxicating discovery that we had no real income whatsoever against which to calculate our costs. I mean that there was no ceiling, no budget, no margin. She simply drew money as one draws breath. Any one of the four banks owned by the firm honored her checks; notes of hand—the merest scribbles on the back of a postcard or on a page torn from an address book—were honored by Nathan, the administrative secretary. She never saw a bill in connection with any of the houses she owned. This contributed a vertiginous singularity to her dealings with money. And now that our fortunes were merged by the Shadbolt document I woke up to find that I too was in the same situation. I had no money of "my own"—

yet what the devil does the phrase mean? At first it was intoxicating, yes, of course, not to have to reflect on costs; but later (I am talking of the period of the crack-up) I began to feel this as a major factor which contributed to her general confusion of mind. She was capable of buying a bracelet for ten thousand pounds and of leaving it in a taxi. When I grew alarmed about her general state of health, and found myself unable to see the elusive Julian face to face, I remember writing a long eloquent memorandum to him which finally wound up on Nash's desk. I emphasized that even the Queen had a budgetary ceiling voted by Parliament, yet Benedicta had none. The confusion and waste were simply due to her total lack of knowledge as to what money might conceivably mean. Julian merely replied to my memo with another, neatly typed and signed in that inimitable hand: "Her doctors have been consulted, and also the principals of the firm. No change need be contemplated for the present." But at this moment I only saw the childish, endearing expression of puzzlement on her face and longed to kiss her. What is more endearing than the capriciousness of a rich woman? O, it is lovely. I might answer the rhetorical question very differently today, I suppose. And heavens, I have had eight years or more in which to ponder the matter, along with more recondite subjects—Charlock sitting at his massvie desk in Merlin House, drawing on his blotter with the golden pen which lived in a fat agate slab. Scribbling on a blackboard in colored chalks.

She turned her white shoulders to me with a sigh. "Do me up at the back, would you please?" And for better or for worse, in sickness and in health, I did, stooping to touch the white skin with my lips. So hand in hand we sauntered downstairs casting admiring glances at ourselves on every landing. Baynes had made up a brown paper parcel of my prehistoric clothes, baggy gray trousers and tweed coats with leather elbow patches and so on: the uniform of the poor sage! He asked me reverently what he should do with them. I was about to tell him to offer them to the nearest jumble sale when Benedicta intervened with an air of crisp decision and said: "Burn them in the furnace, Baynes." Baynes bowed to the heavenly will, and so did I, though I opened my mouth as if to speak. What did it matter? He had found an old French briar in one of my pockets, and this he had set aside. I was glad to see it again, though it was pretty much burned out; yet under the cool glance of Benedicta I found myself strangely incapable of reclaiming possession of it. I thought of the sweet-smelling box of cigars in the drawing room. From now on nothing but the choicest Juliets would touch the lips of Charlock. There was a conveniently placed leather case, already filled, upon the mantelpiece. "I think it had better go—it's pretty used up," I said treacherously to Baynes. He bowed again. "The boots and shoes I have given to the gardener," he said. "They fit him."

So we equipped ourselves with coats and wraps and floated through the front door to find the office Rolls—flatus symbol of the new Charlock—lying at anchor, waiting for us.

Memory refuses to recover the rest of that evening in any detail—behind the stripes and bars of Busoni's music; only toward dawn, lying exhausted beside each other, I awoke with a jerk to find her talking Turkish in her sleep—the strange crooning bubbling tongue which I had once heard her use to her hawk. She was feverish, tossing and turning in bed like someone trying to throw off, in her sleep, the imaginary bonds of some painful dream. But by morning the shadow had fled with fever, and she was in sparkling spirits again. I walked half the way to the office across the spring-fermenting city with its frail sunlight, reveling in the green of the parks, the light rime of hoarfrost on the grass. Well, I was dense with happiness—the poor scientist could have trumpeted his joy like an elephant. Jevons the commissionaire was on duty as usual, stamping and chomping with the fresh cold, clad in his green coat with polished brass buttons, his billycock hat; his huge umbrella lay beside the directors' lift. He lavished his customary hearty pleasantries upon me, and even went so far as to tip me a conspiratorial wink as I passed him with my own black umbrella. It is amazing how quickly one can develop the condescending wave of an umbrella which somehow goes with city clothes. And a bowler! In stately fashion the lift bore me up to the third floor, to the silent and comfortable office from which one could glimpse a corner of St. Paul's far away to the left of the invisible river line. My dispatch box had already been brought up by Miss Tee, its contents neatly arranged in the metal tray for my perusal. The memorandum of the latest meeting upon the subject of the new light-bulb project was already here, duly annotated by the absent Julian and signed by his secretary in his absence. How did he do it, I wondered? I supposed that the minutes were sent to him by Telex. "I am extremely eager to see this project realized," he wrote heartwarmingly, "as it seems one of the most imaginative we have ever undertaken. Please keep it upon the secret list until production department is ready to market. Only one consideration comes to mind. We must remember the prohibitive price of mercury at £150 per 75 lb flask when costing. In this context however I hope shortly to have good news of negotiations going forward in Moscow for supplies of mercury. If we can capture this new market and thus sidetrack the chlorine plants which are responsible for the shortage and high price of this element we should be well on our way towards a signal success. Please press ahead with the first five hundred prototype bulbs."

I rang the manservant in the buttery and told him that for the eleven o'clock break I would very much like a bowl of strawberries and cream with a glass of the finest sherry. Corbin was perfectly used to requests of this kind; he would dispatch an office boy at once in search of the strawberries. I put in a call to Slough to find out how the engineering department was dealing with the new filament and what the first tests had demonstrated. All was well; there was no deterioration in spite of the tremendous load. It was almost too good to be true, things were moving with such speed and smoothness. There was no meeting today and hardly any paper work, so I opened the newspaper and sank into a pleasant daydream about Benedicta and the future—a daydream compounded of such various elements that it would not have been possible to sort them all out into a coherent pattern. At any rate not then.

Later she rang up and said she missed me. *She missed me!* I was overcome. And as far as Benedicta was concerned I found that I liked her all the better for knowing so little about her; this factor contributed something enigmatic to her—to her strangely withdrawn personality which flourished in privacy like some heavy-perfumed magnolia. Everything therefore was a surprise. Had I felt that she was deliberately keeping secret things she might have shared it would doubtless have been different; but her prohibitions and retreats into panic did not suggest this at all. She had thrown up simply the defenses which oversensitive, perhaps even rather neurotic, people throw up consciously against experiences too deeply felt to be the subject of open discussion. Of course at first the tabus were a little bewildering—but then why should someone not wish not to discuss their fathers or past husbands and so on? It was perfectly defensible; doubtless as we got to know each other better these defenses would melt and give way to new understandings. (The strawberries were watery, the sherry indifferent, but I did not care. I was tied to a comet's tail.) And when I arrived back at Mount Street in the evenings there was no shadow of doubt about the warmth and eagerness with which she threw open the door, forestalling Baynes, to run down the steps and embrace me, almost ravenous for my embrace. Thus arm in arm to the warm fire crackling on the hearth, the winking bottles and decanters, and the prospect of a whole evening spent alone together. "Julian telephoned today and told me to send you his warmest greetings." Everybody loved me.

I had noticed that even in the first few days a flock of white envelopes addressed to her had landed like doves upon the hall table. In the morning the office sent her a social secretary to deal with such correspondence, so that when I arrived back

I found an equally massive bunch of envelopes stamped and addressed for dispatch. I sifted somewhat ruefully through them. "Heavens, you seem to know everybody worthwhile in London."

"Those are all refusals," she said. "Besides, I don't see people anymore. I want you to myself. I haven't for ages. Besides you don't want to go out and about, do you?"

"Good Lord no."

"And then after April I shall be in the country where nobody ever comes. Do you see? And you will drive down for weekends or whenever you get a chance. We'll be married there, too, if you agree. Julian has arranged it. Just the two of us I mean, with nobody."

"So you didn't want to escape with me?"

"It wasn't that, Felix. It's just that I can't just disappear like that. I have to stay in touch, you know."

"With whom, with what?"

She looked at me curiously, as though the question were an unexpectedly foolish one: as if she had not expected it from me. "I mean," I went on, "you are not working for anyone; you don't have any real obligations, have you?"

"None at all." She gave a small sharp laugh, a sad laugh as she sat down on the hearthrug before the fire to rest her chin upon her drawn-up knees and stare into the burning coals. Then it occurred to me that it might be something to do with her doctors, and I kicked myself for a prying fool, kneeling down beside her to put my arms about her shoulders. "I'm sorry, Benedicta" I said. She had a trace of a tear in the corner of her eye, but she was still smiling. "It's of no importance. Come, sit beside me and tell me what you have been doing for the firm. Will you? I want to share everything."

This was more easy to do, and most congenial to my mood; and yet, as I started talking about the three first devices which Merlin was to put into immediate production, I could not but feel a sort of helpless despair that they were not more interesting and revolutionary than they were. They were only mechanical contrivances which, however useful, provided crutches for people in need. In the back of my mind I was thinking along more abstract vectors, groping toward something of which Abel is still only a shallow protoytpe. A behavioristic abacus of patterned responses which might respond to the very oscillations of the nervous system—something which might both prophesy and retroprophesy. . . . Nothing was clear as yet; there was so much as yet to be done on the theory of mathematical probability. It made me dizzy thinking about it. But meanwhile my *alter Felix* continued his lucid exposition of the toys for which the firm were to be responsible, and all the time Benedicta listened avidly, as if to music, her head thrown slightly back, eyes closed. And when I had finished—when I had even shown her one of the tiny filaments as some people will show the relics of an operation, a calculus in a bottle—she sighed deeply and put her arms round me, pressing herself to me as if all this prosaic recital had been almost sexually rousing.

"It's going to be marvelous," she said. "You will see."

There was no doubt of it in my mind; nor anything but overwhelming gratitude to this extraordinary golden creature whose head had sunk now to my knees, half fire-tranced. "I'm determined you are going to be happy," I said. "Happy and not scared." Put down that goblet, Felix!

She jumped up at once, startled, and said: "Who said I was scared?" She made as if to walk toward the door but I captured her hands and drew her gently back to the fireplace. "Did Julian say anything?" she said sharply and I answered in the same tone: "Nobody said it; besides I have never met Julian. I thought sometimes you seemed worried, that was all. But it's over now for good. You have got me to rely on." I caught sight of my face in the mirror and suddenly felt foolish.

For good! My clumsy advocacy worked at last; she seated herself beside me once more, relaxed and calm again. Beside the bed that evening I found a couple of books of essays, beautifully bound in green morocco. "I borrowed them from

Julian's flat," she explained. She didn't say when. Each bore a pretty bookplate with the owner's initials entwined and a rebus—an ape climbing a pomegranate tree. Here and there passages of the books had been underscored, presumably by the owner. "Out of the present we manufacture the future; what we dream today becomes tomorrow's reality. All our ills come from incautious dreaming. Trivial or impure dreaming literally rots the fabric of the future. But the dreams of a rarefied psyche help to resolve tensions and build up good sources." I yawned, she was already asleep, curled up beside me with her head under her wing. Drifting now in her direction with half-shut eyes I dreamed I was addressing the politely subservient members of my board on topics of the greatest moment. "The sills of fancy, gentlemen, swell with the following wind of good fortune." I was learning how to raise my voice, to suit gestures to the words, to perorate. . . .

So the brightly etched days rolled by. Julian had apparently returned from his trip abroad, but still put in no appearance at the boards, though his comments upon our lucubrations were as prompt and cogent as ever. I gathered that he did much of his work at home and was hardly ever in his office. It seemed to me strange that he did not make personal contact, if only to shake my hand. In fact I rather looked forward to meeting him. I even suggested to Benedicta that she might ask him to dine with us, but she shook her head doubtfully and said: "You don't know Julian. He is tremendously shy. He hides himself away. I'm sure he wouldn't come. He'd just send a huge shelf of flowers with a last-minute excuse. You know, Felix, hardly anyone in the office has so much as seen him. He prefers to speak to them on the phone." It was intriguing to say the least, and at first I was inclined to think that she was exaggerating; but not so. Then one day he phoned me to discuss some point or other— but from the country. His voice had a thrilling icy suavity. He spoke slowly, gently, in a dreamy way which suggested more than a hint of world weariness—one imagined Disraeli dictating a state paper in just such a disenchanted tone. I expressed my eagerness to meet him and he thanked me, but added: "Yes, all in good time, Charlock. We certainly must meet, but at the moment I am simply worked off my feet; and you have so much other fish to fry—I refer to your marriage to Benedicta. I can't tell you how happy that makes us all."

There seemed nothing for it but to bow to his whim for the time being. But one morning my own phone rang at the office and I could tell from the timbre of his voice that the call was coming from somewhere inside the building. It was Julian all right—by now I was quite familiar with his voice, we had already spoken to each other frequently; moreover I knew that he had an office at the end of the corridor where Nathan, the general admin. sec., presided over his papers. Why, I had even recorded him once or twice for my collection. I thought in playful fashion that I might surprise him, meet him in the flesh. So while he still spoke I put down the receiver on my blotter and stalked down the long corridor to throw open the door of the office in question. But there at his desk sat Nathan only; a small dictaphone, attached to the telephone, was still playing. "Ah you've hung up, Mr. Charlock," said Nathan with mild reproach, cutting off. I felt something of a fool. Nathan switched over and said, "He was in very early this morning and recorded half a dozen conversations. He often does so."

I recounted this incident somewhat ruefully to Benedicta; but she only smiled and shook her head. "You'll never catch Julian on the hop," she said. "Until he decides."

"What does he look like, Benedicta?" I asked. She gazed at me thoughtfully for a moment and then said, "There isn't anything special about him. He's just like anyone else, I think."

On a sudden impulse I asked: "Have you ever seen him?" The question was quite involuntary, and the moment it was out I knew it to be absurd. But Benedicta swallowed and answered: "Of course, quite definitely." But the tone in which she said it struck me as curious. If I had had to "interpret" it in the manner of the inimitable Nash I should have taken it to mean: "I think that the person I have seen is Julian, but I am not absolutely sure." The thought as it crossed my mind however seemed to be ever so slightly disloyal, so I stifled it and changed the subject. "Ah well," I said, "I expect we shall see him for the wedding at any rate." But once again I was to find myself in error, for neither Julian nor anyone else came to the wedding though the house was bursting with presents and telegrams of congratulations.

The wedding! What could have been more singular? I had asked no questions, of course; but then on the other hand I had been asked none. The arrangements were not of my making, but it was to be presumed that Benedicta (if she were not herself responsible for them) had at least been consulted. I supposed that she had decided to get married in the strictest privacy, that was all. Only that and nothing more. Nor had I anyone that I wished to invite. No family. An uncle in America, some cousins in India, that was all.

But it was my first visit to "Cathay," that preposterous, gloomy country house which was to be our home; moreover by night, for the marriage was arranged for midnight. "Cathay" forsooth! With its turrets and fishponds, great park, cloth-of-gold chamber, huge organ by Basset. At the end of a normal office day my fellow directors came in one by one to wish me luck and a happy honeymoon—cracking the usual awkward jokes about visiting the condemned man in his cell, etc. After these so amiable pleasantries I took a taxi home to an early dinner, to find the hall full of luggage and the office car already outside the door. It was piquant, mysterious, rather exciting to be motored down into the depths of the country like this. It smelled of orange blossom and elopements in the dark of the year. I visualized some great house party with Julian and some of his collaborators, perhaps with a wife or two present to balance the forces of good and evil. Indeed I thought that Julian could hardly do less than witness for us. We did not speak much as the car nosed its way slowly through the slippery gromboolian suburbs toward Hampshire. Benedicta sat close beside me with her gloved hand in mine, looking pale and somewhat contrite. After the ceremony we were to drive on directly to Southampton to board the *Polaris*—a Merlin Line cruiser. But the wedding itself was of course to be a civil one. No church bells for Charlock.

It was a long coldish drive with fine rain glittering in the white beam of the headlights, prickling through the greenery of forest land and heath. My initial elation had given way to a certain tender solemnity. "Benedicta," I whispered, but she only pressed my hand tightly and said : "Sh! I'm thinking." I wondered what her thoughts might be as she stared out across the darkling light. Of a past she had confided to nobody?

At last we crackled down the long avenues toward the bowl of golden light which gleamed at the end of the long green tunnels. The house was ablaze with light, and crammed with people all right. A telephone was insisting somewhere. But to my surprise "the people" were all servants. In the rococo musicians' gallery with its moldy Burne-Jones flavor a quintet played ghastly subdued music as if afraid to overhear itself. Butlers and maids moved everywhere with a kind of clinical deliberation—yet for all the world as if they were making preparations for a great ball. A staff like this could have mounted a wedding reception for four hundred people. But I could see no trace of any guests. But a mountain of telegrams lay unopened on the marble tables in the hall, and the preposterous Edwardian rooms leading with an air of ever greater futility into each other were bursting with presents—everything from a concert grand to silver crocks and gewgaws of all sorts and sizes. The mixture of portentous emptiness and reckless prodigality staggered me.

But Benedicta moved about it all with a kind of fiery elation, moth light of step, her face glowing with pleasure and pride. She held her head high against the forest of candle branches and spectral Venetian lusters. It struck me then how foreign she was. I divined that this old house with its musty gawkish features offered a sort of mental association with Stamboul—those rotting palaces in *style pompier* copied and recopied, crisscrossed with mirrors set in tarnished moldings. Shades of Baden and Pau—yes, that is what made her feel so at home, so at one with it all. "But is there nobody except the servants?" I asked, and she turned her dancing eyes upon me for a second before shaking her blonde head. "I told you, silly. Only us." Only us! But we had just passed an enormously long buffet prepared for a midnight supper: apparently the baked meats (I thought in muddled quotation) were destined to grace the servants' hall. It was marvelous, it was macabre. I felt quite a wave of affection for poor Baynes who now advanced toward us with a sheaf of telegrams—congratulations from Jocas, Julian, Caradoc, Hippolyta: his was a familiar face. These brief messages from the lost world of Athens and Stamboul gave me a little pang—they seemed almost brutally gay. Baynes said: "They are waiting for you in the library, madam." Benedicta nodded regally and led the way. The noise of the quintet followed us apologetically. Everywhere there were flowers—but big banks of flowers professionally arranged: their heavy scent swung about in pools among the candle-shining shadows. And yet . . . it was all somehow like a cinema, I found myself thinking. Baynes marched before us and opened yet another door.

The library! Of course I did not discover the fact until later, but this huge and beautifully arranged room with its galleries and molded squinches, its sea-green dome, its furnishings of globes, atlases, astrolabes, gazetteers, was a fake: all the books in it were empty dummies! Yet to browse among the titles one would have imagined the room to contain virtually the sum total of European culture. But the books were all playful make-believe, empty buckram and gilt. Descartes, Nietzsche, Leibniz . . . Here, however, all was candlelight and firelight, discreet and perhaps a trifle funereal? No, not really. A large desk, covered with a green baize cloth, conveyed the mute suggestion of an altar, with its flowers, candles and open registers. Here sunning his shovel-shaped backside stood the Shadbolt, beside the registrar from Weymouth; their clerks stood by to act as witnesses if need be—moldy and dispossessed-looking figures. We greeted each other formally and with much false cordiality. Benedicta gave the signal while I groped in my pockets for the ring.

To my surprise she seemed quite moved by the grim routine of the civil ceremony. It did not last long. At a signal the tremulous Baynes appeared with champagne on a tray and we relaxed into a more comprehensive mood of relief. Shadbolt toasted us heartily; and Benedicta made her slow way through the house to touch glasses with the servants who had also been provided with a little spray with which to respond. It all seemed to happen in a flash. Within an hour we were on our way again, down the long roads to Southampton. It was raining. It was raining. I thought of the blue gourd of the Mediterranean sky with longing. Benedicta had fallen asleep, her long aquiline nose pointing downward along my sleeve. I cradled her preciously. She looked so sly. From time to time a tiny snore escaped her lips.

Dawn's left hand was in the sky by the time we negotiated the sticky dockland with its palpitating yellow lights and climbed the long gangplank of the sleeping ship to seek out the bridal suite on A deck. Benedicta was speechless with fatigue and so was I; too tired to supervise the stacking of the luggage, too tired to think. We fell into our bunks and slept; and by the time I woke I felt the heart-lifting sensation of a ship sliding smoothly through water—the soft clear drub of powerful engines driving us steadily seaward. There was too the occasional lift, and hiss of spray on the deck around us. I had a bath and went on deck—a wind-snatched deck with a light grizzle of rain falling upon it. The land lay far behind now in the mists of a morning, a gray smudge of cloud-capped nothingness. We were on our way round the world. England hull down in the sea mist of dawn. It was so good to be alive.

Just time to return to my cabin and finish the study of the mantis which Marchant had lent me. "Another theory was constructed on the physiological experiments of Rabaud and others; in these it was found that the superior nerve centers restrain or inhibit the reflexive system. The control is weakened by decapitation. The visible result is that the reflexive-genital activity of the headless male is made more vigorous and therefore biologically more effective." Benedicta sighed in her sleep and turned to snuggle deeper into the soft pillows. The same goes for decapitated frogs, while any hangman will tell you that a broken spinal cord will produce an instant ejaculation. I put my book aside and smoked, lulled by the lilt of the ship as she manned the green sea. Then slept again to awake and find my breakfast beside me and Benedicta sitting opposite in a chair, naked and smiling. We were sliding back toward Polis, that was why perhaps—toward those first intimacies which seemed now to lie far back in the past. Did she suit her lovemaking to the country she found herself in? Now as she came to sit cross-legged on the end of my bed I thought back to those ancient kisses and little punishments—the water torture, the wax torture, the frenetic zealous kisses with their wordless pieties —all of them making a part of the bright fabric of the past which must be carried forward into a future bright with promise. And here I was with the creature within arm's reach. Moreover what could well be more delightful than the life of shipboard with its defined routines, its lack of demands upon one's personal initiative? And with it isolation, being surrounded by water on every side. It seemed so soon when we found ourselves sliding past Gibraltar into calmer seas, cradled by light racing cloud and water far bluer than we deserved. She had flowered into a kinetic laziness which suited itself marvelously to the holiday mood. The only interruption was an occasional long cable from Julian about the minor details of some industrial operation; but even those dwindled away into silence.

Three months! But they passed in a slow-motion dream; already the lazy life of the ship had bemused us, sunk us into a tranced nescience. Talk of Calypso's island—I forgot even to make notes, forgot to figure. I read like a convalescent. I was even able to find relief from those half-unconscious trains of reasoning which had always formed a sort of leitmotiv to my quotidian life—so much so that I could honestly say that there had not been a single moment until now when I was not fully occupied with my private thoughts. An invisible censor clad in gum boots strode up and down before Charlock's subliminal threshold—O a far more competent fellow than the graybearded Freudian one. A primordial biological censor this, rather like a beefeater in the Tower of London.

Of course there were interludes in all this uxorious sloth when my alter Charlock reproached me bitterly and pushed me into involuntary attempts to show a leg. At Monte, for example, I rallied sufficiently to consider playing the tables. I collected a mass of those long printed sheaves of paper which record the numbers thrown out by the wheels. They are of great interest to those unwary souls who wish to study form with a view to establishing a system and so breaking the bank. I was hardly less unwary and thought that a brief analysis might—I had been playing about with mathematical probability—ah wretched artificer! But when I suggested this Benedicta came back with a very decisive, "Ah dear no. Have you forgotten that the firm owns nearly all the shares in the Casino? Do you think they would let me lose on my honeymoon? We'd win a fortune, Felix—what would be the point of it?" Indeed! I let the long sheaves float away in the wind and settle in the pale waters.

The firm was omnipresent, though in a queer tactful sort of way; nor do I mean simply that the captain and crew of the vessel knew who we were, and had received instructions to take specially good care of us. It went a bit deeper than that. At every point of disembarkation we were discreetly met by the resident agent and taken on a conducted tour of the place, much in the manner of visiting minor royalty. This was most welcome in countries where we did not know the language and habits of the natives—Cambodia, India for example. Nevertheless I could well understand this unobtrusive tutelage becoming oppressive in the long run. There were a number of state occasions to be observed as well which made me sigh for the anonymity of a hotel room in Florence; a governor here and there bade us to his table: those huge mournful government houses full of sighing chintz and mammoth billiard tables, full of bad pictures and unpalatable cooking. Well, I sighed—we both sighed—but there was nothing to be done but accept and attend. This of course was more marked east of Suez: we were familiars of the Mediterranean, needing no help in Athens or in Jocasland of the tumbled minarets. But Athens was strangely hushed—everyone was away it seemed, either abroad or in the islands. Nor could I get any news of Banubula or Koepgen, try as I would. I had a small fugitive inclination to visit the Plaka and perhaps Number Seven as well, but I dismissed it, telling myself that time was short. But at Stamboul it was no surprise to see a little white pinnace scuttling across the sea to meet us with Jocas steering her—this long before the mists divided to reveal the ancient city trembling among the tulip-topped bastions. I saw the great confiding hand of Jocas come sliding up the gangplank rope like a deep-sea squid; then he was before us, with his shy dancing eye. There was nothing equivocal in the tenderness with which he greeted us, pressed us to his heart. He had brought some small presents like newspapers, Black Sea caviar, Turkish cigarettes and some rare pieces of jewelry for B. So we spent the day agossip under a white awning, watching the city swim up from the deeps. Our lunch was served on deck and Jocas drank his champagne to us, uttering the familiar druidic toasts to bless our union. Benedicta looked ravishing in her new brown skin; the fine hairs shading from temple to cheek had already turned silkworm golden. "I have never seen her look so calm, so well," said Jocas softly in an aside, and indeed it seemed to me to be so. He was full of news of the property and of course the birds and their form. Benedicta questioned him eagerly. Indeed at one point she wanted to stay a week, but the itinerary was already so charged . . . Omar the master falconer was dead, but Said had taken over and was doing very well. He had invented a new kind of lure. And so on. But mixed also in this animated exchange of fact were scraps of news about other friends and acquaintances—Caradoc in New York, for example, preparing to fly out to his new venture. Graphos was going from strength to strength, after having nearly ruined his career because of an infatuation with a streetwalker. And Koepgen? "He is doing well in Moscow; he will have a year or two yet. I know you have his notebooks." As a matter of fact I had one with me on the voyage. "And then what?" Jocas twinkled the gold smile and rubbed his hands. "He will get a large bonus and be free to pursue his studies."

"And that ikon?"

"Yes, we have found the one he wants; it is quite safe, waiting for him. But the firm comes first." Jocas giggled. "It's a lure, eh?"

The liner was scheduled to stay only a few hours; it was hardly worth going ashore for such a brief period; a gaggle of sightseers were rushed ashore, crammed into buses and given a swift glimpse of the great walls of smoking dung. But we sat on deck, talking drowsily, until they returned and the warning siren sent its herds of echoes thundering across the sky. Benedicta was leaning at the rail now, staring down into the water. "In the old days," Jocas was saying dreamily, "they had bird fairs all over Central Europe—singing birds I mean. Her father was a renowned breeder of songbirds, and won prizes everywhere with his exhibits. They say he was the first to think of blinding birds in order to improve their singing— you know, red-hot copper wire. It's easily and painlessly done, they say. He built up quite a trade in cage birds at one time, but the business outgrew it. Now only a few specialists are interested; the fairs have all lapsed. There is no room for them in the modern world, I suppose."

"Did it improve their singing?"

"It would improve anyone's singing; one sense develops to compensate for the loss of another—you know that. Why do they try to find a blind man always for muezzin? It needn't be eyes necessarily. The voice of the *castrato,* for example. He yawned heartily, by now half asleep. "Benedicta," he called, "I must leave you, my dear. I wish I could come too but I can't."

The sight-seeing passengers were panting aboard again led by two steatopygous priests—soutanes stuffed with blood sausage. Benedicta came thoughtfully back to us and said, without any preliminary gambit: "Jocas, did you give Mr. Sacrapant the sack?" Jocas was surprised into a smile as he answered. "Of course not."

"Then why?" she said with a puzzled frown.

"His suicide? But he left a letter listing a number of reasons—mostly trivial ones you would say, even insignificant reasons. Yet taken all together I suppose they weighed something. Good Lord, the firm had no part in the matter." He looked shocked. She drew a sigh of relief and sat down. "Then?" Jocas went on, frowning, as if trying to puzzle out the matter for himself. "We look at things from the wrong point of view. I mean, how many reasons could you give for wanting to go on living? The list would be endless. So there is never one reason, but scores. You know in a funny sort of way he could never get used to the idea of security—it was almost as if he couldn't wait for his wife to get her pension." He burst out laughing in a strange half-rueful way and struck his thigh. "Ah! old Sacrapant!" he said and shook his head. "He will be impossible to replace." I saw the little figure falling.

A bell rang urgently and someone signaled from the deck-house by the bridge. Reluctantly Jocas took himself off, to stand in the sheets of the little pinnace looking up at us with a curious expression on his face—a mixture of affection and sadness. "Be happy," he called across the separating water, as if perhaps he had scented some fugitive disharmony in us after all: and the little craft suddenly reared up and began its glib motion as it raced away toward the land.

"Come," said Benedicta, taking my arm, "let's go down for

a spell." She wanted to go down to the cabin, to lie about and talk or read—most probably to make love: until the first bell went for dinner. Well, but by dark we were crawling through the Straits again bound for the farthest corners of the world. Columbus Charlock! I do not believe that one can love without analyzing—though I know that too much analysis can spoil loving: but here at least nothing but contentment found a place, a luxurious self-surrender which made death seem very far away. That was it, death!

Somewhere there is an album full of photographs of this royal progress—photographs taken, not by us, but by the captain and crew who shepherded us through all the adventures of travel with such docile assiduity. Later a handsome bound volume, with the record duly mounted and in the right order, arrived on the hall table with the compliments of the shipping line. Well then, on the back of bloody elephants bucketing up the holy mountain in Ceylon, wearing weird pith helmets against the sun. Then some tiger shoots in India—Benedicta lavender-pale and slender, with her triumphant little boot upon the head of the beast: the rigor had staffed its snarl into a silent travesty of the last defensive gesture. Smack! Hong Kong, Sydney, Tahiti—the long ritual led us on, offering no demands upon us.

But these superficial records could not deal with everything, take account of everything. For example, unknown to either of us, Iolanthe was also aboard—or rather her image was, the public one, printed on celluloid. Among the films we were shown as we crossed the Indian Ocean was one made in Egypt, trivial and melodramatic, in which to my surprise Iolanthe had a small part. She swam up out of the screen without warning, moving into close-up which projected her enlarged face with its heavily doctored eye shapes almost into my lap. My surprise made me sit up with an exclamation and grip Benedicta's hand.

"Good Lord."

"You know her?"

"It's Iolanthe of all people."

It was not much of a part, it lasted barely half a minute.

But it was enough to glimpse an entirely new person grafted upon the one I had known. After all, the smallest gesture gives a clue to the inner disposition—a way of walking, position of hands, cant of the head. All right. Here she had to cut up food and put it on a plate; then to walk with the plate across a strip of sand, to bow, to serve. In this very brief repertoire of acts and gestures—some so familiar from which I recalled the old being—I saw a new one. "It's a common little face," said Benedicta with distaste and a contempt that extended itself with justice to the whole ridiculous film, with its sheiks and dancing girls. "Yes. Yes." Of course she was right; but how much less coarse, less common, than the original Iolanthe I had known. On the contrary these photographs suggested a new kind of maturity; her gestures had become studied, graceful, no longer impulsive and uncoordinated, fluent. Some of this I tried to express to Benedicta but she did not follow; she turned her cryptic smile upon me and pressed my hand confidingly. "But she is being directed and rehearsed by the *metteur en scene,* my dear: and he probably sleeps with her as well to get her to do things his way." Of course this was true and yet . . . entirely factitious? The change seemed to hold a whole range of significance for me. I was puzzled; more mysterious still, I felt wounded in an obscure sort of way—almost as if I had been tricked. Could I perhaps have missed the most interesting part of my little mistress by the merest inattention? I was nudged into surprise by that short insignificant scene. Moreover, in order the better to analyze my own response to it, I asked for it to be played over again the following afternoon while Benedicta was taking her siesta. No, the astonishment remained. The coarseness, the street-Arab knowingness, had found a point of repose where it could manifest itself calmly as naked human experience. This gave point to a new angle of the head, to the resurrection of a smile which I knew on lips which I knew— but which I had never noticed. Or had they not then been there? Iolanthe! Heavens! I saw the rust-stained marbles rising against the keen skies of Attica. I rummaged, so to speak, among my stock of memories, to find correspondences to match this new personage—in vain. The screen figure corresponded so little to the original that I felt as if she had somehow hoaxed me. My mood of puzzled abstraction lasted until dinnertime, when Benedicta noticed it—for she missed nothing. "I hear you have been visiting your girl friend while I was asleep," she said with a rather cruel smile, her lips curving mischievously up at the corners. "Isn't it rather early in the day to start being unfaithful to me?" It was a joke, and should have been taken as such.

But I wanted to be serious, to explain how confused and puzzled I had been by this parody of nature. O yes I did. Benedicta would have none of it. "You can have all the women you want provided you tell me about it in detail," she said, and a sudden new light, a little grim this time, came into her eye. It was rather annoying for this was hardly the point. Besides nothing could be more distasteful than to provoke the sort of middle-class tiff common to middle-class couples in the suburbs of loathsome capitals. I was outraged by her vulgarity. "It was only a joke," she said.

"How idiotic to quarrel over a strip of film."

"I am not quarreling. Felix, look at me."

"Nor am I." I obeyed. We kissed but with constraint. What the devil was wrong? But we finished the meal in silence and after it stalked up on deck to sit side by side in deck chairs, smoking and musing. "How much do you know about this girl?" she asked at last; somewhat peevishly I replied: "Certainly more than I know about you, even after all this time." Benedicta's eye narrowed with anger, and when she was in this mood she set her ears back like a scared cat.

"I will answer any question you put to me."

"I have never insisted on you answering questions."

"How could you *insist?*"

"Or even ask. I want you as you are, exactly as you are at this moment; I don't care if you are still a bit of an enigma."

She turned her hard blue eye upon me with a new expression which I had not seen before and which I might describe as an amused contempt, and yawned behind her brown fingers. "My poor Felix," she said in a tone which made me long to strike her.

I took myself off to bed with an improving book, but when the clock struck midnight and she had not put in an appearance I dressed again and went on deck to find her. She was sitting alone in the deserted bar, leaning heavily upon it, dozing. "Thank God you've come," she said incoherently, "I can't stand up." She was in fact dead drunk. It was all the more surprising because she was ordinarily a very modest drinker. I helped her laboriously along the deck to the cabin where she sat on her bunk, swaying slightly holding her head in her hands. "On Thursday we touch at Macao," she said. "That is where Max died of typhoid fever. I do not want to go ashore." I said nothing. She went on: "He was a musician, but not a good one. But he had invented something which didn't exist until then—a copying machine for scores, for parts. It wasn't complete, and it took some of the best brains in the firm to develop and market it. Anything else you want to know?"

"Did you have a marriage settlement with him?"

Her eye lit with a sulfurous gleam, the embers of a queer triumph shining through the whiskey daze.

"No," she said; but the tone in which she said it permitted me to construe the words, "There was no need." (I jumped with guilt at so treacherous a thought.)

Then she held up her cupped hands pleadingly and said: "But even if he had been alive I'd have left him for you."

It was not possible to resist her when she was in this mood—sitting like some forlorn collapsing edifice, foundering among its own distresses. I felt crushed under the weight of my self-reproaches. I soaked her patiently in hot water, helped her to be sick, and toweled her back to some semblance of sobriety; afterward she lay, pallid and exhausted, in my arms until daybreak when she was able once more to whisper the little phrase which had become almost a slogan for us. Always after making love she would say: "Let's always, Felix."

◆ ◆ 227

So Macao passed, and with it some of the weight of her private preoccupations; her mood lightened and made room for a new gaiety, a new responsiveness. We had become used to the ship by now and familiar with the habit of life. It was almost as if we had never lived land life. And as we neared our final port of disembarkation we even started to take part in the absurd dinners and fancy-dress dances which we had found so distasteful during the first weeks of the voyage. In fact the night before we reached Southampton we went the whole hog and borrowed fancy dresses and masks from the extensive wardrobe of the vessel. I was Mephisto I think, with eyebrows of jet; she was a nun in a great white coif of starched linen. It was while she was making up her face in the mirror that she said, in an almost terror-stricken tone: "You know, Felix, I may be pregnant—have you thought about it? What shall I do?"

"How do you mean?"

About the blood and all that. It was not very consistent.

She was sitting there in front of the mirror staring into her own wide eyes with an expression of silent panic. Then she gave a long trembling sigh and shook herself awake from the momentary trance, turning away toward the door of the cabin with the air of someone leaving the condemned cell. And all that evening she hardly spoke; from time to time I caught her looking at me with an expression of inexpressible sadness. "What is it, Benedicta?" But she only shook her head and gave me a tremulous smile; and after the dance, when we reached the cabin, she tore off her coif and shook out her golden hair, turning upon me with a sudden air of agonized reproach, to cry: "O can't you see? It will change everything, everything."

That last night we lay side by side unsleeping, staring up into the darkness, our strange voyage almost over.

We stepped ashore in a mist of gray watered silk, to find the car waiting on the dockside. Someone had already been aboard to take charge of the luggage; we had nothing to do except to negotiate the gangplank and take refuge under the

black umbrella the chauffeur held for us. "Welcome back!"
We sat in the back of the car, hand in sympathetic hand, but
quite silent, watching the ghostly countryside whirl away
around us. Gusts of wind stirred the tall trees; heath molded
itself away into heath, dotted here and there by statuary of
soaked forest ponies. At last we came to the big house, which
seemed no longer full of people; but there were fires going
everywhere, and the muzzy smell of old-fashioned central
heating filled the air. A lunch table had been laid for us. It
was a queer sensation to be on land again; I still felt the sea
rocking in my semicircular canals. Baynes was there to greet
us with his air of lugubrious kindness; he had mixed one of
his excellent cocktails, Benedicta took hers upstairs for a
while. I heard the telephone ring, and saw Baynes switch the
extension lever sideways so that it would sound on the first
floor landing, I heard Benedicta speaking, her voice sharp
and animated. When she came down she was all smiles. "It
was Julian. He sends his love to us. He says that you'll have a
pleasant surprise when you next visit the office. We've had a
big success with your first two devices."

That afternoon I motored up to London to my by now
unfamiliar desk, to be greeted with good news that Julian
had promised me. Congreve and Nathan brought me the
whole dossier, including all the advertising and promotion.
"It's a landslide, Charlock," said Congreve happily, washing
his hands with invisible soap. "You sit tight and watch your
royalty scale; there seems to be no ceiling—the German and
American figures aren't even complete and look at sales."

All this was extremely gratifying. But at the back of the
dossier was another folder somewhat cryptically labeled "Dr.
Marchant's adaptation of the filament to gunsighting."
Neither Congreve nor Nathan could enlighten me as to the
meaning of it. When they left me I picked up the phone and
asked the switchboard to try and unearth Julian for me; this
took some time, and when at last I did locate him his voice
sounded a good way off, as if he were speaking from the
depths of the country, I cut short his conventional greetings

and congratulations and at once broached the subject of the dossier. Julian said: "Yes, I was meaning to talk to you about it. Marchant runs our electrical side down at Slough. You may have met him, I don't know. But when we were going into production he at once seized upon your device and applied it to something he himself was working on—a vastly improved gunsighting system. It looks very promising indeed; the Services are most excited by it. We have not moved properly into prototype as yet, but in a month or two we'll have a trial shoot with the Army and see what we've got. I don't need to emphasize the importance of the contracts we might get; and of course your patent is fully protected. It would mean a terrific jump in your royalties. I hope you are pleased."

My silence must have disabused him of the idea, because he repeated the last phrase somewhat more anxiously and went on: "Of course I should perhaps have consulted you—but then you were somewhere on the high seas and Marchant was eager to get going with this infrared electrical device." His voice trailed lethargically away. "I feel," I said, "as though my invention has been wrenched out of my hands." It was marvelous the way he managed to convey the notion of a sympathetic smile over the phone, the kindly touch upon the elbow. "O don't take it like that, Charlock. It isn't the case. It's your device differently applied, that is all."

"Nevertheless," I said stubbornly, spectacles on nose. "Nevertheless, Julian." He clicked his tongue sympathetically and went on with redoubled suavity. "Please accept my humblest apologies; I should have asked. But now the damage is done, so please forgive me, won't you?"

There was in fact nothing to be done but bow to it. "Where is Marchant?" I said. "He is on his way up to you now," said Julian, his voice suddenly fading into a thicket of scratchy interruptions. There was a click and we were cut off. I looked up to find Marchant standing before my desk with the air of an aggrieved collie, tousle-haired and shortsighted behind steel-rimmed spectacles of a powerful magnification, basted with insulation tape. He held out a long limp hand with fingers heavily stained by nicotine and acid. "It's me," he said in his whining disagreeable voice, without removing the wet fag end from his lower lip. "Of course we've met." "Sit down," I said with as much cordiality as I could muster. His whole appearance spoke of the stinks labs of some provincial university—much-patched tweed coat and gray bags: extremely dirty and crumpled shirt with missing stud. He threw a bundle of drawings onto the desk and drew up a chair in order to explain them, pointing cautiously with a silver-hilted pencil. His tweed smelled of wet. I was disposed to adopt an attitude of somewhat boorish resentment toward him, but one glance at his papers showed me the marvelous elegance of his application; he had made full use of the new sodium-tipped contrivance and applied it, with slightly modified mountings, to the conventional sighting screen of a weapon. I listened to his lucid explanation with unwilling admiration. "But then weapons!" I could not help saying at last. "How disappointing. I was hoping my toys would help the human race, not . . . well, contribute to its quarrels." He looked me over, coolly, critically, and with some contempt. Then he lit a cigarette and said: "It's quite the opposite with me. I hate it. Anything I can do to make things harder for it I will, so help me." He exposed a row of uneven yellowish teeth in a ferine grin.

"Anyway," I said with unconcealed distaste, "I must congratulate you, I suppose."

"It's too early," he said. "Wait till we have our first shoot and see if this blindsighting device works out. Nor need you repine too much, Charlock; compared to some of the things the firm is working on, this is . . . why, virtually harmless." The little intercom panel below my desk lit up and buzzed. Nathan's quiet voice said: "Mr. Charlock, more good news. Mr. Pehlevi says to tell you that the mercury contract is secure; we can substantially reduce our price on the new costings."

Marchant was quietly wrapping up his plans and preparing to slide them back into the cardboard tube. His cigarette dangled from his lip. "Marchant, have you ever seen Julian

Pehlevi?" I asked curiously; I found I was addressing this question to more and more people these days. Very few could say yes—Nathan was one of the rare ones to have had the privilege. Marchant depressed his cheek in a grin and shook his head. "Can't say I have," he said. "He keeps in touch by phone."

He hovered for a moment, standing on one leg, as if everything had not been said on this particular topic. "I must say," I said with a laugh, "his damned elusiveness is getting me down—he's like some blasted ghost." Marchant scratched his nose. "Yet," he said, surprisingly, "he must exist somewhere— look at your paper today." There was a daily paper lying unopened in my in-tray. Marchant took it up and hunted for a moment before doubling it back at the financial page and handing it to me to read. Julian had made a speech to the Institute of Directors which was reported in full. "You see?" said Marchant. "Several hundred of those bloody directors must have listened to him for an hour yesterday."

Despite the long tally of successes on every front it was with a kind of subdued melancholy that I drove down to the country that evening. Benedicta had already gone to bed when I arrived. I went up and watched her sleeping by the rosy glow of the night-light, her breast rising and falling, her features relaxed by sleep into an expression of forlorn simplicity. It seemed to me that there were several thousand things I had to tell her, to ask her: yet they were locked up somewhere below the threshold of consciousness. I could not bring them out, rationalize them. What were they? I did not really know—but they swarmed and pullulated inside me like bees from some overturned hive. I watched her thus for a long moment, before turning away and moving silently toward the door. I had my hand upon the panel when I heard her voice say: "Felix." I turned, but she was still lying with her eyes shut fast. "You were watching me," she said.

"Yes."

"I have seen Nash and Wild. They think it is true, I am."

"Open your eyes."

"No."

Two tears welled slowly out from under the closed lids and ran down her aquiline nose. "Benedicta!" I said sharply. She sighed deeply. "But *you* said you wanted a child."

"I do. But I did not know it would be like this."

I dabbed her nose with my handkerchief and stopped to kiss her lips, but she writhed away on the pillow. "I can't bear to be touched, don't you see? Please don't touch me."

I realized in a confused sort of way that a whole new pattern of our relationship had come into being, ushered in by these words. "Go away. I must sleep now." Her tone might well have signified "I find everything about you repellent, disgusting." Her eyes were open now, and they said much that lips could not. In the hall I sat down in a chair and stared hard at the opposite wall, completely bemused and discountenanced. "It will pass, I suppose."

I had just finished dining that evening when I heard the sound of a car upon the gravel drive outside the house. It was Nash, whom I had seen only once or twice before—small, pursy and pink: he stood before the fire somewhat self-importantly, rocking slightly on his heels, and drank a whiskey. We spoke about Benedicta. "She often gets into states of mild confusion or hysteria—but this you probably know. There is nothing to be done, and as yet nothing to get unduly alarmed about. I've brought her a sleeping tablet or two; if you don't mind I'll go up and have a word with her in a minute. By the way, terrible thing about Caradoc."

"'What about Caradoc?"

"Haven't you seen the *Evening Standard?* Killed in an air crash. I couldn't believe my eyes." Caradoc killed! It was like a hammer blow in the center of the mind. Nash extracted a paper from his briefcase and made his way up the long staircase, shaking his head and muttering to himself.

CLOSE MISS AS AIRLINE CRASHES

Sydney

An Australian airliner reported a very close miss with an Eastern Overways DC-7 which crashed into the sea off Sydney yesterday afternoon. The Federal Aviation Press issued the transscript of an exchange between the plane and the control tower. The DC-7 was at 3,700 feet soon after takeoff while the airliner was coming in at 3,500 feet, although not quite at the same time. The transcript reading was as follows: "We had a close miss here. We are turning now to three six zero. Did you have another target in this same spot? About the time you turned over?"

"That's right, Southbound, affirmative. However not on my scope at the present time."

"Is he still on scope?" "No, sir."

"It looked like he's in the bay, then, because we saw him. He looked like he winged over to miss us and we tried to avoid him and we saw a bright flash about a minute later. He was well over the top of us, and it looked like he went into an absolute vertical turn and kept on rolling."

"Air Japan reports a big fire going out on the water. Route traffic control keeps asking where is Eastern six thirty-three. I don't scan him any more."

There were 40 passengers in the crashed aircraft but only four survivors, one seriously injured. So far twelve bodies have been recovered. Units of the Australian Navy are on the scene to lend aid. Among those listed as missing . . . *Professor Noel Caradoc*

The name swam out of the text with paralyzing force, holding me to my chair with my untouched drink beside me.

Nash came downstairs once more to reclaim his drink and to stand beside me in sympathetic silence for a long moment. "Wretched bad luck for us all," he said at last. "I shall miss the old bastard." Then he replenished his glass and turned back to the topic of the moment. "You know, Charlock, on reflection I think I did right; I told her as long as she felt like this she should go away quietly for a while; recover her good spirits in Zurich, say. Get away from you—what do you say? I'm not unduly alarmed, but she has after all a bit of a medical history—and as you know women often get strange and hysterical when they are going to have a child."

"But it isn't even absolutely certain is it?"

"No."

"And besides she doesn't need to keep the damned child if it's going to unbalance her, need she? I don't want to be responsible for her cracking up."

"She wouldn't dream of losing it."

"Are you sure?"

Nash sat down and smiled his sad and wrinkled little smile which was always so unexpected, and gave him a sudden simian expression.

"Yes."

"I am not so sure."

"Anyway, humor her for a while."

"Of course."

No alternative line of action seemed to commend itself; listless and apathetic I walked the little man to his car and watched the headlights wander away down the long leaf tunnel. I walked back slowly into the house, still preoccupied by the image of Caradoc's sudden disappearance from the land of the living. Suddenly the huge house seemed stuffy, confining. I took the paper and started upstairs to bed. On the turn of the second landing a sudden impulse made me look up. Benedicta was standing staring down at me with a queer feverish expression which made her pointed features look almost wolfish. She moistened her lips and said: "Has Nash gone?" I nodded. "And you don't mind if I go away for a bit?" I shook my head. "Thank God," she said with relief. She turned away and disappeared on the instant and I heard the rattle of the key turning in the lock of her door.

By the time I returned the next evening she was already gone, though she had left me a few tender words on a postcard, ending with the phrase: "Believe me, it won't be for long. And then happiness again."

FIVE

T he new life, which displaced the old with such abrupt-
ness, had a somewhat hollow flavor colored as it was by
apprehension about Benedicta's fate with its sudden reversal
of values. But Nash was kind and kept me in touch; she was
well, it seemed, and living in a small chalet in the grounds
of the Paulhaus near Zurich. She was always most composed
when she inhabited a snowscape—clouds, pines, snow—and by
now she had made up her mind about having the child, indeed seemed to welcome the idea. I wrote to her every week,
giving her an account of our doings, but the letters sounded
ominously hollow to my ear; the old scaffolding of such common intimacies and confidences as we had been able to build

was summarily removed. Subconsciously too I suppose I must have felt that the raw new building exposed, like an aborted piece of architecture, the slack and insubstantial nature of my loving. Yes, something of that order. Also it was somehow humiliating to feel myself replaced by a series of couriers who brought me news of her without ever having a direct message to retail. Julian too was kindness itself and phoned me regularly to demonstrate how close he was keeping in touch with events. The weeks deepened into months, and yet time appeared to have slowed up, to be almost standing still. I had left the country and moved back to the town house in order to be nearer to my work, but I went out very little. I knew hardly anyone in London; and during this period I saw most of Pulley, perhaps, for whom I had developed a great friendship—due in a queer sort of way to our joint misfortune in the loss of Caradoc. The Cham, far from being absent, seemed to go on growing as we sorted out his effects and grouped his papers into some sort of order against the forthcoming publication of whatever might be publishable in all this diverse mass. A great deal of scabrous verse, limericks and the like, were scattered about in his notebooks, and these we supposed would hardly be found suitable—though they afforded us great amusement and pleasure: almost as if he himself were present. Strangely enough, too, the putative publisher of the essays on the history of architecture turned out to be—I would never have guessed it—Vibart of all people. One day he strolled into my office, fit and brown and smiling, to grip my hand and, sinking into an armchair, announced that he was "saved." "Saved?" I echoed; the word had all the flavor of religious conversion. "And all due to you, Charlock Holmes," he said, waving his hat and lighting himself, sumptuously, a cigar. This was surprising indeed. "As they say in stories written for housemaids, I have *found* myself; I have left the F.O. thus avoiding a posting to Sofia and I am now— why here, let me give you my card."

"A publisher!" I said, peering at it. "How is this?"

"Jocas Pehlevi," he said with his shy grin-frown. "Some

while after you left he came to see me and said he knew all about my ambitions from you."

"But I never mentioned you to him."

"My dear chap, he could quote some of my conversations verbatim." Perhaps, then, I had recorded Vibart at some stage? My memory held no record of the event, but it is true that I usually made samples of everyone for my voice library —the five vowels, etc. (More of that anon.) Perhaps Jocas had helped himself? "Well I'll be damned."

"But he went further; he said that in his view I was no writer but that I would probably make a good publisher. Now as the firm owned half the Norwegian paper stock . . ."

"Does it? I didn't know, but nothing surprises me nowadays."

"It does. It does. He offered to set me up in business with a young Frenchman here in London. Presto! The first fifteen titles are on the stocks already—among them the stuff you are digging out by your friend whatsis name, Caradoc. Do you see?"

"With no strings attached?"

"The firm never attaches strings," said Vibart in a vibrant histrionic register. "Why should it?"

"You really surprise me. But I am glad."

He became very serious now, putting on his most humble and endearing expression as he puffed his cigar. "So am I. Glad? O Lord, it goes deeper than that. I really feel I am going to fulfill myself. It's really saved everything—you know my marriage was going steadily on the rocks because of my incessant whining? And I was getting more and more costive instead of less. My life was terribly abortive; and now look at me! Aren't I a wonderful figure of a man, a publisher? Large cigar, slight *embonpoint?*" He rose and spread the wings of his coat, rotating slowly before me like a mannequin showing off a dress. We both laughed, and I ordered up some sherry to celebrate this surprising resurrection from the dead. "So you see," he said, "I only dropped in to thank you, and to ask you in my official capacity when the manuscript will be ready for us."

"But I have all the material at home and we are still working on it; listen, you must dine with Pulley and myself and help us sort it—after all, it's your responsibility really, and there are decisions to be taken. Some of the stuff is characteristically comic, too."

A change. This meeting led to at least one or two delightfully congenial evenings in the Mount Street house, reading, sorting and reminiscing over this huge bundle of papers and notebooks. Moreover I was able to supplement much of this material by a series of recordings made at different times—yes, many of indifferent quality, but sufficiently clear for transcript. It was Caradoc alive who lumbered into the circle of firelight before our very eyes, growling and grumbling and perorating. Pulley at times had tears in his eyes, as much from laughter as from tears. "Pulley standing there like a cow, with his udders swollen out, needing to be milked of this abstract transcendental love of humanity—his religion of service. Eh, Pulley, damn you? Ethics not based on metaphysics —that's what it is." "Whee," answered the static.

> Deaf as a piecrust
> Smooth as a sage
> This old man is anyone's age.
> Younger than a schoolchild
> Older than a Norn
> This old man was to the manna born.

This must have been the Nube at some point; crisscrossed with mandolin whirs and tonic sol-fa and snicking of Saint Foutain's painted penis. Then a sudden shift of venue, the noise of a tavern with its clanging cans against butts and the whistle of wind in the trees. Here, rather surprisingly, Koepgen's voice raised angrily—one can well guess against whom. "But you become what you hate too much, you attract what you fear too much." A series of piercing whistles drowned an altercation.

So we listened while the Cham roared on, and Vibart made notes on a pad; we would obviously need to have most of this set down on paper, but the only problem was to find a blush-proof secretary capable of undertaking the task.

It was getting on for eleven when the doorbell rang; Baynes had gone to bed. On the doorstep stood the junior office messenger with a letter. It had come in that evening. I could recognize at once the handwriting of Benedicta—but it was mirror writing; another hand had drawn a line through it and readdressed the envelope to me at the office. I tipped the boy, and excusing myself went upstairs to the bathroom where I opened the letter and unearthed a shaving mirror in which to decipher it. "My son," it opened shakily, with the words thrice repeated. "It is so dark here, down here. The darkest of the three nights and the train has not come in. It goes very slowly when you are waiting but the eyes will always be the same, watching. We will compare notes later, unless I am too bored to exist. In that case good-bye. Julian knows how I feel."

I returned to the firelight, to the room from which all the gaiety seemed to have disappeared. "What is it?" said Pulley. "You look pale." "Bad omens," I said. "Let's have a drink."

It was late when we parted—but for me all the pleasure had gone out of the evening; a massive anxiety had replaced it, anchored in frustration—for there was clearly nothing to be done, to be said, to be acted upon. I grabbed at the chance to walk Vibart across London to his new flat in Red Lion Square for the sake of his company; and when finally we parted I pursued my own walk, erratic and unstudied and frequently turning back upon itself. Vague notions of finding somewhere open which might provide a coffee to drink; but it was either too late, or not early enough. On a hoarding in Oxford Street the post stickers had already begun to glue up the announcements of next week's film. On one hoarding there was half a poster already up, waiting for its twin to complete it, like the missing piece of a jigsaw puzzle; on it there was a girl dressed in black, but split neatly down the middle—half a face, one breast, one leg. It was Iolanthe—or rather so it seemed to me. I peered among the titles to see if her name was there among the credit lines. Yes, there it was, though it too was split in half; but its size indicated that she was a star of some consequence already. The dawn was swarming up now, wind-triggered, opalescent. A few people were out, walking with ghostly step and wearing cadaverous early-morning faces. A policeman eyed me speculatively as I stood, gaping at the poster; he was almost minded to move me on, but I saved him the trouble. I woke a sleeping taxi at the corner of Bond Street and made my torpid way home. The morning papers would bring the world the knowledge of her runaway marriage to the greatest box-office star in Hollywood. Reno. There was no such thing as a private life for her anymore. In *The Times* she looked radiant, but in the evening paper she was more suitably crying with emotion.

Some days later I received a phone call from Marchant to tell me that his new gunsight was ready to be proven. "All things being equal day after tomorrow, early, Salisbury Plain. Can I ride down with you? We'd better take a Thermos and something to chew. Oh, and you know what? Julian says he is coming, so at last you'll see him in the flesh." In the flesh! At last the promise of something to relieve the monotony of the passing days, something to pique my curiosity.

We set off together accordingly in the middle of the night —we were supposed to reach the proving grounds at seven. But as we neared our destination a thick fog began to settle over the world, and soon we were traveling at a snail's pace inside a frosty bowl of yellow light from the dashboard panel. Here and there a corner would lift and the chauffeur broke away and made a dash along the highway to gain ground before the thick white curtain closed again, submerging our powerful headlights in pools of whirling snowflakes. It was lucky there was no traffic at all to intensify our difficulty. Nevertheless we nearly ran into the little cluster of jeeps and staff cars which were waiting at the point of rendezvous. It was eerie to see the bustle of shapes and figures moving about upon this damp screen; the headlights yawned in the obscurity. The chauffeur was anxious about the plain, fearing he would get stuck in the mud; but Marchant was delighted. "What could be blinder than this?" he repeated. "The conditions are perfect." A tall figure emerged with startling suddenness from the veil around us; it was like a swimmer surfacing. "Brigadier Tanner?" called Marchant, and was relieved when the tall personage answered to the name. "I'm glad you've got here," he said. "I've detailed a staff car to guide. We're all set up on the side of that hill. . . ." He laughed in an exasperated way to find himself pointing into blankness. "The minister is coming down, I believe; God knows if he'll ever get here with this muck. How far along did you hit it?" We exchanged fog information in a listless way. It had turned quite cold of a sudden. Marchant had unearthed an old sheepskin coat which gave him more than ever the air of an unbrushed collie dog. We did not dare to wander too far from our car in case we lost it altogether. "Julian is with the minister," said Marchant. "But I don't propose to hang about; we'll get our shooting over and bugger off back to town after we've eaten, what do you say? They can come along anytime and talk to the Army."

At first the brigadier seemed rather reluctant to comply with this view but, when Marchant pointed out that the fog

◆◆ 245

might hold them a prisoner indefinitely and that they might never arrive, he took the point; he would leave a picket on the main road to guide them if they turned up. We were to follow his string of glowworms across the plain; there was no danger of mud, it was perfectly dry and safe.

We moved off in formation, our engines whimpering in bottom gear; the journey seemed endless at this pace. The scout cars had to stop frequently to reassure themselves that they were on the right path; the light carrier behind us was working on a compass bearing which did not square with that of the leading picket car. A conclave of shrouded figures exchanged grim pleasantries and grimmer oaths. "The bloody thing's demagnetized," suggested a cockney voice. Shrouded up like this against the dawn airs they looked like a group of Stone Age figures moving about in the whiteness, engaged on obscure tasks. Now and then a patch of curtain would lift, and the whole convoy would break into a canter, so to speak, for a hundred yards or so. It was getting lighter though; a kind of salmony tinge was beginning to run along the higher reaches of the whiteness—as if something were slowly bleeding to death in the upper sky. The variations in visibility gave human movements some of the quality to be seen in underwater swimming, or else in slow-motion film; the shifting depth of focus teased the eye and dazzled the mind. People seemed far away at one moment; the next they swam up in front of the car as if they had been fired by a cannon. The gradient had sharpened now and we were moving through patches of scrub; earth had changed to gravel on which our tires sizzled agreeably. The chauffeur grunted with relief. He did not believe the brigadier's tales about there being no mud. "You can never trust the Army, sir," he said to Marchant. "I was in it. I know." Marchant giggled and stumped out his nauseating cigarette, filling the car with acrid smoke. "So was I," he said.

At last they were there; suddenly and quite mysteriously materialized upon a lightly sloping hillock—the three tall weapons looking more like combine harvesters with snouts cocked at the sky. The gnomes that tended appeared first in a sort of tableau, leaning forward to identify us—in fear, I suppose, of being run down. Hoarse voices barked orders, answered one another; the brigadier reemerged from the nothingness and opened the door of the car. We followed him across the field to where soldiers in blankets now moved —but with the immortal listlessness of a typical apathy. The ground-glass tones of a sergeant major tried to stir them up with quaint oaths and elephantine jokes. But they moved like somnambulists. Marchant's toy was a clumsy great barrel organ of an instrument whose panels glowed with a whole spectrum of colored switches.

He lurched across to it with a welcoming gesture, arms open, almost as if it had been a girl; then he crouched over it with an overelaborated delicacy, touching now this part now that, manipulating switches, patting it and peering about him shortsightedly as if seeking some sort of reassurance from the sky. Watching him thus so vulnerably exposing the whole range of his naïve gestures, his anxiety, his frail hopes, I had a sudden pang of sympathy for him; and at the very same moment I was swept by a conviction that here was not simply a scientist, but a sort of genius. His whole waking mind moved among abstractions now, like a fish in its element. And I made an involuntary comparison with my own gifts— the mere tinkering with string and wire, the superficial meddlesomeness of the second-rate gift: and I realized that I would have given anything to be Marchant, to belong to his tribe. How trivial my string of elementary devices seemed to me as I took in the feverish engrossed state of my fellow inventor; the very skeletal posture seemed to have the pulse of a different sort of fever running through it—an electrical charge. "We'll have to modify the whole armature, of course," he said. "She's far too heavy. But first let's see if she works, eh?"

We were surrounded by more figures leaning down to tend these metal engines with the air of men carefully watering plants in a high window box. These were the flint arrow-heads of our wretched culture!

I could watch all this activity with a certain bemused detachment, since I could not interpret all these diverse movements; I was like an amateur at a ballet or a bullfight. All I knew was that these stubby snouts raised in sinister elevation against the lightening sky would spit out a momentary stab of flame. The brigadier was counting; he held something in his right hand attached to a long landline. His air was that of a doctor taking the pulse beat of a patient. A plane drowsed languidly overhead, established radio contact and moved off. More orders came harshly out of the mist and a thick snicking of oiled steel. Marchant produced a little box, such as airlines issue to their passengers, containing earplugs, and urged a couple on me. Then came another interminable wait before the shoot began.

When it came I was quite unprepared for it; a tremendous pulsebeat ran through the ground under our feet and ran swiftly away to the horizon in an accumulating wave. The snouts recoiled slowly, with great elegance, hissing, only to return and flame again briefly. Fire and recoil, fire and recoil. The nearest part of the mist had been blown to bleeding patches; there were tears everywhere in the fabric now, it hung down and swirled slowly about. Marchant knelt down staring at his barrel organ, hands over his ears, chattering to himself. A smear of sharp light illuminated a large-scale map over which hovered some disembodied moustaches. Then followed a silence during which a devout signaler communicated with the unseen through earphones, his box of tricks spluttering and crackling. I divested myself of my plugs and turned up my coat collar. Marchant was in a state of high elation. "It's going to be all right; the modifications are nothing," he repeated; he had grabbed the sleeve of the soldier who disengaged himself politely, his attention turned on his signalers. Again. There seemed to be a long moment of suspense now followed by a lot of jabbering in military argot. The brigadier shook hands with Marchant, and as he did so

248 ◆ ◆

an equestrian figure emerged slowly out of the mist on our left with a high degree of improbability and walked his tall horse over to the battery. "It's the general," said Tanner, and went over to give an account of his stewardship. "Well done," said the mounted figure in sepulchral tones. "You can wind it all up now. The minister has got stuck somewhere along the road, waiting for this fog to lift. We'll have to wait and see what he says. I expect he'll put it off until next week."

"Well, that's the lot," said Marchant. We climbed back into the car; he sat beside the chauffeur to take advantage of the light from the dashboard, for he had already resumed notebook and pencil in order to cover the pages with hieroglyphics and drawings. "Sorry," he said apologetically over his shoulder, "but unless I get things down they have a habit of disappearing."

The fog was thinning out quite perceptibly and once upon the gravel road the chauffeur professed to know his way; we were able to dismiss the single jeep which had been delegated to shepherd us back to the main road. It turned aside with a roar and bounced back into the obscurity, leaving us to our own devices. We pressed on slowly with the headlights ablaze; from time to time the chauffeur sounded his melancholy horn—a desolating croak like that of some solitary marsh bird. And then we found ourselves lost again; the gravel gave out and we were rolling softly along grass inclines. Marchant used a great deal of bad language, but added: "Thank God we brought some grub. This can't last forever. Let's press on a bit, eh? After all what is the worst that can happen? We might end up in Cornwall that's all."

"There's no mud yet, sir."

"Well, it's your fault for sending the Army back."

"I'm sorry, sir."

But even as we spoke a miracle started to take place; a wind started to flap from nowhere, lifting huge panels of fog almost bodily, rolling them back upon one another like so many strips of sodden newspaper. Huge rents and whorls and eddies began to appear all round us. In corners the white screen had begun to pour away like suds down a sink, to shiver and swirl like the dust devils of the desert. Huge slices of visibility were thrust upon us, and the sun started to shimmer through the opaqueness. It was like watching the scrambling retreat of an army. Even the terrain looked firm and promising; elated we moved into second gear and gave chase, squeezing down the soft inclines, farther and farther. "A compass, damn it; we should have borrowed one," said Marchant, but I was breathlessly watching the bewitching phosphorescence of the mist retreating from us. Larger and larger grew the spaces, until with a last sudden flick of the wrist a whole valley burst open to the view, radiant with sun and green grass on which glittered a million diamonds of condensing fog. The theatrical effect was vastly heightened by the fact that there, right before us, glowed the melancholy and enigmatic pillars of Stonehenge. Involuntarily we all three exclaimed. We were alone, surrounded by a good square mile of radiant sunlight. "Marvelous!" shouted Marchant. "We'll eat our grub here. Abandon ship, my lads." It was doubly lucky as the chauffeur could now reorient himself in relationship to the stone monuments—we had been traveling at right angles to the correct bearing. The fog was now vanishing with greater speed, restoring the whole landscape to us, stretch by stretch. So it was that in a state of high elation we took our provisions and devoured them among these mysterious blocks.

It was not unduly cold in this frail sunlight. Marchant fell upon the chicken and ham with ardor, speaking volubly as he chewed. "Well, it went off all right, Charlock, didn't it? The only fly in the ointment is that we didn't see Julian." He chuckled mischievously. "But I didn't expect to. I don't. I say, you are not much of a chemist, are you? I'm not being rude, I'm asking." I shook my head ruefully. Alas. "All the better stroke of genius that guess of yours—but I'm not sure that sodium is your answer; I'll see what I can do to improve on it. It's marvelous that you are not a jealous person."

"Alas, I am."

He gazed at me wide-eyed, his mouth full of cress.

"O Lord," he said in dismay. "I did hope not."

We sparred good-humoredly for a while as we ate and gulped the scalding coffee; the chauffeur maundered off among the ruins, still wounded in his *amour propre* by having mistaken his road. "As for Julian . . . well damn him. I don't *want* to meet him anymore." He chuckled. "As a matter of fact I once had the impression that I *had* met him—and I'm not given to fond fancies. But once he asked me to take some drawings up to his flat and leave them. When I arrived there was a singular-looking bird in the lift, very striking in a queer way. Deeply lined face, eyes like dead snails, medium to tall, dressed rather well in a stockbrokerish way, with a spotted bow tie. A brown signet ring. He was waiting for me in the lift. I tried to get him to speak, because then I would have recognized the voice, but he wouldn't. So I simply said: 'Second floor' and let him press the button. I addressed a question to him but he shook his head without speaking and gave me a sort of sad smile—a lost world of a smile. On the second I stepped out and up he went to the top floor. Well, I rang the bell, but the manservant was a hell of a while coming to open the door to me. All this time I could hear this chap just above me in the lift shaft—hear his breathing I mean and smell his cigar. He hadn't got out of the lift, he was just standing there waiting. Well, when my door opened and I was let in—while I was still standing in the hall having the front door closed behind me—I heard the lift coming down again. The servant said: 'You've missed Mr. Pehlevi by a few moments, sir. He's just gone out.' Well now, had I missed him? I wondered."

He laughed again with a schoolboyish elation. "I say, you aren't depressed, are you?"

"No." But really I was, depressed and confused. "As for Julian," he went on, "I've given him up, as I say. But it's curious how a little thing like his obstinate Trappist-like refusal to manifest himself gives rise to rumors. You can never trace the source, of course; it's always at secondhand.

But someone had heard that he was disfigured by lupus and was too ashamed to show up; another chap in the office had heard that Julian was going through a long and complicated piece of facial surgery. There may be something in that one. The Institute of Directors were addressed by a man who had a huge dressing across his forehead, and wore dark glasses. It's rum, I suppose, but I've got used to it. Strangest of all was Bolivar, a weird painter fellow; Julian bought some of his things for the firm. You may have seen them. Well, he claimed to have done a sort of composite portrait of him based on the evidence of those who said they had seen him— what they call an Identikit nowadays, I suppose. On the sly, of course. Bolivar was an awful drunk and lived on some repulsive cat food in a basement room in Campden Hill. He's dead now, poor chap; but during his last illness he rang me up and said that he was going to leave this portrait to me, and that I should find it in the drawer of the bureau in his room. I went round, but he was already delirious and the drawer was empty. I say, Charlock, cheer up. When a civilization has decided to bury its head in the sand what can we do but tickle its arse with a feather?" Marchant raised his pale and grubby finger and apostrophized the sages of antiquity. "O Aristotle, your civilization too was based on slavery and the debauching of minors."

It was almost noon before we piled back into the car to start the homeward journey, and by now almost the whole landscape had come back into sheer focus. The fog had banked up to the north and west but in our immediate vicinity visibility was virtually total. It was pleasant to feel the car at last able to slide up the scale into top gear, and to see the hedgerows sliding by. In the remote distance among the dangling coils of remaining mist moved an ant-line chain of Army cars crooning across the plains; but we had gathered momentum now, and our tires whirred upon the fine macadam. I settled myself in the back, wrapped my coat collar around my ears and fell into a doze. I do not know how long I was asleep, but when at last I woke it was with a start of surprise. We were in the middle of a forest moving in almost total darkness through a fog much heavier than the one we had experienced; moving, moreover, in a long slow string of main-road traffic, taillight to taillight, in a slow forlorn processional. "It's come back," said Marchant angrily. "It'll take us weeks to get back to London at this pace." So it would seem.

We were advancing slowly and circumspectly in measured distances; at some of the crossroads ghostly policemen walked up and down the lines with torches, keeping the files as free for movement as possible. There were long inexplicable halts, followed by short advances, and then new halts. It was on one of these halts that I suddenly saw, in the whiteness of our headlights, the number of the car in front of us; it was Julian's Rolls! We had drawn up almost touching his rear number plate. "My God, it's Julian!" I cried to Marchant. "He must have turned back." And before the matter could be discussed—indeed in quite spontaneous fashion—I opened our car door and lurched into the road. I ran up alongside the Rolls, calling out "Julian" and rapping with my knuckles on the glass of the side windows. But the whole car, like our own, was virtually misted up. Only the windscreen wipers kept a triangle of visibility open in front of the chauffeur. I tried to draw his attention, but he was watching the road ahead and did not appear to see me. I tried the rear glass again, shouting once more, and from inside a hand lowered it about an inch. A voice, not Julian's, said: "Who is it?" I wiped a circle of mist from the outside and said: "Is Mr. Pehlevi in there?"; and from the misty interior the voice— probably that of the minister—answered testily. "Yes, who wants him?" The glass was lowered slowly and I said, some- what foolishly: "Julian, it's Charlock." There were two fig- ures sunk in the dark depths of the limousine, and I could see the face of neither clearly. Just an etching of two black Homburg hats. "I was looking forward to meeting you at last," I went on naïvely. One hat turned to the other, as if waiting for it to take the cue and answer me; but Julian did not speak. I was still hanging there anxiously when there came a hooting of horns and the confused sound of traffic police shouting: "Move along there smartly, please." A torch flashed mothlike from somewhere near. "Julian!" I cried, I wailed. But the Rolls was moving forward now—the whole line sagged forward and peeled itself off softly into the obscurity. The window went up with a slap; I was forced to rejoin Marchant in our car, furious and disappointed. "It's his car all right," I said. "And he's in it. Next time we stop . . ." But we had reached a double crossroads with an island now, with slightly better visibility; the cars ahead were moving to left and right now, the file had thickened and started to disperse down the various lanes. By the time we came up to the faintly glowing beacons Julian's car had disappeared, and we were hard behind a charter bus, hemmed in on either side by small cars. A mournful hooting filled the air. Marchant laughed and slapped his knee. "I suppose you can't catch them," he said to the chauffeur, but the rejoinder was an obvious one. They could have slid away down any of four roads. Once again he had given us the slip.

Characteristically enough within the space of an hour the fog had dispersed again and we were racing away toward London in a fine clear rain. The chauffeur put on a turn of high speed in order to try and catch the Rolls if indeed it were traveling along the same road—the main London road. But strive as we might we overtook nothing that looked like it. Marchant found my disappointment rather comical, and once or twice I found him glancing at me with his cruel sidelong smile. When we arrived back at Mount Street he invited himself in for a bath and a drink; a flock of messages waited for us. Congratulations from the office, presumably on the strength of Marchant's success with the Army; a note from Pulley to say he would come in after dinner—some of Caradoc's drawings had been washed ashore. But most surprising and heartening, there was a short note from Benedicta which was both coherent and very tender, promising that everything would soon be over and that she would rejoin me. I rang up to tell Nash the news, only to find that he was very much *au courant*. "Yes, she's had a splendid period now, a complete change, and the outlook is excellent. By the way, she is convinced it will be a boy. Women usually get what they want, have you noticed?"

Marchant had his bath, though except for damp hair awkwardly combed back toward his ears one would hardly have guessed it. We joined each other for a drink by the fire; and he asked if he might play the piano for a moment before taking himself off. He attacked several of the more complicated preludes and fugues of "the 48" with great assurance, but with a total lack of sensibility, working at them like a woodpecker or a cobbler at his last. "Poor Bach!" I said. "I know," he said cheerfully, "I know." But he seemed to derive great enjoyment from this somewhat awkward operation; he wagged his head about as he played. When he stopped to light a cigarette I said: "You have never been married, have you, Marchant?" He looked at me slyly, his hands poised to resume playing. "Good Lord, what a question. No. Why?" I refilled his glass. "An idle question," I said. "I was wondering why not." "Why not?" he repeated, as if trying the question, so full of novelty, upon himself for the first time. "I've never felt the need. I doubt if real scientists ever do—the need for these charming articulated mummies. At least, I think we belong to a dispossessed tribe, all our affective life is passed in the head; and then, again, after forty you begin to feel out of date and out of sympathy. Do you care for this age particularly? I mean, once our hero was a Saint George doing in a dragon to free a damsel; but now our hero seems to be a spy doing in a damsel in order to escape the dragon. The genius of suspicion has entered the world, my boy. And then, what do you make of the faces of the young? As if they had smashed the lock on the great tuck box of sex only to find the contents had gone moldy. Sex should be like king's drinking, not piglets at teat."

"My goodness," I said, delighted. "You are an old-fashioned romantic, Marchant. I would never have guessed."

"I was once in love with a little female butcher, a pretty widow. But you know with all the handling of the meat her little paws had got the fat worked into them. White little plump mortuary fingers. When she touched me I could feel her handling those swinging carcasses. I was cured, but not before I had made some very valuable scientific observations on her. You know the pharmaceutical boys down at Lund's working on the firm's perfumes. I was able to turn out a cream for old Robinson which is second to none for rough or chapped skin. But I had to leave her all the same, the girl in question."

"A sad story."

"Perhaps; but it illustrates another extraordinary fact about this game. Your best discoveries are always accidental by-products of a search for something you never find; you set out to hunt something and presto, along comes something else, something quite unexpected. Did I tell you about our bottled sweat project—we call it that for a joke? It's still experimental which means nonexistent. It's interesting in a farcical sort of way. Toller works on perfumes, as you know; well, Nash came up with some Czech psychiatrist's notion that all perfumes contained a kind of built-in echo of human sweat, and that some types of sweat, male sweat, contained a sort of paralyzer which women could not resist—like cats with valerian. It was a complicated and wordy essay this, but it advanced the idea that the irresistibility of Don Juan was not due to looks or charm, but due to his smell. All Don Juan types are ugly and stunted, says this chap, who had run over a few psychoanalytically. But they all had a smell which spelled out danger. It sounded silly, of course, and the team busy making things for women's armpits got a hell of a laugh out of it. But Toller and I ruminated a bit; we started to do a leisurely survey of sweats, every kind of sweat: a woman with her period, an athlete after a race, sun sweat, fear sweat. You will hardly believe how much smell changes according to

256 ◆ ◆

circumstance, temperature and so on. For years we played about this notion; I can't say we were entirely serious. It was a by-product of the scent business. It was a rest and a change from worrying about what smell makes women irresistible; what, we asked ourselves, makes a man irresistible?

"The actual chemistry, the analysis, was fearfully complicated, a real challenge; we had to devise a sort of scent log. And for a long time we were at sea. We used what we knew of the rest of the scent range—from garlic to magnolia blossom. Then one day I had a glimmer; fundamentally women want to be raped I think, taken by force; things haven't changed much since the Stone Age. On the other hand, as the biological left hand of the partnership responsible to the tribe for childbearing, they had developed a heavy load of conscience about it. In order to really give in it had to be a fashion which unequivocally excused the lapse. In other words they had to be *frightened* almost to the point of insensibility before they could clear themselves with their own consciences. Our hypothetical Don Juan, then, had this paralyzing gift. He could scare them into surrender by his scent. All right, laugh; but sometimes these crazy ideas have a point. It was a sort of rape mixture we were after. Where to find a laboratory of smell? It suddenly occurred to me (do you know the smell of schizophrenes, of epileptics?) that all of the kingdom's top rapists are locked up in Broadmoor! Nash arranged for us to send in a small team to hunt around among them, and see what we could find. Well, after four years' work we have, very tentatively, isolated something which might break down into this vital secretion. Women beware! From the sweats of paranoiacs we have husbanded something which will permit your lasciviousness full play and your consciences rest! It has no name at the moment and the quantity is small; but we have put it out on test for a tryout."

"Do you mean you have a lot of London bobbies walking around smelling like goats and making women drivers turn dizzy at the wheel?" Marchant gave his characteristic giggle. "Of course not. They would never get near enough to do the damage; what I *have* got is a willing experimental team of fifteen provincial hairdressers, women, who have agreed to wear nothing but this stuff for six months. Now they are always bending over their clients. Moreover there is always fug to help things along. We shall see what effect if any that has. Might start a wave of Lesbianism in the blameless purlieus of Norwood or Finchley. Then we should feel our little extract was the real thing."

He banged down the piano lid and stood up, groping for his briefcase in order to produce a dirty handkerchief wherein to blow his nose. "I'd offer you some," he said, "but you wouldn't need it, being a married man of consequence and place." There was no hint of bitterness in his tone—it was simply a lighthearted sally: but to my surprise it stung me. Taken unawares by an overwhelming sense of futility and inadequacy I heard myself saying: "Yes. I am Mr. Benedicta Merlin, no less," in tones of savage irony. Marchant looked at me keenly and with a new sympathy. "I didn't mean anything by what I said," he told me apologetically, "truthfully."

"I know you didn't."

"Good."

I poured him a stirrup cup to show that there were no hard feelings. "Listen," I said, "I wonder if later on you would let me pick your brains a bit; indeed you might help me build it. When I've sorted out my library of voices—it will take ages. I wanted to build a sort of sound bank based on phonetics. I can already build up voices from a sort of sound bank—based on the vowel sounds. A sort of embryology of language. Just like Cuvier deducing his whole animal from one bone; sometime I'll get around to developing it, but I'd need help on the practical side—the electrical wave mechanics side. For the moment I'm snowed under with other projects."

"So am I. But of course I will."

"But this is something of my own, outside the firm. I wouldn't, for example, tell Julian about it."

He walked slowly toward the door, brooding. "I wonder,

Charlock," he said, "if you aren't under the same misapprehension as I was; I mean in imagining that he runs the firm. He doesn't, you know. He has to fight tooth and nail sometimes for his own ideas about how things should be done, and very often he is overruled by his own boards. No, nobody runs the firm, strictly speaking; it's a sort of snowball with its own momentum now, the bloody organization. I pity Julian, in fact; to be so powerful and at the same time so powerless."

"Truthfully I am beginning to dislike him," said I.

"Ah! the father figure," he said cryptically. "I think that's a waste of energy. You are in it now, you are part of it, rowing with the rest of us. Myself I would have got nowhere without the firm; they picked me out of a provincial university. I would have spent my life in a senior common room babbling about Rutherford forever had it not been for them. As it is I am marvelously free to give of my best; once they even gave me three years off to travel. No, Merlin's is a godsend—at least for me."

So might it have been for me, I thought, had I not made the mistake of marrying into it. Or was that really the reason? The whole problem of Benedicta rose like an overtoppling wave and engulfed me. I shook my head doubtfully. "Well," said Marchant shaking my hand "thanks for being decent; and count on me when you want anything."

I watched his slight figure disappearing down the street, with its queer slanting stride. The telephone was ringing. The telephone was ringing.

We always think that we are thinking one thought at a time because we have to put them down one under the other, in a linguistic order; this is an illusion, I suppose. Here I was talking to the office while my hands riffled the colored pages of a weekly magazine which dealt with Iolanthe's new conjugal life in a turreted Hollywood mansion bearing a fair resemblance to parts of "Cathay." Her swimming pool, her bedroom, the expensive scents, the loaded racks of clothes, the press cuttings, the emptiness of the mirror world. She herself looked pale and tired, clad in riding boots. Expression of a frail old-fashioned devotion which no longer had any place in our world, but which the screen still perpetuated as a herd echo. Her husband looked palatable and superficial. I wished her luck. O yes, I did.

Summer passes, autumn comes; and with it the news that Benedicta had produced the intentional man-child, who was to be called Mark. (I was not consulted on this point among others.) Shoals of telegrams like flying fish, cases of champagne. Moreover she was planning to return for Christmas. Nash pronounced her in excellent health, but advised me to make no move, to let her do things at her own rhythm. "It is maddening and worrying for you, I know that," he added with sympathy. "But it will come right, I am sure, with time." In the meantime there was only one thing to do—to become absorbed in my work, the classical response. My list of trophies mounted gradually, one success following another, but with an ease and rapidity which somehow had the hollowness of an illusion. Entangled in its coils I felt a sort of heartbreak as I found myself harking back nostalgically to the promises which the past had once sanctioned—Istanbul huddled among her veils of mist. All the more poignant because distance in time had cast all these events in the brilliant colors (memory-induced) of half-fictions. Small fragments broken from the bright screen of days passed with a different sort of Benedicta, a woman who might seem forever unreal to me now; naturally with fear comes misunderstanding, with anxiety the sense of separation, of drifting apart. Unless. Unless what? An outside chance of reversing the immortal process.

Hippolyta came to London somewhen about now to nurse a broken ankle. Sitting before the fire, crutches beside her, she was staring bitterly at the face of Iolanthe which adorned the cover of a glossy magazine. It was startling how much she had aged—perhaps the crutches by association made it seem so? No, there were great meshes of white at her temples. Crow's-feet, reading glasses and so on. Nor was she the only one, for "Charlock, you've changed," she cried: and breaking out, as if from a mask of witch hazel, her face flowered once more into that of the impetuous inquisitive Athenian. Yes, of course. I had been putting on weight, my hair was badly cut, lusterless and dandruffy, my suit unpressed. "Longer cigars, shorter wind." But we embraced until she winced from the pain of her leg. "Wiser! Sadder? Have you seen this new face?" She pointed ruefully at the star. ("The body dries up, the mind becomes toneless, the soul reverts to chrysalis; the only providing power lives on and on, independent of a dogmatic theology. The only thing that does not wear out is time." Thus Koepgen.) She smiled up at us like a mummy, and tapping her face with her glasses Hippo said, with the same downcast expression, "I get more and more jealous of less; she gets better and better, Felix. She is a real personage now. Have you seen her new film? I've come over for it specially. I shall choke with rage, but I must see it, I must see them all.

◆ ◆ 261

It's become an obsession. I hunt among her expressions for the traces of Graphos."

"Graphos!"

"Yes. And to think that all that time I didn't know that this common little fiend enjoyed the real thing."

She lit a cigarette with steady hands and blew a great plume of smoke like a denunciation. "And now he's dying slowly, out of reach of everybody. Nobody knows as yet, he is still active. But he knows." She poked up the fire with one of her crutches. I said "Graphos" on a sort of grace note. She smiled. "He explained it to me. You might say it was hate at first sight—the only form of love they could know; they had the same values, were both frustrated in the same affective field. But they did not have to *pretend* to each other. It lasted like that, for ages and ages. And, to my humiliation, I did not know. Does one ever? I rebuilt his career, poor moonstruck me." She used some very bad language in Greek; brief tears came into her eyes. "And now I am obsessed with her because of it. But never mind, she has made her mistakes, even though she now wears her sex like an expensive perfume. Aha, but the man *she* married creaks, *creaks*. I am glad. There is no joy to be got from *him*. It's malicious, but I can't help being pleased."

"No. That's not you, Hippo."

"It is. It is. And what galls me worse is that she is *articulate* now; I stole some of her letters to Graphos. You see how low one can sink? I can remember parts by heart, like where she says: 'As for me, having been in a sort of clinic of love, a captive when young, and forced by circumstance to take on everyone, young or old, I missed the whole point. My understanding remained unkindled. The sex act misses fire if there is no psychic click: a membrane has to be broken of which the hymen is only a parody, a mental hymen. Otherwise one can't understand, can't receive. So very few men can do this for a woman. You, Graphos, did this for me. Though I never could love you I'm grateful.' "

She banged her crutch on the floor and turned the journal over on its face, Io's face.

Well we dined there, by the fire, plate on knee; and there was a kind of luxury to talk about the past which for me had become prehistory--yellowing snapshots of the Acropolis or Byzantine Polis. After dinner Pulley and Vibart put in a short appearance, and though our talk gathered a superficial animation we could still feel the hangdog death of Caradoc looming over us. It was a deeply felt physical presence--not only because all his papers were stacked up there on the sideboard. It would only have increased the sense of constraint to have played out his voice upon my machines, so I did not try to. But there was news of Banubula who might be coming soon to London to have his prostate looked at. "In the morning he still retires to the lavatory for an hour with a churchwarden clay pipe and a bowl of soapy water. There he sits in silent rapture blowing huge iridescent bubbles and watching them float out over Athens. In harmony with himself. Only he still moans a good deal about not getting into Merlin's. Otherwise no change."

Vibart had just returned from a visit to Jocas who was also recuperating from a fall and a fractured hip. Picture of him bedridden before a huge fire taking castor oil out of an old-fashioned soup spoon; having his toenails trimmed for him by the eunuch. Almost mad with boredom, and unable to read, he had hit upon a solution—a model railway. His little trains ran all round the house, and around half the garden. Carried from point to point in a sedan, he passed his time agreeably in this fashion.

But at last talk lagged; Caradoc ached on like a bad tooth. The decanter was empty. They took their leave, reluctant to leave the evening unachieved, yet realizing they could not revive it. Hippo stayed on to gossip and meditate. "Will you come with me? I have located four other films in the provinces in which she plays. I am here for a week—all too short for London." I agreed, feeling curiously stirred by the idea; apart from the brief glimpse on board the vessel of love I had seen nothing of Iolanthe. She pressed my hand; we spoke of other things, and I mentioned the dead boy in Sipple's bed. Who was finally responsible, both for the deed and for hushing the matter up? She did not know; and I could sense that she was telling the truth. "Sipple had threatened to do it because the boy was going to blackmail him. Fifteen all. But later he said it was done while he was out. Thirty fifteen. Yes, it was a brother of Iolanthe, and her father, who was in Athens that weekend, had also threatened to punish the boy. Thirty all." She gave a little groan and patted her head. "There seem to be a hundred reasons to account for every act. Finally one hesitates to ascribe any one of them to the act. Life gets more and more mysterious, not less."

"I must say I thought that she herself might have . . ." I gazed in abstracted fashion at the doelike face of the world star. "I wonder if the firm knows."

"You must ask Julian."

Later, of course, I did. He said something like: "You know most questions become more macro or micro, more Copernican or Ptolemaic: they don't stay still, the pendulum is always on the move. They change as you watch. And always the answer proposed, particularly by an organization like the firm, is provisional, short-term. We have to accept that." There was an overwhelming sadness in his voice. I was so touched by his sadness that I almost had a lump in my throat.

"Questions and answers" she said with bitterness. "How should I explain you loving Benedicta Merlin?"

"Easy. It was like breathing in."

"And now?"

"Exactly. I am all confused."

She gave a cruel little laugh. "Ah wait," I said reproachfully. "It still goes, on my side."

"No woman can stand her," she said. "You know that."

Of course I knew that. It wasn't easy to explain the sort of mesmeric influence Benedicta exercised over her witless scientist. "A form of hysteria I suppose; in the Middle Ages it would have been classified as possession."

"They say that the firm has her regularly burgled in order to offset her tremendous expenditure against insurance!"

"Malice," I said.

"Very well, malice."

There was a ring at the door; I had ordered her a taxi, and now slowly and reluctantly I helped her hobble to it. She turned in the street and said: "Shall we tomorrow afternoon? Please."

"Of course we shall." She meant the film of Iolanthe. Away she rolled with a wave of a white glove and a tremulous smile.

All at once the house seemed very old and damnably musty, like some abandoned tomb which the grave robbers had not spared. I got out one of the firm's calendars—huge meretricious pictures of colonial landscapes—and marked off the days to Xmas. I supposed I should have to make some preparations to receive her. Or should I just leave it to chance, let her walk back naturally into the circle of our common life if you could call it that like one who had only left the room for a few moments? I wondered. I wondered.

But the pilgrimage to the shrines of the love goddess intervened among these preoccupations—poor Hippolyta's week of self-torture and admiration; riding to suburban cinemas in Finchley and Willesden where the sacred mask was being exhibited in a series of hieratic roles which, superposed at such speed one upon the other, and with such variety of age, situation, landscape, hypnotized me hardly less absolutely. Sitting in musty seats, inhaling dusty floors whose peanut shells crackled underfoot: in afternoon flea pits, holding the white glove of Hippo and watching, heart in mouth—well no, I couldn't any longer use the prop of her name as a memory aid. Iolanthe had slipped away, far beyond me now, out of sight of Number Seven, of Athens, the Nube. She brought to this new silver life a gravity, authority, distinction, even a tender mischievousness which bewitched; she had refined her potential for gesture and expression in some radical fashion. No. No. This creature I did not know at all. I whispered her name once or twice, but it raised no echo. And yet it was with real concern for her true self that I watched this mammoth distortion of Iolanthe into a world fetish. (Hippo gasping after some great scene, saying "marvelous," touched to the quick.) But my goodness, the responsibility she had taken upon herself was frightening. She lived by the terms of this mock art, lived a travesty of a life passed in public: as much a prisoner of her image as any of us to the firm. She couldn't walk down a street to post a letter unless she was disguised. I saw in the flash the sad trajectory of her new life, the life of a priestess, with a clarity that no further information could ever qualify. It was all there, so to speak. Even what she told me herself afterward added only detail—even the worst things, like having to dress up and "really act" when she wanted to be alone, out of the glare of the following press-men. For example, even to visit their securities in the bank vaults twice a year—a ritual the husband insisted upon: it lulled his sense of insecurity. Then about how one day the child gets locked in a safe, suffocated, brought out dead—all that stuff; and running down the street from the hospital in tears there comes a snap from a street photographer and a tendered card. "Your picture, lady?" He did not notice the tears under the dark glasses. Well and then pacing a long low-ceilinged room with her new camera-shy walk, so painfully learned from a ballerina, she says piteously: "Why should I not love this life, Felix? It's the only real life I have known."

Indeed. And then Hippo saying savagely: "If it were an art form she would be really great. Thank God it isn't. I should be even more angry."

"How can we know?"

"Why it's aimed at the mob."

"And?"

"And!"

Then later over repulsive tea and buttered toast in some small café she explained in more detail. "You see, the majority must always be denied the higher pleasures like art, etc. which in our age it feels entitled to. It's not a matter of privilege, my dear. Just as literacy doesn't confer the ability to really read—so biologically the many are unfitted for the rarest pleasures which are travestied by Iolanthe; lovemaking, art, theology, science—they each contain whole lives, silver lives, encapsulated in a form. They exist for the maker and his few subjects. She exists for everyone. When we speak of the destruction of an ethos or a civilization we are describing the effect on it of the mob discovery of it. The mob wants it, but it must be made palatable. Naturally the efficacy becomes diluted. There you have Iolanthe."

I was not sure at all about this. I had spilled butter on my tie. But inside I simply ached with vexation at never having met Iolanthe.

But there was no news until the day before Christmas when Nash rang up very chirpy. "Well, here she is at last," he said with his false-sounding heartiness. "All safe and sound."

Flowers! In my benign way I had always thought of her returning to Mount Street; but Nash dispelled the illusion. "No, she's in the country. She wants you to bring Baynes down to her if you will—you will go down this evening, won't you?" I said I would, though I had to disguise a distinct pique that Benedicta had neither bothered to inform me of her arrival before the event—nor telephoned me to tell me of her whereabouts. However I swallowed the toadlike thought as best I could, and went out to buy such presents as might be deemed suitable to the season. It was sleeting, the taxi driver was kindly garrulous; there was, as usual, nothing that I could give Benedicta, for she had everything—nothing, that is, of any real value or worth; things such as paintings or books would not have felt to her like presents. It was going to be an unbridled yuletide. The shops were all lighted up with a ghastly artificial array of colors and forms which signal the triumphs of commerce over religion. Loudspeakers everywhere were playing "Silent Night," pouring the spirit of the Christ child over everything with this amplified crooning of organs and xylophones: into the frosty streets with their purple-nosed crowds of milling hierophants, busy buying tokens of the miracle—poor pink-witted, tallow-scraping

Socialist mobs. It was cold. It was biting cold. I was angry. The latest jazz hit sawed at the frosty air, with its oft-repeated refrain:

She's as sweet as a tenderized steak
And I'll conquer the world for her sake.

In all this tremendous tintinnabulation Charlock walks, the "self-inflicted man" of Koepgen's fable, wondering what he might buy as an offering to the season. There's something wrong about a philosophy which doesn't offer the hope of certain happiness. Despite man's estate (tragic?) there should be at least a near-guarantee of happiness to be dug out of the air around us. In Selfridges the air hovered and lapped us, impregnated with the heat of our bodies and breath. Pressed in sardine fashion on all sides I let myself drift slowly down the carpeted streams. Our predispositions reveal themselves very accurately in our *mœurs*. Never mind. I bought some expensive gifts and had them elegantly wrapped; then swollen with these acquisitions waddled back to the doors like a woman at term, crushing up my paper as I went. The crowds milled and swirled. "Freed from the economic whip, we will not steer your bloody ship." Nor could I find another taxi. I had to walk almost all the way back to the office where the duty car was waiting for me. At Mount Street, Baynes was waiting; he had already packed for me. I looked around to see if anything had been overlooked, gasping a bit, like a goldfish fallen out of its bowl onto the carpet.

But by now, with the falling evening temperatures, everything had become stringently real—for heavy creamy snow was falling, showers of white inhaling the white lights of cars, fluttering like confetti from an invisible proscenium of heavenly darkness. Speed and visibility got into lock step; we slithered down Putney and away into the spectral ribbons of main road which led us ever deeper into what now slowly became an enchanted forest—a medieval illustration to Malory. To beguile the time I played over some prints of recent voices which were destined for my collection; it was strange to sit watching the snow while Marchant's somewhat squeaky voice . . . "The war, my boy, meant all things to all men; full employment, freedom from the wife and kids, a fictitious sense of purpose. Blame your neighbor for your own neurasthenia and punish him. It was all real, necessary and yet a phantom. The reason why everyone loved the war was simple: there was no time to think about the even more pressing problem namely: 'Why am I making a mess of my life?' I had had the time, but not the good sense. I threw myself into this delicious amnesia which only wholesale bloodspilling can give. Thirsty Gods! What hecatombs of oxen. Hurrah!"

It was late when we arrived, hush-hushing down the white avenues toward the strange house, where every light seemed to have been lit and left to burn on in tenantless rooms; who went round and turned off all those lights, and at what time? The lake had frozen iron-stiff and here a great fire of oak logs sparked and hissed in the center of it, near the island; several dozens of muffled figures skirred about it on skates. There was even a colored marquee with fairy lights where some were drinking steaming colored drinks—presumably hot lemonade, since it was past the drinking hour, and even considerations of Christian charity could not be expected to sway the habits of mind of lazy bureaucrats and publicans. Nevertheless it was a grateful and heartwarming scene in this desolate property to have a few villagers amusing themselves. From time to time would come a pistol crack from the ice, and a fissure would trace itself with soft rapidity, like someone running a stick of charcoal across the whiteness. Shrieks and laughter greeted these warnings. Baynes shook a sage head and muttered something like, "It's all very well, sir, but a few minutes' thaw and they'll all be in the drink."

The car drew up, the doors opened. The hall and all its galleries were hung with dusty bunting left over from other festivals; there were a few servants about, engaged on unobtrusive tasks, but not many. Yet from the light and the decorations you would have said that Benedicta expected a great company to descend on us. No such thing. Moreover she had gone up already. No glittering cars disgorging madonnas in evening gowns, no monocles glittering, no sheen of top hats.

I mounted heartbeat by heartbeat. The bed she lay in was like some fat state barge with its squat carved legs and damascened wings of curtain drawn back and secured with velvet cords. The light fell upon the book she was reading, and which she closed with a snap as I entered the room. The child lay in a yellow cot by the chimneypiece—a small indistinct pink bundle, thumb in mouth. We stared at each other for a long moment. Though her regard was sad, almost humble in its directness, I thought I could detect some new quality in it—a new remoteness? She was like some great traveler who had come back finally after many adventures—come back to find that his experiences overshadowed the present. Sitting at the foot of the bed I put my hand upon hers, wondering if she were ever going to speak, or whether we should just sit like this forever, gazing at each other. "The snow held us up," I said, and she nodded, still staring into my eyes with her sad abstracted eyes. She had made herself up carelessly that evening, and had not bothered to take the makeup off; the pale powdered face looked almost feverish in contrast to the thin scarlet mouth. "You know," she whispered at last, "it's like coming back from the dead. It's so fragile as yet—I hardly recognize the world. So tired." Then she took my hand and placed it upon her forehead saying: "But I am not feverish, am I?" She trembled as I embraced her softly and went on. "But you know there is something else to be got over now between us. It's very clear. How patient can you be?" She drew down her frowning brows over those wide-awake eyes and stared keenly, sternly at me. Then she pointed at the cot in the corner. "Have you seen?" To temper the ominous intensity of this monologue I crossed the room and stared dutifully at the child. She had turned sideways upon an elbow now, and her concentrated gaze held a strange hungry animal-like quality. She resumed her full voice to say—with a sort of dying fall: "He has come between us now, don't you see? Perhaps forever. I don't know. I love you. But the whole thing must be thought over from the very beginning."

Over and above the numbness I felt only a sudden rage; like a wild boar I could have turned to rend the world. Benedicta gave a sob, a single sob, and then all at once was smiling again: a smile disinterred from forgotten corners of our common past, full of loyalty and fearlessness. She shook two pellets out of a bottle. They tinkled into a shallow glass which she held out for me without a word. I filled it from the tap in the bathroom. She watched them froth and dissolve before drinking the mixture; then, putting down the glass, she said, "The main thing is that I am really back at last." A church bell began to toll from the nearby village, and the clock by the bed chirped. "I must feed it," she said—it seemed to me strange the use of "it." I turned away, muttering something about going downstairs to dine, and she crossed the room with a sudden purposeful swiftness to take up the child. I left her sitting cross-legged in the armchair by the bed, holding "it" to her breast, absorbed as a gypsy.

Downstairs the grizzled Baynes was waiting for me; he had organized my dinner, knocking up a couple of servants from the deeper recesses of the kitchens. I could see he was dying to question me about Benedicta but resisted the impulse like the perfectly trained servant he was. I settled down to this late repast with a sense of anticlimax, but to put a good countenance upon it all—the long solitary table I mean with its colored candlesticks, the absence of Benedicta—I made some rough notes for a speech I would soon be having to deliver to the Royal Society of Inventors.

Afterward I betook myself to the log fire in the hall; and while I was sitting there before it, half asleep, I heard the traditional cannonade upon the front-door knocker, followed by the shrill pipe of waits whose voices were raised quaveringly in a painful carol. It was a welcome diversion; I went to the front door and found a small group of village children standing in a snow-marked semicircle outside. Their leader held a Chinese lantern. They were like robins, pink-cheeked and rosy. Their infant breath poured out in frosty tresses as they sang. I sent Baynes hotfoot for drinks, cakes and biscuits, and when the first carol ended invited them into the warm hall with its big fire. It was bitterly cold outside, and they were glad to huddle about the blazing logs with small bluish fingers extended to the flame. The teeth of some were achatter. But the warm drinks and the sweet cakes soon restored them. I emptied my pockets of small change, pouring it into the woollen cap of their leader, a tough-looking peasant boy of about eleven: blond and blue-eyed. As a parting gesture they offered to sing a final carol right there in the hall and I agreed. They began a ragged but full-throated rendering of "God rest you merry, gentlemen." The house echoed marvelously; and it was only when they were halfway through the melody that I saw an unknown figure stalking in military fashion down the long staircase; a tall thin woman with gray hair, clad in a white dressing gown, which she clutched about her throat with long crooked fingers. Her narrow face was compressed about a mouth set in an expression of malevolent disapproval. "You will wake the child," she repeated in a deep voice. She came to a halt on the first landing. "Who are you?" I said. The waits came to a quavering halt in midbar. "The nurse, sir."

"What is your name?"

"Mrs. LaFour."

"Can you hear us upstairs?"

She turned back without a word and began to remount the staircase. There was nothing for it but to disband the carol singers and wish them good night.

When I reached my room sometime later it was to find pinned to my pillow one of Benedicta's visiting cards; but there was no message on it. I slept the sleep of utter exhaustion—the kind of sleep that comes only after a prolonged bout of tears; and when I woke next morning everything had changed once more—like the shift of key in a musical score. A new, or else an old, Benedicta was sitting on the foot of the bed, smiling at me. She was clad in her full riding outfit. Every trace of preoccupation had vanished from this smiling reposed face. "Come, shall we ride today? It's so beautiful." The change was breathtaking; for once it was she who leaned down to embrace me. "But of course."

"Don't be long; I'll wait for you downstairs."

I hurried to bathe and dress. Outside the country snow-scapes were bathed in a brilliant tranquil light. There was no trace of wind. Occasionally a tall tree let fall a huge package of whiteness which exploded prismatically on the roofs of the house. And now even the house itself seemed suddenly to have woken up, to be full of a purposeful animation. There was a servant actually humming at her dusting; the hall tables were piled with telegrams and packages. This was more like it. The horses were at the door sneezing white spume. Benedicta was giving some last-minute orders to Baynes about lunch. "Julian rang to wish us everything, and so did Nash," she cried happily as she pulled on the close-fitting felt hat with its brilliant jay's feather. She seemed to have restored, with a single smile, a hundred lost familiarities. It was hardly conceivable.

We set off briskly, swinging across the meadows in the snow; though we were upon the path of a traditional ride well known to us, the snow had baffled boundaries and we were forced to work from memorized contours, munching across this abstract whiteness into woods whose trees had become wedding cakes. And everywhere, as if developed mysteriously from a secret print, we could study the foot-marks, trace the movements, of animals which were normally invisible: cuneiform of hare and squirrel and field mouse scribbled into the snow carpet. A whole geodesy of the in-visible life which surrounded our own. The shallow ford was frozen, and I dismounted to lead my horse, but with her customary rashness she forced her own mount through, revel-ing in the crunching ice under its hooves. We rode westward toward the Anvil following the long intersecting rides formed naturally by the firebreaks, now outlined and demarcated clearly by the contrasting snow and forest. Once toward the top of the Anvil we turned along the down, and here the going became riskier. A rabbit warren could have spelled a heavy fall or a broken leg for a horse. But Benedicta defied sweet reason; she turned her flushed face to me and laughed aloud. "Nothing can happen to me anymore, now that I have told you the truth, how we must separate. You see, it has freed me to love you again. I am immune from dangers today. " And she set herself into a breakneck gallop across the white surface leaning ever closer into the drawn bow of her horse's neck. So we came at last without mishap to the little inn, the Compasses, whose clients, dazed by the bounty of this winter sun in a windless world, were standing about in the snow outside the tap room to drink their brown beer. We tethered at a convenient hitching post and joined them for a few moments to drink hot lime and rum. Benedicta's arm was through mine, pressing softly against me, as we leaned against the fence. "They put me in a huge canvas jacket like a burnous, with long sleeves to wrap around one; it was always when I wanted to write to you. I felt so safe in there. The canvas was heavy—you couldn't poke a needle through. I felt so safe, just like I feel today. Nothing can happen."

"When do we separate? Do you want to divorce me?"

She frowned and reflected for a long moment; then she shook her head. "Not divorce," she said. "I couldn't do that."

"Why?"

"It's hard to explain. I wouldn't like to lose you because of many reasons; the child must have a father, no? And then from the point of view of . . ." She stopped just in time; perhaps she caught a glimpse of the expression on my face. If she was about to say "the firm," it would have been just enough to make me lose control of myself.

I replaced the glasses on the gnarled counter and paid for the drinks; we remounted and moved off, more slowly now, more soberly. Benedicta's eyes were on her own white hands holding the reins.

"If I stay here until spring you could come at weekends."

"I suppose so."

"It's only the sleeping business I can't manage; I'm still a little fragile, Felix. Ah but you understand everything—there isn't any need to explain to you. Come, let's gallop again." We broke once more into this breakneck pace, swerving down the long rides, hurling up petals of snow behind us. "I shall leave tomorrow," I called across the few feet which separated us—our laboring horses were neck and neck.

She turned her bright smiling face to me and nodded happily. "Now you understand I have confidence in myself. Tomorrow, then."

The city seemed exhausted and deserted by everyone, abandoned to the snow; not less the rows of empty offices in the Merlin Group's offices. The heating had been turned off or frozen and for a few days I had to content myself with an electric stove trained upon my feet. My secretaries were on leave, as were the servants in the Mount Street house. I had my meals at the club, often staying on as late as I could in the evening, spinning out time with a game of billiards. The late-night ring of footsteps on the iron-bound roads . . . But yes, Benedicta sometimes rang, full of afterthoughts and moribund solicitudes; one could feel the heavy ground swell of the resistances licking the sunken rocks—the steep seas of Nash's little pet, the unconscious. He at least was in town, in bed with a cold; I dined with him once or twice, taking care to admonish him when I did. "Theology is the last refuge of the scoundrel." I had read it somewhere among a friend's papers. I also spent some time on the Koepgen scribbles which yielded their linear B after prolonged scrutiny, thunderous aphoristic flights like: "A great work is a successfully communicated state of mind—*cosa mentale*" and "The poet is master of faculties not yet in his freehold possession—his gift is in trust. He is no didact but an enjoiner." Crumbs, I said to myself, crumbs! And we talk about nature as if we were not part of it. I could see the influence here and there of a writer called Pursewarden. Nor could I interest Master Nash very much in such lucubrations. "You see, my good Nash, reality is there all the time but we are not: our appearances are intermittent. The problem is how much can we swallow before closing time?"

O but it was a miserable period. . . . I lay choking among my frustrations. "I know it is miserable," said the great man. "But sudden swerves aside are part of the pattern. The recovery will go on steadily, you will see. Do nothing to alarm her."

> *All ye graceful midgets come*
> *Softly foot it bum to bum*

I suppose that in an abstracted sort of way I had begun to hate Benedicta! Even now the idea surprises me; indeed it may not be true. A form perhaps of inverted love, a famished ingrown vegetable love fostered by exhaustion and the sense of perpetual crisis. I had several beautiful photographs of her hugely enlarged and framed—for my bedroom at Mount Street as well as for the office. Thus I was able from time to time to rest a reflective eye upon that long grave face with its confederate eyes. Emotions that refused to maintain any stability of pattern.

I went down for several successive weekends, heart in mouth, briefcase in hand, soft hat on head—to be greeted by the new composed Benedicta; a quiet, kindly, slightly abstracted woman whom I vaguely recognized. All her thoughts were for the infant prawnlike Mark, a mere series of bone twigs as yet: but upon whose small thoughtful face I seemed already to see etched the first pull, so to speak, of the sparrow-chested intellectual he would doubtless become. They would send him to Winchester, he would be filled with notions, learn to control his emotions as well as his motions, become a scholar. . . . It was desirable, desirable. Later he could help me on lasers. Dear Mark, Matthew, Luke, John, bless the bed that I lie on. We sat on either side of the fire with the cot between us, discussing neutral topics like elderly folk sunning away a retirement. Benedicta. In the emptiness of my skull I howled the name until the echoes deafened me; but nothing came out of my mouth. It was almost with relief that I returned to my papers of a Monday—to the flat in Mount Street where Vibart and Pulley at least were visitors, where Marchant came to expatiate about the power of light to carry sound waves—the principle which I was afterward to adopt for Abel. A single laser beam, etc. He covered the grand piano in blue chalk formulae and I had to have it Frenchpolished again. But wait, there was one surprise.

Pulley came into my office on tiptoe, pale to the hairline with wild surmise. "Felix," he whispered, waving *The Times*, "unless you did it *he's still alive*."

For a moment I did not follow his drift; then I followed the shaking finger down the column of Personals until by godemiche, I struck . . . *a mnemon*. I read out in astonishment: *"Lazy dwarf with sponge cogs seeks place in animal factor's poem."* I gave a cry. "No, I didn't do it, Pulley. He must be *alive*." The word rushed about the room like a startled pigeon. Caradoc! But Pulley was speaking so fast now that he was spitting all over the place. "Not so loud!" he cried in anguish. "If it's true it means—O the silly fool—that he's escaped; yet how typical not to be able to resist . . . O Felix." His eyes filled with tears, he wrung his long soapy fingers together. "Why?" I cried, and he answered, "If Julian sees this—do you think Julian would ever let him go? No, he'd set to work to find him, to inveigle him back, the silly old bugger." I thought furiously. "Nonsense," I said, seeing the whole thing in a flash. "We could easily tell Julian . . ." And the phone started to ring. We looked at each other like schoolboys caught masturbating. Pulley went through an extraordinary contortion, pointing to the phone, then to his own lips as they spelled out a message in dumb show. I nodded. The same idea had come to me. I picked up the instrument.

Julian's quiet warm voice filled the earpiece; he spoke in a calm, thoughtful, amused tone. "I wondered if you had seen *The Times* as yet? It has one of those oddities of Caradoc's in it today."

"Yes," I said, "Pulley and I thought it up as a sort of obituary to an eccentric man." There was a long pause and then Julian yawned. "O well, then. That solves the problem. Naturally I was a bit puzzled." Pulley writhed. I said effusively. "O naturally."

"You see," said Julian dryly, "one can be sure of nothing these days. There were several survivors from the crash; we've heard no more about them. Our man on the spot was away. And then of course some of his papers *have* been washed up." I agreed to all this. "Well," he went on, his voice taking a sly tinge, "I only wanted to ask." He rang off. We sat on, Pulley and I, discussing this new development in hushed tones. It was not long before the phone rang again and Nathan asked if Pulley was with me, as Mr. P. wanted to talk to him. I ran my fingers across my throat and handed him the instrument. Pulley, all subservience, sibilated his information into it, the sweat starting on his forehead as he spoke. Then he put it down and stared thoughtfully at the blotter before him. "He's not convinced," he said hoarsely, "not at all. Wants me to fly out and get at the truth." Then he flew into a characteristic rage and banging the newspaper with his palm said: "And this bloody fool is probably sitting in a brothel in Sydney, thinking he's escaped from the firm. I ask you." He rippled with moral rage.

"You'll have to go."

"I shall have to, I suppose."

Go he did. I drove him up to the airport myself next morning grateful for a chance to escape from the office. Pulley was dressed as if for the Pole, his pink stoat's nose aquiver at the chance of having a holiday from an English winter. Dismay and uncertainty had replaced our original excitement, for inquiries had revealed that the mnemon had been posted in New York—perhaps before Caradoc had started on his journey. I watched with affection the gangling figure of Pulley traipsing across the tarmac, turning to give one awkward wave before climbing into the bowels of the aircraft. Outside the bar I saw Nash hanging about, waiting for an incoming flight, and we decided to have a coffee together. He looked at my face quizzically and said: "Things are not going too well as yet are they?" I made a face and briefly sketched an ape swinging from a chandelier. "Frankly, Nash, I have almost made up my mind to get a divorce. Nothing else will meet the case." Nash drew in his breath with a groan of dismay. "O Lord," he said, "I shouldn't do that. O no." Then he cheered up and added: "As a matter of fact I don't think you could even if you wanted. Felix be patient awhile."

Patient! But it was really my concern for Benedicta which kept me bound hand and foot. I drove back recklessly, half soliciting a crash—always the weak man's way out. But safely back once more I allowed the tranquil little lift to carry me upward to my office. My fervent secretary looked up and said: "Promotion has been ringing you every few minutes since I came in." Promotion department consisted of three exophthalmic old Etonians, who lived in a perpetual susurrus of private jokes, and an intrepid Bremen Jew called Baum who smoked cigars and looked freshly circumcised each morning. Between them they schemed up ways of marketing Merlin products. Baum's voice was deep and full of forceful enthusiasm: "You remember the idea of having the biggest Impressionist exhibition of all time at London Airport—sponsored by us?" Vaguely I did. I vaguely remembered the memorandum which began, "In our age nothing has proven itself so useful to merchandising as the genuine cultural product. Merlin's has found that nothing pays off so well in terms of publicity as the sponsoring of art exhibitions, cultural gatherings, *avante-garde* films." The latest of these ideas was to sponsor an Impressionist exhibition of mammoth dimensions at the air terminal—offsetting these cultural trivia with a huge display of Merlin products. "Well, yes, Baum, what about it?" Baum cleared his throat and said: "Well, guess who we've got to open it? I have the telegram of acceptance before me."

Iolanthe! It seemed extremely improbable. But, "her new film opens in London at the same time and she has agreed to come. Isn't it wonderful?"

It was indeed—a wonderful conjection of commercial and aesthetic interests. Buy a lawn mower while you sip your culture. "Good," I said. "Very good. Masterly." Baum crooned. "The entry will be free," he said. I waved my paws and barked like a chow. "What did you say, Charlock?" Woof, Woof. Iolanthe's new film was called *Simoun, the Diva*. Somewhere, down deep inside, a new and urgent irritation against Julian had begun to materialize. It had its point of departure in a chance aside of Benedicta's, when she said: "And Julian is in full agreement that he should go to Winchester." He was was he? I studied with savage attention that fluent hand which had engraved a few words upon a recent paper of mine. I tried the old graphologist's trick of tracing the writing with a dry nib, trying to feel my way into the personality of the writer; absent yet omnipresent, what sort of a man could this quiet voice represent? And did he simply regard me, like everyone else, as a sort of cat's-paw to be telephoned whenever he wished to issue an order? Why would he not meet me? It was insulting—or rather it would have been if everyone else had not been in the same boat. And yet . . . that voice could never tell a lie, one felt; it inspired the confidence of an oracle. Julian was good. I tried to brush aside my annoyance as a trivial and unworthy thing. Who knew what pains and sorrows Julian himself had had to endure? And where would I have been had it not been for his farsightedness? It was thanks to him that my professional career . . . Nevertheless it came over me by degrees—the idea that I might force the issue, actually waylay him. Face to face I could discuss Benedicta, and the issues which had grown up around us and were threatening my concentration on the tasks vital to the firm. Damn the firm!

When the office closed that evening I took a taxi to the

little square in which he lived—there was nothing secret about his address, it was in *Who's Who*. Sepulchral trees, a little snow. The Rolls and the liveried chauffeur at the door raised my hopes of finding him in; but I did not wait to ask the man, who sat stonily at the wheel with the heating purring. I took the lift to the second floor and rang twice. I was let in, already prepared to see Ali, the Turkish butler—a heavy torpid man with the head of a stag beetle; prepared too to hear the soft plosive jargon he talked, squeezing the words up into a cleft palate.

He was not sure about Julian's movements, and had received no instructions for the evening. I asked if I might wait awhile. I had already phoned Julian's club to ascertain whether he were dining there or not. There was a fair measure of probability that he might come back here, if only to change for dinner—suppose him to be invited out. It was not late.

I examined the fox's earth with the utmost attention, surprised to find how at home I felt in it. It was a sympathetic and unworldly place—a relatively modest bachelor flat with a fine library of classical and medieval books, opulently bound and tooled. A bright fire of coal burned in the grate. The three armchairs were dressed in brilliant scarlet velvet; on an inlaid card table with its oasis-green baize center stood a decanter, a pack of cards, a pipe, and a copy of the *Financial Times*. The tips of his slippers peeped out from under one of the chairs. A sage-looking black cat sat upon a low wicker stool gazing into the blaze. It hardly vouchsafed me a glance as I sat down. So this was where Julian lived! He would sit opposite me over there, in a scarlet chair, wearing slippers and cooling his mind with the arid abstractions of the world markets. Perhaps he even wore a skullcap? No, that would have spoiled everything. The cat yawned. "For all I know *you* might be Julian," I told it. It gave me a contemptuous glance and turned back to the fire.

A small upright piano gleamed in the far corner of the room. A bowl of fresh flowers stood upon it, together with some bundles of sheet music. The tall goose-necked alabaster lamps with red velvet shades made a pair, echoing and chiming with the red velvet chairs. Yes, it was atmospherically a delightful room; the good taste was unself-conscious and unemphatic. The pictures were few but choice. Everything hinted at a thoughtful and eclectic spirit. One felt that its owner was something of a scholar as well as a man of affairs.

So I sat, waiting for him, but he did not come. Time ran on. The servant brought me a cocktail. The fire burned on. The cat dozed. Then I noticed, standing on the little escritoire in the corner, a small framed photograph. It had been clipped from the *Illustrated London News,* and it depicted a group of people leaving St. Paul's after some national memorial service or other. The size of the screen was not very fine and the result was a somewhat vague photo; but I noticed Julian's name among those printed in the caption. At last a picture of him! I went carefully along the second row, name by name, until I came to the fifth figure. It gave me something of a start, for the picture was surely that of Jocas. Or so it seemed. I cleaned my spectacles, and taking up a magnifying glass which lay to hand I subjected it to a close and breathless scrutiny. "But it is Jocas!" I exclaimed aloud. It was damnably puzzling—there were the huge hands, even though the face was shaded by the brim of a hat. I found the servant standing behind me, gazing over my shoulder at the picture with an expressionless attention. "Is that really Mr. Julian?" I asked, and he turned a glossy and vacant eye upon me, as if he hardly understood. I repeated the question and he nodded slowly. "But surely it's his brother Mr. Jocas Pehlevi; there's some error."

He moved his tongue about in his mouth and pressed some air up into the cavity below his nostrils. He had never seen Jocas, he said; as far as he knew it was Julian all right. I was nonplussed. Of course it could have been a mistaken ascription, a journalistic error. "You are sure?" I said again, and he nodded expressionless as a totem. He shuffled off and left me staring at this singular picture. I finished my cocktail and set the glass down Then my eye caught sight of another small door in the farther wall. It was ajar. I pushed it open and took an inquisitive look into the tiny adjoining room to which it gave access. It was a little workroom, with an overflowing desk. But what surprised me was that on the farther wall, beautifully framed, was a gigantic picture of Iolanthe, an enlargement from her Greek film. She stood, looking down, hands gravely clasped, on the temple plinth of the Wingless Victory, with all Athens curving away under her to the sea. I had hardly time to take this all in before a clock struck somewhere. I was dying to explore further—I wanted to see the bedroom, have a look at the clothes in the wardrobe and so on. But the noise startled me in burglarish fashion; I turned, and then the telephone began to ring in the hall. I heard Ali answer it with his gasping and grunting delivery—he must be conveying the fact of my presence. And sure enough, he appeared in the door and beckoned me away from my investigations toward the phone. How familiar were the lazy precise kindly tones. "My dear Charlock, fancy you being there. What a disappointment for me." Sometimes it was Felix, sometimes Charlock. "It was another vain attempt to see you," I said lamely.

"My dear fellow." He spoke mildly and yet with a scruple of genuine pleasure in his tone—as if in some obscure way I had actually conferred a compliment on him by coming here unheralded. "It's the weirdest luck," he went on, and the dramatic pointing, so to speak, of his voice, suggested the presence of a cigar between his teeth. "To miss each other once again. Do you know, I had definitely planned to stay in this evening? Then at the last moment Cavendish rang up about an urgent decision which had to be taken about a merger up north—and dammit here I am at the airport, waiting for a plane." He laughed softly. "But is there anything urgent I can do?" So calm, so friendly, so serene did he sound that I felt all of a sudden guilty: as if I had tried to take an unfair advantage of him in hounding him down. My voice faltered in the instrument as I said, "I wanted to discuss

Benedicta with you, in very general terms of course." He coughed and said: "Oh that!" with an evident relief, as though the subject were already trivial, or else out of date. "But I know about all your difficulties from Nash—all of them! I was going to tell you how grateful I was—we all are—that you are treating these unfortunate matters with such patience and conscientiousness. It's heroic. And you have even put aside the notion of divorce for the present—for her sake. My dear chap, what can I say? We will make it up to you in any way we can. All our sympathies are with you."

In the scratchy background I could hear a voice from a loudspeaker intoning plane numbers—the faintest intonation of a muezzin from a tulip mosque. I could feel that he had half an ear cocked back, waiting for the flight number of his own plane.

"I wonder why you hide from me?" I said at last, with a sort of graceless aggressiveness. Julian gave his quiet surprised laugh; he sounded so fond, almost tender—as if mentally he had put his arm through mine, or around my shoulders. "My dear Felix," he said with loving reproachfulness. "Answer me," I said. "Go on."

"Above all you mustn't exaggerate," he said. "Once or twice I might have found it inconvenient, but for the most part it was sheer coincidence—like tonight for example."

"Would you have come home if you had known I was here?"

"It's too late to say. The fact remains that coincidence kept us apart tonight; how can I say what I *might* have felt? That would be hypothetical merely." I rapped my knuckles on the polished wood. "Verbiage," I said. "You wouldn't have come; perhaps even you *did* know and deliberately sidestepped me." He clicked his tongue in reproof.

"Come now," he said plaintively.

"No, I wouldn't put it past you; the thing is—*why?* I sometimes wonder what you can have weighing on your mind." He gave a small groan—a satirical small sound. "In the age of the detective story one could hardly do less. But I fear you are building up a house of cards. Just imagine me as real, awfully prosaic, but a trifle shy—almost to the point of eccentricity if you wish. Truthfully."

"No," I said. "It won't fit."

"Good Lord, why not?"

As I had been talking I had been sifting through the silver bowl which stood by the telephone, telling over the thick pile of white pasteboard invitations addressed to him—embassies and clubs, individuals and societies. I knew that an office secretary came down every morning from the firm to deal with his social correspondence. He had neatly annotated the top left-hand corner of each card in that beautiful secretary hand of his. On some he had written "Refuse pl" and on others "Accept pl."

"Not too shy," I said—feeling at the same time a trifle ashamed of myself for prowling around his private domain in this way—"not too shy to accept lunch at Buckingham Palace to meet the Persian Trade Mission." He gave another exasperated chuckle and said, without heat: "But, Charlock, for the firm's sake I have to, don't you see? I can't afford to do otherwise: besides an invitation from Buck House is really a command, you know that." Yes, I supposed that I knew that: and yet . . .

Come," he said in his coaxing, conciliatory tone, as if he were speaking to a child. "Have some confidence in me, in my good intentions toward you. I haven't failed you yet, have I? Have I?"

"Quite the contrary," I said, with very real despair.

"And you know how deeply we are all concerned about Benedicta. Believe me, you are not the only one to care for her. Jocas must have told you about this unhappy pattern which repeats itself, no? But it's intermittent, it never lasts for long. You should base your hopes on that, as we all do. As for our meeting—why, better luck to us both next time, that's all I can really say." I grunted. "Ah, there's my plane coming up." A vague burble of sound from a loudspeaker swelled up slowly behind his silence. "I must be off," he said, with a little sigh. "Will you tell Ali to dismiss the car? Thank you. Well, Felix, good-bye for now." A faint click, and we were once more cut off.

I went back to the fire to finish my drink and reflect upon the little picture in its silver frame. The cat had disappeared. I heard the manservant doing something in the kitchen. I sat in bemused fashion, staring into the fire, almost asleep now. Somehow, I thought, I must get a glimpse of Julian's hands, if only to slake my curiosity. At least he could not deny me that! It was strange to feel like a suppliant, like a beggar: and then suddenly again to be overcome by rage or remorse. The moment I heard his voice a wave of sympathy was elicited. I melted. It was baffling, this polarity of feelings—and I supposed, to adopt the formulae of Nash, that the whole thing was due to nervous strain, mental weariness which hovered about the central problem of Benedicta. The Victorian word was still the most expressive—brain fag. Where we cannot establish the etiology of a disease or of a course of human action—when, for example, the providing brain and the sustaining nerves are out of whack—we can always slap a clinical term on it, give it a name even if the name is meaningless.

I had drunk more than one cocktail from the silver canister before it occurred to me to look at the time; it was not as late as I'd thought. I set out to walk across London to Mount Street. A fresh tormenting wind blew, the parks rustled. In my mood of prevailing despondency I hardly noticed my feet covering the pavements of the capital, between the dark brown houses; slow and regular as breathing. And the half attention I could devote to the life around me cast a curious kind of glow about ordinary realities—making them seem disembodied. In Bond Street the back of a lorry blew down and out fell a hundred gilt chairs. They tumbled out like a river and gave the illusion of dancing with each other on the pavement before subsiding into eighteenth-century curtsies. They had obviously been bound for some embassy ballroom. Then later, in a narrow street, a woman dropped a big leather purse which exploded on the pavement scattering hundreds of halfpennies. Almost at once the passing crowd, like an ant file diverted, started to help her gather them up—they had rolled everywhere, even into the center of the street. Within the space of a breath everyone was transformed into a snail picker or mushroom gatherer. The woman stood looking vaguely around her, almost tearful, holding her bag open; one by one the kindly helpers filled it with the coin they had gathered. I stood and simply watched. Thence onward to the dry click of the key in the door, to the ministrations of silent servants, to my tapes and papers. We were still not finished with the Cham, thank goodness. "Modern architecture reflects the dirty vacuum of the suburban mind." Yes, but other voices had to be cleared off the track, vexatious and interfering voices—many of them unidentified; but some of these baffling irruptions were singular enough to be worth preserving One voice, for example, which said; "When Merlin was dying of GPI he had his Rolls brought out and sat by it in a wheelchair touching it, as if rubbing cold cream into its glossy velvet skin." Who on earth could that have been?

There remained such a lot to do—so many confusing diversions to be followed up or to be eliminated. In such a chaotic collection, spanning such a long period of time, the problem of ascription had become a formidable one. It was all right where I had captured a distinct voice saying a distinct thing— a voice made recognizable by its familiar timbre—like that of Caradoc. But what of the droning quotations which so frequently supervened; and sometimes even the background noises which gave substance and point to what had actually been recorded? My little dactyls worked loyally enough transcribing all they overheard, but with faulty transmission I was left often with huge sheaves of confusion—speeches one could not faithfully ascribe to one person or another. And yet many of them too good to tear up. It was like some mad accumulator building up its energies to supply a mnemonic museum. . . . Goodness, that was it. Somewhere in the midst of these studies, wallowing in this mountain of white paper, I had the idea which later led to the building up of Abel, the computer. It was only a germ, then, though in the succeeding months it began to take sharper form. The raw materials of phonology are relatively simple if reduced to an alphabet. But if the actual phoneme—so I thought in my muddled fashion—could be translated, by a conversion table, into vibration . . . why, poor Charlock, in terms of frequency, could sort out the authors of this voice fest and bring scientific order into chaos: not even chaos, just a misnumbering of the data? It was all horribly vague; I still had much to learn from Marchant of electronics. I might even go so far as to make people seem explicit simply by marking down the tonalities of their ordinary speech. Who knows? A new sort of interpretation of the human being in terms of his vocal chords?

At any rate anything would be better, however factitious, than to surrender all this equivocal but often amusing or instructive babble to the dustbin. We were making a beginning with Caradoc, and for a specific purpose. But even here the identification was becoming questionable. It was mixed up with other things—which might have been his—pronounced in other voices, or in different keys. It was in a way as if his personality (now dead) had begun to diffuse around its edges, become less distinct, less easy to grasp in terms of an individual psychology. He was entering into his own mythology now; and of course our own mistakes of ascription might completely falsify him by adding to his massive incunabula of obiter dicta examples of Koepgen or others. These were the irresolute ideas which crossed my mind as I plugged in and watched the little creature begin to sick out her pages for me onto the expensive carpet—a human ticker tape from the strong rooms of memory, of destiny.

To what degree is pattern arbitrary? Please help me, little faithful dactyl, with your pretty claws, please help me. I marked slowly and with as much conscientiousness as possible the voices that I knew, using a letter of the alphabet for such of my friends as I could. But often these cursed toys had been left running when I was not there. Both Caradoc and Iolanthe had been shown how to play with them. It was no wonder that there were so many puzzles to be sorted out.

Come, a drink, my boy, an abacus of the steeplejack
Winch me in a drink, contemporary moods your beanstalks
Gaff me a zebib, (K?) are the sky
Harpoon me a gin (C) (K?)

Poets; put your
sperm to work

his death is still fresh (?)
paint Ah do not touch
a mystic who likes his breakfast my balls have bells Wang Shu
in bed would you say? (?) while your balls have little
ad hoc bells, so ting-a-ling
cherished master as you pass
in your swansdown sampan
(C)

Fundamentally every woman
wants to give birth to an One lesson women teach is that
upper-class child, my dear. it is possible to be superb in
(H) mind without being at all
intelligent. (K)

Little gold ear-rings in the
shape of a guillotine, darling; Eros defused will save
they all wore them under the the human race. (K)
Terror. Look how pretty.
(B?) My ancestors, yogically untrained, died
through the eyes as they say; hence me,
look, a house, a museum, a brothel.
(?)

So the labyrinth of this intermittent record poured out of the little machine to spread themselves on the carpet, to be gathered and stacked like sheaves; later our three bent heads would try to puzzle them out, to listen to them played back, to dispute their authorship. And some which were only holes in sound. For example, simply a sweet long sigh—the unmistakable sigh of Iolanthe in my dark room. She must have had someone there while I was out? A door opens, a match scratches, someone sees the wooden pattens. Graphos' voice—

but in a whisper so that I cannot say for certain it is his: but certainly speaking Greek says, "These are your shoes, then?" The silence scratches on for an age; the bed creaks. Later came the equally unmistakable clank of the bath tap and the sound of running water. Yes, some of the scratched parts could themselves be human sighs, luxurious sighs to correspond with simple acts—a voice whispering "Ah" or else (I am not so sure) "Ah, mother." Such faulty transcription defies significance; some of those dreadful crepitations could be the sucking of a breast. My little instrument whirrs on transcribing nothing—nothing in darkness. This is one tape I shall be able to destroy without compunction. Iolanthe!

Sitting among the tall columns of blue cigar smoke I meditate on this broken record of a past which is still not too far away to be revived and recaptured; which can still be compared to itself for example—memory against records. Only the faults in human memory cause the doubt and distortion. Where neither memory nor machine is completely sure you often get this kind of tentative ascription on the page. Palimpsest.

after all nature is big-breasted
indiscreet, undiscriminating, ample, a spender . . . why not you?
why not you?

          (C or K)

Zoë Pithou
"the life of the jar"
think of it, for the mind
needs housing space

          (C)

I do not usually like the type
but if he is rich he must be
very nice   (H)

you talk of the prodigality
of nature; but the old bitch
in spite of those swollen dugs
is really lean as a bedrail,
all the superfluous fat is
melted off her in her war to
the knife with history.

          (C or K)

All change for Moribundia!
ah the beautiful anguish of change!

          (C?)

a dialogue in whispers, but
the transcription very faulty;
a few phrases, among them:

the present overtaking the   "But must he die—can't you make
past bit by bit and falsifying it   him disappear?"
all the time, breath by breath;
seeing it through the spectrum   O God what have I done?
of death one supposes.   (K)
                                                          (?)

such salient facts as self-trans-   Come in. Lock the door.
formation, the pursuit and identi-   (?)
fication of dead selves, the accom-
modation of the idea of death—   I don't know, I shall never
these are the capital preoccupations.   know.   (?)
All the rest is tinsel.   (K)

To wake up with a start at two o'clock in the morning,
surrounded by these growing hillocks of paper: to switch off
and crawl girning up to bed. Only to echo on, I fear, in the
dreams and fevers which crowded the skull of the happy
weed. Did I say happy? Ah, Charlock infelix—why ever did
you let your fancy stray along these unbeaten paths, lured by
the idea of razors which sharpen themselves as they cut, of an
electronic Braille vibrating through the sensitive fingertips of
blind men? All those hybrid voices filtering through my toys
afflicted their creator's sleep. A confused jumble of historical
echoes—for once dead everything sleeps in the same con-
tinuum: a historical reference from Pausanias or a remark by
a modern streetwalker—"a public mouth from which the
lipstick has been gnawed"; or a line here and there of poetic
aphorism—"poetry which modifies uncertainty awhile." Somewhere walking hand in hand with a girl among the great
stored stones of Delphi which seemed to yawn at post-Chris-
tian relics—the Goth of a yawn.

Or as in the film where the Parthenon by celluloid moonlight seems fashioned in a modern soap; and Io's face faceless
with the interior preoccupations of the silent stone women
with snail locks. Stone head with ring? "Once a cut lip which
kissing gave back salt and wine, pepper and loot." On airless
nights in the desert Benedicta and I climbed into cold
showers and then without drying took the car to ride over the

coiling dunes, to let the moon dry us out. "Death like hair, growing by inchmeal." Voice of Hippo: "Of course they are starving; the humble always have the biggest wombs." And then Julian's chop logic (*I must see his hands.*) I awake with a cry, the telephone is ringing; but by the time I reach it it has gone dead, the caller has rung off. Dozing off again I dream that I enter my office to find a loaded revolver lying on my blotter.

Nevertheless . . . I nearly had him next day at Crockford's; I had discovered that he often dropped in for a flutter. Indeed that very evening he had lost an impressive sum. But I was just too late; he had been spirited away by a phone call. There was still the butt of a cigar burning in the silver ashtray by an armchair. The manservant showed it to me as one might show someone the bones of a martyr. I watched the cynical smoke curling upward in the warm air. The tables were buzzing—all these people had seen him, he had been there standing shoulder to shoulder with them, or sitting smiling over a hand, really existing.

Then again I overheard a clerk telephoning some bookings to Nathan; Julian was going to Paris in the Golden Arrow. I noted the numbers of his reservation and with a light heart (and lighter head) I went into the Strand and, somewhat to my own surprise, bought an automatic with six cartridges. I must have looked vaguely furtive, like a monk buying a French letter. Nor was it anything to do with aggressive notion—rather those of self-defense. But the action puzzled me a little. I sat at my desk and cleaned it respectfully, waiting for the taxi which would take me to Victoria. But once again I was bedeviled by traffic holdups. I burst past the ticket collector and broke into a ragged gallop, for my train was sliding smoothly out of the station. Coach six. Coach six. I redoubled my efforts. A window seat, number twenty-six, about the middle. Panting, I glimpsed the six on the side of a dining car and drew level with it. But the machine had gathered speed now and I had to put on another spurt to gain

on the coveted carriage. Right down to the end of the platform I held it, gaining only inches.

Yes, I drew slowly abreast of Julian's seat, but just not
enough to see his face; *but I did see his hands!* They were not
the hands of Jocas, no. Very fine, small, white, Napoleonic
fingers, holding a cigar. The hands of a manipulative sur-
geon, intricate, subtle fingers; but no face, I could not reach
the face. I collapsed on a trolley at the end of the platform.
Strangely enough I felt elated and a little frightened, perhaps
even a shade triumphant. I had seen his hands, at any rate, or
rather one of them. I left the automatic in a litter bin outside
the station, burying it under some sodden newspapers. Its
existence in my pocket was a puzzle which would not yield to
analysis; yet once rid of it, the neuralgic pain between the
eyes abated. I went down for a shilling wash and brushup
for the sheer curiosity of examining my face in the mirror. I
looked amazingly well and quite handsome in any ugly way.

Yes, it was with a distinctly new feeling of relief that I
found my way back to the office, to the plush-carpeted cage
where I was surrounded with all the paraphernalia of the
creative life. (Some new protos had appeared: I pawed them
appreciatively.) The secretaries chirped in that white light
(which turned fair powdered skins to buckram), excited by
the quaint wheels and cogs. Quite suddenly I had lost all
interest in Julian, in his identity; my mind had put him
aside. I stood at the window, staring out at the beautiful
austerities of my winter London, wondering about the sym-
biosis of plants and jingling the change in my pockets. I jest
of course, for the backdrop of my consciousness was still
crammed with the ominous images of the country house
where Benedicta walked, with pale concentration, as if waiting for something to explode. She strained to listen to something which was just beyond the reach of human ears. She
might even say "Hush" in the middle of a conversation; and
once as I walked across the hall toward her I found her eyes
fixed upon something which was behind me, something
which advanced toward her as I did. She shrank away from

me; then, with an effort of will, shook her head as a swimmer does to clear the water from his eyes, and reemerged, smiling and normal and relieved.

Then one afternoon I arrived to find a long line of hearse-like buses drawn up outside the office, and the whole staff of Merlin's in a ferment. I thought at first it was a funeral; everyone was dressed up in their best black. Extraordinary characters whom I had never seen before in my life poured out the nooks and crannies of the building—all clad with sepulchral respectability; they represented the differing totem clans of our establishment—the accounts men like cassowaries, the legal men like warthogs or rhinos, the policy-makers like precious owls. Baum, superbly clad and ringed in a fashion which reminded one of a blue admiral flirting its wings, was busying himself with the organization of this tramping crowd, now rushing to the window to assure him-self that the hearses were being filled in an orderly manner, now marching up and down the corridors, tapping on doors and calling hoarsely: "Anybody there?" Clearly someone of national importance had turned up his toes. Baum caught sight of me and started: "You'll be late," he cried tapping his sideburns. "What the devil is it?" I cried, and the good Baum lowering his head to an invisible lectern uttered the re-proachful words: "The great Exhibition, Mr. Charlock. You mustn't miss that." I had completely forgotten about the affair. I could see Baum running a reproachful eye up and down my town clothes. "Come as you are," he said. "There won't be time to change now. I'll tell your chauffeur."

So I set off following this long cortege of apparent mourners across the star-prinkled snow-gashed London, jerked to a halt everywhere by traffic blocks (Baum gesticu-lating furiously), skidding in mush and viscid mud. Had it been a funeral cortege, whom would we have elected corpse? Fortunately there was a well-stocked cocktail bar in the car, and I reinforced my resolution with a couple of strong whiskies, filled now with a sense of resignation. By the time we reached the white billiard table of the airport the snow had thickened and dusk was falling. The white lights of cars crossed and recrossed caressing each other, as if making recognition signals as insects do with their antennae. Some mad draftsman had drawn black lines and parabolas everywhere on the whiteness, so that the whole place looked like some plausible but tentative geodetic diagram. We settled on the central building like a flock of starlings. But inside all was light and space and warm air.

The exhibition area was roped off by a silk ribbon. Everywhere stood policemen. Baum had told me that the insurance on the pictures was so huge that practically the whole CID would be needed to guard it. It was very well done, I suppose. The hessian walls with their treasures confronted a wall of equal length and height which contained specimens of Merlin's choicest products. I could not help chuckling—perhaps too loudly—and was quenched by the flashing eye of Baum. We clotted up in slow fashion to wait for our guests, milling slowly round, ill at ease. No drinks as yet, no smoking. Much pulling down of waistcoats, shooting of cuffs, adjustment of collars and ties. Some slid on the polished floors. I looked down at the notes my chauffeur had handed me to study a list of the guests. Everyone, literally everyone. Now through the swinging snow-silhouetted doors came the Lord Mayor of London, and the senior members of the diplomatic corps. Ye Gods!

And was that an illuminated address he held in scroll fashion upon his bosom? The police teemed like perspiration. Nor were the Worshipful Companies outdone by this social display—for here came the Fishmongers, Skinners, Cordwainers, Tanners, Logrollers, Straphangers, and God knows who else. All pink, all suitably embaubled, all determined to see justice done to the arts. As for the diplomats, they provided the overture, so to speak—so enormously complacent, so relaxed, so Luciferian in their elegance. They recognized each other in the crowd with little false starts of surprise and mock cries of astonishment. "Fancy meeting you . . ." They hugged each other with circumspection like actors who "when they embrace, hold each other's wigs in place." More snow and more lights. I gradually backed away into the crowd, found my way through a curtain into a small bar which was serving the ordinary passengers. Drink in hand I peeped out upon the dark superstitious horde. And Iolanthe? Well, rumors of her impending divorce were in all the papers together with moody pictures. I suppose it must be the same in all fashionable love affairs conducted in the public eye—when the attraction wears thin you are left with a heap of soapsuds and a film contract. The hum of the company rose up into the glass roofs as if from a hive of bees: or "as sharp-tongued scythes gossiping in the grass." I was feeling unsteady but secure. I yawned.

At last came a swirl of movement outside the great doors; six huge cars settled simultaneously, mothlike, spreading their wings. The police were all expectancy now. A brilliant star flash of pink light colored the whole scene—a desne brilliance which gave all our waiting eyes huge shadowed orbits. Cameras began to tattle; the smaller flash of light bulbs dotted this aurora borealis with harsh white smears. "There she is!" cried someone. "Where? Who? There! Who?"

The doors fell back and she advanced slowly in the center of a semicircle of businesslike-looking people, perhaps armed guards? A hundred times more beautiful, of course, and set in the pattern of dark-suited men like the corolla of some rare flower. The famous crescent-shaped smile. She walked slowly with soft and hesitant tread, as if unsure of her role, looking about her almost beseechingly. In a twinkling the foyer was brimming with uninvited lookers-on—passengers, desk employees, hairdressers, pilots . . . The police started to try and prevent this intrusion. The spacious hall diminished in size until they were all shoulder to shoulder.

Iolanthe advanced with all the shy majesty of a pantomime fairy, certain of her applause and yet still a little diffident about it—I mean the thunderous clapping which swelled up to the roofs. The huge wet false eyelashes set off her features to admiration, giving them shape and grace. Her dress was shot with some sort of bright rayon which made it seem lighted from within. O, she was wired for sense and sound—nor could she escape an expression of alembicated piety as she advanced toward the waiting dignitaries from whom she would unlock the mysteries of Monet, Manet, Pissaro. . . . And this was the girl who had once asked me what a Manet was. ("It says here that she bought a Manet—is it a sort of motorbike?") I hoped she would tell the mayor that it was a motorbike. Vaguely, in a shuffling manner, a line of reception was being formed. I was about to duck back into the bar when Baum appeared and caught me forcibly by the elbow and all but frog-marched me into this forming line, whispering, "Please, Mr. Charlock. Please," in an agony of supplication. I hadn't the moral courage to bolt; so found myself elbow to elbow with my fellow slaves in the direct line of march. I closed my eyes for a while to restore my composure and judge how much I might be swaying; but no, I was all right.

The radiance moved inexorably toward us in slow camera time. It was possible to see how really beautiful she had become—factitious beauty I don't doubt, but very real. The smooth skin had burst from its mask of egg white fresh as a chick. Smiling eyes and modeled nose. Moreover she accepted her presentations with a modest distinction which won one as she floated effortlessly down the long line of dignitaries. Kallipygos Io, acting the third caryatid for all she was worth. The cameras traversed lecherously across our numbed faces. I was tempted to close my eyes on the ostrich principle in the hope that she would not see me; but I saw the critical gaze of Baum upon me and refrained. The radiant light was upon me at last and here she was with beautifully manicured fingers extended toward me. "*Xaire*, Felix," she said, in a low amused voice, and the little sparks of mischief took possession of the centers of her eyes. Perhaps there was also something a little proudly tremulous there too—she was half pleased and half ashamed of all these trappings of success. I replied hesitantly and in a Pleistocene Age Greek to her greeting.

She depressed her cheeks in the faintest suggestion of the old grin and went on, low-voiced, looking about her to judge whether anyone in the line understood what she was saying. "I have been wanting to see you for some time past; I have much to tell you, to ask you." I nodded humbly and said, "Very well," which sounded stupid. I could see Baum swelling with pride, however, and this encouraged me to add, "As soon as you have time, as you wish." Iolanthe wrinkled her brow briefly and said: "Thank you. Quite soon now." Then she passed slowly along to where the mayor stood panting and mopping.

She made a speech, brief and wise, and obviously written for her; she did not mention motorbikes in it. Then with a huge pair of dressmaker's scissors she cut the ribbons. We all poured reverently into the Exhibition behind her. In the heat of battle the mayor had forgotten to deliver his reply to her speech; he stuffed it into his tailcoat and followed manfully. There was nothing further to keep me and I made my way back to the bar for another drink to wait upon her departure—for she might conceivably ask for me again and I didn't want to hurt Baum. Through the curtain I kept a sharpshooter's eye on the proceedings, so intently, indeed, that I hardly heeded a thump on the shoulder from behind. Then, spinning round, I found myself face to face with Mrs. Henniker. "My poy!" The last person in the world I was expecting to see! She extended a hand rough as a motoring glove and pumped mine violently; she spoke with untold vivacity. She had not changed by a day—but yes; to begin with she was dressed in country tweeds and natty brogues, a black pullover and pearls. Neatly smart. Her hair had been cut into roguish curls and dyed reddish. She smelled rather heavily of drink, and there was a slight vagueness of eye and speech which suggested—but this might have been sheer emotion at seeing me again. Her skin was rough and red and windblown. She was carrying several folders and a notebook. She moved up and down on her heels with triumphant delight. To my question about what she might be doing there she jerked her head in the direction of the Exhibition and said: "With her. I am Iolanthe's secretary." Then, draining her glass at a blow: "The minute she could she wired me to come to her. She has been a daughter to me, and I . . ." she broke off to order another round, "have been a mother to her." There was no suspecting the deep emotion with which she made me this confidence. "Well I'm damned," I said, and Mrs. Henniker gave a harsh cackle of laughter. "You see," she said with gleaming eye, raising her glass, "how strange life is?"

We had several more drinks on the strength of this, and it was only when the goddess was leaving that Mrs. Henniker jumped to her feet and exclaimed that duty called. "Can you come to Paris next week? She prefers to meet you there—because of Julian." I jumped. "Of course I can come to Paris." Mrs. H. shook her red wattles and said, "Good, then I'll get in touch with you with all the details. She will have to dress up, you know, and meet you in a cafe or something. I expect she'll explain everything to you. But she's mobbed wherever she goes. And there's no privacy in the apartment. I'll ring you. Ah, my poy, my poy."

I drove back to London with a certain pleasurable perplexity, in the company of Baum who was beside himself with joy at the great success. Full justice had been done both to the painters and also to those superior titillations of the thinking mind like the Merlin lawn mower. "You must have been very moved to see your work bang opposite the great masters," he said. "And she was so beautiful I felt quite afraid. Do you know she gets a million dollars for every film now? A million dollars!" His voice rose in a childish squark of amazement. "She was like a flower, Mr. Charlock." Yes, an open flower filled with synthetic dew. "A dedicated artist," went on Baum impressively. Indeed. Indeed. Full of the *feu sucré*. I was jealous of her success.

It is all very well to be flippant; the truth was that even from the glimpse I had had of the new Iolanthe I had gathered the impression of a maturity and self-possession which made me rather envious. She seemed to me to be very much her own woman leading a life a good deal more coherent than mine. And yet it had been a pretty good mess had it not? I picked up an evening paper at the corner and took it home to dinner, the better to study the pictures of her and of her husband; it was still in the rumor stage, of course, this impending separation, but it remained undenied, which gave it a certain flavor of validity. Well, all this was nothing to do with me. After dinner Julian rang up and startled me—I mean that I had almost forgotten his existence, and the fact of his voice resurrecting thus caused me a real surprise. He talked about the Exhibition, asked me if it had been a success and so on. I described as much of it as I could; and I had the impression that he positively drank in anything I might have to say about Iolanthe. He seemed to linger over anything concerned with her.

Then he modestly cleared his throat and said, almost humbly: "She was your mistress once, wasn't she?" I replied: "No, not this woman. That was quite another girl. She's completely changed, you know." Julian's voice sank a tone. "Yes, I know," he said, "I know." There was a long silence, then he said: "Has she asked to see you? Will you be meeting?" But, made cautious by long doubting, I replied: "No. We have nothing to say to each other now; I don't think there is any point." He grunted, and I could hear him light a match. "I see. By the way, I hear that Benedicta hasn't been too well this last week. Nash has gone down to see her." I supposed that meant some more deep sedation. I said nothing. Benedicta rose with my gorge until I was filled with a sensation of nausea.

"In the meantime," said Julian, "I want you to spend a few days in Paris." He gave me the details of some negotiations which were going on; I duly noted them down on my blotter. "Very well," I said. "Very well." And that was that; he sounded as if he were speaking from Dublin or Zurich. I returned to my fire and my cigar, full of a certain mild surmise. (To bow or not to bow, that is the question?) Before going to bed I sent a night letter to Mrs. Henniker, asking her to phone me at the office on the morrow.

But it was Iolanthe's voice which came over the wire, heavy with sleep. "Henniker is off today so I thought I'd ring you . . ." she began, and then switched into Greek, in order, I suppose, not to be understood by the casual switchboard operators. "I want to give you a number to ring when you come—I hope you do. I am here for another month at least. I'm so looking forward to it. When do you think you will come? Friday and Saturday I have free." So the appointment was made, aided and abetted by the chance which was to take me to Paris anyway. My spirits rose at the prospect of a short change from snowgirt London—even though it would mean lodging at the Diego which was owned by the company and where everything was free. I know. Everyone hates the Diego—its spaciousness confers an infernal anonymity upon its residents. But then I had some trivial details about patents to discuss: and this was the ideal place to discuss them, for it boasted of elegantly appointed conference rooms smelling of weary leather and Babylonian cigars. Threading and weaving about its great entrance halls with their flamboyant marquetry were grouped all the traditional denizens of the international world of affairs—Arab potentates with black retainers poring over maps of oil fields, gamesome little bankers from the USA moving on hinges, forgotten kings and queens, gangsters, revivalists and fleshy brokers. The never-stopping hum of critical conversations, anguished bids, political lucubrations, arguments, disagreements, hung heavy on the air. All this variegated business fauna pullulated. Diego buzzed with a million conflicting purposes, schemes and schisms.

I conducted my business with dispatch and moved into the fourteenth where I had once lodged as a youth; it was still there, the old Corneille, though it must have changed hands a hundred times since. Still the same high reputation for general seediness and defective plumbing; but modestly priced, and with rooms backing onto insanitary but romantic courtyards, and tree-tufted. Also there was my old room vacant. It was in reality Number Thirteen, but in deference to public superstition it had been renumbered Twelve A. The old telephones creaked and scratched, half transforming the melodious laugh of Iolanthe when at last I reached her. "Listen," she said, "you know my problem about being mobbed—she told you? I daren't show my face except over a cop's shoulder. And so I have to dress up a bit to enjoy any sort of privacy." She sounded however as if she enjoyed it. "And this apartment is useless; here I am watched." I groaned. "O God," I said, "not you too. Must we then meet heavily veiled or in false beards? And who watches you anyway?" I groaned again. "Julian!" I said with bitter certainty. She laughed very heartily. "Of course not. It's my husband." Out of the window Paris was in the grip of a magnificent early spring thaw, gutters running, trees leafing, birds loafing. The scent of pushing green in the parks, the last melted drops running from the penis of the stone Pan in the public gardens. "Well what, then?"

"I am going to act Solange," she said gaily.

"Solange?" I was startled. "What do you know about Solange?"

"Your little girl," she said. "Everything you told me about her has stayed in my memory like a photograph."

"I told you about Solange?" This was really surprising; Solange had been a little grisette with whom I had lived for one brief summer—actually part of the time here, in this room. But when could I have mentioned her to Iolanthe?

"You have forgotten," she said. "You told me all about her, making unfair comparisons with me. I remember being depressed. She was so this, she was so that. Besides I didn't realize that it was all Paris snobbery. In those days everyone simply had to have a love affair in Paris or risk being ridiculous. But I didn't know that—you took advantage of my ignorance. Nevertheless I listened carefully, always anxious to learn. And I have never forgotten Solange. And what is more, I shall prove it to you. At eleven-thirty. The Café

Argent isn't it?" As a matter of fact it used to be the Café Argent all right; then back here for those tender little maneuvers which by now I had so completely forgotten that I had to make a real effort to recapture the fleeting expressions on the white peaky face of my little Parisienne. "Good God," I said. It seemed an extraordinary thing to bring up; one never knows what lumber one has shed like this—lumber which has been preserved in somebody's memory. Tons of this detritus thrown off by a single life, flushed away one thinks: but no, someone has recorded it—sometimes a chance remark, sometimes a whole case history. "Very well," I said with resignation. "Come and act her then."

She did it to such good effect that for a moment I did not quite believe it—of course she could not look exactly like Solange: and there were quite a few young women sitting along the *terrasse* even at that time of day—laid up like trinkets in some peddler's tray. But then Solange! It was only when the waiter brought me a little slip of torn newspaper with a question mark on it, indicating the sender of the missive by a jerk of his head, that Solange burst out of the tomb and into that warm spring sunlight. Solange of the powder-blue skirt badly cut, the dove-gray shoes much worn, the yellowing mackintosh, color an uncut manuscript: cheap beads, crocodile handbag, mauve beret. Rising she came toward me with that heavily whitewashed face and over-made-up eye, with that flaunting yet diffident walk. (The diffident part was Iolanthe herself.) *"Je suis libre, Monsieur."* Among those shy students, Germans, Swiss and Americans, the little monotonous whining voice, the dire sadness covered by the deliberately pert smile. "Iolanthe," I exclaimed, "for goodness' sake—what next?" She burst into a characteristic peal of common laughter as she sank into the wicker chair beside mine, putting her handbag on the table between us. She clapped her hands to summon a waiter and demand a *coupe* in her marvelous tinfoil tones. "Go on," she said, "tell me I can't act. *The Times* says I can't act." But the brilliant impersonation of Solange held me spellbound. Of course she was wigged—brown bobbed hair with two points at her dimpled mouth. Certainly she would never be recognized like this. "You see?" she said, slipping her arm through mine as we sat. "So we can be free to talk. Tell me everything that has happened to you." I should have answered perhaps that while much seemed to have happened in fact catastrophically little had. Where to begin anyway? I tried my hand at a brief sketch of my fortunes; there was much that she already knew. She listened carefully, attentively, nodding from time to time as if what I said confirmed her own inward intuitions. "We are in the same boat," she said at last. "Both rich, celebrated and sick."

"Sick, Iolanthe?"

"In my case physically."

"And mine?"

"You've taken the wrong road—I knew you would even then: always in your cards I found it: and then yourself—you always saw real people as sort of illustrations to things—glandular secretions. I felt that you'd never get free, and then later when I heard you had joined Merlin's my heart went down and down. I know what it has cost me to free myself from them. I knew you'd never do it."

"Why should I?" I said sturdily. "It suits my book very well." She looked at me with dismay, bordering on disgust; and then her expression changed. She realized that I wasn't telling the whole truth. "Merlin's made me what I am," I said sententiously, feeling quite sick to hear myself talk such twaddle. Now she began to laugh. Ouf! It seemed as if the whole conversation were going to take a wrong turning. "Come, let's walk," I said. As we passed the Café Déme she insisted that I enter it to see if there was any message from Solange on the postboard. Sure enough there was, in typically bad French: she had had it planted by Mrs. Henniker. "This is going too far," I said with poor grace. "Now we better go back to the hotel and . . ." An expression of sadness came into her eyes for a moment and then was swallowed by her smile. Taking my arm once more she fell into step. So in leisurely fashion we crossed the park, quizzing the statues, talking in low voices now, inhabitants of different worlds. "And so you are free, as you call it? What does it mean to you, Iolanthe?"

"Everything; I just needed it. But it has cost me a great deal—in fact my company is hovering on the edge of bankruptcy all the time—thanks to Julian of course. He could not bear to see me free."

"Do you know Julian?"

"I saw him once—just a single look we exchanged, a look to last a lifetime. I knew then that he loved me—indeed in a perverse way all the more for crossing him, for breaking free. With my first money I set up my own firm, chose my own parts. Julian has tried to break us because—again perversely —his only way of getting me would be by owning me, having shares in me." She laughed, not bitterly but ruefully. "If you men didn't prey on women where would you be?" she added smiling. "But Julian's expression was so strange that I even tried to learn to draw in order to reproduce it."

"How did you meet?"

"We didn't; our audience research people said that there was one of my fans who was always there, never missed a single film, often saw them over and over again for weeks. They wanted to make a newspaper story of it; but the journalist was told by his proprietor that Julian had had the story stopped. Then they pointed him out to me at a fair."

For some reason I felt jealous of this.

Across the Luxembourg, the children's play-pit and so on slowly down, drawn by the inexorable strings of our Athenian memories. There was much to surprise me; it was like coming upon a bundle of letters one had read in cursory fashion and thrust aside into a cupboard corner—and now on rereading discovered to be full of things which had escaped notice. For example: "It puzzled me afterward very much to think how much I thought I loved you then. I did love you, but for singular reasons. Ultimately it was your lack of understanding which enabled you to occupy this place in my mind—your very indifference in a queer way. Since you could be objective, cool, and consequently *considerate*." (O dear, this is the mere vermiform appendix of love.)

"At times I thought you quite contemptible as a man, but I never wavered. You don't know, Felix, how little a woman hopes for in life—for an iron ration only: *consideration*. We haven't enough confidence in ourselves to believe that we could ever be loved—that would be butter and jam on the bread. But the bread itself? A woman can be won by simple consideration; she will settle for that when she is desperate. Look, you took my arm in the public street, though all Athens knew I was a street girl. You dared to be seen with me, opened doors for me. What chivalry, I thought! Everyone will believe us to be engaged. But of course later I realized that it had no special connotation for you—it was pure absentmindedness and ignorance of the mentality of small capitals." She laughed very merrily; I turned her friendly face round to embrace her, but she groaned with pain, and said her wounds were not yet healed. "You used to talk about going from the unproved to the proved in your work; but later I realized that with each new discovery the so-called proved is falsified. It collapses. The whole thing is only a funk-hole process—necessary because you are weak."

I didn't care about all this, inhaling the warm Jupiterian air, the leaves, the crunching passersby who walked as if upon a tilting deck, or else were dragged widdershins by huge dogs on heat. Intuition can become a conditioned reflex? "And then," she went on, "I heard what you'd done, and I crossed my fingers for you. I half believed that you might decide for independence one day like myself. But when I saw your face the other day I knew that you hadn't made a serious effort. You had the same funny stillborn look you always had; I was tempted to kiss you very hard, very triumphantly, simply because Julian was there in the crowd."

"Julian was there?"

"I *think* it was Julian."

I kicked some pebbles about for a moment wondering if I

shouldn't become angry. "I don't much like this sort of curtain lecture coming from you," I said at last, "with its boastful idea that you have done something very special; you who supply a surrogate mob culture with vulgarized versions of classics watered down by pissy-witted *cinéastes*. . . ." Iolanthe looked at me with delight. She said: "It isn't the point; even if it had only been a small dressmaker's shop in the Plaka instead of a film company. It means living without deceptions, awkward secrets, living in the round. The real freedom. *My own*."

I laughed contemptuously. "*Real* freedom?" She nodded briskly. "Inevitably you would ask yourself how real you were; you would think that it isn't just the firm which confers an illusory reality upon you. O I'm not saying the firm is anything but benign; it helps you toward what you want to do, to achieve."

"Then why all this Quaker-maid nonsense?"

"I've angered you," she said sadly. "Come let's talk about other things. You know Graphos is dying; now he would have been worth the love of some greathearted woman if his health had not spoiled his mind. It's typical of the cynicism of fate that he should imagine he loved me, and still does. And I like him too much to deny that he does. After all, he educated me, taught me to see—in spite of his perverse habits and tastes."

We had come to the doors of the old hotel; I took my key and we mounted slowly, arm in arm. She chuckled as she gazed round her. "It's typically your sort of room," she said. She went to the grimy window and stared out into the foliage. It was raining now, quite a storm of rain. "Do you remember the spoiled picnic on the Acropolis when the sky seemed to come down in whole panes of molten glass and our footsteps smoked on the marble?" She kicked off her shoes and lay down beside me, setting a pillow in the nape of her neck, lighting a cigarette. It needed only a lighted candle and an ikon. . . . Ikons, the portfolio of the collective sensibility. I imagined them as I dozed. ("There is no God and no plan: and once you accept that you can start to identify"?) She lay quietly with her eyes half shut. I had penetrated again the cardboard, the outer cerements of the worshiped mummy. Above all, one should not make a mythology out of one's longing.

My hand sought out hers and pressed it; we were half dozing, reconstituting, like archaeologists with every drawn breath, a past which had long since foundered. The arcane clicks and whistles of the little owls; mountains of gauche leaves blowing in the parks. The firm was like one of those great works of art which perish from overelaboration. ("The greatest happiness of the highest few is what nature aims at, the great aristocrat.") The white mice I have cut up, starved, tortured on behalf of science—as Marchant might say; some people one can only convince by drawing blood. I kissed the nape of her neck softly and lapsed into inertia, dozing by her side while she quietly talked on and on in sweet leaden tones. "It's a terrible thing to feel that one has come to the end of one's life experience—that there is nothing fundamentally new to look forward to: one must expect more and more combinations of the same sort of thing—the thing which has proved one a sort of failure. So then you start on the declining path, living a kind of posthumous life, your blood cool, your pulse steady." She pressed my finger to her slow calm pulse. "And yet it is just the fruitful point at which some big new understanding might jump out on you from behind the bushes and devour you like a lion." Small sighs, small silences, we were like people drugged; without any sexual stirring we had reverted to the prehistoric mode of an ancient intimacy.

"It's a sort of curse, you might say, for I've brought little comfort to anyone; and some I have gravely harmed. Not voluntarily, but simply because I was placed at an axis where all their lives intersected. That Hippolyta—I had to act to deceive her. And others, like that poor Sipple. Whenever I am in Polis I look him up as a sort of expiation, though we never mention my brother."

"What on earth about Sipple?"

She rose yawning and stretching to seat herself at the mirror; she took off her wig and began to comb it softly. "I thought you knew about that boy; he *was* my brother; I was obliged to kill him."

It was like a pistol shot fired in the quiet room. She turned round to me smiling, with an air of patient fidelity. "And poor Sipple has had to bear the odium. He is going blind, you know. He has become a perfume-taster. They dab those little flippers of his with scent and he tells them how to mix their perfumes. He is studying to be received into the Catholic Church, of all things."

"But why, Iolanthe? Why on earth?"

"That's the sad thing—in order not to let my father take it upon himself; he was a very rash, violent little man, and he had vowed to punish Dorcas. To the Virgin, you know. I knew that he would be obliged to do it, if only because of his vow. I could not let him go to the grave with that upon his conscience—a man of sixty-five. So I stepped in to shield him; and Graphos had it all hushed up. I suppose the idea of atonement is a lot of conceit really—who can say?"

"As arrows fit the wounds they make!" She crossed to the bed and placed a lighted cigarette between my lips; so we stayed silently smoking for a long while, staring at each other.

Then she began to speak of her father's death. He at least was unaware of what she had done for his sake. The scene rose so vividly before my eyes—the little house with its cobwebs, its table and three chairs before the fireplace. A dying peasant wrestling with a death by tetanus, closing up slowly like a jackknife. "Have you heard someone scream with their teeth firmly locked together—an inhuman screaming like a mad bear?" And stumbling, knocking over the furniture. He would not submit, fought death every inch of the way. And the rigor setting the body in such strange shapes. He was like a man wrestling with riding boots too small for him. And then the candles smoking; but even dead he wouldn't lie down. Up he came each time they pushed him down like a jack-in-the-box. The piercing lamentations of the villagers. But it was no go, he wouldn't fit. Finally the village butcher had to be summoned to break up his bones like a turkey in order to coffin him properly. But now there was sweat on Iolanthe's brow, and she was walking slowly up and down at the foot of the bed. They tied a ribbon, a green ribbon, round his arm before the barber bled him. There was so much blood in that withered old arm. "He wouldn't give in, you see." Then she paused and went on. "The little house is still there, it's mine, but I daren't go back. I left it just as it was, the key in the hole by the coping of the well—but you remember, don't you? If ever you go that way will you visit it and tell me about it? I'm sufficiently Greek to feel that I might return one day when I am much older—but how? Someone must exorcise it for me. Felix, if you did that I should be grateful. Will you?" She was so earnest and so beseeching that I said yes, in my futile way, yes I would. And of course now it's too late, as it always is.

"Meanwhile I am here," she said with a rueful bitterness, "the most beautiful woman in the world they say. O God."

She has gone such a long way away now, dissolved among the shadows of time; only her masks are preserved in the tin cans that crowd the lumber rooms of the bankrupt companies. Iolanthe now is an unidentified wave to sadness which reaches out for me whenever I see a slip of blue Greek sky, or a beautiful late evening breaking over the Plaka. And then the horror and sadness of the way in which she said "Look" in a voice of a frightened child; and ripping open the cheap bodice showed me the bandaged breasts plumped out with their surgical wadding, and taped like hot cross buns. "I haven't completely healed up as yet."

"Cancer?" I exclaimed; but she shook her head and replied: "Not yet at any rate. It's even more ironic. Last year in Hollywood they brought in a new treatment for falling breasts—injections of liquid paraffin. It was all the rage. But mine went wrong though I am not the only one, Felix."

She sat down at the mirror once more to adjust her

disguise, saying tonelessly: "Now I have brought you up to date." Subjects of calendar time trapped in the great capitals of the world. I let Iolanthe sink deep into my reveries; down she went and down like a plumb line, turning and rolling through the subaqueous worlds of memory and desire, dissolving and disappearing from view.

"Come," she said at last, "enough of these postmortems. I have ordered a hire car to wait for us at the office. Let us drive into the country together, have lunch, lie on the grass, forget, pretend."

"Forget," I said, and suddenly remembered Benedicta. "I must just ring the office and see if there is any news of Benedicta; she hasn't been very well of late."

"Benedicta," said Iolanthe. "They say that it is all because she drugs. I heard it ages ago and it may be true. Apparently Julian . . ."

I felt my scalp tingle with rage; it climbed my spine to burst in the center of my mind like a black bubble of fury. "I do not want to hear his name anymore," I said. "I implore you."

"Very well," she said calmly, and kissed me—the sort of kiss that might soothe a refractory child. I banged Number Thirteen shut behind us as we went downstairs.

We came back in the late evening, and she was careful to adjust her disguise before crossing the pavement to the glass doors of the apartment house. Outside lay the film company's Rolls, with the usual small knot of onlookers hanging about it. Its presence always signified that she was inside and might at any moment emerge to be driven somewhere. It was quite miraculous to see how swiftly the crowd gathered—people seemed to spring from the very pavements: she had only to leave the lift and appear in the soft red light at the end of the corridor for the ferment to begin. Autograph books would flash. It was necessary to clear a track for her. Then as she sat back in the car, noses would be pressed grotesquely against the windows; avidly the parched faces would inhale her, drink her up. But little Solange looked like some shabby dressmaker and not a head turned as she unlocked the tall doors and, once safe inside, blew me a kiss and rang for the lift.

I walked for half the night by the river which mirrored the opal-studded floors of the dark heaven powdered by stardust; cold, it was cold. The spring day had foundered back into a subzero night which made me glad of a heavy overcoat. I roamed the deserted bookstalls and the dark ships along the riverfront with a sense of confusion and loss; I should have been sobbing, I imagine, but what is one to do if the tears pour inwardly, if the amateur face expresses nothing? All that I deserved was some dirty unknown old woman with a gold tooth and shrunken thighs to drain my semen in an instant, pocket the money and scuttle downstairs again to her lamppost; but even this seemed merely an act of bravado, an attempt at a self-inflicted wound which hardly penetrated the thick carapace of my narcissism and self-regard. Smelling of dirty underlinen, rubber and sweat; nor could I assuage the thirsty hounds of introspection which were licking my bones. In a bookshop window I read a phrase from an open volume of Flaubert: *"On ne saura jamais ce qu'il a fallu etre triste pour entreprendre de ressusciter Carthage."* I read it over and over again; perhaps if I had had my wits about me I could also have become a master of corkscrew prose? I walked on and on until my legs would carry me no farther; then I took a taxi back to my musty room, to spend the rest of the night sleeplessly doing battle with the giant shapes of a nightmare which paralyzed my breathing and my will. My own groans woke me, and I remembered Benedicta saying: "But I suffer from daymares, Felix, *pavor diurnus,* as Nash calls it; it is harder to wake from them." (At midnight the quantity of carbon monoxide in the blood reaches its maximum.) As always when she was talking honestly one had the impression of truth barbed with a ferocious tenderness. Next morning I scribbled a note to Iolanthe promising to visit her again, and pleading that urgent business called me back to London. In some unanalyzable fashion our meeting had upset me, had knocked the props from under my self-esteem. It was hard as always to leave Paris—hard, grimy and metallic city where civilization is always dragging its anchor; harder still to face cold London with the sullen ferocious visages of the young half hidden by hair.

> *the big syringe*
> *the shrunken penis*
> *is all they offer now*
> *to Venus*

No, it won't do; deep in the penetralia of one's self-regard there was an arrow pointing toward something which had remained unrealized and unachieved—though how to formulate it without making a model I knew not. Nor should I let the calculated despair of this realization drive me toward any violent solutions—violence is for the weak. But then, Felix, it is precisely because of your weakness . . . Someone said once that Julian was obsessed, not with dying, but with rotting; he could not face the idea of that (was it Iolanthe or Koepgen?). Nor could he submit to having his entrails removed, his body embalmed. He hit upon the notion of having a steel, airtight coffin built for him by Gantry, the famous makers of office safes. I had one in my office which closed with a slight puff. A Gantry with an elaborate combination system whose code I am always forgetting.

High summer to autumn the year went by, its clock time not matching the slow accretive growth of the buried decisions I meditated; but they were so inchoate as to have to be disinterred, brushed clean, examined—dug up like the bones of dinosaurs. The flora and fauna belonging to such bones must be imagined, their world visualized. Externally nothing had outwardly changed. Life still held its unhurried glacier pace. Iolanthe wrote once or twice and I tried to answer, sitting before the blank paper for ages biting a pen. What I most needed to say would not rise to the nib. I gave up the struggle. Banubula, in search of female hormone I suppose, paid me a brief visit and for a few days carried me back to those remote unhurried epochs when we had both time and will to devise, to execute. Also the sacramental whiff of Polis and Athens. Jocas had been shot at by a eunuch and in returning the fire had killed the man; elaborate and exhausting litigation about restitution was still going on. Graphos was much worse; he spent all winter at the Paulhaus now, but the treatment availed him little. Hippo had "gone so white." Well, so had we in a way; both the count and I found our temples turning. I was sorry to see him go, in spite of his perpetual moaning about not being able to join the firm. ("But why on earth should you *want* to join it?" Banubula stroked his nose. "Well, because of you all; look at you, you are all so happy.")

Benedicta still lay at anchor, not noticeably better or worse; still hovering between white depression and sudden bursts of tender enthusiasm—attacks of almost total lucidity one might have called it. Yet always lying for half the day in the darkened rooms, blinds drawn, candles fuming. "I suddenly realized one day that real people had become shadows—without any substance as egos." It was well expressed, but I was tempted to answer, "Except Julian, I suppose?" Then self-reproach, of course, and bad dreams in which Julian sat by my bed, a small vampire-snouted man, staring at me with two live coals. I knew, of course, what all these women lacked —a tablespoon of fresh poet's sperm breathing salt air and seed into them. It can work wonders with a sensitive woman. What we all lacked, it seemed to me—and here I was mentally copying Koepgen with his ex cathedra judgments—was the mythological extension of human personality. I remember him saying, in front of a statue of the old king who went on sleeping with his dead wife for months: "And do you dare to imagine that there isn't a real historic personage buried underneath each mythological one?" It was all very well. I went to New York, to Rio, conferring my intellectual bounty on them in well-shaped discourses.

And then, quite unaccountably (or so it seemed, it was so

sudden) Pulley walked into the house in Mount Street one evening with an air of rare distraction. He had found the front door ajar, as I had been expecting Marchant to come and talk chemicals. A new cadaverous Pulley; without even greeting me he crossed the drawing room to the sideboard and poured himself a stiff whiskey and soda. "Well," I said. He looked at first blush as if he had been beaten up—his forehead was all blue and bruised; moreover his skin was yellow, as if he were just getting over an attack of jaundice. But no, he said, the bruises were due to a fall downstairs and the yellowness due to a bug he had picked up "out there" and for which he had been under treatment by Nash. "Just got back from Zurich this morning to find my digs in an awful mess." He sank into a chair sighing, and giving me a yawning grin with very little grin in it—a funny rictus really.

"Pulley, what have you been up to?"

He shivered a little and said: "They gave me drugs at the Paulhaus, drugs for bugs, old man. And now I don't know what I've told them, at all I don't. I can't remember. It worries me. Did I tell them the truth? I didn't mean to. Anyway, I'm not really sure it was him—Robinson."

"Wait a minute. Stop this babble. Who is Robinson? And where?"

"Sorry," he said with contrition. "Either it was Caradoc or it wasn't Caradoc, and it was only a glimpse. I was sure it was at first; then when I left I suddenly grew doubtful. Maybe it was Robinson after all, the old man. But I'll begin at the beginning. The smell of copra—do you know it? I can't get it out of my nose. Specially rotting copra mixed with a little oil and bilge. Day and night vomiting about in a little boat smelling of singed gym shoes. I'm not saying it isn't all very beautiful, it is: but I'd prefer to see postcards. The damp in those islands, my boy, the damp winds, damp clouds, steamy jungle. And the diet, chunks of pig and breadfruit inadequately cooked and very badly served on leaves. After about a month I'd had enough. Moreover I'd cleared the few survivors, visited them as from an airline insurance company.

There remained a man called Robinson, a defrocked clergyman they said, who had gone native and retired to a tiny little island miles from anywhere. He had been on the plane, or so the passport people said, and had crawled ashore and disappeared. Presumably he had gone back home again; but the last copra boat had gone ages since and the next wasn't due for a while, so I just had to cool my heels in Pyengo.

"A more godforsaken dump I never hope to see; and if the ladies are kind as they are reputed to be, it's all very well. Only you should smell the local cold cream they use on their bodies. That also takes getting used to. However there was sunshine, there was a sharkless lagoon, and the foodstuffs arrived wrapped in old *Times'*, so I made do with it until I could catch the boat for Robinson's little island. Apparently he had quite a tidy copra crop to be collected and some shells. So an occasional visit was on. Anyway there I stuck and waited, slowly getting athlete's foot in my armpits. Nor did such inquiries as I could make offer much hope. In fact the whole thing seemed a waste of time. I didn't sleep very well; the blasted trees make such a noise. Also they said the season would soon be breaking, and I had visions of being stuck altogether. However at last it came, the boat, and the skipper agreed to take me; but he emphasized that Robinson absolutely refused to allow people ashore on any terms whatsoever; the crew were allowed to ship the copra and clear off. There were signs tacked up everywhere saying: 'Strangers forbidden.' I said I would take a chance on it; but I didn't feel too elated as apparently Robinson had a gun and was quite likely to use it. He had once fired at a suffragan bishop who tried to come and draw him back into the fold.

"Well, one has to take risks; and after all that time waiting I felt I really should. The voyage was hell for smell, the sea was oily, everything appeared to be rotting all round us. Three days it took and at last we came to the tiny little island and drew into a rusty iron pier with a crooked crane. The ship tooted to tell Robinson that we had arrived but nobody answered, so the crew just swung off and began to load the copra which was lying around fairly neatly laid out for them; also several big boxes of seashells. I walked up and down for a bit in a hesitant manner, keeping my eyes skinned; but nobody appeared, and the skipper seemed to think that nobody would. It was often like that, he said. He pointed over the hill and said that the village was somewhere over there; and so I started to stroll in the direction he indicated. It was quite pretty and quite green with patches of cultivation here and there; I had been told that the total population of the island was about sixty souls—enough for the harvesting and all that. There was rather an exceptionally large hut standing some way outside the nearest village-shaped cluster and I went toward it, imagining it must be the chief's or Robinson's. All the way along I saw notices tacked to the trees saying: 'Strangers absolutely forbidden. Danger' which didn't sound too reassuring. However on I pressed. As I got nearer to the big hut I saw that there was an old man sitting on the steps, an old man with a mane of white hair. He started when he saw me and gave an inarticulate cry, as if of rage. I waved my hands in a peaceable and pleading manner, like a soldier waving a white flag of truce, and called out in English: 'Is Mr. Robinson here? I have only come for a moment to ask him a question.' My dear Charlock, that was absolutely all. My range was fairly extreme, but I did get a good look at him. He was simply covered in hair, beard to his waist, high-foreheaded sweep of mane backward, loincloth, and rough thonged slippers made of some bark or other. His eyes were small and bloodshot, and at this moment regarded me as a cornered and wounded wild boar might.

"Everything seemed to come together in a confused sort of focus—you know how it is in moments of excitement? And some of the things I saw in that few seconds I didn't take in until afterward, when I was on the run. For example that he had two small kids at his breasts, *he was giving them suck, old man.* I could even see some of the milk trickling down among the hairs on his breast, white as coconut milk. It seemed to me that it was Caradoc all right. I mean that at that precise moment it seemed so; later I lost confidence in my judgment. A woman appeared at an upper window, large and rather handsome, and clucked something at him. All this happened in a twinkling. I called his name once in an uncertain sort of way. Then he put down the kids and picked up a gun which was lying beside him and opened fire. A bunch of leaves from above my head fell with a crash on me. There was no time to argue; it was a near-miss. I took to my heels with the shells knocking up the stones all around me. Once I thought I had been hit, but it was gravel thrown up by the shots—but it hurt. It must have been a six-shot twelve-bore, for he sent all six whistling about my ears, some damn near. I cleared the brow of the hill with thumping heart and galloped down to the pier where they had just finished loading. I took refuge in the deckhouse until the ship drew anchor and set off. I feared he might follow me down to the harbor and take a potshot at me there.

"Well, this whole thing, sort of instant snapshot stuff, had a strange sort of effect on me. It wasn't just the unexpectedness, the fright and so on. I felt as if my mind had been, for one brief second, unfrozen; and even later when it went back into deep freeze again, the experience left something, a nagging something. I'm not much good at expressing these things. Later, of course, when I got very ill I had all sorts of feverish delusions about us all, about the firm. Julian had me flown back to Zurich where they could look after me. But God, the drugs were strong—I'm still woozy from them. And then that old fool, Caradoc or Robinson? Yes, but it *was* Caradoc. It is touching in a way—I saw how clumsily, how shakily he had tried to escape, to leave his body behind so to speak. Why on earth should he do it? The firm is everything to me; it's a livelihood, and a creative way of earning one. And yet, Felix, and yet . . ."

He gazed at me with sallow concentration from the fireplace, fingering the bruises on his forehead and sucking his teeth. "Another thing I didn't know I'd noticed until after we set sail was the sort of house he was living in there. It wasn't like most of the architecture of the place—it was canted upon piles. You don't remember, do you, how Caradoc used to talk about the theory of Sarasin that the proportions of the Parthenon corresponded in a way to the pile buildings in Celebes? He used to go on quite a lot about it, and often drew it in the sand for us. No, you've forgotten? Well, anyway, it's this sort of shape if I remember rightly." He took out a colored pencil and sketched in the following figure on the back of a newspaper.

No, I had never seen it before. "Ah, well," said Pulley with resignation. "That was what he had been building for himself. It would prove nothing to anyone else, but to someone who knew Caradoc it would be conclusive. You see, he just could not resist making mnemons and building houses. Try as he would. And he'll always be found out because of it." He paused for a while, finished his drink, and said, "I don't know whether I told them all this, I couldn't judge. All that Julian said when he was thanking me was, 'Well, the case is closed, then.' But did he mean it, that's the point? Ah! That's the point."

The case is closed. "I don't know," said Pulley. "Perhaps we should act out ourselves more." He strolled about fiddling with things on the tables and mantelpiece. "But I could never dream of trying to get out," he said sadly. "But in your case, Felix, I—"

"Me?" I said with some indignation. "Why pick on me?"

"I wasn't; but somehow I have always wondered about you—from way back at the beginning, I mean. Whether you really belonged here, with us."

"Well I'm damned," I said, and the surprise was genuine. It was suddenly borne in upon me that there must, after all, somewhere, be people who didn't belong to the firm. Pulley showed his huge teeth in an infantile grin. "You are one of the few people," he said, "one can honestly distrust in this outfit. I would confide anything in you, I think."

"And you feel I should get out somehow?"

"Oh, I didn't say that exactly. I don't know quite what I feel about anything anymore, I'm so damned tired after all this drugging. And I still occasionally get the weeps for nothing at all. So don't ask me leading questions. Besides, Felix, is there really *time* to worry? One minute you are fretting over your income tax, and the next you are staring up from the bottom of a pinewood coffin. Heavens, stay put, old boy, stay put."

"Stay put, you tell me now."

"Well, unless you feel too hampered. Lots of us do. The weak usually resort to acts of senseless violence. I remember old Trabbe—he ran out with a fireman's ax one day and buried it in Julian's car. But they cured him and sent him abroad. And poor Mrs. Trabbe—after she died the servants started wearing her frocks and shoes, surprising everyone and giving pain. O well!" He yawned and stretched. "I must be getting along now. It's been good to see you; we must meet again soon, eh? When things don't feel so damned precarious."

His eyes had a haunted look which somehow I misliked; his walk, too, was the walk of an old man. I accompanied him to the door and suggested that he might like to move in with me for a few weeks, but he shook his head slowly. "Ah, thanks," he said, "but no. Cheerio."

I stood at the door and watched him wander off down the street toward the nearest tube station. He did not turn round and wave on the corner as was once his wont.

I had some difficulty in running Julian to earth—if that is the expression—but at last I found him weekending somewhere in the country. My call caught him in mid yawn. "Ah good, it's you, Charlock," he said. "I was wondering who it might be."

"Julian," I said, "I've come to a decision which I want to discuss with you. In itself it may not seem very important, but it is extremely so to me." Julian coughed and said: "Well you know you can always count on me." It sounded not at all sententious. I took a breath and went on. "I have decided to give one of my inventions away to the public—to *give* it away, do you see? Simply, unequivocally donate it." He said nothing, and after a pause I went on. "Recently in playing about with some chemistry work in the lab I tumbled upon something which one might really describe as a boon to the ordinary housewife. It costs nothing, or almost nothing to make. It will completely transform washing up."

"Well, for goodness sake take out a pat—"

"Ah but listen. This I propose to *give* away. I propose to write a letter to *The Times* describing how anyone can, for the price of a pennyworth of common salt, make this . . ."

The timbre of Julian's attention seemed to shift and deepen. He sighed, and I heard a match click, followed by a puff. "I'm glad you decided to discuss it with me first before doing anything," he said. "What is the point of it, after all? At a penny halfpenny it would still be a boon—as a Merlin patent. Do you think we are dealing hardly by the public? By comparison with other firms I should have thought . . ."

"That has nothing to do with it. I simply feel that for once in my life I must make this gesture, *give* something freely, you see; something which is the fruit of my thought, so to speak. Can't you see?"

"I follow what you mean," he said coolly. "But nevertheless I can't quite see the motive. You have given the world so much through the firm, Charlock."

"Not given, Julian. That's the point. Sold."

"There is a pleasing touch of religiosity about your idea," he said dryly. "I commend you." He sounded serious but weary.

"I know it sounds trivial, but for me it represents something momentous, something I haven't been able to imagine for years—an act."

"The married man dreams of divorce," he said oracularly, and I recognized a Greek proverb in translation. "And the scientist thinks of science as a pretty girl with two cunts. . . ." He was wandering, playing for time. Then a little more sharply came: "What am I supposed to do about this idea—agree? How can I, Charlock? Indeed I wonder why you consulted me. You know that you are raising much more than a personal question? It smells of precedent. Indeed, whatever I said, I doubt if the firm would agree: and I am not the firm, as you know, only one of the camel drivers, so to speak, in the general caravan. Anyway thanks for being honest enough to tell me what was in your mind."

"I always felt I could talk to you as man to voice," I said.

"Irony was always your long suit, Charlock. Always."

"Anyway, now you know what I've decided."

Julian cleared his throat softly and let a pause intervene;

when he came back to the charge he was dreamy, reflective, unincisive. "I wonder if you have really thought about it—no, it's a pure impulse of generosity on your part."

"On the contrary: the fruit of a long interior debate."

"Hum. Have you considered, for example, your articles of association with the firm? This would cut across our agreement which is valid, if I remember, for some twenty years more at least."

"Twenty years." A shiver ran down my spine. Yes, I knew it all right—but uttered out loud like that it produced a chilling effect.

"It wouldn't work," said Julian at last in a more wide-awake voice. "It would lead to some costly and tedious litigation, that's all. And you'd lose, the firm would win. Contractually you are tied for everything."

"We shall see," I said, but I felt my voice falter. Julian went on suavely: "You know, don't you, that there is a whole string of charities supported by us in part or in full? Merlin's staff are encouraged to contribute to them—why don't you? You could make over the whole of your salary to them if you wished. Ask Nathan to show you the bound volume with the lists."

"I've seen it." I had. There was a huge vellum tome the thickness of the Bible listing all the charities to which the firm contributed.

"Well," said Julian, "wouldn't that do?"

"No."

"Why not?" He was almost peevish now.

"We get income tax relief on those—it's a company ploy."

"I see! My goodness, you are hard to please."

He puffed away another long silence and then asked: "What is the source of all this unrest, Charlock; where does it come from?"

"I have simply come to a point where I must make a gesture, even the feeblest of free gestures, to continue breathing."

"It must be due to some misconception about the nature of

◆ ◆ 323

the firm. I feel in all you say a funny kind of moral bias—an implied criticism which cannot be wholly just. Are you just being pharisaical, holier-than-thouish?"

"No, I'm being holier-than-meish for a change."

"What I'm trying to say is that the firm isn't just an extension of moral qualities, a product of a wicked human will, of a greedy mercantile spirit. It goes deeper than that. I mean, it has always existed in one form or another. At least I suppose so."

"What a sophistry! The firm is not the world."

"I'm not so sure. I'm not saying it's an easy thing or a gay thing; but it's a fact of nature, man's nature. One can't blink the firm, Charlock."

"Nature!"

"It must correspond to some deep unexpressed need of the human psyche—for it's always been there. We should take it more coolly. It's not in itself malefic, it is just neutral, a *repoussoir*. It's what we make of it. . . ."

"So the slave is born with his chains, is he?"

"Yes. Some can free themselves, but very few. I couldn't. If you believe in free will or predestination, for example—"

"Cut out the homilies," I said.

"Well, who imposed the firm on you, then?"

"I did. Out of ignorance."

"Not really; everything was clear from the beginning; your eyes were wide open."

"Like a three-day kitten."

"I don't see how you can want to back down at this stage."

"Even in prison they get remission for good behavior."

"But damn it, you might wake up one day and find yourself in charge of the firm, or most of it; Jocas and I won't live forever, you know."

"God forbid!"

Julian said, "Ach!" in an exasperated sort of way and then became mild again. "The firm isn't inflexible," he said, with a faint tinge of reproach. "Despite its size it is a pretty fragile thing, a bundle of long wires stretching out around the world. But it is all based on one slender item—the spinal column of the matter: that is the sanctity of contractual obligation. If you abrogate that you begin to damage the essential fabric of the thing. Naturally it will try to protect itself like any other organism."

"I *must* do this thing, I tell you."

"You will end up by building up a delusional system about being persecuted by the firm—the poor thing does not merit it."

I ground my teeth.

"Anyway," he went on, "there is no pressure the firm can bring upon you in the immediate sense; but it would certainly counter any such move as the one you have outlined. It's strange, you still seem to think of it in terms of personalities; but it has long ago outgrown the personalities which created it—Merlin, Jocas, myself: we are already merely ancestors. The firm is self-subsisting now, rolling down its appointed path with a momentum which neither you nor I can alter. Of course he that is not with it is against it, and so on. In other epochs it might have taken other forms. But man rests, unchangeable, unteachable, and the firm is cast in his mold—*your mold, Charlock!* Ask and it shall be answered! Prod the old sow with a stick and it grunts." He paused and his voice sank softly into the tones of a twilit resignation. Under his breath, in a whisper which I could just catch, I heard him say: "And Iolanthe is dying?" He sighed, he was talking to himself. A long silence fell.

"You are still there, Charlock?"

"Yes."

"Well, I think all this must come from your sense of impotence aggravated by success; such feelings always result in rash moral judgments. You have never succeeded in doing the abstract work for which you pined—though that was not our fault. And you have worked up a grudge against the firm in telling yourself that it is caught up in the nets of base matter, is exploring and adapting matter, expropriating matter."

"And the results?"

"My dear, I can do nothing, nobody can. Yes, we can make small adjustments of stress or direction or emphasis. But the wheel turns in spite of one. Come, grow up, Charlock. The firm won't bite, you know."

"I am still waiting to be convinced," I said grimly. "All this is special pleading."

It was, of course and yet in another way it wasn't. It made sense on one level, nonsense on another. I had not yet succeeded in penetrating to the basic fallacy in these contentions. In a funny way, too, I thought him—Julian personally —innocent of any intention to delude. He believed what he said, and consequently it was true, not for me, but for him. Perhaps even objectively true? My reason was spinning like a top. The vertiginous sense of failure was so intense that it had got mixed up with my breathing. I was suffocated. I heard Julian put down the receiver and walk away a few steps; then in the silence I heard some music begin to play— the opening bars of a Schumann concerto. "As an honorable man," he said, "who abhors all exaggeration, I do not know what to tell you."

How many of these ideas would remain waterproof? I wondered. Julian was sighing again. "What about Iolanthe?" I said cruelly. (Marchant said that ideas were simply nags; one rode about on them until one tired of them, then tied them to a tree and fucked them.) "Iolanthe," he repeated slowly, accenting the word wrongly. "What of her?" In my almost drunken state I could not resist a further threat. "A creation of the soap-flakes mind," I said. "Nobody would believe it to see her picture in your flat." Julian smiled invisibly. "An artist," he said, and, "A smile to make one rise in one's stirrups."

"I might even leave England," I said, "where the national sloth has reached the brain cortex."

Julian coughed. All of a sudden his voice became bony and determined; a sort of cold fury possessed it. "There is only one solution for you—to stop inventing altogether, to retire on your winnings—I will not call them earnings, for without us you would be penniless today. Abandon the game altogether." Then his voice changed again; it sank into a lower register, it became merciful, tender, calm. He whispered almost to himself. "Who can gauge the feeling of a man in love who is forced to sit and look on at the steady deterioration of a fine mind and lovely body? We must celebrate the people who set us on fire."

"Julian," I cried, "is this your last word?"

"What else?" he said with such world-weariness, such inexpressible sadness, that I felt a lump come into my throat. Yet at the same time gusts of rage and frustration were still there in my mind, I could not still them. "Mountebank! Actor!" I jeered. Yet he did not seem to have heard me—or at any rate the insults produced no recognizable reflection in his tone.

"Graphos," he said, "could only love a weeping girl. If she did not weep she must be made to—so he said." All of a sudden I recalled a chance remark of Io's to the effect that only the free man can really be loved by a woman; I wondered which of us she might have in mind? Ah which?

I had said it before I knew the words were out of my mouth—without any premeditation whatsoever. "Julian, for how long has Benedicta been your mistress, and what is the name of the drug?" I heard him draw his breath sharply as if I had run a thorn under his fingernail. "Do you hear me?" I said lurching about drunkenly and laughing coarsely. Silence from his end. It was war now to the very knife, I felt it. Yet the silence prolonged itself into infinity as I stood there. "Julian," I said again, "you don't need to tell me; I shall find out from her." There was the dry crisp click of the receiver going down, that was all; and I stood with the seashell of emptiness to my ear, mumbling to myself; for somehow these stupid remarks had set fire to my mind, illuminating a whole new area of unmapped action. The key—*of course*—the key to everything was Benedicta! I could do nothing that did not encapsulate her consent, her agreement. Before any problem could be settled I must settle the problem of this wife of mine. "By God," I said to myself as suddenly the fact dawned upon me. "Of course." How unjust I had been to her! I was filled with remorse all of a sudden. I had never really talked to her, explained to her, tried to enlist her support for my plans. . . . I must rush to her side to explain everything.

But by the time I reached her Benedicta had already taken one of her characteristic leaps forward into triumphant unreason, eluding more successfully than ever the vain pursuit of her doctors or her lovers.

The slim three and a half liter Lethe lay outside the office—a birthday present from the firm; its glossy black snout pointed downstreet like a lance laid in rest. This elegant missile could sway silently through traffic, and climb effortlessly into the hundreds with a faint blue snarl. For the most part it made only the noise of cremated silk—which is to say, no noise whatsoever. Its brief insistent horn copied the note of a trumpeting goose. I tell you the intoxication of driving this deft shooting star across London soothed away my anxieties. Cool winds came off the river at Hammersmith; cloudy sunshine feathered on the last of the daylight. It would be dark before I arrived. It was dark when I did.

The house presented its usual aspect of tenantless animation—as if the owners had gone out to the pub for a drink leaving all the lights on, the radio on, the fires unguarded. It was the servants' day off no doubt. The lake was still. In the vague enthusiasm of my self-discovery (that I still had the power to conceive of independent actions) I was ill prepared for anything out of the ordinary. I could think about nothing but my own feelings: about how to make them clear to poor Benedicta. So much so that I hardly took in at first the bloody spoor which here and there marked the scarlet staircase carpet; nor the trail of dummy books which lay anyhow on the landings—an obscure paper chase of empty titles like *Decline and Fall* and *Night Thoughts* and *The Consolations of Philosophy*. Up I went and up: not sufficiently attentive to be alarmed, more puzzled. Yet here and there—it was like following a wounded lion to its lair—I came upon a red pugmark freshly impressed in the carpet. What could it mean? How on earth could I guess that Benedicta had been at that double toe of hers with a kitchen knife?

Well, the bedroom door was ajar and pushing it softly open I entered, to stand upon the threshold and contemplate the new Benedicta in her latest yet oldest role. I vaguely surmised that her period had surprised her, that was all. But everything was quite different. She was standing on the bed naked, her arms raised in rapture, her face burning with gratitude and adoration; it was clear that the ceiling had burst open to reveal the heavens, clouded and starry, with its vast freize of angels and demons—figures of some great Renaissance Annunciation. The ceiling had withdrawn, had become the inverted bowl of the heavens. She was talking to the figures—at least her lips were moving. In the heavy pelt of the bed you could not discern the torn foot. She was surrounded by an absolute snowdrift of paper, torn up very small. Most of it was my transcripts I suppose—I recognized the paper I use for dactyl. But there were other things, letters on lined paper. Cupboards hung open with clothes pouring from them. Her dressing table was cluttered with fallen cosmetics. The elegant little leather boxes with trees—her *postiche* and wig boxes—lay about poking their tongue out at us. It was memorably silent. The trance could have been indefinitely prolonged, one felt; the figures in the frieze held up their hands to bless, or to point to breasts, or crowns of thorns. But they were benign, they were on her side, and her tears flowed down her cheeks in gratitude. In the bubble of this enormous concentration there was simply no room for me, nor for my preoccupations. I stood gaping at this tableau until she caught sight of me out of the corner of her eye and turned slowly in a puzzled way—the wonder widening in concentric rings upon her white face, as if I had thrown a stone into a pool. I suppose I must have stammered out something, for she stared keenly at me and then put a finger to her lips. A look of sudden panic intervened now with astonishing rapidity and clutching her ears she screamed once: "I've gone deaf." Then just as suddenly dropped her hands, calmed and smiled wickedly.

This called for restraint of some sort, though nothing could be more angelic than the cool sweet smile of the demon. Underneath it, too, far down below the surface, one recognized the look of a wounded animal, say a cat which tries to say: "I have a thorn in my foot. Please help." Borne on a clumsy tide of scattered and conflicting emotions I surged awkwardly forward, mumbling, arms outspread in the travesty of an embrace, unsure what the contents of my gesture might be—to embrace, to restrain, to comfort? All three, I suppose. In the corner there was a telephone torn out of the wall which hinted at strength which that slender body did not appear to own. "You see how it is?" she whispered, and slipped from the bed to elude my arms. The operation was more delicate and awkward than I had supposed; like when a swallow flies into a room and one tries to expel it without damaging or frightening the creature. Well, so we walked round, full of an awkward stateliness. Once or twice I almost caught up with her; her attention jumped for a moment from me to other objects in the room. But it was never absent for long, and she continued to elude me in a deft unhurrying fashion. And so out on the landing, with only a pause to topple a small statuette; and down the long staircase, saturated in the loneliness of this dreadful situation. Where the devil was everyone? Normally the house was full of servants. She slipped through doors, shutting them behind her to delay me; as I entered I would see her leaving the room from the far end, still looking at me over her shoulder to make sure I followed, expressionlessly seductive. She was heading steadily across the mansion toward the eastern side—toward, in fact, the old gun room with its glass cases stocked with weapons. My concern deepened, my pace increased, but she held her distance. Then, as she disappeared into the gun room, she managed to find a key to turn. I was locked out. Under the noise of my impotent banging and cajoling I could hear the sliding doors of the glass cases being opened; then a crackle of paper and carton which instantly translated itself into a vision of Benedicta stripping a cartouche of shells. There were several drawers full of them. I began to sweat; then I remembered that there was a second door, a mere hatch, which led into a tiny bar built into the corner of the room. This was a swing door, and I rushed for it; but the delay had given her just enough time, and when I barged through it was to see her quietly slipping out from the farther end of the room with a gun under her arm.

She had chosen the second ballroom—the huge gilt one—now polished like a skull and empty of everything but its mirror and grand piano. She was standing in the center of it, waiting for me to appear in the doorway, quite calm and composed. A few streaks of blood only—toes are relatively bloodless—marked for progress across the polished floor. But there she lounged, as if waiting for the machine to flick clay pigeons into the sky. It was no use calling her name. Inevitably, too, I feared at that instant that her target would be myself, framed by the gilt doorway in all my ineffectualness. But if by any chance the idea had not entered her head, I did not wish to provoke it by a sudden move. I stood rooted, expecting to receive the twelve-bore charge in the stomach; but she swung up and away and round, confronting the long chain of mirrors which lined the somber room. As she let fly she began to recite the Lord's Prayer in a shaky broken voice—a small thread of sound among the explosions. "Our Father which art" (bang) "in heaven hallowed" (bang) "be thy name" (bang). And so forth. She had picked upon a repeating pump gun, a six-shot. The noise of the smokeless shots was deafening, wit-scattering. I felt dizzy and faint, all my impressions fused together in a dazzle; and yet with the part of one's mind which remains attentive and critical I could not help noticing the voluptuous thwack with which the charge burst into the mirrors, embedding itself deep in the reality of the nonmirror world, shattering her image. A plump sound like someone beating up a swansdown pillow.

The rest doesn't translate so very well. I had picked up, I don't know how or where, a short ashplant—perhaps with some vague instinct of self-defense. I suppose I rushed at her—but it must have been with the toppling sliding motions of someone on ice, for the floor was glossy. Vaguely something in the nature of a football tackle. I locked my arms round the defiant nakedness and together we stumbled and fell to the ground, the gun pressed between us. Indeed, the last discharge went off as we were falling and its hot breath burned my forehead; the barrel was fiendish hot too. So we rolled over and over until she released it and sent it skittering across the floor. Then to my surprise I began to beat her with my own weapon, but beat her precious hard across the back and buttocks. A sort of voluptuous rage must have possessed me—I was beating Julian, I suppose. And for her part she lay, pale and with an expression of content almost, eyes shut, lips moving in prayer—like someone accepting a well-merited punishment. It was frightening, also sexually exciting in a dim sort of way. But an end was soon put to this disgraceful scene, for by now the room was filling up with people.

The two governesses were upon us, witchlike and purposeful in their rusty black clothes; they hardly spoke as they set about separating and shackling us. Then frightened supers like Baynes, gobbling and swallowing. And lastly fussy Nash with his calamitous concern.

I was sick and feverish and upset—and now very much out of place in all this babble. Nor was the solace of strong drink very much in keeping with so hysterical a mood. I could not sleep in spite of it. I lay awake most of the night, listening to the faint sounds which betokened more purposeful activities than my own in other parts of the house: the telephone ringing, the voice of Nash. "Yes, he's here. I've put him to bed." I laughed grimly to myself and shook my fist at the ceiling. It did not need much imagination to translate the keening of rubber tires on gravel in the first dawn light; that would be the limousine with the drawn blinds. Soon Benedicta would be beginning that eternally repeated journey back to the land of the archetypes. "Our Father which art in heaven." By craning my head out of the window I could verify these hypotheses. The child would be in front with the harpies. Benedicta would be carried, heavily veiled, like a statue of the Virgin Mary. I don't say it wasn't all for the best. I don't say it wasn't all for the best. *Om*.

SIX

Human attention is fragile and finite; won't be mastered; can't be bribed; is always changing. . . . Ah, for one moment of that total vision which might reorder the whole field and make it significant. I suppose from the outside it must have seemed like a progressive melancholia—I mean, resigning from the firm (no reaction to this) and locking myself up in the country in a desperate attempt to abdicate, along the lines suggested by Julian. *Not to invent anymore.* Somehow one day one must try and stop being one's own little hero—eh, Charlock? You can do it for a year or two at most without faltering. It's all very well, solitude and misanthropy. The beard I grew was patched with white; it gave me a startled look. I had to buy heavier lenses for my glasses. I was drinking a good deal and smoking too much. But it was a pleasure to let my appearance run to seed, to wear torn pullovers and knee-bulged gray bags. Nor was I completely cut off, except from Julian; he was biding his time, I supposed. I spoke to others on the phone, long conversations full of *non sequiturs*, yes, and common-room pleasantries. And all the time, unknown to my conscious me, that bloody old mass of wires I have called Abel was maturing. A certain resignation set in, too, walking about in the snow, hammering out Bach, skating in a deep muse upon the frozen waters of the lake. Well, so be it; if I must occupy myself, what better way? Besides, who would ever understand poor Abel, his foggy calculus of human potentials based upon the first caveman chirp of the human voice? I was also preparing my revenge on Julian.

You may say that such an instrument could not possibly predict; but the future is only the memory of the past extended into the future. The backside of the moon of memory, if you like. The prediction of stars in the sky as yet undiscovered by the lens—that is a fair analogy. From the birth cry to the death rattle most lives can be plotted. I shall spare myself the eight lines of maths which resume this statement—crisp pothooks, shell of the cosmic egg. How little one needs to divine the human potentials in a single given life; translate through vibrations back to memory and thence to situation. Something the pundits of the firm will not fathom. When they take Abel apart they will be left with a mute collection of wires, like a human skeleton. Where is the soul of the machine? they will cry. Ah me! An invention as singular, original and definitive as the telescope. *E pur si muovi*, and so on.

The proof was in the pudding; and I had a pitifully small abacus to work with—just the people who had collided with me like rogue stars: just their sayings, vision and the few facts I knew about them. I took over the big musicians' gallery for my keyboard, mounting the long and complicated panel of my fascia in the manner of some huge cinema organ; behind it was the library with its transmuting system. What is better than reading the stars? Why, listening to them in their transports of love and pain, music of the spheres echoed by diluted animals. It all grew out of my little magnetic boxes—a lot of it scratchy as hell. Sitting there in the tremendous loneliness of the silent house (I had sent most of the servants away), I sat, a lean and bearded man, switching from life to lie. It took ages, of course; more than three years before I managed to obtain the first coherent response to my data. In this way I hoped to prosecute the opening moves of my war upon Julian—my persecution of this hidden man. I had thought of other things, but they were schoolboy pranks— messages in invisible ink slowly printing themselves on astonished blotters. But Abel was better. With him I could scry and scan. Much of it was not very palatable—but is truth ever palatable? I discovered much too about myself, about my inadequacy with women. O it was terrible to see the real truth about Benedicta; she was to be pitied, not to be hated. And the quiet Iolanthe's deathbed cry: "How little I have managed to live, and that always in hotels. There never seemed to be enough time, and now . . ." I should have carried off these women in my teeth to devour them at leisure on a piece of waste ground. But then women cannot help being predatory—to take up with one is to inherit a mink farm.

Mark came, my son—how strange the word sounds! But he sheered away from me, sneaking round corners to avoid encounters. I saw him, a pale thin little creature with stick-ingout ears, walking solemnly to church between those two black harpies, as if between warders. It was clear that they had had their instructions. The boy was doing some sort of preparatory work for an entrance exam though still barely out of kindergarten. I could pick him up on Abel, but dimly. I saw him, *heard* him, sitting at my desk in Merlin's—a pale small-boned young man with a widow's peak. But that lay far ahead as yet, after my own . . . disappearance. This was foggy, with more than a hint of suicide about it. But talking of suicide, since the word has cropped up, I remember Mark's own little effort. I was working very early one morning when I happened to glance out of a window in time to see him walking down toward the lake. The earliness of the hour struck me—it was barely light. He had a slice of bread in his hand and was apparently about to feed the swans. I was about to turn away when something about his walk aroused my curiosity; it was so stiff and stilted, as if he were forcing himself to advance by sheer willpower. A moment later and he has walked right into the icy water, wading slowly outward. Heavy sleet was falling. I shouted twice but he did not turn. Suddenly the comprehension of what he was doing dawned upon me and I raced for the door. The cold struck one amidships. He was moving steadily into the deeper reaches, already almost up to his neck. In spite of the blazing freeze I plunged after him, gasping with pain. I just reached his head as the water rose to his mouth, and grabbed him. He was blue and contorted with cold, crying and snickering. I half pushed the little creature into my shirt and crawled laboriously back to land with him, myself half fainting from the cold. Through his little blue prawn lips he was saying, "They are trying to keep me away from you." Over and over again. I plunged for the downstairs bathroom with its hot taps, in a delirium of cold and anguish; plunging him into the hot water to soothe his numbed limbs. Then I slumped down on the bidet opposite him and wept; I wept my way right back to my solitary childhood, back to the breast, back into the very womb which is the only memory we know about. He wept too, but commiseratingly; and presently I felt his small pale hand touching my head, patting me, consoling me. I did not need to ask who or what was trying to keep him from me. So we sat for an age, staring at each other. Then I toweled his pink frail body back to life, alarmed at his slenderness, his shallow lungs. Our clothes fumed upon the radiators. Waiting for them to dry I said, "Would you like to work with me on Abel?" and his eye lit

340 ◆ ◆

with a frail gleam. He sighed: "They wouldn't let me."
"Then they mustn't know, Mark, that is all. You must find
times like this, too early or too late for them."

And so it was, he became very famulus, sneaking down
before first light to spend two engrossing hours among my
lights and wires. It was difficult at first to teach him the first
principles of the thing; but later he mastered the whole
system and crawled about my organ loft like a powder
monkey.

"What is Abel really?"

"Well, one day you will want to know about us all, about
your past and mine, about your future."

"Will I?"

"Almost certainly. Everyone does. Here look at the pro-
gramme manual—do you see the different bays marked
'When' 'Who' 'Why' 'Where' and 'If'?"

"*If?*" he said with surprise. "Why *If?*"

"It's the most important question of all in a way—it can
change all the others: just one tiny grain of *If*."

It was a pleasure too to have someone to talk to; and as we
worked I gave him the whole pedigree of Abel, starting with
the *Theaetetus* and its block of wax in the human soul eager
to imprint itself with every perception, thought, emotion;
the whole theory of Platonic memory and all that blubber to
which the child listened with wonder and a certain understanding. The only thing was that I had to warn him against
the Julian dossier—how to be careful; because when I had
finished with Julian I knew he would walk into my trap and
come down to find out what there was to know about himself.
What man could resist reading a secret report on himself? It
was the second panel on the left with an inviting red button.
I pushed it open for Mark—in order to make certain that he
understood—and together we stared into the barrels of the
loaded twelve-bore I had lashed to a stand and wired for
action. I would leave this behind me when I left. Mark gazed
at it wonderingly, and then at me, his small blue eyes narrowed as he tried to assess the meaning of this present. But he

said nothing. "You won't give me away?" I said, feeling so sure of his love for me. He shook his head proudly.

So we opened up several of the channels and completed the elaborate programs which would bring them to life—if that is the scientific word. I don't know when I have been so happy. Nor was the business kept a secret; Nash came and had it all explained to him. He looked very strange, declared that he understood, and tiptoed away again. If he did not tap his head significantly before my eyes he perhaps did it before the eyes of others. Marchant also came—but he turned pale and gnawed his lip, whether from jealousy or contempt I do not know. Yes I do, though. I had pitifully little on him and I hadn't really assorted the field with any thoroughness but up in the predictor came the word "plagiarism." I wanted all this guff to filter back slowly to Julian, and it did. But that was only the beginning.

Then unluckily Mark was caught; one of the harpies in a wizard's dressing gown stood sibilating in the doorway of the gallery. "Mark, you have been *told* over and over *again*." She reached out a hand like a spade. I watched with a sort of recondite insolence, tipping the bottle of lemonade to my lips. Mark allowed himself to be led tamely away, head high, lips white, ears pink—the captive rabbit. It seemed useless to protest, so I did nothing, secure in his confidence. He stepped high and proud, and did not turn his head to say good-bye.

Well: and then what? Why, a whole winter lay before me of ordering and scrying—on a much firmer wicket than John Dee ever was. Fires blazed everywhere, the snow blanketed everything. And now *Julian* was being persecuted. His *own* voice was ringing him up! "Is that Julian?" "Yes." "This is Julian too." It had been pretty largely given out that Abel was some sort of electronic hoax; but truth is relative. It was far less accurate than I would have liked to hope, but nevertheless I found I could use it. After all, the planchette is no good without the hand, the crystal ball without the sorcerer's eye. Yes, I could see backward and forward along the tragic ellipse of these segmented lives, to come up now and again with partial fragments of truth. At times my nets were full; at times I had to empty the small fry back into the stream. Goodness, but enough came up to fill Julian with alarm. He tried to ring me several times, and I was delighted by the concealed agitation in his tones. How did I know what I knew? Truth to tell, by the merest divination in the name of Abel. It took hardly any time to convince and disturb him because I fell upon some trivia which proved themselves accurate within days of Julian's voice telling him. Perhaps all this might prove a useful guide to the stock market or the racecourse? I made Julian ask Julian this in a slightly bitter tone. But then inexorably I began to edge toward his private life—the field of his emotions and hopes. Ah, I wanted to reduce him slowly, with infinite slowness; already I scented his weakness. He was like a drowning man. At times too I was overcome with remorse to be so brutal, for now he was really suffering. And I brought the whole weight of my tortures to bear upon the sick Iolanthe, upon her silent native death. He had heard enough by now to suspect that the rest might well become true. And then Graphos too: the sad footsteps of Hippo echoing on the lino of some gravid hospital corridor. The ignominy of the acetone breath, the legs gradually filling up, turning gangrenous. So carefully kept, those legs, in gray woolen socks. He had been *warned* not to try and cut his own toenails, for the slightest wound . . . But Graphos was not used to obeying others. He always knew better.

I had written to Iolanthe, promising to exorcise her house provided she came with me; but the letter arrived too late and she burned it along with many others. All this comes of a strange meeting I was to have with Mrs. Henniker on the Zurich plane. Her face had been hollowed out by suffering, scaled and pared to the bone by the sleepless nights she had spent at the bedside of Io. The tall steel bed against a window full of Alpine stars and tumultuous grass. One candle burning before an ikon—no need to say which. Shaken by a kind of involuntary sobbing which contained no more tears—she had used them all up. At first nobody knew except Julian *of course*. Whenever she was ill she was registered at three different clinics in order to enjoy some peace and anonymity at a fourth. Well, there by candlelight reciting her past and peering with those wild enlarged eyes into the fastnesses of the future, the pinewood coffin. *Tunc*.

It was so slow, the simple declining into the final pens of sleep, without too much pain, too many numbed regrets. Rolling down the green slopes of death, moving faster and ever faster, turning through the slow spirals of consciousness toward the heart of the fire opal. All night long now Mrs. Henniker sat beside the bed, her stone-colored eye fixed upon the face of the white woman who had become her daughter; all night upright in an uncomfortable steel chair, the whole building silent around her, save for the shuffling shoes of the night nurse—one for the whole floor. From time to time the patient's eyes would open and wander about the ceiling as if seeking for something. Her lips might move a little, perhaps even tenderly smile. I would have liked to think—I *did* think —that she was picturing both of us crossing to her father's island in the blue fishing boat. A church, cypresses, sand-colored jetty, box dwellings of colored whitewashes, the pink-toed pigeons crooning. Up and ever up to the abandoned barn where his whole life had been lived, had completed its simple circle. The well overgrown with moss now, the marble wellhead grooved by the cable which for centuries had drawn up the sweet water. One loose stone extracted revealed the hiding place of the key. Let us suppose we entered on tiptoe— entered the smelly gloom of the apple-charmed room full of unbroken cobwebs—the room he died in. Somewhere along the line, at this exact point, everything about my life threatens to become successful; everything takes a turn for the better. A fresh wind fills the sails—so Abel tells me, but always adding the rider, "a delusion like so many others, that's all." Then the field goes blank again and the hints about suicide come up. It would not last, you see: could not last.

Well, on and on she sits, Mrs. Henniker with her hanky

344 ◆◆

screwed up in her hand, her red horseface gleaming with sweat. If I could convey with how much dazzling longing I gazed upon the face of Iolanthe dead—why everything would burst apart, catch fire, disintegrate. The little green book which fell from the bed had no underlining in it to serve as a guideline to her last thoughts—perhaps she did not have many. Henniker carried it away for me, together with a lock of that famous hair—the sentimental relics which human children so cherish: the evidences of memory which are supposed to endure as long as the last unshed tear. Her eyes, did they fall upon the passage which I was now reading out, my own lips moving stiffly along the lines? *"Vous êtes lié fatalement aux meilleurs souvenirs de ma jeunesse. Savez-vous qu'il y a plus de vingt ans que nous nous connaissons? Tout cela me plonge dans les abîmes de rêverie qui sentent le vieillard. On dit que le present est trop rapide. Je trouve, moi, que c'est le passé qui nous dévore."*

Perhaps it was the eyes of Julian rather which traced and retraced these faltering lines written in the hand of the aging Flaubert; for Julian inevitably was there. He came in silently, unannounced, just after midnight, softly putting his briefcase on the floor. In her confusion Henniker saw only a batlike figure in a black suit and a soft black hat. He motioned her to silence and indicated that she might leave the patient to be guarded by him. Without a word all was understood. With a sigh Henniker crossed to the low divan and plunged into a deep sleep. One thing only she noticed. Iolanthe did not open her eyes at all, but all of a sudden her face quivered and her hand came softly across the white sheet toward Julian's small, childlike hand. So they sat silently with her feverish fingers resting upon his. Of course I asked how he *looked*, but her answers were vague; she had received a dozen conflicting impressions. Terribly tired and old, an ashen face, the crater of an extinct volcano; or else some great quivering bat of pain clinging by his wings to the steel-tubed chair. Or else . . . But it is useless, useless. Whenever it is really necessary Julian appears, and one knows it: but often only after he has gone.

The night wore on and on into the milky opaqueness of dawn; the white fangs of snowscape glittered in all their fruitless splendor. All nature dozed and even Julian felt his head drooping. It must have been after one of these transitory catnaps that he woke to feel the full massiveness, the charged weight, of her changed status. Death had made her fingers so heavy, it seemed, that he almost had to prize his own out from under them. Just that. He did not move anymore. Mrs. Henniker snored faintly. He continued to stare intently at the white profile she presented to him with such motionless intentness. Even when a drowsy fly settled on the eyeball he could not move.

But they were not to be spared the final indignities which the press reserves for events such as these. Somehow the secret of her whereabouts had leaked out. The clinic was ill-equipped to protect itself against sixty such persecutors, especially at such a time of day. They burst through the swing doors with all the vulgar assurance of the tribe, overwhelming the dazed duty nurse, deaf to all protest. Some even limbed over the balcony from the garden. The candle-lit silence of the room was filled now by their hoarse reverent breathing, the shuffle of their feet, the hiss and splash of their bulbs. Even now Julian did not move; he sat exhausted in his chair. And in some singular way they did not notice him, for not a single glance or question was addressed to him; and in all the photographs which smeared the dailies of the world there was no trace of his presence—the chair seemed to be empty. Why go on? The planned obsolescence of the human body, etc. Mrs. Henniker slept right through it and was only woken by a banged door. Julian had gone. "The unlucky thing," he said later, "was her loving you; it was completely unsuitable, and anyway you did not care." I cannot answer these charges anymore. A fearful horror and exhaustion seizes me. I am guilty of nothing—in fact that's really what I am guilty *not of*. Then later in the gutter press to read of her grave being robbed. They said that fans had done it—it is true that fans will stop at nothing. At any rate it could hardly have been Julian; nor ordinary robbers, for her jewelry had not been touched. Hair, though; there is a high market value for the hair of a goddess. What she sought was not love but the frail combining of hopes with someone—but how was Henniker to know this? She had choked me with a phrase and I sat there staring at her feeling as if I had swallowed a toad.

It is very still here. *Om.* I said *Om.*

SEVEN

It has been wearing, this brief period of lonely inertia in Athens, waiting for Koepgen to appear. I don't know why I felt I ought to see him before . . . before getting on with it. I kept an eye on the favorite tavern; that too is much the same. One window has fallen in, and the vine had got mildew. The widow is dead, but her son carries on. I have been walking about a good deal at night—the brutal velvet Athenian night with its harsh rancorous music and game smells. I can't record thoughts anymore, the spool seems to have run out. The whole bloody thing has begun to seize up in my head like an engine. And then, bang, tonight I ran into him—the pocket Silenus in the monkish gear. A streak of brindle in his hair.

But no surprise at seeing me. We sat silently for a while devouring each other with our eyes; I noticed he was rather drunk and hastened to join him in that blessed state. "I knew you'd come." Nodding owlwise and tipping the blue tin can. "You want to hear about me, my story." I did actually. A vague nervous curiosity had possessed me, for in spite of my fairly extensive data upon Koepgen I could hardly get anything out of Abel except fictitious-sounding aphorisms. "The ikon and all that—your farty fairy tale." His eyes danced, he leaned his back against the whitewashed wall of the tavern. "My God, Charlock," he said, "I am really free. I took ages to earn it, but I stuck it out and got an honest discharge. Free, my lad!"

I raised the wine can and almost let him have it on the crown of his head—so sick was I of the meaningless four-letter. "They've treated me very well," he said. "But that isn't the strangest thing. Yes, I found my ikon at last—and what I took to be some sort of mystical awakening waiting for me turned out to be the most prosaic thing imaginable." He laughed very heartily. "My father's will was gummed into the back of it, together with the deeds for our property in Russia —if ever they decide to give it back to us."

"Where, though?"

"Another fantastic thing—Spinalonga."

"The leper island? The one off Crete?"

"The very same. I got the Church to post me there when Jocas told me and sure enough I found it there. It was the damnedest thing. And it wasn't all. There was a little old man, one of the lepers, who was dying and I was asked to help send him down with all the usual formalities. But he took ages to die; and in his delirium he talked away whole nights. You know, he was English; he told me—what next? He told me he was *Merlin* himself."

"The devil he did."

"It was certainly his name; but how could I tell if he was THE Merlin or just someone of that name? Eh? But he knew a great deal about us all, about Benedicta, about you; and indeed he twice sent you a message through me. I was not lying, Charlock. Wait a second and let me recall." He guzzled some more wine with its bitter twang. Wiped his lips with bread and went on. "He said *'The firm only exists to be escaped from. Tell Charlock.'* What do you make of that? Then on another occasion he said: *'There are two kinds of death open to the living. Tell Charlock.'*" I sat looking incredulously at him, but feeling somehow cheered up in a confused way. We clapped hands for another beaker of the thought provoker. "In his view he said the firm was something different for each of us; it was something like memory for you—its banked funds too great to be exhausted by promissory notes."

"To the devil with it all."

"I know what is in your mind," said Koepgen seriously, "but you ought to visit the little house before you decide. And you ought to realise that such an act—"

"Shut up, Koepgen," I growled, baring my fangs.

"I know, I apologize. The free should never moralize to the bound. Let's talk of something else. Let me tell you about a stroke of luck I have had; you remember the translations you helped me with? Of my poems? I sent them in anonymously to an agent. They have been accepted without any *piston* whatsoever. Straight off. Like that! I received the contract today. Look!" I took the wad of paper from him and glanced at it. Then I looked at him in slowly dawning horror. The firm was Vibart's. The contracts were signed by Vibart's partner. Was it possible that the fool did not know? I stared keenly, reverently, tenderly into the eyes of the poor foolish little man and swallowed my Adam's apple a number of times. Should I tell him? "No," cried my *alter Felix*. "Not a word."

"Well, we must drink another one on this," and Koepgen echoed my clanking pledge with his own, his eyes full of the tears of fulfillment. We sat until very late, until the violet sky went lilac and started to bleed; until the waiters were snoring on windowsills. Then we clambered down the hill past the Acropolis.

Well, I had made my decision. I would visit Io's house before deciding how and when.

Nash was always at a loss to account for the depression which welled up in him as his car turned slowly along the axis of the hill, along the double avenue of elms. But the man in the dark suit who sat beside him looked at it all with a studied coldness; Julian had been relatively silent for the first part of the journey down. But in the last few miles he had begun to muse again after his usual fashion. "It isn't beautiful," he said, as if reading Nash's thoughts. "I agree. The grandeur is too Byzantine. It could never be a home for anyone, I suppose." Nash changed gear, shaking his head. A frown anointed his cock-robin's face. "It's not her fault," he said. "She has made a wonderful recovery, you must agree; in spite of so much bad news, the death and so on."

Julian lit a cigar and said: "Presumption of death isn't quite the same thing. Without a body to show for it. You need as much body to die as to live. In the case of Charlock— we will have to wait upon the evidence. At any rate the Mediterranean always gives up its bodies. I think we'll find him, if he is to be found. It's only a matter of waiting awhile." He coughed and settled himself deeper in his seat. They had come down to inspect the curious toy in the musicians' gallery. ("An abacus of the intuition—can you

354 ◆ ◆

make one?") That and other little matters had to be gone into. Julian went on softly: "It's like those legends of the Hesychasts—to die and leave an empty grave. One must beware of Charlock."

"Oh dear, I don't know," said Nash and Julian replied coolly.

"You are not expected to know; you are expected to exist, to be."

"That's the whole trouble."

The lake was of dark and dirty jelly. The swans floated about like white lanterns. The paint had peeled along the benches. Under this lowering sky the skin of wet leaves lagged his tires. Nash was fastidious as a cat when it came to his car; he could not bear things sticking to his paws. He found a stick to poke at them while Julian stood in the drive, debating heavily. "We will deal with the child first," he said softly. "He may know how the thing is booby-trapped, as obviously it must be. At least we can ask." Nash grunted. He had found a bracelet on the gravel, which he put into his overcoat pocket. The manservant let them in with a silent inclination of the head and they passed together down the long corridors and up the spiral staircase to the room where Julian proposed to interrogate Mark. Nash thumped heavily along behind him, puffing a little on the landings, with a curious air of fugitive derision on his face. "I'll go and see Benedicta, then," he said, and turning left where the landings intersected, marched away toward the bedrooms.

As usual Julian, that master of effect, had chosen a place of interrogation worthy of a practiced inquisitor. It was an old cobwebby boxroom with a single uncurtained window looking out across the park. Here an old-fashioned high-backed chair had been placed facing the window—a chair with so tall a back that when Mark did come hesitantly into the room all he could see of Julian was a pair of white hands lying softly, negligently on the arms of the chair. Nothing else. The high back hid even his head. Mark had been marched down the corridors of the east wing by a nurse and introjected into the room at a given signal. He stood now, anxious and pale, with his feeble countenance made whiter than usual by the daylight outside. "Yes, Uncle Julian?" he said when his name was uttered. "Yes?"

Julian put on his slow, suave reptilian voice, letting the words uncoil by themselves, musingly. "Mark, you helped our dear Felix build Abel, didn't you?"

"Yes."

"Is there a booby trap of any sort in it: something that might explode and injure someone?"

Mark began to breathe very heavily and his face took on an unwonted expression of determination, of awkward resolution. The man in the tall-backed chair stayed heavily, ominously silent as if he wished to give time for some reaction to these inappropriate emotions to set in.

"I won't tell you. I promised," said the boy at last.

"Then if someone should get hurt you might be to blame?"

"I promised."

"Then if someone should get hurt you might be to blame?"

Mark watched the slow spirals of cigar smoke rise in the eddyless air of the musty room. "I am asking you," said Julian suddenly in a voice so sharp that the boy started. "I am asking you." Mark hung his head. He was hovering on the edge of tears now. Julian resumed his suave impartial voice. "Mark," he said with infinite slowness, "you know the story of the Princes in the Tower?" Mark nodded and breathed out his "Yes" into the silent room. "Very well," said Julian, "I'm glad you do. It's not a pretty story. Now, Mark, I am going to ask you something else. Is there any safe way of dismantling the trap?"

After a long interior struggle Mark once more delivered himself of his half-choked affirmation. "Good," said Julian, "and you know how to do it, don't you?"

"Yes, Uncle Julian."

"And you will help us, won't you? We cannot afford to lose that machine by some clumsy accident."

"There's a switch," said Mark haltingly. "I was shown it."

Julian heaved a great sigh of relief. "Then that settles it," he said. "You will do it for us, won't you? You see, Professor Marchant and I want to have a look at the machine. It's a very beautiful and original work—the best thing Felix ever did. The firm can't afford to lose it. If you would do that this morning, I could come down this week with him and we could put it into motion."

A long, deafening silence fell. Mark stared at the spirals of smoke curving upward towards the dirty ceiling.

"Very well, Uncle Julian. I'll do it now, if you wish."

"That's my boy," said Julian with relief. "That's a good boy."

"Can I go now?" said Mark.

"Of course you may."

"Good-bye, Uncle Julian."

"Good-bye, Mark, and thank you very much."

Benedicta was still convalescent, still only half up, half out of bed. She was forbidden to move about too much in case the palpitations set in again. Nash sat by the bed full of hopeful optimism. "You are very much better," he said, and reached for his small prescription pad and fountain pen. "We'll have you up and about in a day or two." She watched him carefully as he wrote with small feathery strokes of his pen. Her pale long face was set in a helmet of unkempt blonde hair. She was dressed in greensleeves fashion—a vague smock gown with a gold rope sash round her slender waist: the attire of a Victorian poetess, one would have said. A small heart-shaped watch ticked on her breast, attached by a brooch in the form of an octopus. She half reclined, surrendering her pulse to Nash, brooding heavily the while.

"Marchant rang me up," she said abstractedly. "About all the tapes by Felix which they found on the beach with his clothes. He has been through them very carefully. The last one is a bit of a puzzle though. He says that there is something recorded which one *could* take for the sound of oars, a squeaky rowlock. But it's all very hazy. Do you think that Felix is really . . . .?"

"We can't think anything," said Nash hastily. "I was discussing it with Julian today. We must wait. We have all the time in the world now, all the time in the world."

But it was when the dark shade of Julian stood before her, gazing at her from the foot of the bed, that Benedicta recovered some of her wonted animation of look; her eyes stared into his with a sweet burning intensity. His mere presence seemed to ignite her, to return her to the order of coherent things; her indisposition slid from her like a mummy wrapping. "Julian," she said, and her voice took on a thrilling resonance.

"Mark is going to cooperate," he said in his lazy musing way. "And that is one point we have cleared. Now then, for the rest, Benedicta: Nash and I both feel that as you have made such a splendid recovery we must take advantage of it. I have spoken to Jocas and he is quite on our side. You must have a decent rest. Go to Polis for a while and leave us to settle up all the details at this end. Will you?"

"If you wish," she said. "If you wish, Julian."

He rested his elbows on the end of the bed and looked down abstractedly at her pale beautiful face. "You could also be useful to us if you wish," he went on slowly. "There is a young German baron, a botanist, traveling about in Turkey with his yacht. He has found a flower which he says could give us something like perfect insect control in a natural way. . . . I won't bore you with the details. But the firm must try and secure him. You could take the provisional contracts with you when you go, so that Jocas can get to work persuading him. He seems rather doubtful about joining."

"Of course I will," she said with a curious furtive, wolfish look, beginning to bite her nails as she listened.

"But there's no hurry," said Julian. "We have all the time in the world, all the time in the world."

The sound of a distant report, muffled by the heavy walls of the building, was barely loud enough to pierce the hard integument of Julian's abstraction or of hers. She still stared at him with admiration and pity, and gazed down at her as he had always done—his eyes full of an impenetrable sadness. It was left to Nash to sit up in his chair and say: "Surely that was a shot?"

Lawrence Durrell

PROSPERO'S CELL

Prospero's Cell is an enchanting picture of Corfu as Lawrence Durrell and his wife knew it before World War II. Early in 1937 the Durrells took an old house in the north of the island. They sailed, gardened, observed nocturnal fishermen at work, watched religious processions that were "like a flower bed moving," relished the island's wines and festivals, its history and people, its golden sands and ancient olive groves. Then, in 1941, lying on the deck of a war vessel bound for Crete, Durrell left behind him the mellow light of Corfu "with a regret so luxurious and so deep it did not stir the emotions at all." "*Prospero's Cell*," wrote Freya Stark in *The New York Times Book Review*, "is still, I believe, one of Lawrence Durrell's best books—is indeed, in its gem-like miniature quality, among the best books ever written."

REFLECTIONS ON A MARINE VENUS

Reflections on a Marine Venus is "a companion to the landscape of Rhodes." Its title refers to a marble statue (period uncertain) that fishermen dragged up in their nets from the bottom of Rhodes harbor. To Lawrence Durrell, assigned to Rhodes as an information officer in 1945, the statue, "gravely meditating upon the works of time," seemed the presiding genius of the place. Under her sign, he wrote these luminous pages, evoking not only the island's spectacular past (the building of the Colossus, the arrival of the Crusaders) but also its shimmering, sun-drenched present. "This book conveys an impression of Greece that is almost tactile . . . a presentation which sparkles with an intense brilliance and fire"—*Christian Science Monitor*.

Lawrence Durrell

THE DARK LABYRINTH

Seeking peace and fulfillment, a band of English people embarks upon a Mediterranean cruise. Their journey ends abruptly on Crete—in the very labyrinth once inhabited by the Minotaur. Trapped by a sudden landslide, only a few of them are able to escape; others remain immured in a darkness from which there is no return; still others, penetrating the maze, find at its end a new life upon the roof of the world. . . . Here, for Lawrence Durrell's many readers, is one of his early novels, showing already that richness of style and powerful sense of destiny that were to find their supreme expression in *The Alexandria Quartet*.

POPE JOAN

Pope Joan is Lawrence Durrell's adaptation of the notorious Greek classic *Papissa Joanna*, the story of the only female pope. The story's source is the old belief that in the ninth century a girl disguised as a monk made her way from Greece to Rome, was elevated to the throne of St. Peter, and ruled over Christendom for a time as Pope John VIII. Interest in this legend (if it is a legend) was revived when Emmanuel Royidis published his sparkling and irreverent book in Greece in 1886. In the present version of Royidis's work, Lawrence Durrell has given us much more than a mere translation. This *Pope Joan* is a masterpiece in its own right—a dazzling blend of fantasy and scholarship, witty, ironic, and full of prophetic vision about women.

SICILIAN CAROUSEL

A motley group of tourists takes a carousel-like whirl around the rim of Sicily. In homage to his late friend Martine, who had often urged him to explore the island, Lawrence Durrell joins their tour, which is appropriately named the *Carousello Siciliano*. The result is this sparkling book—a volume to put beside Durrell's previous "islomania" works about Cyprus, Corfu, and Rhodes, for here are not only the madcap adventures of the multinational sightseers bouncing up and down in their little red bus but also Durrell's own explorations of the fabulous, many-layered civilization of surprising Sicily.

Peter Ustinov
DEAR ME

"Dear me!" says Peter Ustinov as he traces the history of his ancestry, a mad tale of revolutions, dangerous border crossings, suitcases stuffed with money, and wild coincidences; recalls his ambivalent relations with his father, a journalist and spy; relives the vicissitudes of his career in the theater; and, indeed, recreates all the ups and downs of a life story so rich in droll and colorful anecdotes that even Ustinov could not have invented it. Primarily known as an actor, having made his debut as a pig in a school play, he has in his fifty-odd years also been a film and opera director, playwright, novelist, producer, and short-story writer, as well as one of the world's most brilliant conversationalists. This last talent is shown to perfection in these scintillating memoirs, which, incidentally, include delightfully witty verbal portraits of Laurence Olivier, Edith Evans, John Gielgud, Ralph Richardson, Charles Laughton, and David Niven, among many others.

Simone Signoret
NOSTALGIA ISN'T WHAT IT USED TO BE

Provocative, passionate, intelligent, and witty, Simone Signoret leads several lives. In private, she is the wife of the celebrated actor and singer Yves Montand. As a political activist, she has traveled widely, involving herself in important issues and encountering such leaders as Nikita Khrushchev and Tito. As an actress, she has created unforgettable characters in films like *Room at the Top* (for which she won an Oscar) and, most recently, *Madame Rosa*. Starting with her life in Paris before World War II and through the Nazi occupation, her debut in films, her marriage, and her international acting successes, Signoret tells a story studded with famous names, filled with courage and drama . . . a story she shares fully in this vital and warmly human memoir.

Daphne Fielding

THE DUCHESS OF JERMYN STREET

This is the story of the remarkable Rosa Lewis, the real-life heroine of the Masterpiece Theatre television production *The Duchess of Duke Street*. Outspoken, high-spirited, and delightfully madcap, the "duchess" began her career as a kitchen maid and ended it as the owner of the venerable Cavendish Hotel, well known to a long succession of the famous (or sometimes infamous) in the brilliant Edwardian and Georgian period.

Philip Magnus

KING EDWARD VII

King Edward VII, subject of the major television series *Edward the King*, was the most charming, impulsive, and colorful of monarchs. Rigorously educated under the stern gaze of his mother, Queen Victoria, and the Prince Consort, Edward was utterly untrained in affairs of state when he came to the throne in 1901 at the age of sixty. Meanwhile, his romances and his love of gambling had been ill-kept secrets. During the troubled years of his reign, however, he succeeded in enhancing the prestige of the British monarchy as it adapted to the needs of the first years of the twentieth century.

Edgar Johnson

CHARLES DICKENS
His Tragedy and Triumph

In this definitive biography Edgar Johnson depicts not only Charles Dickens but also the colorful world around him. William Makepeace Thackeray, Benjamin Disraeli, Thomas Carlyle, Alfred, Lord Tennyson, Edgar Allan Poe, George Eliot, and even Queen Victoria are among the players in the drama of Dickens's life—a drama in which he himself appears as one of the most complex figures of his time, a man whose political and social crusades are as compelling as his literary achievements.

V. S. Naipaul

A HOUSE FOR MR. BISWAS

"*A House for Mr. Biswas* can be seen as the struggle of a man not naturally rebellious, but in whom rebellion is inspired by the forces of ritual, myth, and custom. . . . Though he has married into the family (the Tulsis), Mr. Biswas remains an outsider and refuses to follow the family in their habitual devotions; he won't be recruited, and he has a perfect terror of being enslaved. He is not submissive, and many times in the novel makes a solitary stand against the others. His victory is in liberating Anand (his son) and in dying in his own house. . . . It has Dickensian largeness and luxuriance without any of the Dickensian sentimentality, apostrophizing, or preaching"—Paul Theroux.

Also:

IN A FREE STATE
THE LOSS OF EL DORADO
MIGUEL STREET
THE MIMIC MEN
MR. STONE AND THE KNIGHTS COMPANION
THE MYSTIC MASSEUR

Frederic Raphael

THE GLITTERING PRIZES

This witty and sardonic novel is based on the much acclaimed television series. From their student years at Cambridge University in the 1950s to the onset of middle age two decades later, a small and talented group of men and women pursue "the glittering prizes" that success in an acquisitive society can offer. Although they achieve varying degrees of material wealth and spiritual poverty, none of them will ever forget those heady, golden days at Cambridge spent unraveling the knots of friendship and in exploratory sex and badinage. "There are many stories here, and in all aspects of writing, this book goes beyond simple entertainment"—*Publishers Weekly*.